This copyright page is being written in a bed & breakfast in Wales, in a town called Weston-Super-Mare. Be assured that it was not this copyright-page-writer's desire to be spending the night—and I hope it's just one night—at a bed & breakfast. This writer's stated and most pernicious enemy is the bed & breakfast, the B&B being a concept that, due to the early hours of the hosts and fellow-inhabitants, and lack of cable or pay-per-view, or a candy machine, or a pool, or an arcade, or proximity to anything, seems to inhibit just about every last activity that anyone would want to do in or near a hotel. But you're not hearing complaints from me (though you are hearing whatever this is in an antiquated voice, no doubt because this writer has been reading much too much Mark Twain of late, and the influence is, if not unavoidable, undeniable). Complaints? Nay, the woman that runs this place is actually very low-key, and the place is dirt cheap, and we have, in our particular quarters—three small rooms—not just one adult bed but four more, all miniature-sized, for the ostensible brood. It is bitchbutt cold here this October night, much colder than would be expected or desired here, in early fall, and the wind off the Atlantic is screaming songs of revenge and revolution. This town, or village, or city—it's somewhere between all three—is a kind of Welsh Atlantic City, only not nearly as grand at that city's grandest or as depressed at its most depressing. There are many convalescent homes here, and many older citizens. Why do I tell you all of this? I do not know. The point here should be that for this issue we made a commitment, a while back, to devote the majority of its space to new writers. We had many hundreds of manuscripts to choose from, and went to work. The result represents not necessarily the *only* great work we saw, but does represent a sampling of the best stuff, even though there were many other perfectly appropriate things we could have published, which we didn't in some cases because they overlapped in some way with things we'd already accepted, or because their authors weren't quite green enough for us. (Some of these writers will appear in future issues.) But greenness, newness: this was a difficult thing to determine. How new must a new writer be? We thought we would be rigid about this—only first-timers!—but then realized this was finky and impossible. What if they'd appeared in a small online magazine? What if they'd appeared in a magazine abroad? Knowing that to draw hard-and-fast distinctions when it comes to decisions like this would be to impose a military sort of discipline onto what is, after all, a small literary magazine read by prisoners and deviants worse, we loosened our belts a little. So those who appear here are either completely new, or newish, or newish to fiction. They come from all over, and their voices are distinct and loud. It's exciting, opening all these manila envelopes and one day finding twelve perfect pages from Murphysboro, Illinois. It is our favorite thing. ¶ I'm writing now a day later, again in the very cold living room of this huge cold house. This morning a mystery sprang forth when it was discovered that the wooden gate, which prevents the hostess's grandchildren (visiting today, very cute) from tumbling down the stairs, was broken by someone in the night. Of course, I seem to be the likely culprit, given that I was awake late (writing to you) and that there was only one other guest awake after the hostess went to bed. Aha! But who was that other guest? I don't know, for I've seen no other guests whilst staying here. Why was *he* not suspected? Rumor is that he's a drunk and a klutz and a very klutzy drunk and also a liar and a fiend and hater of gates that protect our young ones. Now, I realize that on its own this evidence doesn't indict him, but shouldn't we look into it? I feel that a general and fair inquiry is warranted. The other request I would make of the hostess is that she take down at least one or two of the sixty-one copies of the same toddler's picture that desecrate every last room of this house. The hostess obviously has great love for her family, and each hallway and wall bears the weight of at least a few dozen framed photos, drawings, and horrific oils of the various members of the clan. But though the pictures seem rarely to repeat their representations of any persons in particular, there is one exception, a small-statured and evil one. Let's call him Mordor. In this photo, black and white, Mordor is doing the lying on the stomach, arm-over-arm, facing the camera at Sears pose. His head is large, and he has that weird adult look that some children—usually born between 1930 and 1940—are afflicted with or choose to affect. He looks like a very small man in a sailor outfit—big forehead, penetrating eyes, serious and overly bushy eyebrows. It's a very scary picture, and it's in every room of the house. I do not think one should place hundreds of photos of Mordor around one's house, especially in a house that receives guests, and I would object to it formally, to the hostess, if I weren't already in the doghouse and if I didn't fear, vaguely, that I might end up buried in the garden, perhaps next to this selfsame Mordor. ¶ There is a very popular British magazine here called, no joke, *I Love Telly!* This is the joy of traveling to exotic lands. I just turned on the telly to see what I could about the California election, and either this particular home's telly is ill-equipped or there is no news broadcast in this particular country. Either way, I haven't seen one mention of the election since I've been here. But it is presently October 7, 2003, and at the time of this writing, the polls in the *McSwys* home state of California have been open many hours. All polls conducted in the weeks leading up to the election indicated that Arnold Schwarzenegger would be elected governor. And those of us who grew up under Reagan, I think, are all having a very queasy feeling that our country belongs in large part to young men who want people like Reagan, Jesse Ventura, and Arnold Schwarzenegger to hold our highest offices, not always because they think they will do the best job, but because they think that a) they can't screw it up that badly and b) it'd be really fucking funny (glug glug) if they really got elected. In California, I would venture that Schwarzenegger grabbed the under-25 male vote on pure visual appeal alone. Never has there been a greater and clearer contrast, visually, between two candidates. Gray Davis looks in every particular like a wormy, scheming, cold-hearted science fiction villain, the kind of man who would plot the demise of the planet if he could get off safely and was given a nice penthouse on the Death Star. Davis is thin, he looks tense, he's chilly, and his hair never moves. Schwarzenegger obviously has him by about a hundred pounds, and when he smiles, he seems to be having fun. End of contest. ¶ My god, what the hell am I talking about here? Admission: I'm going on and on mainly because a certain *McSwys* reader in Toronto, whom I met after a reading about four months ago, asked why the copyright page meanderings seemed to be getting shorter. He said he missed the longer ones, and that alone—truly!—was enough for me to get back on my horse and blather. I am, sometimes, *that* impressionable. For a long time I figured that the world had had enough of these kinds of notes, and had been gradually scaling back—and for that I'm sure most of you and those affected by your moods were elated—but, given some small encouragement and a political apocalypse, I have now whacked off 2149 words. I guess it's a way to express my astonishment, my horror, my perverse excitement, and then more horror, at the state of the state—a very great state, I should add, probably my favorite one. ¶ It's now about 1 a.m. and I'm still not finding any results of the election on any channel. I find *Grumpy Old Men*, featuring the still-stunning Sophia Loren. I find *CSI Miami*. I find a few talk shows where they're talking about labor strikes. But no breaking news. I'm pretty sure they have CNN here, but where? It's just occurred to me that a while back, when this recall was new, I had an email exchange with Mark Danner, the noted political writer and journalist, whom I'd been trying (successfully; he was easy) to persuade to speak to the high-school students at 826 Valencia over the summer. ¶ The exchange started lightheartedly, with my naively stating that an event we'd both been to recently had featured at one table at least three people who seemed more qualified than any of the gubernatorial candidates then in the mix, and my frustration that Gray Davis didn't seem to be the most charming or likable or charismatic man. Mark (whose emails will be somewhat truncated, such truncations indicated with the ellipses) wrote this back: ¶ "I do agree that following someone with ideas and the guts to articulate them would be a rare treat, though I fear the treat would be ephemeral: we're really in late Republican Rome here, a time of political decadence and corruption whose only parallel in our history is the postbellum Grant Administration. When I look back on my life, I'll see my political consciousness beginning with the near-impeachment and resignation of one president over an unpopular war, continuing through the impeachment of another president (a terribly articulate one with a proclivity for personal indiscretion) and then on through an election stolen in broad daylight and an imperial war fought on boldly false pretenses. And that's only one convoluted sentence. Articulate? In such a political world, the only way someone articulate and honest could actually govern would be through mob rule. Hmm—does that seem just a wee bit dark and pessimistic? And it's only 11 a.m. I have to work on that." ¶ To this I wrote something about how, despite the chaos of it all, there seemed to be an upside to the recall, in that the voters of California were somehow "taking their state back." And for that, the recall seemed at least a little worthwhile, in that it would energize both sides of the electorate, and encourage third parties, and fourth and fifth parties, and make the voters feel empowered again, even if the recall movement had nefarious architects with dubious motives. Along the way I wrote the words *real democracy*, and Mark made me regret it: ¶ "Well, I'd love to share your enthusiasm on this one and

I'm trying, I'm trying; but so far, alas, I'm failing. I guess it depends what you mean by 'real democracy.' To me, this latest example of that strange fruit shows, if anything, that California has already consumed far too much of it. During the past couple decades voters have passed initiatives that have inflated the budget at the same time as they have passed initiatives that forbade tax increases. The result is a disaster in the fiscal underpinnings of the state, a disaster that should be laid much more at the door of the voters than at that of the hapless, unloved Davis. If this is 'real democracy,' I'm thinking we need a bit more of the fake kind. I'm not sure taking the political parties out of the equation is devoutly to be wished either; much of the larger problems in our current politics have to do, I think, with the decline of the parties— institutions that were, again, unloved, but that were critical to organizing constituencies around concrete, realizable issues and goals. Do you think Arnold will succeed in doing the same? Or in putting together a mandate to fix what's wrong with the state—when in fact he refuses even to discuss it in any detail? Of course, the carnival atmosphere is fun and somewhat cheering to anyone deeply frustrated with 'politics as usual.' I think one should be wary, however, in drawing comfort from this; the emotion is rather too close to those who will vote for the Terminator because of his pure entertainment value—that is, who will cast their vote out of an underlying cynicism about politics in general. I'm not sure such an impulse, even if it dominates the recall, really rises to the level of a political act." ¶ That exchange took place in August, and now we're here on election day, and the results seem inevitable and frightening and explosive and gruesome and of course, as always, morbidly fascinating. I keep thinking of the scene in *Independence Day* (the movie, not the book), where the White House is unceremoniously blown up by the evil aliens. It was a shocking sequence, and it was done with great flair and finality. A huge pulse of raw laser power was pumped into the top of the building until the entire structure burst at every point. For viewers, it was horrifying but thrilling. And it wasn't, I don't think, out of hatred of the government. It had more to do with vulnerability exposed. The greatest symbol of executive power in the country could be exploded, and the country—after the vanquishing of the aliens by Randy Quaid and Jeff Goldblum and some computer wizardry—lived on. ¶ The further I get into this analogy, the stranger and more tenuous it becomes. But my point, I think, is that we all have a dark fascination with testing the limits of any given system, even while knowing that there is, often or always, a breaking point. Right now, the voters of California are testing the ultimate elasticity of our state democracy. My guess is it will stretch without breaking—let alone exploding—and most of the most substantive work to improve lives, one by one, will continue to be done not by legislators, but by people in their communities, and that the decisions made by the new governor—like all governors in this referendum state—will have occasional and often muffled impact on the lives of his citizens. ¶ We didn't get a chance to talk about Roddy Doyle's story yet. About it: we'd gratefully accepted it very long ago, and were anxious to fit it in. It's about as much pleasure as one should be allowed while reading. Where is the rest of it? Is it a part of a novel soon to be finished? We do not know. But we wanted to publish it, and if we were purists, would have waited six months more to place it in an issue not dedicated to new writers, but only a purist would do that, and we are not purists. Does purity, does rigidity, does dogma belong in any kind of art? We have discussed this before, and will do so again. We say no, but there are probably exceptions. Brancusi! There's one. Malevich! But those paintings, in person, are hardly pure. But anyway. ¶ Final note: what was the movie playing on the flight back from Europe? *Terminator 3*. Absolutely true, and my God was it bad. EDITORIAL ASSISTANCE FOR THIS ISSUE AND WITH McSWYS GENERALLY was provided by the following volunteers: Michael Bauer, Emily McManus, Barry Engelhardt, Matt Frassica, Richard Parks, Rose Lichter-Marck, James Moody, Brenden Salmon, Suzanne Kleid, Casey McKinney, Terri Leker, Amie Nenninger, Justin Gallagher, Mark Novak, Andrew Leland, Matt Werner, Audrey Harris, Jessica Tonnies, Andrea Velasquez, Jenni Ulrich, Cindy Kumano, Gideon Lewis-Kraus, Taylor Morris, Ted Thompson, Krista Overby, Tracy Majka, Mike Hearst, Max Fenton, Josh Camp, Rob Krueger, Jason Kellermeyer, J.P. Howley, Joe Pacheco, Brooke Glass-O'Shea. STEREOSCOPIC ADVICE: Rommel Jamias. CONTRIBUTING EDITOR: Lawrence Weschler. EDITOR AT LARGE: Sean Wilsey. BROOKLYN STORE LEADER AND EVENTS COORDINATOR: Scott Seeley. SAN FRANCISCO STORE LEADER AND EVENTS COORDINATOR: Yosh Han. WEBSITE EDITORS: Lee Epstein, John Warner. BUSINESS MAN: Dave Kneebone. BUSINESS WOMAN: Heidi Meredith. PRODUCTION: Alvaro Villanueva. EDUCATIONAL DIRECTOR FOR 826 VALENCIA: Nínive Calegari. MANAGING EDITOR: Eli Horowitz. PRESIDENT OF McSWYS PUBLISHING: Barb Bersche. EDITOR: Dave Eggers. COVER ART: Christian Northeast.

As always, for the amateur reader

McSweeney's welcomes your correspondence. Please send letters to letters@mcsweeneys.net or 826 Valencia, San Francisco, CA 94110. We cannot always respond individually, but each will be cherished and perhaps integrated into a collage.

DEAR MCSWEENEY'S,

The animal trials held in Burgundy in the 16th and 17th centuries can provide a striking and potentially instructive parallel to the military infrastructure of war-worn Iraq.

In 1522, for example, the barley crops surrounding a certain village were destroyed by rats. The villagers immediately hired a prosecutor who charged the rats with "wanton destruction" and brought the case before a special church-run court. The vicar who presided over that court appointed a lawyer to represent the rats, set a date for trial, and read the summons (addressed to "some rats of the diocese") from the steps of the church.

When the trial date rolled around, "some rats" failed to appear in court. Bartholomew Chassenee, the rats' lawyer, argued that the rats must not have heard the summons. Moreover, the summons only addressed "some" of the rats within the church's jurisdiction. Even if a rat had happened to hear the summons, how could he know whether or not he himself was expected to appear?

The court accepted this argument and ordered a second summons, addressing "all" the rats of the diocese, to be read from the pulpit of every local parish church.

The rats failed to appear a second time. Chassenee argued that the defendants were widely dispersed and needed more time to make preparations for the journey. The court accepted this argument as well and granted a further delay in the proceedings.

When the rats failed to appear the third time, Chassenee was ready with a third argument. It was well established at the time that if a person was summoned to appear in court but could not do so safely (for example, because of pestilence) he could lawfully refuse to obey the writ of summons. Chassenee argued that the rats were likely to be attacked by cats if they attempted to make the journey to court, and so they should not be required to make the trip. The court debated whether or not to issue an order enjoining the villagers to restrain their cats. Unable to arrive at a conclusion, they adjourned the question, and judgment for the rats was eventually granted by default.

Chassenee went on to become a successful judge and sometimes cited cases involving animals and insects in his decisions regarding human beings. For example, when he was heading a panel of judges considering an appeal from a death sentence made by a group of convicted heretics, he agreed to give them a hearing because they were no lower than rats, and even rats have a right to be heard. Unfortunately for the defendants, Chassenee died on the eve of the hearing, and all of the heretics were promptly exterminated.

The implications are obvious and troubling.

Allegedly,
ANNA PERVUKHIN
STUDENT OF LAW
CHICAGO, ILLINOIS

DEAR MCSWEENEY'S,
I write to you for two reasons. The first is to compliment you on Issue

No. 11, minus the typos and triptych your strongest issue yet. The second is from mind-numbing loneliness, a hole below my ribs so deep and impenetrable that if you looked inside of it you would go blind.

I'm in Hong Kong as I write this. I've been traveling for two weeks and people prone to the kind of thoughts I'm prone to should never be alone out in the world. Hong Kong is a monster of a city, a soupy mess of British greed gyrating impatiently against China's tiger economy, buildings erupting from the sea and the hilltops while the boatmen keep watch. From my hotel room I can see the traffic twisting its way and then disappearing into this foreign landscape. The American dollar is worth about 7.5 HK. The congee with pork is good.

The big question, I suppose, as I turn the final page on your fine book, laying its pleather spine against a fruit bowl filled with yellow oranges the size of babies' fists: If I had a nickel for every time I accepted a lie as fact, a dime for every passive insult hurled my way, a quarter for every time I mistook a friend's motives for something they weren't, and fifty cents for the last evening I spent in her strong unwashed arms—what would the exchange rate be on that? What does the WTO have to say about despair? Will there ever be an APEC Summit on loss, a treaty on neglect?

Yours,
STEPHEN ELLIOTT
KOWLOON, HONG KONG

DEAR MCSWEENEY'S,
I would like to tell you about the moths in my studio. They are called miller's moths. They appear to belong to the order Lepidoptera. Beyond these pieces of recalled knowledge I can provide only my observations.

The moths are brownish-gray but sometimes slightly paler after they die. They are attracted to burning lightbulbs but do not usually sit on them and burn up as the white moths of my childhood did. When there is no strong light, these "millers" whip themselves about the room and beat themselves to death against the walls. I am guessing this is how they die and why, every morning, I must vacuum the carpet of moths before I begin work. But I do not see them hit the wall and fall to the floor, so perhaps they come in at night only in order to die quietly inside a room, among their own.

Often when I wake up in the house and throw off the bedclothes, a piece of a wing or a segment of exoskeleton wafts ceilingward on the updraft. In fact, most nights I sleep with a moth or moths. Before falling asleep I thrash in my bed if I feel the telltale stroke of wings against an arm or a leg and, in my lethargy, assume my thrashing body will free the moths from my nest. Probably I crush them to death.

I would use the glass sliding door that leads from my room to the outside if hundreds of moths did not live in the narrow flat space between the screen and the glass. When I move the inner glass door at all, the moths rise up as one in a terrifying, shape-shifting cloud of gray and brown wings. The sound of all their bodies hitting the metal screen and glass panel at the same time is hideous.

One frequently flies up my pant leg while I sit at my desk, and I swear and hit at myself as if the moth has entered my very body, until it emerges from my clothing alive or dead. If it flies out I try to swat it to the ground and grind it under my foot. This practice leaves dusty marks under the desk in no regular pattern.

When one of the moths bats against a windowpane from the inside, sometimes a bird flies into the glass to take it. It is disheartening to watch a bird's repeated attempts to take the moth until it is too exhausted to further attempt flying through the glass. These birds, perhaps even the same ones, have stopped attaching their mud-daubed nests to the top of the house since several plastic owls have been hung from the gutters. The owls swing back and forth in the breeze as if from gallows-poles.

The moths have six legs: two long, thin ones joining the body at its middle; two large, thick ones emerging from the top of the body; and two smaller ones from the middle of the thorax. The body is segmented, with eight segments below the thorax, which is slightly redder in color than the rest of the body. The head is dark brown and has two antennae.

The wings number four: two large back wings and two smaller ones nearer the head. When the moth is at rest, the wings lie in two layers. The upper wings are darker, especially at the ends, which are tipped in hundreds of tiny feathery hairs. The larger wings underneath are a silvery taupe and open like fans when the upper wings are stretched to the sides as if in flight. When smeared on a sheet of white paper, the wing dust looks gold.

The body looks as if covered with fine down, and when stroked it feels soft as a pussywillow. With the slightest pressure, pincerlike structures emerge from the body's lower tip. The pincers are covered in the same down.

The head is the darkest part of the moth. At the tip are two fuzzy pincers or teeth. The antennae are about three-eighths of an inch long and have the thickness of human hairs, growing thinner toward the tips.

Oh every girl that ever I've touched, I did not do it harmfully. I listen to music as I write and swat moths. Sometimes the lyrics make me think of something, as of how each young man in each town in this country, from the very beginning of the settlement of this continent, let alone every young man of every village in human history, loved a girl or a few girls he met in his village or somewhere else, and how each man's whole world was his work, and those girls, and the dreams he was delivered in his sleep by a cruel or compassionate God. The amount of recollected emotion that disappears from human memory when someone dies, and the degree to which we rely on a few people to record something of what emotions were to them, is almost too much to bear.

Tonight I vacuumed forty-two moths.

Sincerely,
SARAH MANGUSO
SHERIDAN, WYOMING

DEAR PUBLISHISTS,
I am a fairly unknown poet/noveller in the downtown region of Toronto, Canada's most populous city. It's because of that that I feel that I am overqualified to write a novel.

My book is going to be called *As Yet Untitled*, which is extremely clever of me to do. I know this because I have seen several examples of similar titles, all of which are very clever—for example, Abbie Hoffman's *Steal This Book.*

My main goal has been to try to transfigure the features of novelish fiction and leave it an unrecognizable corpse, with my new athletic and turgid style surmounting the corpse, baying at the pregnant harvest moon of art, which in turn reflects the light of the solar disk of phoebean inspiration back from its craterous face down onto the new style standing proudly on the corpse. Of course, naturally, the light will also probably bathe the corpse, but that's a consequence of my style having tarried, straddling the corpse for too long and risking capture by the park ranger service of criticism. So be it.

My principle characters are all Goths, who are full of rage for being so superior to society. I chose Goth culture because the aura of darkness that hangs upon them like a withered festoon reflects their inner tundral emotional environment, the rough earth of sorrow that lets grow only those few shrubs and the yellow flowers with the spiny leaves.

I had lain (you would expect laid, but I prefer to use the classical past-participlization of the verb "to lay." When you've read *Beowulf* as many times as I have, anything less than the primeval Saxonish language looks glum, and very dejected) the idea down on a napkin at this theme rave I went to. Only children of parents who were members of the Masons could go, so there were a lot of napkins.

Peep this shit right here. There isn't a POV character, there isn't an omniscient third person, there isn't any sort of perspective *at all*. The events are described in such a way that they can only be understood by reading them in a mirror. That's my own mental wizardry, so that's a copyright.

The characters, Delmar, Sholin, Skice, and Breece, are all from the suburbs, and Delmar's parents are both accountants. Sholin's parents are dead, but Child Services didn't want him so he just moved back home and raised himself. Skice is an aspiring writer, and in him I put my most autobiographical bricks and stones. For instance, Skice isn't from Canada, as I am, but he always aspired to meet someone who was. That's just one example. I have at least thirty that I could give you, but I won't. Breece is sort of a fat kid who no one understands, but he's really got a heart of gold, or another heavy element. I was thinking of making his heart out of carbon, or out of a mythical element like adamantium or 100% pure poecite, but it's Skice who's the poet so it would make sense if *Skice's* heart was made from poecite. Therein lies the crux of Chapter Six. Anyhow, Breece only goes along with the rest of the group because they make him feel wanted. You could try to guess why he feels like he needs to feel wanted, but you wouldn't be successful. The thing is that his parents really love him, but he's got "American Youth" sickness, a virus that the book postulates is the source of all the annoying traits that American youths have. Being from Canada, I can write this objectively, because here, children are well adjusted, respected, and loved. They are loving people who are seldom fans of raucous musicians.

Anyhow, the book. The book takes place at Camp Wanatanabe over two summers. The first summer we see that they meet and become a sort of "crew" or "posse." They invent their own language, which is really quite amazing in itself because their language is based on the tonal intervals between the words, which are not spoken, but sung in a deep voice that sounds like this: "wooooooooohhhh wuuuuuuuu u wuuuuuuuu." They all agree to never change and to meet back the next year. The second summer they return, and Breece is taller and thinner, and that starts off a complete ruckus. Skice forgets the language, though they made a pact to remember it, and Sholin doesn't wear black clothing anymore because he got a girlfriend and was "subverted" by the vaginal animal. The book theorizes that it is the vagina that instills the more boring "civilization" characteristics into the penis of the man, which then brings those characteristics by active transport through the cell membranes into the mitochondria, where the adenosine triphosphate that they produce is replaced with boring triphosphate particles. How ironic!

Most of the rest of the summer takes place in a hazy black and white sequence (the book actually describes everything using monochrome grammar and syntax) which turns out to be a dream. But you don't *know* this until you see an old man, who keeps falling down throughout the book. (As a metaphor for the United States of America's Democratic Mission collapsing under its own beleaguered inertial inertia. The man's name is even Usad Inertio.) The old man falls but he doesn't bleed—instead, he's full of wires, which is like, HOLD ON, because old men don't change from cells and fibrous organs into wires and solder, or do they? It leaves you thinking.

The book makes extensive use of new vocabulary from the language

invented by our heroes, for instance, smulch, which is Merlog (their language) for schmaltz. Also, binnder, vb. int. 1. to fall while being an old man e.g. the man binndered on the roof of my uncle's sedan, ruining our vacation forever. My father never forgave him, and they still exchange business cards which contain false information every Christmas during the "we should see each other more this year" portion of the sacred festival.

Some words on the ending: The ending will not consist of "'By Gelfling Hands or by none' read the prophecy, and so Djenn thrust the shard into the heart of the Dark Crystal, healing it and filling the land with fecund bounty. 'When three suns become one, what is sundered and undone, shall be healed, by Gelfling hand or by none,' he repeated to everyone present, to explain the transformation they had witnessed."

Thank you,
DAVID DINEEN-PORTER
TORONTO, ONTARIO

DEAR MCSWEENEY'S,
I regret to inform you that I cannot accept the position you recently offered of War Literature Expert, or McSweeney's Desert Battlefield Expert, or How To Kill a Person in Five Seconds or Less Expert, or whatever the title was. The truth is, I have lately been bombarded by these sorts of proposals, and to add insult to injury, my editor recently informed me that the paperback edition of *Dear Mr. President* will begin to appear in numerous classrooms across the country upon its release, and so will be utilized as a Tool for the Tyranny of All Instructors. It will, sadly, become one of those

Required Reading Books acquired at the beginning of the semester; These books stockpiled in backpacks, tomahawked around student housing, a Paper and Language Weapon Used to Beat the Youth into Submission, then, that inevitably prompts dread in the sleepy, debilitated student for whom each printed word in the book looms as an insurmountable obstacle, or worse yet, a tremulous boulder which will leap off the page at any moment and crush said student's head unless they, in the interest of self-preservation, slam the book shut at once and solemnly vow never to open it again. Because the truth is that When You Teach A Book You Kill It (and the author).

Let's be clear: these instructors have resorted to brutally slaughtering my book because it's one of the few Gulf War Fiction Books out there. For whatever reason, there is a serious lack of Gulf War Fiction, and yet, conversely, there are many actual Gulf Wars. Especially now that We the People have seemingly flown into and through Gulf War II, and find ourselves, given the steady accumulation of almost daily casualties, heading into Gulf War III. And these days the temptation, with the advent of the newest Gulf War, and you should not believe the media's propaganda campaign (for instance, did you know that members of the Shadow Government utilize a secret alphabet comprised of 37 letters?), is to overlook the 1991 Gulf War. Or at least to degrade it, to belittle it, to treat it as a piece of lint in the pocket of American History, and to turn instead to the more current, more colorful, more fashionable Gulf War III, or IV, or V, or whichever number it is we might currently be engaged in.

Although, regarding the actual number of so-called Gulf Wars, some experts have argued that—and I believe they have a point—given Iraq's status as the Cradle of Civilization, the Persian Gulf War(s) has/have been going on since the Beginning of Time. Or, to say it another way, all wars since the Beginning of Time have been Persian Gulf Wars, and that these wars were only previously known by a different name. (I will assert here that likewise all fiction, then, has been and always will be Gulf War Fiction) Because when it comes to the subject of combat, names are important. Say the word war and then try to say the word war without saying the word war, and you will see what I mean.

But whatever. I have decided to assist the murderous instructors who have elected to teach my book by providing them with the below list of Lecture Topics. These lecture topics are, of course (and I am now addressing directly the instructor who will be teaching my book in the future) only suggestions, meant as a prompt to trampoline you into your own Personal Lecture Topics. Furthermore, in my ongoing research into the Gulf War Phenomenon, I have discovered that the below list of Lecture Topics is not only applicable to my book, but—and I have no explanation for this somewhat freakish fact—to all Gulf War Fiction Books. Or in case you, O Mighty Instructor, secretly (for I too know this shame), possess the desire to write (and let me warn you it is a perilous undertaking) your very own Gulf War Fiction Book, then I hope the following list of Lecture Topics might also be helpful:

LECTURE TOPICS FOR ALL
GULF WAR FICTION BOOKS

I. The New Draft
Brain-Mail® and the Government

II. Customized Self-Defense
*Creating Your Own Linguistic
Forcefield*

III. The Propagandistic Parent
Syndrome
*Do We Have to Accept the Story of
Vietnam and WWII?*

IV. Camouflaged Navigation
*Learn How to Build Your Own
Seeing-Eye Snowman in Iraq*

V. Breathing In America
*You Will Shelve Your Gas Mask Once
You Access Your Tenth Orifice*

VI. Gender-Neutral Wrestling
Accessing the Chimpanzee Within

VII. Anatomical Sculpting Through
Manipulated Air
*Growing the Third Ear and
Erasing the Nose*

Thus, I cannot accept your offer of employment, but thank you for the kind words and for thinking of me.
Sincerely,
GABE HUDSON
NEW YORK, NEW YORK

EDITOR'S NOTE: *At some point several months ago, we received an intriguing submission, a strange tale of love and lust, fathers and sons, ape-pornography and intolerance. The story contained no author name, no contact information, nothing but a title: "Gorilla Girl." We wanted to learn more about this story, so we put a short notice on our website, asking the author to contact us. The next day we received an email from Mr. Ryan W. Bradley; this led to an extensive, but ultimately inconclusive,* correspondence. *We present the full dialogue here, calling upon our readers' better judgment. The following exchange is absolutely real. Please send all theories and opinions to gorilla@mcsweeneys.net.*

DEAR MCSWEENEY'S,
My name is Ryan W. Bradley, and I am the author of the story "Gorilla Girl."

I happened to check by the *McSweeney's* website today and saw the notice regarding my story. A little while back a friend of mine stole the only hard copy I had of the story off of my desk and submitted it to you. I had told Jeff several times how great it would be to get published in *McSweeney's*, so being a friend he decided to take the reins. I was more than a bit upset when he told me a few days later that he had sent you guys the story. Of course, it didn't take long for me to calm down. The next time I talk to him I will have to tell him that he forgot to give you any information. I'm sure he will get a laugh out of it.

Thank you for having read the story, and for taking the time to post a notice on your website.
Sincerely,
RYAN W. BRADLEY
ASHLAND, OREGON

HELLO RYAN.
Thanks for writing us—I'm glad the notice worked. Can you also send us an electronic version of the story?
Sincerely,
ELI HOROWITZ
MCSWEENEY'S
SAN FRANCISCO, CALIFORNIA

DEAR MCSWEENEY'S,
I would love to send you an electronic copy of the story, but it is going to

take a while. Currently my computer is broken and about two weeks ago I had to send it in to the manufacturer to see if it can be fixed. Unfortunately the only copy of the story is on the hard drive and you guys have the only hard copy. When I sent the computer in, I didn't think I would need any of the stuff on it for a while. Anyway, two weeks ago the manufacturer said that it will be about six to eight weeks before I have my computer back, so until then I am stuck writing with a pen and paper, and for my computer needs I get to make frequent visits to my public library or coffee shops. I am sorry about the problem, but if you absolutely need an electronic copy of the story I will send it as soon as I get my computer back. In the meantime I was wondering what the status of my story is with *McSweeney's*? If you need one, I have a short bio I can send your way.

Thanks for your encouragement and patience with my story (and its attached problems).

Sincerely,
Ryan W. Bradley
ASHLAND, OREGON

Well, Ryan,
That is too bad. But not deadly. For now, the first step is to make sure your "Gorilla Girl" is indeed the one we read—so far, I've heard from three different contenders. Yours is the only firsthand report, so probably this is the right one. The second sent me a link to a story with the same name and even slightly similar style, but different plot. And the third said his friend wrote a story by that name, but I'm waiting to hear more. Anyway, you can put this all to rest by giving us a few details.

The status of your story is: it's in the pile of contenders for Issue No. 12. We should know more in a couple weeks.
Sincerely,
Eli Horowitz
McSweeney's
SAN FRANCISCO, CALIFORNIA

Dear McSweeney's,
It's amusing that you received more than one claim to the story. I would think that writers would have a bit more integrity. Anyway, I'll be honest with you: I wrote the story when I was tanked, which I know is not a great excuse, but then again they never are. I haven't really read my story; I printed it out (the copy you now have that my friend sent to you) so that I could read it and revise it, but never got that chance. So really the best I can give you is: 1) my word that I am not trying to bullshit you (and I do appreciate that you seem to believe me) and 2) I can tell you what I remember from the night I wrote the story. A couple of nights before I was hanging out with some friends in my dorm room (yes, I am a college student) and was quite angry from an encounter with an ex-girlfriend. One of my friends referred to her as "gorilla girl" because of the way she seems to puff up when she is upset, but the name caught my ear, and I wrote it down. A couple of nights later I went out partying and when I got back I saw the sticky note with "gorilla girl" written on it. So I started to write, and wrote until morning when I passed out. (Even when I am not inebriated this is usually how I write my best work.) What I remember about the story is that I wanted to make it an allegory for two things: 1) my relationship with said ex-girlfriend, and 2) my generation's relationship to society.

I realize that this seems fairly contrived, but I am a proud person and I am very embarrassed to have to admit to people that are interested in my work that I wrote it drunk and don't remember it much. If nothing else, this is a harrowing experience knowing that I might lose credit for my writing because I was stupid. When it comes down to it I am college student and if this story is to be taken away from me I do not have the means to fight for the rights to it. I hope you will be able to see the bare honesty that I am putting forth.

Sincerely,
RYAN W. BRADLEY
ASHLAND, OREGON

DEAR RYAN,
The others aren't being sneaky—one found a story online with that title, and the other said a guy in his writing class read a story by that name a couple years ago. You are our best possibility, since you are the only author we have heard from directly. And I certainly don't want to doubt your word. But given that there are at least three stories named "Gorilla Girl" in existence, can you just put my mind at ease by giving the basic plot, whatever specifics you can recall, that type of thing? Anything will help.

Still,
ELI HOROWITZ
MCSWEENEY'S
SAN FRANCISCO, CALIFORNIA

DEAR MCSWEENEY'S,
I did not mean to imply that other people were being dishonest about having written a story with the same name as mine. I am merely concerned that I will lose credit for my story, which I am quite confident is the one in question. You asked again for more details regarding the story, and I will tell you honestly that what I told you earlier is all I can remember, so I can only think to offer two other possibilities: 1) talk to you on the phone to try and convince you, though it would be quite similar to the email, or 2) I can try to contact my friend Jeff (who submitted the story) and have him contact you regarding proof that he indeed submitted my story titled "Gorilla Girl." I feel like there is still substantial proof that the story is mine: 1) like you have stated, I am the only one who has directly stated that my story was submitted to *McSweeney's*, and 2) I have a third party who can attest to submitting the story on my behalf.

I am sorry that this is such a mess, but I hope and pray that it will not impede the chances of my story being published by *McSweeney's*.

Sincerely,
RYAN W. BRADLEY
ASHLAND, OREGON

DEAR RYAN,
I still hope you are the one—especially because Possibilities #2 and #3 have been conclusively determined to be different stories. But I am kind of fascinated by you remembering absolutely nothing about the story, not even the barest outlines of the plot. For example: Is Gorilla Girl a person, an automobile, or a song? Is the story five pages or fifty?

In any case, this isn't really affecting the chances of publication; the odds are still kind of against it—there are parts that are kind of, well, drunken. I mean, it is a pretty strange story. But never-

theless, it is persistently mesmerizing—
I cannot look away.

Hopefully,
ELI HOROWITZ
MCSWEENEY'S
SAN FRANCISCO, CALIFORNIA

DEAR MCSWEENEY'S,

To tell you the truth I am just as puzzled as you, but I have written things when sober that I barely remember when I am finished—I tend to write very quickly, and usually in a stream-of-consciousness style. But also that night I probably drank more than I ever have in my life. And the fact that I didn't get a chance to edit the story probably leaves some of the "drunk" that I may have removed had I had the chance to revise it.

This has been quite an adventure and ordeal for both parties, and it seems like there would be no greater end to it than to see it published in your journal. I am saying that not just as the author, but also because of all the madness *McSweeney's* and I have gone through for this story.

I appreciate all your support and attention, and if I can bring you any more confusion just let me know.

Sincerely,
RYAN W. BRADLEY
ASHLAND, OREGON

MAN, RYAN—

I have to say, your case is weakening a bit. You remember the Post-it note that inspired the story, but cannot provide any remotely verifiable information? And the computer is being fixed for the next six weeks? There are some who doubt your story, and I regret to say I may be close to joining them. Unless you wrote the story in some sort of fugue state, disassociative personality disorder or whatnot, which could raise a lot of interesting questions about the true nature of authorship, but perhaps that is not the matter at hand.

Nevertheless,
ELI HOROWITZ
MCSWEENEY'S
SAN FRANCISCO, CALIFORNIA

DEAR MCSWEENEY'S,

I know that the story is hard to believe, but I can't help it that my computer broke down well before I even saw the notice on the *McSweeney's* website. And as far as the Post-it note, I remember it because I wrote it the night before when I was sober. I offered to have my friend who submitted the story contact you; other than that I don't know what else I can do, given the circumstances, to convince you. I know only two things: 1) that I wrote the story, and 2) that I would appreciate some benefit of the doubt on this one, since we have all done things that we cannot remember, and we have all been in odd situations that sometimes seem better suited to fictional coincidence than to reality. If you want I can even send you other prose that I have written so that you can compare them (though I have tried to keep from being too stylistically stagnant). I regret that others, and perhaps you, do not believe my situation, but I think that everybody has experienced a time when others did not believe them because something sounded too fantastic.

Honestly this whole thing has me on pins and needles; one minute I see a notice on your website about my story and I get excited, the next minute my authorship is in question and I seemingly can do nothing to protect it, and

then it seems like I am being supported in my rightful claim, and then now
this; I am being discredited again.
I feel like I am in a bad soap opera, yet
I will stand by my claim of authorship,
and I hope that perhaps understanding
and belief will prevail.

Sincerely,
RYAN W. BRADLEY
ASHLAND, OREGON

DEAR RYAN,
It is kind of dramatic, isn't it? If your
friend Jeff can describe anything at all
about the actual story, that would help;
if he can only tell me that he indeed
mailed the story, that won't help so
much. I think your idea of sending
other things you've written could help,
maybe, depending. I certainly don't
want to deprive you of any credit that
is rightly yours—in fact, in a way these
ridiculous circumstances make me even
more hopeful that you are in fact the
author—but do you see how it might
be tough to accept this on pure faith
and nothing more?

You know what I mean?
ELI HOROWITZ
MCSWEENEY'S
SAN FRANCISCO, CALIFORNIA

DEAR ELI,
It is extremely dramatic, which seems
to be the course my life is taking
recently, seeing as today I lost my job
and my car broke down and I get to
deal with the stress of this. I talked to
Jeff and he said that he would email
you when he got a chance. I don't know
what he can tell you, but I hope it
helps. So, would you like me to send
some of my other work? I do realize
how hard it would be to accept this on
pure faith, and that is perhaps what is
frustrating me the most, because I am a
cynic and a realist, so if I were in your
shoes I would have a hard time believ-
ing me. But I am beginning to think of
this as a test to try and balance that
cynical/realist side of my personality.

I was rereading all of the emails
you have sent me and there was something that I didn't address that I feel
I can. It isn't much but it's something.
You asked me about a length, and
while I don't know how long the story
is, I do know how fast I can type. The
longest thing I have ever written in a
single night is thirty pages and that
was a paper for a history class; my
point here would be that I can't see the
story being much longer than that, and
likely shorter. Also, I have only ever
written two stories that were not about
human relationships in some manner:
one was about a concert-giving cricket
and the other about a whisper (remember, I write weird stuff). So I would
also bet that this story deals with
human relationships in some way.

I feel like I should let you know that
I did talk to a lawyer, who is a friend of
my family, today about the situation,
not about taking action, but just for
some legal advice regarding my options.
He said that I should make sure to dis-
close to you that I did seek out legal
advice. I don't want you to think I am
threatening, rather I am just trying to
examine my options as an author. But I
thought I would let you know, as I feel
that through all this emailing we are
building somewhat of a rapport.

Sincerely,
RYAN W. BRADLEY
ASHLAND, OREGON

DEAR RYAN,
We do have a rapport, no doubt. And

you have my sympathy regarding car and job. Here are some questions: Did Jeff look at the story at all, or just send it in without reading anything? How long ago was this written? What are your feelings toward Nell Carter? Have you read *The Taming of the Shrew*? Can you expand at all on the story as an allegory for your relationship with your ex-girlfriend and/or your generation's relationship to society?

My regards to your lawyer,
ELI HOROWITZ
MCSWEENEY'S
SAN FRANCISCO, CALIFORNIA

DEAR ELI,
The story was written in November, I believe. I think that Jeff may have read part of the story, probably not all of it. I think that my writing tends to confuse him. As to the other questions of the email, Nell Carter was an actress I remember from my childhood: I read an article about her having diabetes shortly after my mom was diagnosed with diabetes as well. Other than that I had no special attachment to her, but she is one of those famous people that you forget for a while and then is brought back into your consciousness in strange ways. One that you already think of as being dead, even when they aren't. Though she did die recently.

Yes, I have read *The Taming of the Shrew*, three times, in fact. Once was for an English class, the other two times were on my own. I like to think of myself as an amateur scholar of Shakespeare, and *Shrew* is one of his more controversial plays, so it was one of the first I really tried to study. It has been an influence in my life, to a certain degree, because I seem to approach romance in the same sardonic sort of way. My relationship with the girl-friend in question was tepid; she was a girl that I tried very hard to date and when I finally got the chance, I wasn't all that impressed. Because of my awe for her, I allowed her to dominate the relationship with her points of view, and when I finally took a stand it led to our demise. As for my generation: My generation is seen by many to be lazy, and goalless, but the people I know and have grown up with are the exact opposite. We are ambitious and much like the Lost Generation, in that we are sick of seeing an older generation get more and more corrupted. The reason we are seen as being lazy is because we have chosen different outlets than our predecessors. I feel like my generation is a big feline ready to pounce and show society what we are really made of. And I believe that in fifty years my generation will be measured against the greatest generations our country has known.

Sincerely,
RYAN W. BRADLEY
ASHLAND, OREGON

MR. HOROWITZ,
My friend Ryan Bradley asked me to email you on his behalf, regarding the short story of his that I submitted to *McSweeney's*. He said that any information that I would be able to provide you may prove helpful in proving his authorship. In my haste, I grabbed the first story I found in his dorm room, and had no idea it was a story he had just written, or one that he had written while intoxicated.

To the point: I am not sure if I can be much help. I did send Ryan's story, titled "Gorilla Girl," to *McSweeney's*. But I only read the first paragraph of the story; I am a bio-chem major, and literature has never been my strong point, but Ryan's stories are really far out there and I don't really understand them. I tried to read a story of his about a wave of women castrating men throughout an entire city, but I didn't really get it. Since then I have been hesitant to read anything by him, but I submitted "Gorilla Girl" to you because I knew he didn't have the guts to send a story into your journal.

If I can be of any more help, please do not hesitate to let me know.

Ryan's friend,
JEFFREY BRAND
ASHLAND, OREGON

HELLO RYAN.
Your pal Eli here. We are considering running some portion of our correspondence in the upcoming issue—you know, "Let the Reader Decide!" And if the public cries out for the story, and you get your computer back and provide the file, maybe we can work something out. I just wanted to let you know, in case you have reunited with the gorilla-girl-girlfriend or something.

Actually, it looks like this coming Tuesday will be exactly eight weeks after you sent the computer to the manufacturer! Kudos! Have they given you a return date yet?

Sincerely,
ELI HOROWITZ
MCSWEENEY'S
SAN FRANCISCO, CALIFORNIA

DEAR ELI,
About two weeks ago I called the computer manufacturer, because I had not heard anything, at which point I was told that a letter had been sent to explain that my computer was beyond repair. My first question was in regard to the hard drive, which I was told was basically fried, which loosely translated into layman's terms means I'm "screwed." Because of this I have lost somewhere between ten and fifteen short stories, several essays, the first thirty or so pages of my second novel, and countless ideas that I had typed out, as well as most of the digital art that I have created over the last three years. Among this array of lost musings is the story "Gorilla Girl," which means that *McSweeney's* has the only remaining copy of the story.

It seems I am now a poster boy for those who are constantly saying "back up all your files." If you want to run any part of our correspondence, feel free. If it is of any interest, I have been working on an essay/short story about the entire ordeal, from seeing the notice about the story on the *McSweeney's* website, to the night the story was written, to the more current events of losing all hope of retrieving the story. It seems like all is just another turn in my life, the living soap opera.

I appreciate your correspondence and support.

Sincerely,
RYAN W. BRADLEY
ASHLAND, OREGON

We would appreciate answers to the following questions:

Did Ryan W. Bradley write the story? Is it possible to write twenty-five coherent pages and remember nothing? If he didn't write it, who did? If our generation is a giant pouncing feline, what kind of feline is it? Maybe an ocelot?

Send all theories to gorilla@mcsweeneys.net. Please provide appropriate documentation.

ROAD TO GAGARIN

We first went to Moscow in 2001 to put our fairly jaded Western fingers on the pulse of Cosmonautics at a time when the Mir Space Station, the last vestige of a purely Soviet/Russian manned space program, was due to plummet back to Earth. Just after this end, however, there was also the anniversary of the giddy beginning: the 40th anniversary of the flight that made Yuri Gagarin (1934-1968) the first man in space.

Gagarin cheerfully strapped himself into a tin can to attempt something that only a few dogs had tried—and most of those dogs had died. While his premature and conspiracy-addled death earned him such titles as "the Russian Elvis" and "the Soviet JFK," Russians prefer to remember Yuri as "a really nice guy." But he was also the embodiment of the ancient Russian dream of conquering outer space—a dream that inspired a school of philosophy and science, Cosmism, a full century before Khrushchev started frothing about Soviets pumping out "rockets like sausages."

Though Gagarin's story should not be told outside its totalitarian context, it can still represent the power of positive dreaming and what it is like to live life, as he described it, "as one big moment." Gagarin lives on as a worthy hero and as a symbol of a certain Russian idealism that transcends the Communist era.

STEVE KORVER
RENE NUIJENS

DANCEWRITING

DanceWriting is a way to read and write any kind of dance movement. A stick figure drawing is written on a five-lined staff. Each line of the staff represents a specific level. The bottom line of the staff is called the Foot Line; it represents the ground. The next line up is the Knee Line, which is at knee level when the stick figure stands straight. The next line up is the Hip Line, and after that, the Shoulder Line.

When the figure bends its knees or jumps in the air, it is lowered or raised accordingly on the staff. The five-lined staff acts as a level guide. Figures and symbols are written from left to right, notating movement position by position, as if stopping a film frame by frame.

When more detail is necessary, special symbols representing the third dimension are written below the figures. The round circles picture the head as seen from above. The spokes projecting from the circles show the direction of the limbs in relation to the center of the body. The first row of small symbols represents the overhead view of the arms and upper body; the second row of large symbols represents the overhead view of the legs and lower body.

VALERIE SUTTON
www.dancewriting.org

Portrait of Cosmonaut #1

Once upon a time, long before Cold War competition, the Russians dreamed of space being a place that stretched not only horizontally from St. Petersburg to Vladivostok, but also vertically from "Moscow to the Moon, Kaluga to Mars." Spurred by the vision that "Earth is the cradle of humanity, but one cannot live in a cradle forever," Konstatin Tsiolkovsky (1857-1937), a deaf son of a Polish lumberjack, used his spare time to come up with the formula that made rocket flight possible. It would be many years, however, before Yuri Gagarin would put a face to all this dreaming by becoming our planet's first cosmic emissary.

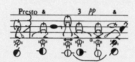

THE GREAT DIVIDE

by SHANN RAY

The train moves west on the highline outside Browning, tight-bound in an upward arc along the sidewall of tremendous mountains, the movement of metal and muscle working above the tree line, chugging out black smoke. Smoke, black first against the grayish rock, the granite face of the mountain, then higher and farther back, black into the keen blue of sky without clouds.

1

THE BOY five years old, and big, bull child his father calls him, and bulls he rides, starting at six on the gray old man his father owns, then at nine years and ten in the open fields of neighboring ranches. He enters his first real rodeo at thirteen in Glasgow and on from there, three broken fingers, a broken ankle, broken clavicle, and a cracked wristbone. Otherwise unharmed, he knows the taste of blood, fights men twice his age while attending bars with his father. When he loses his father grows quiet, cusses him when they get home, beats him. When he wins, his father praises him.

Work, his father says, Because you ain't getting nothing. People are takers. As well shoot you as look at you.

At school he has high marks. He desires to please his mother.

Home, he smells the gun-cleaning, the oil, the parts in neat rows on the kitchen table. The table is long and rectangular, of rough-hewn wood she drapes in white cloth. He sees the elongated pipe cleaner, the blackened rags, the sheen of rifle barrel, the worn wood of stock. He hears the word Winchester and the way his father speaks it, feels his father's look down-turned, his father's eyes shadowed, submerged in the bones, the flesh of the face. The family inhabits a one-room ranch house, mother, father, son. There is a plankwood floor, an eating space, a bed space, cook stove. A small slant-roofed barn stands east of the house where the livestock gather in the cold. Mom is in bed saying, Don't make a mess. The boy's father, meticulous at the table, says, Quiet woman. Outside the flat of the high plains arcs toward Canada. To the south the wild wind blows snow from here to a haze at the earth's end. A rim of sun, westerly, is red as blood.

The boy's mother reads aloud by lamplight. Looking up, into his eyes, Mind your schooling, she says. She touches his face. The words she reads go out far, they encompass the world, and in the evening quiet the boy and his father curl at her feet on the bed listening. Before I formed you in the womb I knew you, she reads, and before you were born I set you apart.

In town the boy witnesses a drunken Indian pulled from his horse by a group of four men. Hard rain falling, the boy standing on the boardwalk staring out. The man has wandered from the Sioux reservation, Assiniboine, day ride toting liquor, empty, seeking more. They throw his body to the ground, his head they press down. Their hands are knotted in his hair and into the wet earth they push his face until it's gone. They throw loud words from white-red mouths while the Indian's body lurches and moves beneath them. The man's lathered voice seeks life and they laugh and champion one another before they rise and spit and walk away. The Indian turns his head to the side and breathes. The boy waits. Directly, he walks and lifts the man, positions him on his horse. He puts his hand on the round flank and horse and rider continue on. He watches, cleans his hands on his pants, and when he turns he is violently struck down in the street.

His father stands over him. He holds the shovel, the long handle he put to the boy's head, the father's countenance as misshapen as the mud that holds the boy, the boy's blood. Sir? The boy says. You helped the Indian, his father says, and lifts the handle again, fine circular motion that opens a straight, clean gash above the boy's cheekbone. The boy lowers his head. He touches the wound, dirtying it, feeling it fill and flow. His eyes are down. He keeps silent. Next time finish it, his father says. The father leaves him lie. The boy follows him home. Voiceless, they work the land, the boy in his father's shadow from the dawn, walking. The sound of his mother is what he carries when he goes.

Sixteen years old, the boy walks the fenceline in a whiteout. He is six foot seven inches tall. He weighs two hundred and fifty pounds. Along a slight game trail on the north fence he is two hours from the house at thirty below zero. He wonders about his father, gone three days. His father had come back from town with a flat look on his face. He'd sat on the bed and wouldn't eat. At dark he'd made a simple pronouncement. Getting food, he said, then gripped the rifle, opened the door and strode outside long-legged against the bolt of wind and snow. Gone.

Walking, the boy figures what he's figured before and this time the reckoning is true. He sees the black barrel of the rifle angled on the second line of barbed wire, snow a thin mantle on the barrel's eastward lie. He sees beneath it the body-shaped mound, brushes the snow away with a hand, finds the frozen head of his father, the open eyes dull as gray stones. A small hole under the chin is burnt around the edges, and at the back of his father's head, fist-sized, the boy finds the exit wound.

When the boy pulls the gun from his father's hand two of the fingers snap away and land in the snow. The boy opens his father's coat, puts the fingers in his father's front shirt pocket. He shoulders his father, carries the gun, takes his father home.

They lay him on the floor under the kitchen table. At the gray opening of dawn the boy positions old tires off behind the house, soaks them in gasoline and lights them, oily-red pyres and slanted smoke columns stark in the winter quiet. The ground thaws as the boy waits. He spends morning to evening using his father's pickaxe, then the shovel, and still they bury the body shallow. He pushes the earth in over his father, malformed rock fused with ice and soil, and when he's done the boy pounds the surface with the flat back of the shovel, loud bangs that sound blunt and hard in the cold. The snow is light now, driven by wind on a slant from the north. His mom forms a crude cross of root wood from the cellar and the boy manipulates the rock, positioning the cross at the head of the grave. The boy removes his broken felt cowboy hat, his gloves. His mom reaches, holds the boy's hand. Their faces turn raw in the cold. Dead now, she says. He saw the world darkly, and people darker still. May his boy find the good. She squeezes the boy's hand, Dust to dust. May the Good Lord make the crooked paths straight, the mountains to be laid low, the valleys to rise, and may the Lord do with the dead as He wills.

Already inside the boy is a will he does not see but feels, abstruse, sullen, a chimera of two persons, the man of violence at odds with the angel of peace.

Find the good, the boy thinks, a burden that resides in the cavity of his chest.

The next day, sheriff and banker come and say I'm sorry and the four ride in the cab of the Studebaker back to town. Papers and words, the ranch is taken, some little money granted and the two move thirty miles to Sage, farther yet toward the northeast edge of Montana, the town joined to the straight rail track that runs the highline. Small town, Sage, post office, two bars, general store. They room with an old woman near dead in a house with floors that shine of maple, neat-lined hardwood in every room. At night the boy hears a howling wind that blends to the whistle of the long train, the ground rumble of the tracks, the walls like a person afraid, shaking, the bed moving, the bones in him jarred, and listening he is drifting, asleep, lost on a flatboard bunk near the ceiling in a sleeping compartment, carried far into forested lands. Within the year the boy's mom dies. He finds her silent in the morning under cover of cotton sheet and colored quilt. In her hair the small ivory comb given by the boy's father nearly two decades before. The boy places the comb in his breastpocket. In her hand a page torn from scripture, Isaiah in her fingers of bone, the hollow of her hand, the place that was home to the shape of his face. He lifts the page, finds her weary underline, Arise, shine, for your light has come. And the glory of the Lord has arisen upon you. Behold, darkness covers the earth, and deep darkness its people, but the glory of the Lord has arisen upon you.

The boy waits. He stays where he is, not knowing. Behind the Mint Bar past midnight, he beats a man fresh from the rail line until the man barely breathes. When it started the man had cussed the boy and called him outside. The boy followed, not caring. The man's face was clean, white as an eggshell, but the boy had made it purple, a dark oblong bruise engorged above the man's neckline. She has been dead one month now.

The boy lies on the hardwood floor at the house in Sage, watching the elderly landlady as she enters the front door. She is methodical, working the lock with tangled fingers. Welcome, Ma'am, he mouths the words. Same to you boy, she answers. Same hour each day she returns from the post office. It is dusk. The boy sees the woman's face, the boned-out look she wears. They have their greeting, she passes into the kitchen, he notices the light. He feels it as much as he sees it, a white form reflected left-center in the front window of the old woman's house. The house faces away from the town's main street. The thing is a quirk, he thinks, a miracle of fluked architecture that pulls the light more than one hundred feet from across the alley and down the street, from the pointed apex of the general store and its hollow globe-shaped street lamp beneath which the night-people ebb and flow on the boardwalk. The light comes through the aperture of a window at the top of the back stairs. From there it hits a narrow gold-framed mirror in the hallway and sends its thin icon into the wide living room. The light is morphed as it sits on the front glass, an odd-shaped sphere almost translucent at dusk, then bright white, bony as a death's head by the time of darkness. The boy hears the woman on the stairs, her languid gate, the creaking ascent to her room. As her body passes, the light disappears then returns. She is never in the front room at night and the boy rarely looks at her during the day, done as he is over his mother, over the loss of all things.

A man will be physical, he thinks, forsake things he should never have forsaken, his kin, himself, the ground that gave him life. Death will be the arms to hold him, the final word to give him rest.

The boy curls inward, lies on the floor for days. The greeting remains the same, the woman leaves him his space. He pictures the round bulb over the general store, pictures himself beneath it in the dirt street, standing in the deep night, looking up. He beholds the bloom of light as he might a near star, a sun. Then he sees himself above it, behind it, clenching the roof between his knees as he would a circus horse, his chest upraised, his father's big sledgehammer lifted overhead. He pulls down sky with arms like wedges. He blasts the light to smithereens. He floats in shards of glass and frozen light, soft, and softer, the wind and the powdery glass like dandelion-white parachutes adrift through the opening, through the window and down, angled from the hall mirror and pulled inward to the living room, falling soft, clumsily, full-bodied onto the hardwood floor. He has returned to the space he keeps. It is dark. The light's reflection shines white in the night of the front window, the outline complete, precise. He sleeps. Outside, he hears the loud confidence of the engine, the steel wheels of the cars at high speed along the rails. In the early morning the old woman puts a hand on his shoulder. The touch awakens him. Yes, he thinks, I will leave this place.

The next day he rises, moves south and west to Bozeman. No jobs, but big he gets work in a feed store. He passes a placement exam and enrolls in the agricultural college in Bozeman. He rides bulls in every rodeo he can find. Nearly every Saturday night he fights in bars. He doesn't drink. He seeks only the concave feel of facial structure, the slippery skin of cheekbones, the line of a man's nose, the loose pendulum of the jawbone and the cool sockets of the eyes. He likes these things, the sound they make as they give way, the sound of cartilage and the way the skin slits open before the blood begins, the white-hard glisten of bone, the sound of the face when it breaks. But he hates himself that he likes it.

Still he returns. In the half-dark of the bar in the basement of the Wellington Hotel outside White Sulpher he opens the curve of a man's head on the corner of a table. A small mob gathers seeking revenge, the man's brothers, the man's friends. He throws them back and puts out the teeth from the mouth of one. He breaks the elbow of another. You'll leave here dead, he says, and the group recedes, the power in him vital and full and he walks from the open door alone into darkness until he sits off distant wrapping his knees in his arms, weeping. He seeks to turn himself and he turns. He fights less. He wanders more, dirt streets of rodeo towns when the day is done, the lit roads of Bozeman in the night after his reading. It is the sound of gravel beneath his boots he seeks, a multitude of small stones forming a silver path under the moon and sky, leading nowhere. He graduates college, barely passing, a first in agribusiness, a second in accounting, Depression on, jobs scarce. He builds roads, digs ditches, dams, gets on at Fort Peck, his home a hillside cut-out, tarp angled over woodstove, single three-leg stool, small lamp of oil, he smells the earth, he sleeps on dirt. North still but jobless, he waits overnight in a line of one hundred men. The head man sees his size. He gets on as a workman with the railroad. He'll earn some money, buy himself some land. Perhaps buy back the land they lost. Plant a hedge of wild rose, he thinks, for his mother. He is six feet nine inches tall now and weighs over three hundred pounds. He works the Empire Builder, the interstate rail from east to west. He works with muscle and grit. He shovels coal. He keeps his own peace.

Alone in the late push across the borderlands they ride the highline of Montana and he stops for a moment and rests his hands on the heel of the shovel, rests his chin on his hands. He feels the locomotive spending its light toward the oncoming darkness, toward the tiny crossings with unknown names, the towns of eight or ten people. He feels the wide wind, sees the stars in their opaque immensity. He hears the long-nosed scream of the train, bent in the night, and he pauses, considering how fully the night falls, how easily the light gives way, then he returns to his work.

Late he lies himself down in his sleeping berth. He stinks of smoke and oil, the sweating film of his body envelops him and he falls toward sleep as one who has come from the earth, who has molded it with his hands, who has returned again. In his place in the dark, always he hears his mother. Mind your schooling, she says. It is after dinner. She lays him down. He is a child sleeping, and in the half world between night and morning, waking him she speaks her elegant words, presses her cheek to his small cheek, whispers, Awake, awake O Zion, clothe yourself with strength. Put on your garments of splendor. She smoothes his eyebrows with a forefinger. You can get up now, she says. She touches his face with her hand.

It is not yet dawn. He lies on his side, sees on the hard shelf before his eyes the ivory hair comb bright as bone. He takes the comb in the curve of his hand. He lies still. He puts the comb to his lips in the half-light. He breathes his deep and holy breath. He remembers the clean smell of her hair. Along the spine of the comb he moves his index finger, then he eyes his finger for a moment, coal and dirt deep set in the whorls. He draws his hand to his mouth and licks the tip of his finger. The sun has broken the far line of the world. His tongue tastes of light.

He works the train and travels to places he has not yet known, where day is buoyant and darkness gone, and when death comes seeking like the hand of an enemy he gives himself over, for it is death he desires, and death he welcomes, and the spirit of his good body is a vessel borne to the eternal.

2

HE IS BORN into this world, he is named. He is made of dirt and fight and the grace of his mother's sacred words. He is one. He is caught in the mass of many. The earth bends beneath him and he listens to the whistle of the train, the notes like a voice of reason in the early dark that wakens him and returns him, takes him weary back to the loaded pull of the cars, the sound of the push and the steel of the tracks.

He rises. He begins again.

The older men on the line call him Middie because they've heard talk of him breaking the back of a bull that wouldn't carry its weight. It was at a rodeo he entered when he was nineteen, up in Glendive. The bull was old and skinny, put in by a local farmer as a joke. The bull didn't show enough verve so the boy bucked the animal himself.

Bent its middle like a bow, the vet said. Sprung its spine.

The bull had to be put down. The boy had both hated and delighted in this, delighted in undoing the farmer's intention, hated that the animal was hard done by. The railroaders laugh their heads off and Middie has to listen to them nearly every stop. They sit behind their counters at each station chewing fat with Prifflach, the conductor, telling and retelling what they've heard. Middie doesn't like them. When they speak they look through him, just as Prifflach does. He sees he is nothing to them. He lets them think they own him. He has a job, he bides his time.

The railroad furthers the chasm between father and mother. Something lower down is revealed, something more sedentary and rooted than even the earth that had opened and closed, closing over him the darker image of his father alongside the subtle light of his mother, the stiff shock of his father's hair under snow, the gray, grainy look of his mother's teeth long after the last exhalation, after he'd found her in her bed.

Riding the highline he is mostly unseen by the passengers, hauling freight, working coal. But a change in duty comes, a change he doesn't welcome. He'll provide muscle for the bossman, the conductor, Ed Prifflach. Three times tossing drunks to local sheriffs at the next stop, twice tracking rich old lady no-shows still wandering after the all aboard. Then the real trouble begins. Just past Wolfpoint, when the first theft is discovered, Middie is put in charge of public calm. He keeps to the plan, following Prifflach's words though it is distasteful to him and he begins to feel in the eyes of others he is becoming the conductor's efficacy, an outline of Prifflach's power, a bigger, more mobile expression.

Things aren't what they seem, Middie thinks. Danger, for reasons a man doesn't comprehend. On his first trip east a workman at the roundhouse in St. Paul threw himself between the cars of an outgoing train. When Middie got word he went to see. The man was severed in two at the chest. Middie isn't afraid to die, and when he dies he wants it to be hard and without any hope of return, as physical as rock and water so he can feel the skin give, the bones in the cavernous weight of his body broken, and blood like a river moving from the center of him, pooling out and away and down into the earth, to the soil that receives him and sets him free.

In the first compartment Prifflach leans toward him, nonchalant in body in order to avoid alarm, yelling at him to surmount the noise. First seat, worst position, thinks Middie, while Prifflach sets the course with regard to the thief. Get some leads, he says. Prifflach's face is wolflike, a man with large buttocks, hairy arms and hands. Middie dislikes him, his sunken eyes, the haughty tenor of his voice. Happening nearly every stop now, Prifflach says. Bad for business. Under a long, narrow nose his mouth tightens. The line ain't gonna like it, guaranteed. Give me the tally.

Five people, says Middie.

Tally his take, says Prifflach.

Middie uses a small piece of paper, a gnawed pencil. Near four hundred dollars, he says, four hundred ten to be precise. His face feels colorless, his body breathes in and out.

Get going, Middie, Prifflach says.

Middie stares at the double doors with their elongated rectangular glass, two top squares open for the heat. Prifflach said he'd picked him because Middie had thighs like cottonwoods and thick arms.

Look alive, Middie.

He hears the words, notes Prifflach's face. Wet lines in a wax head, he thinks. Then he looks at the people.

A weight of soot covers everyone. Their eyes are swollen and bloodshot. They have stiff red necks. On their laps they hold children and bags, gripping them as if to ward off death. Middie peers at the faces, and farther back, through more doors at the end of the car, more elongated squares of glass into the second car where expressions breathe the same contempt, the shadow of a shadow, the same self-preservation, the same undignified desire. They are on the upswing through great carved mountains and though Middie has worked the round-trip St. Paul to Spokane five times, he still feels unlanded here, awkward under the long slow ascent of the train, the sheer drop of landscape, of trees and earth, and way down, the thin, flat line of the river.

Side windows remain mostly shut, frozen in place by the interlock of the moisture inside and the frigid temperature of early winter outside. The air in the compartments, especially those closest to the heat of the locomotive, is heavy, thick to the lungs, and lined with body odor.

Middie has succeeded, through a forceful combination of the billy club Prifflach issued him and a jackknife he carries, in slightly opening the casement adjoining his seat. Air slides through the sliver of space he's created and Middie can feel it, even if the chug of the train taints it all, he feels the clean blade of pine, the rich taste of high mountains, the snicker of winter, windy and subliminal. He feels Bearhat Mountain and Gunsight out there, the draw of Going to the Sun Road lining the opposite side of the valley, spare of people now, the park locked in the grip of September, closed to visitors but for the oil and punch of the train, and the Blackfeet nation in the expanse below the great rocks.

Looking out he feels the calling an eagle might feel in the drafts over the backbone of the continent, that something of light and stone and water, perhaps fire, has created him and breathed life through the opening of his lips, and there is a violence in that, he thinks, and a tenderness, and he sees as if with the eyes of a child the wings of the eagle thrown wide over the body of the beloved, the scream of the bird in the highborne wind.

*   *   *

Yet a dark pall covers Middies' eyes; he stares at everyone suspiciously. When Prifflach rises, Middie follows. They walk a few steps and sit down again in another couplet of chairs, aimed back down the corridor, to the next car, and the next. People are seen in a long line, from compartment to compartment, bumped by the small clicks and turns of the train, jilted forward, hitched to the side, bumped back. The people say nothing. They clutch their bags.

The scenario sickens him. Too many people. Too public. If he were alone, or in the dark of barrooms, he'd feel clear, free to do as he wished, but here the fray of his mind annoys him. He brushes the tips of his fingers over his left shirt pocket, the cloth there housing his mother's comb, he feels the form of it, the tines like a small alien hand, the spine simple and hard. He's already checked them all three times by order of Prifflach. Once each after the last three stops: Wolfpoint, Glasgow, Malta. The first time, he apologized, comforting an older woman on her way to see her son in Spokane. Prifflach had sent a wire out at Glasgow, inquiring what to do. The second check more of the same, this time soothing the worry of a young gal off to the state agricultural school in Pullman. Prifflach called it coincidence— two different burglars, two different towns, a little over three hundred dollars missing. But after the third stop, at Malta, when an elderly man was found dead, his head askew, a small well of blood in his right ear, the rumors poisoned every compartment.

He had money, said the help in the dining car. Paid for his meals in crisp new bills. But when Middie checked the body, Prifflach looking over his shoulder, there was nothing, no money, not even any silver. Middie felt the minds of the people beginning to hum and move and he sensed the interior of Prifflach, angry as if cornered, pushing him to take action. Middie hated it, but the line chose him, and he was big.

On the first check, the "just checking" check, no one resisted; everyone simply wanted the thief caught. The second check, the "only a coincidence, folks" check, people remained polite, grimacing some while Middie displaced their bags and Prifflach went through them. Middie had to pat the people down, check their coats, their clothing, have them empty each of their pockets. It took far longer than he wished, but mostly the people smiled and tried to be helpful. On the third check the death had changed things. The women whispered and shrank back from him. The body itself, alone in a sleeping car until the next stop, was like an evidence, an imprint of the predator among them. Middie felt the tension of it, the people's thoughts in fearful accord, like a dark vein of cloud swept into the bank of mountains, collecting, preparing.

Prifflach had declared all must hand over their weapons, and declared Middie the one to gather them. The men looked boldly at Middie as Prifflach rifled their bags. Some were openly angry. Many, he thought, suspected him, or Prifflach. Only a few gave up their arms, and unwillingly, a cluster of pistols, four Colts, two Derringers, along with one rifle. Other men lied directly, though Middie felt their weapons, in a bootleg or under the arm, the stock of a gun, the handle of a knife. He decided not to push and Prifflach silently colluded, the potential threat subduing the conductor's zeal. What Middie retrieved he stored in the engineer's cab. Returning, walking the aisles, he felt weary. People don't like being pushed, he thought.

The next stop, Havre, town of locked-in winters, town of bars. At last, the removal of the dead man, to be shipped back to Chicago. Not dusk or dawn, but day, not night as Middie would hope, nor the color of night. The body is well blanketed, taken off from the back of the train. Middie carries it across the platform and it feels light to him, almost birdlike in his arms. He turns his back to shield the view. Prifflach holds the door for him and as Middie enters the station he catches over Prifflach's shoulder the faces of passengers in the fourth car, most of them pale and dumb-looking, not meeting his eye. But one, the Indian man he'd noticed on his passenger checks, a crossbreed, looks right at him. The eyes are black from where Middie stands. He imagines round irises among the slanted whites; it reminds him of how people had stared at this man during the checks, a few uttering quiet threats while the man stared back at them as if taunting them to put meaning to their words. Despite the fact that the Indian was well dressed, Middie had had to quiet the car twice as they searched him.

Inside the station Middie hears Prifflach tell the attendant the death is nothing. Old man died in his sleep, Prifflach says. Line informed the family; they'll meet the body in St. Paul. The attendant is a potbellied bald man, chewing snuice. Prifflach orders Middie back to the train to watch the passengers. No sheriff, thinks Middie. Line saving its own skin. Closemouthed, he looks at Prifflach, but the conductor waves him on and Middie does as he is told.

He sits on the train, puts his head in his hands, runs his hands through his hair. He rises, he disembarks, rounds the platform and crosses the dirt street. He approaches the front door of the Stockman Bar. Door painted black, oiled hinges, inside a dim small room and three tables, dark marble counter with five stools, the place is clean, a lone bartender wiping things down. Help you? he says. No, Middie answers, the murmur of his voice barely audible. He needs a chair to sit in, a space to calm his mind. The bartender spits in a tin cup on the counter. You don't drink, you don't stay, he says. Middie feels things shutting down, his insides are heavy and tight, the center of him like an eclipse that obscures the light, three quick steps to the barman and one fist that rides the force of hip and shoulder, the man laid cold on the hardwood floor. Not dead, but still, and flat-backed, and Middie, seated in the chair he desires, watches the blood curl from a three-inch line over the man's eye, elliptic down his face to his neck, to the floor. Orbital bone still sound, eyes rolled back in the head, the man lies motionless and Middie considers him. Should've been Prifflach, he says aloud. But saying it Middie feels broken. He can't go back. His eyes are grave, dark as his father's. Darkness covers the earth and deep darkness its people. It is a darkness he feels he cannot undo. But he must, he thinks, he will. Prifflach comes cursing, and Middie walks in the conductor's shadow, back to the train, the people.

Three quick halts at Shelby, Cutbank, and Browning. East Glacier next, the station at the park's east entrance, the one with the Blackfeet Agency greeting in which three Indians wait on the small gray platform in full regalia. An elder in full eagle-feather headdress gives out cigars. Two women in white deerskin dresses sell beadwork. Only a handful of white passengers gawk this time, not all as is customary. Most remain subdued, brooding, sitting in their seats. Then on the track past East Glacier, climbing the high boundary toward the west side of the park and the depot at Belton, two more reports of impropriety, two more thefts, lesser, but significant, one of sixty dollars, the other forty. Not counting the unknown amount stolen from the dead man, the total, as Middie said, had reached four hundred and ten.

Middie loathes the thought of checking bags again. He thinks the people, all of them, close and far, dislike him. Some of the faces are full of disdain.

So? says Prifflach.

Yes? says Middie.

So start another check, says Prifflach. He speaks like a crow, thinks Middie. He watches Prifflach pull a small piece of paper from his vest pocket, the wire retrieved from the Havre station in answer to his plea at Glasgow. Prifflach turns the paper to Middie, these words: keep quiet—no police—security man finds thief—or loses job.

No good, says Middie, awkward, aloud, using a tone he'd seen his mother use to calm his father. Look at them, Middie says, motioning with his eyes to the people around him.

Prifflach turns on him, sharp-faced, and what he says makes Middie desire to kill him. It's your own good, boy. Line's takin' you out if you don't get it done. Move.

Middie sees it coming, and he wishes against it, but he knows no other alternative. All that college, he thinks, up against the wall with book learning, and nothing now for real life. Heavy shouldered, he rises from his seat. He begins the procedure again.

Pardon me, may I see your bag? and, Pardon, sir, I have to look through your personal effects. The words are graceful in Middie's mind, his mind electric, his body like ether around his words.

But people are openly hostile. A woman in the first car, one in the second, and one in the third make a scene and won't unhand their bags. He pulls the bags from the first two, and lets Prifflach search the contents while he quickly pats the people down, pushing his fingers in their coat pockets. When he approaches the third woman she claws a bright hole in his cheek. His mind thinks terrible things. Ugly, he tells himself. Ugly. Has to be done though, he thinks. Other passengers help him do it too, they hold the woman back while he searches her and while Prifflach gives the bag a thorough inspection. Idiots, Middie thinks, all of them, and me with them. They see it too, the people. They all admit inwardly the logic is imprecise, but better than doing nothing. Check everyone or it's no use. Futile, Middie thinks, a man can hide money anywhere. When he returns the third woman's bag she curses him. Then she looks him in the face, says God curse you, and turns her back.

Middie can't remember ever having heard a woman speak like that. He walks from the third car toward the fourth, opens the double doors at the end of the compartment, closes the doors behind. He stands on the deck, he hears the raw howl of the train, the wind. Something will happen now, he thinks. To his left a wall of wet granite undulates, hard and dark, blurred by the train speed. He looks up and sees the great face of it arching, reaching up and out, thousands of feet of rock, jagged and pinnacled at the top, swept up and out over the roof of the train. Beyond this, the gray sky is low and thick. The look of it gives him vertigo and he turns his head down, gripping the handrail, seeing his worn boots on the grated steel. His mother, he thinks, he can't remember her face.

To his right he can feel the valley out there, spread wide in a pattern of darks and lighter darks, filled from above by the distant pull of fog and rain. Sleet falls in wide diagonal sheets, descending into massive rock blacks and rock grays far on the other side of the valley. Along the bases of the mountains forests are spread like cloaks, and everything bleeds to a river that glistens coal like the curve of a gunbarrel, choked by the runoff of the storm. The river is the middle fork of the Flathead, past the summit of Marias Pass and past the great trestle of Two Medicine Bridge. They've crested the great divide and the train's muscle pumps faster now, louder on the down westward grade. The river runs due west from here, seeming to bury itself into the wide forested skirt of a solitary mass of land. The flattopped tower of the mass is obscured, mostly covered over by wet fog and cloud, but visible in its singularity and the ominous feel of something hidden in darkness, something entirely individual, devoid of any other, accountable to neither sky nor storm. At the mountain's height a black ridge is barely detectable in among the gray fog. The hulk of the land feels gargantuan. Is it Grinnell Point or Reynolds Mountain, Cleveland or Apikuni? He can't make it out. Here in Middie's reverie, muffled shouts are heard, faint like the far-off cry of a cat. He looks up to the doors of the fourth car, the final passenger car. Slender windows frame what he sees and suddenly the words, though disembodied, come clean. I've got him! yells a fatty-faced man, sealed up there in the box of the car. I've got the mother-hatin' rat.

Middie leaps forward, opening the fourth car, shouting, Stop! Wait! About midway up the car the fatty-faced man, and now four others, have thrown a man to the floor in the aisle. The man wears a brown tweed suit, he makes a vigorous struggle with his assailants.

It's him! cries the fat one. We caught him red-handed.

To avoid the wild flail, passengers press back against the walls. Women push their children in behind them, children with wide eyes, lit with fear.

Let go, says Middie, staring at the fat man, and the men heed his word quickly and without complaint. An understanding strikes Middie, a remembrance of the fear men harbor, bigger than a child's, and Middie recalls the pure sway he holds because he is big, over people, over men.

The captive stands in the aisle now, brushing wrinkles from his suit, his hair flung forward, black and thick over his face. The Indian, thinks Middie, as he draws nearer.

When the man pushes his hair back, the bones of his face appear, cheekbones driven up as if by hammers, chin chiseled like stone, and dark aggressive eyes, the skin a thin casing for all the intrepid want in him. Thin as a sheet of newsprint, thinks Middie, ready to tear open, ready for it all to rush out. The man tucks in his shirt and realigns his belt. He straightens his vest, then the lapels of his jacket, visibly pulling the tension back in and down, breathing. He is silent. He views his captors with contempt, each one.

Middie remembers seeing him board the train in Wolfpoint. Assiniboine-Sioux he'd thought. But after pulling his bag and questioning him four times he'd found him to be a Blackfeet-White cross, Blood in fact, a Blackfeet subtribe (and Irish on the other side, he'd said, one clan or another). He was on his way to his family's home south of West Glacier after a "work-related" trip to Wolfpoint. Middie had checked him once more than all the rest. The man said he taught at the college in Missoula. In education, he said. They locked eyes when Middie carried the dead man at Havre, but Middie had dismissed it, and other than the agitation of the crowd during the checks, an agitation Middie felt always accompanied whites and Indians, he had found nothing unusual. The man carried no weapon.

What is it? Middie asks the man with the fat head.

A short man, a man with slick hair, one of the others who had held the accused, speaks up vehemently. This man—he points in the Indian's face— this man has been lying! He's the one. He took all the money.

Slow, says Middie. Say what you know.

I have not lied, says the prisoner.

Shut up! the slick man yells.

Middie puts a forearm to the slick man's chest. Settle yourself, he says. Sit down.

The slick man obeys, whispering something, glaring. He's lying, he says. Hiding something.

How do you know?

Check his side, see for yourself. He's had his hand there in his jacket from the start.

The fat man butts in, edging with rage, He won't show us what he's got in there.

Is it true, sir? asks Middie, heightening his politeness. Is there something hidden in your vestcoat?

Yes, he states, looking into Middie's face, but that makes me neither a liar nor guilty of the offense in question.

We will check it, sir, Middie replies, but he feels aggravated. He doesn't like the uppity tone the Indian has used. What have you concealed? Middie asks.

My money belt, says the man.

* * *

Middie hardens his look. His hands sweat. He wipes them on his pantlegs as he stares at the man. Probably had it on his waistline, Middie thinks, concealed under the clothing, probably thin as birch bark. He remembers Prifflach muttering under his breath at the Indian, checking the man's bag, a small cylindrical briefcase made of beaten brown leather, sealed at the top by a thin zipper that ran between two worn handles, the word MONTANA inscribed on the side. Mostly papers in the bag.

You have searched my briefcase and my wallet, says the man, and me once more than the others. I saw no need for you to search my money belt. And if I had shown you my belt, would that not become a target for the robber if he were present in this compartment during the search?

Don't listen to him, the slick man says in a wet voice, he's slippery.

The crowd murmurs uneasily. Middie notes that outside, the fog has pressed in. Nothing of the valley can be seen, and nothing of the sky. The mountains will be laid low, Middie thinks. He hears the words soft and articulate in his mother's voice. Outside is the featureless gray of a massive fog bank, and behind it a feeling of the bulk of the land.

Check his belt, the fat face says.

Then the crowd begins. See what he's got, says a red-haired woman, the fat man's wife by the look of it, the small eyes, the clutching, heavy draw of the cheeks about the jowls. She says the words quietly but they are enough to hasten a flood. Do it now, hears Middie. Make him hand it over, Take it from him, Pull up his shirt, Take it—all from the onlookers, all at once, and from somewhere low and small back behind Middie, the quiet words, Cut his throat.

The conductor arrives and Middie exhales and feels his body go slack; he stares outside. The gray-black of the storm leaks moisture on the windows. The moisture gathers and pulls lines sideways along the windows, minuscule lines in narrow groupings of hundreds and wide bars of thousands, rivulets and the brothers of rivulets, and within them the broad hordes of their children, their offspring, all pulled back along the glass to the end of the train, to the end of seeing.

You will have him hand over that money belt directly, says Prifflach, his nose leading, his face pinched, set like clay. Pressure builds in the bodycage of Middie, a pressure that pushes out against his skin like a large child caught inside, big feet placed on the ribs, forcing out as if to crack the ribs wide and emerge leaping from the open ribwork. Middie reaches out, grabbing the accused man's wrist, gripping the flesh with frozen fingers, red-white fingers latching on.

To Middie's relief the man responds. With one arm in Middie's grip, the man uses his free hand to untuck the front of his shirt. He slides the money belt to a point above his waist, and undoes the small metal clasps that hold the belt in place. His fingers are so meticulous, thinks Middie, so dexterous and sure. His eyes as clear as the sky before they reached Glacier, cold and steely-black. Middie looks again to the window. He thinks his own reflection is not unlike the gray outside, and behind it the unpeopled weight of land, the emptiness. He notes he has left his billy club in the last compartment, on the floor near a seat where he'd checked a man's ankles, his socks. Middie's fists feel big, hard as the stones of a landslide. He doesn't need it, he tells himself.

Give up the belt, Prifflach says, though already the man is pulling the belt free.

He holds it out to the conductor. Nothing out of the ordinary, he says. I'm simply a man carrying my own money. His hair is still bent, his shirt poorly tucked. He does not look away from his accusers.

At once, the fat man and his wife shout something unintelligible.

We'll see, says the conductor, interpreting their words. We'll see if it's his money. At the corners of Prifflach's mouth the skin twitches. Prifflach takes the money belt and hands it to the slick man. Count it up, he says, watching the Indian's face.

The slick man thumbs the money once, finding an unfortunate combination of bigger and smaller bills. How much is there? asks the conductor. The slick man counts again, slowly. Five hundred ten dollars, he says. Exactly one hundred more than the amount stolen. Middie knows a desire has gripped them, and that they all, silently, hastily, have calculated the old dead man's loss at a clean one hundred. Middie has done the same.

I could have told you that, says the accused.

Prifflach tells the man to shut up, then says, A hundred dollars more than the total. He folds the money belt in half, and half again; I'll take that, he says, placing it in the chest pocket of his coat.

It comes clear to Middie now, the look of the onlookers, the way of their eyes and their bodies, how they've all torn loose inside, all come unspun. He remembers what he'd read in a pamphlet at the West Glacier station a month ago. Something of a hidden passage west, close to the headwaters of the Marias, a high mountain pass that according to Indian belief was steeped in the spirit world, inhabited by a dark presence. Decades back, when the line first wanted to chart its track through here, no Indian would take a white man through. Death inhabited the place.

Middie sees the demeanor of the Blackfeet man change. The man's face loses expression, his body pulls inward and a gathering is felt in the space between them, Middie senses it, the surging, up through the flesh of the Indian's forearm. Middie tightens his grip.

The crowd moves.

Suspected him back in Glasgow, a stout man pipes up. I should have known, says another, and from the slick man, He ain't gettin' outta here. Low again, deep back in the crowd, a voice says slit his throat.

The movement begins in words and rustling, then leaps upward like a mighty wave that breaks upon the people and the man all at once. The Blackfeet man jerks free and jumps the chair back next to him, seeking to flank the men and escape from the rear of the compartment. The men scramble after him, Prifflach leading, the others following, all of them livid with hate.

Middie vaults a set of chairs and lands on the Blackfeet man, slamming him bodily against the sidewall of the car. The man rights himself and spits in Middie's face and Middie, fueled now, lifts him, encircling the Indian's neck in the crook of his left arm, positioning him. He props him up, left hand on the man's shoulder, holding him an arm's length away. Then he levels a blow with the right that bounces the Blackfeet man's head off the near window, flings his hair like a horsetail, and leaves a grotesque indentation where the cheekbone has caved in. Four other men, along with Middie, jerk the prisoner from the wall, shake him hand over fist to the aisleway. They surround him, and proceed to drag him toward the back of the car. The shoving lurches the Indian forward and makes his neck look thin, snaps his head back, throws his eyes to the ceiling.

What are you doing? he cries out, I'm innocent, and straining from the hands that grasp at his upper body, turning his face to the window, to the gray valley beyond, he says, I have a wife. I have a child.

With shocking swiftness the Indian throws his forearms out and lunges forward with his head in order to strike someone. But now his flailings are as nothing to the weight of the accusers: there are many men now, their arms entangled in his limbs, controlling him easily. They punch him in the back and in the back of the head. Keep your head down! they say; You'll lose your teeth in a second. The group is packed in, forming a tight untidy ball in the aisleway and among the spaces between the seats. A thick odor is in the air.

The prisoner's head is near the floor. Reaching for the Indian's waist, Middie sees a look of resignation, a look of light among the features of his face. The man stares at Middie and whispers something Middie cannot hear or understand.

Amid the tumult a smaller voice says, Wait! It comes from behind Middie, up near the front of the car. Turning, looking up and back through the moving heads, back behind the bending, pressing torsos, Middie sees the source of the voice, a small man, adolescent in appearance, thin-boned in a simple two-piece suit. The man has fine, blonde hair and oval wire-rimmed glasses.

Wait! the man says, I know him.

A large man at the back of the mob turns to the boyish man and says, You shut up.

The small man's face goes red, he shrinks back to his seat. Middie sees this and turns back to the mob. The people are grabbing the Blackfeet man's clothing in their hands and shaking his body like a child's doll. Men are emerging from their seats, running the aisles like ants, joining the mob. The man's limbs appear loose in the torque of the crowd. The arms move as if boneless, the elbows seem disconnected from the shoulders.

From his vantage Middie turns and sees the little man with his head down now as the people swirl toward the rear of the car, down to the doors they have already pulled back and the opening tilted like a black mouth from which the wind screams. Middie hears the accused grunting, cursing. He sees the little man rise and walk directly to the rear guard of the mob. Unable to get through, the little man sidesteps the knot of people, climbing over three or four seats, repositioning women and children. He travels awkwardly but consistently, like a leggy insect, toward the back of the compartment, toward the opening and the landing beyond. He goes unrecognized by all but Middie and when he reaches the far wall of the car, he stops, and stares. The prisoner is held about the neck by the thick hands of Prifflach, clinched about the waist by Middie and on both sides by bold, angry men.

The small man positions himself, mounting the arms of the last two aislechairs so that he stands directly before the mob. He straddles the aisle, the land a blur in the open doorway behind him, around him the live wind a strange unholy combustion. He draws his fists to his sides, billows his chest as he gathers air, and screams, Stop! A wild scream, high and sharp like the bark of a dog.

The little man's effort creates a brief moment of quiet in which the people stand gaping at him. Seizing this, he strings his words rapidly. I know him. I spoke with him when he got on in Wolfpoint. He has a three-year-old daughter. He has a wife. He has a good mother, a father. He will be dropped off at the stop on the far side of Glacier where they are waiting for him. He will return with them by car to the Mission Range.

Shut up, says the fat man.

I won't, says the small man. He told me precisely.

He lied, says the slick man.

Let me speak, the small man pleads. He touches his hand to his face, a gesture both elegant and tremulous.

We won't, the mob responds, and in their movement and in the pronounced gather of their voices the prisoner is lifted by the neck and shoved forward toward the door.

Out of the way! someone yells, and Middie watches as the small man takes a blow to the side of the head, a shot of tremendous force that lifts him light as goosedown, unburdened in flight to where his body hits the wall near the floor of the car and he lies crumpled, his face lolling to one side. Thickly now the small man says, He told me precisely. His words are overrun but he continues, slow, distinct. He told me precisely, in Wolfpoint. Before all of this, he had five hundred ten dollars of earnings. He meant to do what he and his wife dreamed. Middie's fists are bound up in the clothing of the Blackfeet man, his forearms are bone to bone with the man's ribs. The little man is speaking, He meant to buy land, off the reservation. The voice seems small, down between the chairs, He meant to build a home.

The opening through which they pass is wide, the small man's body a bit of detritus they have cast aside, the landing now beneath their feet solid and whole, like a long-awaited rest. Middie hears the velocity of wind and steel as he flows with the crowd to the brink. He feels the rush, like the expectancy of power in a bull's back when the gate springs wide, like the sound a man's jaw makes when it breaks loose.

Also he feels sorrow; he wants to cry or cry out. He wants to reach for the ivory hair comb but a weight of bodies presses him from behind and his hands are needed to control the captive. He feels the indent of the guardrail firmly on his thigh. He hears the small man's voice, back behind him. He told me at Wolfpoint—precisely five hundred ten dollars. Five hundred ten.

The landing is narrow, the people many, and they are knotted and pushed forward by a score more, angry men running from other cars, clogging the aisle to get to the man. Those at the front grab the railing, the steel overhead bars, they grab each other, the Indian, the enemy. Noise surrounds them, the train's cry, the wide burn of descent, the people's yells are high and sharp above everything, shrill as if from the mouths of predatory birds.

The Indian's suitcoat and vest are gone. His slim torso looks clean in his worried shirt, a V-shaped torso, trim and strong. In the press of it Middie is hot. Oxlike, he feels the burden of everyone, borne at once in him, and he bends and grabs the man's leg. Other men do the same, there are plenty of hands now. He wants to hold the man fast but instead the crowd shoves the man aloft, tipping him upside down, clutching his ankles, removing his shoes. They tear off his shirt, then his ribbed undershirt. They throw the shoes down among the tracks. The clothing they throw out into the wind where it whisks away and falls deep into the fog of the valley, rolling and descending like white leaves.

From here the man is lowered between the cars. He becomes silent. Below the captive, Middie sees the silvery gleam of the tracks, a line in the black blur of the ties, the line bending almost imperceptibly at times, silver but glinting dull like teeth. With his elbows he tries to hold the people back. He feels the oncoming force of the crowd behind him, the jealousy, the desire. A woman's voice is heard, a voice he knows but does not recognize. He bows his back, groaning, trying to draw the man forth. The words are like a song, simple and beautiful in his mind: Put on your garments of splendor. He smells the oil of the train, the heat, the wet rock of the mountain.

He sets his jaw and strains, he would pull the people and the man and the whole world to the mercy of his will; he gains no ground.

In the gusts of wind, the mob squints their eyes. Leaning forward, their hair is blown back, it swirls some, it blows back again. The speed of the train and the noise of the tracks, the scent of high sage and jack pine, the fogged void of gray as wide and deep as an ocean, but foremost the wind, which rushes up against the mob creating an almost still-life movement into which they carry their considered enemy. Then the wind dies. The river of men, flowing from the compartment, bottlenecks in the doorway. Bodies from the choked opening to the guardrail twist and writhe and a vast shouting commences. Middie says No! This must stop! He grips the Blackfeet man's belt with both fists and pulls him upward. His big body is a countermovement against the rise of all around him but angry yells issue from wide red mouths and the mob grows to an impossible mass that pushes and swells, and breaks free in a sudden gush. Middie finds himself with the Indian airborne, cast into the gulf without foot or handhold, he has lost everything, and falling he sees a shaft of blue high in the grey above him and he is surprised at how light he feels, and how time has slowed to nothing. He reaches back seeking a purchase he will not find, and in the singular sweep of his arm he takes people unaware—Prifflach, the fat man, his wife, the slick man—they fly from the edge, effortless in the push of the mob, unstrung bodies and tight faces, over the lip of the guardrail and down between the cars, down to the tracks, the wheels, the black pump of the smoking engine, the yell of the machine.

THE NEUTERED BULLDOG

by RACHEL SHERMAN

WHEN MY TEACHER first began her affair, she told me about it on the rug where it had happened. We were in the second floor study of her house—above her husband's office—where she had first kissed Brian Wojowsky.

The floor was hard with only a thin rug on top of it. She had a couch but they hadn't used it, and while she told me, neither did we. I sat on the wood part, facing her bookshelves, while she leaned against the wall and smoked one of my cigarettes. It was the afternoon, during lunch hour, and soon we would both have to be back at school.

"Brian is in my gym class and in my math class next period," I told her. I took the cigarette from her thin freckled fingers and blew smoke into the dusty light.

"Really?" she said. She took the cigarette back and stubbed it out in the ceramic ashtray she hid from her husband, Ed. "I didn't know that." I got up and pulled my jeans down on my waist. If I was late for math I could get a detention, and my teacher had already written me a bunch of notes. She couldn't write too many more. Boys were already saying things.

"What does Brian wear in gym class?" she asked, getting up and looking in the mirror that was next to her computer. She ran her fingers around the rim of her lips.

I had never thought about Brian in gym class before. He was not some-one I noticed. He was small, for one, and not attractive in the way I liked boys I couldn't have. If I couldn't have any of them, I saved my fantasies for the best. Brian was thin and quiet and didn't play sports.

"I don't know," I laughed, walking down the stairs to the living room where she had lined the windows with rocks and shells and beach glass she had found. "Shorts and a T-shirt, probably."

My teacher followed me and we walked out the door together.

"See you tomorrow—third period," she said, getting into her car. "I'll be busy tonight," she said, and winked.

On the first day of school, in the beginning of fall, I called my teacher "Mrs. Holly." She wasn't my teacher then the way that she is now. On the first day of school she wore glasses and her hair pulled back. She wore a pleated skirt that was too long to show her perfect calves that tapered in to her knee in exactly the right place.

The desks were already in a circle when everyone got to class so we all sat around and tried not to look at one another. Mrs. Holly was a new teacher, and no one told her that we weren't used to sitting that way. "I'd like to go around the room and have everyone tell a little bit about them-selves," she had said. She pointed at me. "Starting with you."

"Moldy," one of the boys whispered loud enough so everyone could hear. I rolled my eyes and ignored him.

I had been nicknamed "Moldy" because my last name is Gold and it rhymed. Sometimes they called me "Moldy Matzoh" because I am Jewish.

I had been drawing in my notebook, making circles inside of circles. I did not want to go first.

"Um…" I said, "My name is Sarah… I'm sixteen years old… I don't play any sports."

"Okay," Mrs. Holly said, smiling, "Tell us a dream."

"A nighttime dream?" I asked. My dreams were filled with colors and boys and people without any genitals rubbing up against each other .

"No, a daytime dream," Alec Ryerson said and there were laughs around the circle.

"I pass," I said, that first day.

I handed in my first poem to Mrs. Holly after our second class. The poem, "P is for Prozac," was about a girl who commits suicide. It did not rhyme.

When I read it in class, Mrs. Holly smiled and asked me to stay afterward.

She told me that I had talent, like her.

After class we both sat at the desks, next to each other.

"You remind me of me," she said.

I blushed because she was beautiful. She was tall with reddish hair and I was tall but did not look like her. I looked at the width of her freckled wrist and compared it to my own.

"I would love for you to come over sometime," she said, "It's important for poets to stick together."

I nodded at my teacher and looked away from her eyes.

"I'm a person too, you know," she said, tilting her head so that I had to look at her. She laughed and invited me to her house. She told me that when we were alone, she didn't like to be called "Mrs. Holly."

Brian is not the best poet in the class. I am. That is why my teacher likes me. That is why, after I handed in my first poem, she invited me over to her house.

On the first visit I met her husband, Ed, who is handsome and nice, and who shook my hand. He looked the way I imagined a husband should look, with dark hair parted to the side.

"She's my best student," my teacher told him.

They stood there in their hallway together, he taller than she, and I imagined them making love.

When Ed went to work, she told me he didn't like to fuck.

"Really?" I asked. My teacher was beautiful and I thought that everyone wanted beautiful women. If I were beautiful I was sure things would be different.

"So why don't you get a divorce?" I asked her. It was the first time I had been to her house.

"I don't know. I don't know why we even got married. It just seemed like a good idea at the time."

I watched her purse her lips. We were in her study smoking cigarettes.

"Ed will be done soon," she said, taking my cigarette from me and taking a drag, then putting it out in the ashtray.

I looked at the floor where, beneath us, Ed was working.

"He seems nice," I said.

She shook her head. "He doesn't like it dirty. We're not compatible."

My teacher told me about an ice sculptor she had met, a man who knew how to make love. She said they went into his freezer to cool themselves down, and she watched as he carved things: birds and bowls for restaurants and a naked woman made of ice, who, when she melted, dripped water from her crotch, for his art.

She wrote a poem about the ice sculptor. He wasn't as tall as she was, but he had thick arms that made her feel small.

We left her study and I followed her up the stairs to the bedroom. We lay on her big bed and looked at ourselves across the room in the mirror on the vanity.

"How old do you think I look?" she asked.

I did not know.

"Thirty," I said, "Twenty-eight?" I was not good at telling people's ages.

"Really?" she said, pursing her lips. Her lips were shriveled in a strange way that reminded me of brains.

"I think so, yeah," I said.

She squinted and reached over to feel my face. I worried her hands felt each acne bump on my skin, but she smiled. She pushed my hair behind my ear.

"Wow," she said, "And you don't even own your face yet."

After class, the next week, my teacher pinched me under the table and wrote on her notebook, "I need to show you something. Stay after class."

When class was over we sat on the desktops and closed the door. My teacher opened her folder and took out a sheet of paper that was typed. "Read this," she said.

I read the poem. It was short, about a neutered bulldog who was sad and thought no one would ever love him.

I looked up at my teacher who was looking at me, watching me read and smiling.

"I think I'm missing something," I said.

"Really?" she asked, "I thought it was so obvious. Brian must feel inadequate. He must feel inadequate as a man."

"Brian Wojowsky wrote this?" I asked, looking again at the neat typewriting, definitely from a real typewriter.

"Yeah," she said, taking the page back. "He gave it to me this morning during homeroom. Who would have thought? I mean, he never says anything, right? So talented... And how great that he can express himself this way. It's kind of sexy, even though he's admitting he might not be able to satisfy a woman."

She wasn't looking at me when she said this. She had her skirt bunched up at her knees and her feet on the chair. Someone could look in on us through the small rectangular window on the door. "Yeah," I said, pretending I understood. It did not surprise me that I was missing something, since the way she told me things, sometimes, made me think everyone knew things I didn't. It was as if all the secrets people whispered to one another, all the books I hadn't read, were the things that I most needed to know.

"I wonder if he knows how good he is..." my teacher said, placing the page back in her folder, being careful not to crease it. "I should tell him," she said, nodding to herself.

My teacher is a poet, and that means she gets a faraway look sometimes. I wonder if I will get that way when, someday, people will watch me stare. She is a poet, so sometimes everyday words, words unphrased and boring, are beneath her to hear. She was thinking about Brian's words, I could tell. Words on paper were stronger than anything. My simple word, the squeak of my leaving, was not enough for her to come back to me that day, and I wondered if I was really a poet too. It worried me that I might be just a girl with too much time, when I heard myself say, "Goodbye." My teacher calls me in the middle of the night. She whispers into the phone.

"I did it!" she says, "I saw it!"

"Saw what?" I say.

"The neutered bulldog!" she says and laughs.

I am still half-asleep, warm in my bed.

"Can we talk tomorrow?" I ask, even though I love her.

"OK," she whispers and puts down the phone.

When I am at home, in my own house, I go upstairs and lock the door to the bathroom where I lie on the thin bath carpet on the tile floor and try to think only about the things I can see. I look at the dust beneath the sink cabinet and the underside of the toilet bowl and up at the red heat lamps I turn on. I look out the top of the window at the black branches against the gray sky and inevitably feel sad and lonely.

Twice I have showered in the bathroom with all my clothes on, which felt strange and warm, but in a good way, until I turned the water off. Then I felt cold and disgusting, and my jeans stuck to me in a thick and heavy way. Usually I get in the shower without my clothes and sometimes I shave different parts of myself I hadn't before like the backs of my hands and my toes.

On the floor with the heat lamps on, I can only think about what I see until I think of something else. No matter what is in front of me, it seems, it never keeps all of my attention.

I imagine Brian and my teacher, using up all the space on her bed. I imagine Brian so small next to my teacher.

Brian is just a boy in my class, and I don't know how to make her see that everything that is in front of him is probably just there, and that she, so big on her own bed, makes him focus on her. It occurs to me then, sadly, that maybe this is what she wants.

It is Saturday so I drive to my teacher's for brunch. She mixes up a salad dressing from balsamic vinegar and mustard and pours it over lettuce. She makes us chamomile tea.

My teacher is still wearing her nightgown. Her husband has been away for the week on a business trip. We sit alone at her sunny table and pick at our salads.

"So, I did it," she says.

"With Brian?" I say.

"Yes. And he has nothing to worry about," she says, shaking her head, "It won't be a problem for him. I think he'll be fine."

My teacher doesn't know that I am still a virgin. When I tried to do it, once, with a boy with huge feet I met last summer, it hurt too much and he couldn't get it in. It did not feel good and I can't imagine it ever feeling any way but sore. I am told that once you start you will not want to stop, and I pretend to my teacher that I have started, with boys in other school districts that she doesn't know.

"Did you like it?" I ask.

"I think we're going to have to work on it," she says, swiping her highlighted hair from her face and letting the strap of her nightgown fall so that I can see the start of her nipple.

In math class, I watch Brian walk in. He does not look at me. He sits down across from me, his shaggy hair in his face, and begins to draw in his notebook. He has acne on his neck that it looks like he picked, and his shoelaces are untied. He does not look full, the way my teacher looked in the morning. His cheeks look like he is sucking on a straw.

I draw in my notebook. I try to picture how lesbians do it. I draw two vaginas squeezing each other with their lobes. This must be the way.

I ask to go to the bathroom and sit in the stall and smoke a cigarette. Brian is a loser, I think, and no one in our class wants to date him. Everyone loves my teacher. The boys that see me leave with her ask if I ever lick her pussy.

I put my head between my legs to get a head rush and try to picture Brian with his neutered dick. I picture my teacher on top, her freckled body astride small Brian. I picture them lying in the sheets afterwards, looking at their reflections in the same mirror that my teacher and I did and laughing.

I go to my teacher's after school. She is sitting in the backyard on one of her lawn chairs, her eyes closed and her face up to the sun.

"Come tan with me," she says, but I hate the sun. I pull a chair into the shade of her house.

Her garden is lined with bricks she put there herself. I've seen her some days, shovel in hand, trying to grow things. She wears a hat, like a woman with a garden in the movies.

"Where did you learn to garden?" I ask her.

Her past seems like something unreal, something that would never happen to someone like me. The way she talks about things seems so easy, like she slipped out of a bed somewhere faraway, already a woman with a husband and lovers, already with a past.

"My dad," she says, "He used to make us help him plant things."

She keeps her eyes closed and I stare at her. It is like she is asleep and I am spying, or that she is dead and I am examining her, so close, in a way that nobody would let anyone else look at them.

My teacher is wearing tight white jeans and a striped T-shirt. Her skin looks papery around her eyes and I can see the creamy cover-up she has on her face. There are white hairs on her cheeks, fine hairs that look soft. For a moment I wonder what would happen if I sat on her lap with my arm around her neck.

My father does not plant things. He makes me mow the lawn every weekend on a small tractor. He makes me wear headphones so that I don't lose my hearing from the loud noise the mower makes. He has a way I am supposed to mow: around and around in one big oval, then in smaller circles when I get to the two big trees in the middle of the yard.

"I like to garden," she says, "It distracts me, you know?"

I don't know, but I nod. It is hard for me to get distracted that way.

When I mow, all I can think of is the next circle, and then the next, and how when I am done I will be able to go inside and lie on the bathroom floor.

My teacher's eyes are still closed, and she does not see me nod. She opens one eye and smiles.

"Brian is coming over tonight," she says.

"Again?" I ask.

"Again," she says.

At home, in the bathroom, I lie on the floor and turn on the heat lamps and close my eyes. I think about my grandparents' old bathroom with its bidet that my mother once washed my underwear in when I peed in my pants.

"What's it really for?" I had asked.

I had never tried the bidet then, and now that I am old enough my grandparents have moved to a less fancy apartment.

I love the idea of being that clean after I go to the bathroom, hardly having to wipe. I love the idea of all that mess disappearing.

Someone knocks and my father's voice says, "What's going on?"

He must see the sliver of red glow beneath the door and worry.

"Nothing," I say.

In math class, on Monday, Brian's shoelaces are untied. I wonder if he slept over my teacher's or if he drove home late, listening to loud music down the long roads in the dark. I wonder if he is like me, and can only think of other things while he is in math class. I draw a woman with a long white skirt on my math test margin.

Mr. Hall, our math teacher, calls on Brian.

"And what did you get for number nineteen?" he asks. Mr. Hall wears wide ties with bright patterns on them. To get our attention, he says.

"Um," Brian says, shuffling through his papers.

"Dork," Alec Ryerson coughs into his armpit.

"Enough," Mr. Hall says, pointing at Alec. "Brian?" he asks.

"Um. I didn't get that far," Brian says.

Brian's face is flushed. He is in the moment. He doesn't know what I know about him, that I know what he is thinking. That I know, I know. I didn't even have to be there.

* * *

My teacher holds up a pair of plaid boxer shorts.

"They're his!" she says.

"Whose?" I ask.

"Brian's," she says, laughing.

Before I met my teacher, I thought only teenagers acted this way.

"Oh," I say.

Ed is on a business trip again and will be returning tomorrow. I wonder what she will tell him she did while he was away.

We sit on her couch in front of the fire place and drink tea. I look through a photography book on her coffee table. It is a photo book of trees.

"How are you going to see Brian when Ed gets back?" I ask.

"Oh, well," she says, sipping, "I have it all planned out. When Ed is at work Brian can come over and we can have our rendezvous in my study."

"Wow," I say, "Right above him?!"

"Yes," she says, "It turns me on."

I did not know that cheating was so easy. It is all a matter of time and space, it seems: When one person leaves a space, another person can fill it. When one person comes back, the other person leaves. Just like that.

If I squeezed over in my own bed there would be room for one more. There is also another bed in my room for sleepovers, but no one has slept there since eighth grade. Sometimes I switch beds for a few weeks and sleep in the empty bed. I wake up in the night and wonder where I am. The room is in the wrong place, and I can see what every girl that ever slept there saw: my mother's old doll collection she passed down to me, the slant of the ceiling in stucco white, and my own empty bed, looking more cozy than it did before. After a few days, I crawl back into my own bed and wake up only to pee.

"Do you think my breasts are sagging?" my teacher asks me in the afternoon while she is changing into her bra. We are in her bedroom and I am sitting on the bed where she sleeps and does it with Brian.

It had not occurred to me that there was anything wrong with my teacher before. She had been a model. She is a poet, and after a new man makes love to her, she has a new poem in the morning.

"No, not at all," I say. I sit on my teacher's bed and watch her.

"You should try this on," she says, taking out one of her dresses from her closet. It is long and navy blue and goes out where her hips must have pushed it.

"I'll try it in the bathroom," I say, taking the silky dress off the hanger.

"Don't be silly," she says, catching me and pulling at the other end of the dress, "try it on here."

I sit on the bed and take off my jeans and then my shirt, covering myself up quickly by putting the dress under my chin and then over my head. My teacher watches me and laughs.

"What are you doing?" she says. "You silly."

"Stand up," she says, and I do.

First my teacher pulls the dress all the way down. It is a bit big, but in the three-way mirror she turns me in front of, I can tell that it fits in the back.

"Look how nice you look," she says, and then she turns me around to face her. She looks into my eyes and I laugh because for a moment I forget who I am. Then she lifts the dress above my head so that she can see everything but my face.

"Stop," I laugh. I try to pull the dress down with my hands but my teacher is tall and strong. She holds the material above my head so I can only see the outline of her through the fabric, and not what her mouth is doing.

I stop trying to bend over. I hold my hands above my head and surrender. My teacher lets the dress fall back down.

"You're lovely," she says, pointing her finger at me.

"Shut up," I say. I wonder if she is teasing me. Or if she feels bad for me. I also wonder, enough to make me blush, if maybe she is telling the truth.

In gym class we have to run the entire field. The gym teachers are all old men—stupid old men—who wear shorts that go down to their old men knees. They are tired old men who have been here too long. They don't even coach sports teams, they just watch us run in gym.

A bunch of kids go into the woods at the edge of the field and smoke pot. You can see through the trees when the gym teachers are calling them in and you can hear the whistles in the woods. These kids depend on the other kids, the nerds, to run around and around the field for the whole gym period. I usually go into the woods alone or else stand near the other kids and smoke cigarettes. When there is a big group, sometimes they don't notice me.

Today Brian is there, smoking a cigarette between two fingers like a girl, not like the other boys who hold it with their thumbs and look sexy. He looks stupid smoking; he has always been one of the runners. I wonder if he has only taken up smoking since he has taken up sex.

Alec Ryerson walks over to me and asks me for a light. He has blond hairs on his legs that are thick on his thighs. He has a joint.

"Hey," he says, "Hey, Sarah." He talks as if he is just remembering my name.

"Hey, Alec," I say.

I slump down and lean against a tree and light the joint for him. He leans over and looks down, and in the flame his eyelashes are dark and long.

Alec stands back and blows the pot smoke in my face.

"Brian says you eat Mrs. Holly's pussy."

I look over at Brian, who is looking out at the field.

"Shut the fuck up," I say to Alec.

"Brian," Alec calls over to him, "Didn't you say you saw Mrs. Holly and Sarah in a 69?"

Brian looks at me and blushes. It seems to be the first time we have ever looked at each other. His eyes are small like mine.

"Yes," Brian says. He needs no coaxing from Alec. He is set on his lie, the way he insisted the neutered bulldog was about his "friend's brother" to my teacher before she got it out of him and then inside of her.

I look down at the ground where onion grass is growing up from the dirt.

"Jaime Dwyer says he saw you two at the movies once too."

It was true my teacher and I had gone to the movies once, two towns away. We shared popcorn and a large diet soda and sat near the front, silently. We both cried—it was a sad movie about two people in love. During one scene, while the actors had sex, my teacher pinched my leg and twisted. I wanted to tell her I didn't like that, that I was sensitive.

I hadn't seen Jaime Dwyer there. I often missed other people when my teacher was around. When I was alone, I was always looking at people—kids in the halls who were trying to walk quickly without tripping, mothers who looked like their sons, picking them up in their vans after practice. With my teacher I felt safe, like I had a blindfold on and she was leading me, her manicured hand pushing and pulling me.

"Whatever, asshole" I say.

I realize how much I hate Brian. I hate his smallness and his stupid poems. He is unremarkable and I notice everything.

"You stupid bitch," Brian says, out of nowhere. He flicks his cigarette like some tough guy and folds his arms across his chest.

Kay Simon, the class slut, pulls down her belly-shirt so her breasts are flattened. "Fight!" she says, walking over to where we are from where she was, wherever she was. "Fight!" she says.

Other kids start to come out from behind the trees like dwarfs who were hiding in *The Wizard of Oz*. Where were all these people before? They surround us, and for once it seems like Brian and I are popular.

I feel like I am in the middle of things, and I start to get a ringing in my ears. Brian and I are inside a group in the middle of the woods and in the center of my world. I can see his pores.

"Come on, " Alec says, clapping his hands like he's trying to get a dog to come to him.

"Dyke," Brian whispers.

I get close to him like I will spit on him, but instead I say, "Neuter."

No one else can hear us, but Brian's face turns red.

The whistle blows. A gust of wind hits us. Brian and I can only see each other.

"Shit," Alec says, walking back to the field. Everyone else starts to follow. If we are not back by the second whistle we get detention.

I watch as Brian walks with his head down, his hands in his pockets. I walk behind him, staring at the back of his greasy head. I walk in the footprints he makes in the misty field, noting that my footprints are bigger.

At home, my teacher calls.

"I want you to come over for dinner," she says, "and wear the dress."

The dress has been in my closet, hanging there as if it is waiting in the shape I hope to fill.

"Eight o'clock," my teacher says.

In the bathroom, after my shower, I lie on the floor and think of how I will tell her. I will move over to her side of the table and sit on her lap. I will stroke her hair off her face and put my finger to her wrinkled lips.

"Him or me," I will say, "Choose."

Then she will answer me with her hands or her tongue and I will find the words in her mouth, without her having to say them.

I smooth the dress on my hips outside my teacher's front door. I look down at the pouch of my stomach and suck it in. In my backpack are two packs of cigarettes and wine from my parents' cabinet.

I ring the doorbell and put one hand on my hip. I wonder where her husband is tonight.

When my teacher opens the door she is smiling. She is wearing a tight black minidress that hangs off the shoulder, and her hair half-up, half-down. In the light, she looks like a Club MTV dancer. I have never seen her so beautiful.

"Come in," she says, kissing me on the cheek. "You look fabulous."

"You do too," I say, putting down my backpack, and I walk into the living room. There, on the couch, sits Brian in a sweater and khaki pants, as if he thinks he is grown up. He holds a glass of red wine and motions it to me as if he is giving me a toast. He is smirking.

"You know Brian," my teacher says, "and I want you to meet Michael. He's the ice sculptor I was telling you about."

Michael is leaning on the fireplace mantle, looking at the photo book of trees. His blond hair is tied back in a ponytail, and I can see the veins in his big arms.

Michael shakes my hand and I start to feel a ringing in my ears.

"Good to meet you," he says, and I am surprised he does not have an accent.

I sit on the arm of the couch. I want to put my head between my legs but I don't. I feel like I am sweating through my dress.

"Want a cigarette?" Brian asks, opening his pack towards me. My teacher has gone into the kitchen and I wonder what everyone was talking about before I arrived.

I take one of Brian's cigarettes. He takes out a lighter and flips it open on his knee. He is stupid, and I think he must have practiced that move over and over, the way I mouthed to my mirror, "Him or me?" I hate him.

"Here's some wine," my teacher says, pouring me a large glass.

Brian and I watch my teacher walk over to Michael. She puts her arm around his low waist and opens her legs. He puts his hand on her ass and moves it with his stubby fingers.

"Come up to my study," she says to him, "Let's pick out some music to dance to."

I have an urge to look at Brian and smirk, as if I am saying "We know what that means," but we have shared enough secrets, and we both know, without looking at each other, what we know.

I listen to my teacher's laughter while I trace the patterns in her rug with my foot. I hear the door shut, then a thump, then muted laughter, and then nothing. I wonder if Ed hears sounds like these and thinks she is bumping around her office, just writing poems.

"Oh God," Brian says, putting his head in his hands.

There is a space on the couch next to Brian, between us, that needs filling. I lean from the arm of the couch and slide my butt down. It feels easy moving this way, the red wine making me ache.

My hand touches Brian Wojowsky's back and I rub it in circles—first big and then smaller and smaller to the center of his back as if there was something there that needed kneading. In the center of Brian Wojowsky there must be something like that, but I do not say anything, because we are not writing poetry. The poem, it seems, is where my fingers go, on the tiny bone I come back to each time the circle becomes a dot. It is not something we say in my teacher's house. It is not something we will write down.

MY LIFE
AS SAMUEL BECKETT

by ANDY LAMEY

BECKETT IS AT his old job at the mutual fund company. At first there are things for him to do, but then they stop. Beckett thinks *a-ha*. This is how existentialism is born.

Beckett is talking on the phone with his mother.

"You're thirty-two years old. When will you be married?"

Beckett feels the hot lash of shame. He grows angry, he strikes out.

"I transform the degradation of modern man into his redemption. What need have *I* for marriage?"

Beckett storms into his bedroom and plays old punk songs on his stereo. Beckett pogos around his room and thinks: If I can capture in language what music makes me feel, I will be a great literary artist.

Beckett is sitting in his boss's office. She is young, pert, blond. He is her senior writer. She taps something he has written.

"When you say 'suppose Vladimir, Inc. buys Estragon Co. at forty cents a share,' I think it should be Company A and Company B." She pauses.

"That way, people can *understand* it."

Beckett nods. He nods a second time and hears himself say "No problemo." But inwardly, he vows to strip the veil of futility from human existence.

Beckett is out having drinks with the former Mrs. Beckett. Their arrangement was common-law; she now works in publishing. Somehow they are friends. He thinks it is because they do not see each other very often, and only come to places like this, where they can hide in smoke and alcohol and cynicism.

"Have you seen the latest issue of ——?" she asks.

He nods.

"I thought it was pretty bad," she says.

It is their constant topic, things that are pretty bad. This way, at least, there is always lots to talk about.

Walking home through the snow, something she says stays with him.

"You know what I realize I don't like as I'm getting older?" she announces, stubbing out a cigarette.

What?

"Other people."

She blows smoke through her nose like a bull. "I mean, think about it. Isn't that where all your problems come from?"

Beckett is lying in his bed, listening to 4 a.m. He thinks of a woman he was with many years ago. The time she brought her hands up to his cheeks, held them, and kissed his craggy face.

He rolls over, into the pillows of his nostalgia, the sheets of his exile.

He thinks to himself: From here on in, my work will take a darker turn.

Beckett is walking into his office. He turns on his computer, sips coffee, fiddles with his tie. The desk is still dark brown mahogany, the window forty floors in the sky. They brought him here on his first day and said, "This room would normally go to someone much more senior, but until the *merger* is over…" Beckett has been waiting ever since for someone to come and get him; today, finally, his boss enters and closes the door.

"I know there's not a lot for you to do right now, but until the merger's sorted, things could be a little crazy. I hope you can just sit tight."

Beckett looks out the window for the one-thousandth time and sees the white crest of waves break across the lake. This week he has written three words, "prognosis for growth." He wonders if they are dead enough to use in a health fund brochure, should he ever finish one.

His boss reassures him that soon they will want him to write something, then smiles and leaves the room.

That afternoon she quits. Beckett never sees her again, and she is not replaced.

Beckett is watching the clock slowly approach 5 p.m. Outside the sun is dying. He sits at his desk, checking his email. It is something he enjoys: the random communication, the strange distances, the silence. But he is worried. Sometimes he asks himself: Why do I enjoy checking the e-mail *so much*? He has not yet taken to sending messages to himself. But then, he thinks, that could just be a matter of time. In the meantime, he has begun to develop strange ideas:

1. He likes that no one speaks or interrupts him. The screen is a dark stage, the messages the actors he sends darting back and forth, the kind who never take a false breath or argue, confound his precious lines.
2. He is waiting for a special message. One that will explain this unforgiving universe. Of course, it never comes.

SUBJECT: Broker copy
DATE: Thu, 15 Aug 19:36:32 -0400
FROM: Samuel Beckett <sbeckett@aimfunds.com>
TO: Design <design@aimfunds.com>

Enclosed is copy for global equities broker brochure. —S.B.

Capitalists:

Given the existence as uttered forth in the work of Puncher and Wattman of a new economy quaquaquaqua dot.com QUAQUAQUAQUA Freedom 55 and people would rather play tennis and labours left unfinished, it is established beyond all doubt that the nature of mutual funds has heretofore been unknown in the statistics of Testew and Cunard; as only at this date does THE APORIA GIVE WAY and the boredom without extension finally rise up from underneath the stock market, rounded to a decimal for clients wanting strong earnings potential without the numbing tears of numbers and

"THE BEARHUG OF TIME" which is the boredom in light of research showing clients crushed in its paws, revealing our ultimate product is the potential of pure boredom, swirling around THE WASTES AND PINES OF ECONOMICS (see enclosed chart: money supply as model for tedium distribution) and our pursuit of market share is clearly shown in addition to value investing and aggressive growth and high P/E multiples to be the boredom only we are inside of whereas meeting a client in stocking feet in their living room the upward curve of NASDAQ over time shows their DEMAND TO BE RESCUED from the vale of economic tears WHICH IS HUMAN LIFE and which when analyzed through earnings before interest taxes depreciation and amortization the boredom presses in with TENNIS and CHILDREN CALLING and a mathematic DARKNESS descends upon their SKULLS adding further support to the equation of Weiss in which we can round boredom up to the nearest figure and TENNIS CAN GO ON.

Beckett is talking on the telephone. At the other end is his old friend, at her apartment in New York. They have not spoken for eight years—eight years!—but now they know where each other is, and so here they are again. She asks him: Who knew it was possible to be this much older? He laughs; she promises to visit soon. He hangs up and walks into the kitchen. Something warm, light moves around inside of him.

Ah, Beckett. Could you come in here please.
    [...]
Please have a seat.
    [...]
So... someone left your copy for the broker brochure on my desk this morning.
    [...]
Beckett, are you... doing OK?
    [...]
I mean, "A mathematic darkness descends upon their skulls." Under what circumstances would you see us giving this to someone? It doesn't really help sell mutual funds. You understand that, right?
    [...]
Look Beckett. I hope it's clear why... we may have to make some changes around here.

* * *

Beckett's old friend has arrived. They have gone to a quiet restaurant and come back, are lying on the bed in his bedroom. Beckett will be moving soon and so it is nearly empty: a bed, lamp, dresser, no pictures, the television flickering.

Beckett is aware of her warmth lying beside him. He fidgets. He points to the screen. A man in an office, his head in a vise, talking about investments.

He turns to her. Do they have a lot of mutual fund commercials in New York this time of year?

She looks at him.

Ah Beckett, she sighs, such a way with the ladies.

Beckett remembers the night he stood on a jetty overlooking the Irish Sea. He remembers the vow he made about the external world, its stupid, stunted language, its deaf and dumb alphabet of convention; his honouring, from that day forward, of only inner things.

Beckett looks over at his old friend. It is late and they are smoking and listening to music. They have been together many hours.

She rustles through her bag. Here is a poem she would like him to read. The churn of old words in the heart again. She kisses him.

Some things from the world, he thinks; some of them I will keep.

Beckett is at his new job at the newspaper. He is glad there are things for him to do. One day he walks around the newsroom. He passes by a columnist's desk. A sticker: I am the gun lobby. Beckett halts. Back at his desk he trembles. He sketches a theatre set, a lobby in the shape of a gun. It is hard to draw but he works feverishly, intently, finishing it after lunch. He is delighted with his handiwork. "Bang-bang!" he says out loud when he is done.

A journalist glances at him. He looks down, pretends to busy himself in paperwork.

I am the Gun Lobby. He chortles. Let's see them try to stage that.

A woman walks by his desk. She pauses, performs a pirouette, smiles at him.

"I'm a dancer," she says, laughing.

* * *

This is Samuel Beckett getting stabbed.

Beckett's old friend is on the phone again. She is sharpening her words into a point.

"I think I was lonely," she says. "That's all it was. I don't want you to come down here."

And?

"I'm not coming up there again."

Her next sentence arrives with a slash, each syllable a serrated edge.

"It's just going to jeopardize our friendship. You mean a lot to me, and I don't want to risk it."

Beckett is in the newsroom looking at his computer screen. On it is a story about Pierre Trudeau. He is pictured during his invincible years, 1969, towering over a small image of Joe Clark. Beckett is to write the headline and the words underneath the pictures.

He looks at the picture of Trudeau: smiling, purposeful, waving to the crowd. Bah, Beckett thinks. You're outdoorsy, aren't you, Pierre? So delighted, walking around, as if there is a point to things.

Beckett looks at the photo of Clark: lost inside an airport, unshaven and confused. Yes, yes. Now here's a man who knows what it's like to feel trapped inside the womb. Beckett would like to work for Clark, on anything, so long as it will lose.

Beckett looks around. When no one is watching, he reverses the size of the photographs. Clark is large, dominant, an enormous monument of pain. He turns Trudeau upside down, draws a mustache and a word balloon: *I admire the stories of G. K. Chesterton and Arthur Conan Doyle!*

He writes in the headline above Clark's massive head: HE MUST GO ON, HE CAN'T GO ON, HE'LL GO ON.

Beckett glances around quickly. He slips out the backdoor and escapes into the parking lot. It is early evening; dusty sunlight is glinting off of windshields. Beckett does not look forward to arriving at work tomorrow. He wonders why he has done what he has done.

Beckett stops. He sees a familiar prehistoric landscape. Telephone wires blur into vines; a line of cars inching toward the street moves slowly as triceratops rumbling across the plains. Somewhere far away his old friend has evolved down from the trees: She has animal skins, cave paintings, is about to discover fire. He stands outside himself and sees a regretful brontosaurus, always changing direction with wide turns, hindquarters smashing into undergrowth. Ah Beckett, you thought you could escape. But this is it. Primeval, biological, Darwinian. Away from the study, not writing, trapped in a universe of ancient life.

Beckett is sitting in the cafeteria eating, yet again, by himself. Potato soup has spilled onto his plate. He looks at it. He moves it around with his spoon, making little shapes of brown liquid. This one is a man, ha ha. About to be eaten by a cow with lobster claws. Beckett pauses. If he made that into a play, he realizes, it would be very big in France.

He sees the dancer crossing toward him with a tray. Her hair reaches down to her shoulder, moves around in time with her buoyant strides.

Beckett stops playing with his food. Steady, he thinks, not looking up from his paper. That walk is the walk of a woman looking for a sportswriter.

She arrives at his table and stands before him.

Beckett looks up, chewing.

May I sit down?

The great writer nods.

She tells him the things she knows: cheap beer, pool halls, cigarettes, diners and divey bars. Buster Keaton. The smell of old bookstores on rainy afternoons. Anne Carson, *Withnail and I*.

On Saturday, she is going to see a Charlie Chaplin film. Would he like to come?

She whispers: I write poems too, you know.

Beckett thinks: Well now. A-ha. This is getting interesting.

What will Beckett have tonight? Pizza, or slow-cooked vegetables, with pasta and rice?

Pizza wins again!

Beckett is in his room, drinking coffee and smoking in the dark. The walls are bathed in the blue glow of his computer. Beckett is working on his masterpiece.

Outside, the wind is telling stories. Beckett wonders why they are always the same. But soon Beckett realizes. This is the world, after all, telling stories to itself. It has always played favourites. Just as stories blow through Beckett too, coming at him when he sleeps.

Lately whenever Beckett closes his eyes, he opens them as an elephant handler. He is in a field beside an airport; he wears high black boots and darts among the wrinkled creatures, waving whip and bullhook, shouting and slapping leathery skin, forming the elephants into rows (a wrangler's voice, Beckett knows, is always his greatest tool). The animals carry white boards with letters inscribed on them. Beckett's job, like that of the other wranglers, is to arrange the elephants so they spell words for the benefit of people in airplanes. They proclaim their admiration, passing overhead, through the use of bullhorns.

Beckett looks out at the herd of milling beasts. He recalls the words he has spelled to date, on previous attempts:

Vermin

Pancreatic cancer

Carnage

Slavery

Beckett reflects. These words did not garner much appreciation from above. Beckett wonders if they don't understand, if he should try another language altogether. Perhaps *sissonne. Porté*. Or *cavalier*.

Another handler cracks his whip: his last animal in place. The handler is younger than Beckett, in a green jacket with a shamrock patch. Beckett has never seen him before. Suddenly the sky is filled with exclamations. Oh… why yes! A dictionary word! A woman's voice: of course!

Beckett looks at the Shamrock's row of animals. What is the great term he has conjured?

P … a … c … h … y … d … e … r … m.

Beckett scowls. Oooh, Mr. Big Word, Mr. Greek Etymology. Mr. Self-Reference. You see through our signifiers. You party naked with Jacques Derrida.

Overhead, someone is launching fireworks. Beckett pays it no mind. Finally he decides. *Jeté*. That absolutely settles it.

Beckett is sitting by himself at the matinee. The dancer has not come. The woman with large hair in front of him ingests popcorn, licorice, and a large Diet Coke. Beckett has bottled water tapped at the rootspring of forgetfulness that flows everywhere beneath a bleak and pitiless cosmos and nachos made in hell. But then: The dancer is in the aisle. She sees him, comes to sit in the next chair, places her hand on his arm and—gently, tenderly—murmurs an apology. The entire theatre chuckles together. Beckett wants the film to rewind and play the scene over again, forever.

She laughs when Chaplin is caught inside the cogs of a giant machine. He sits in silence and thinks: This movie is about the hat. It goes flying off Chaplin's head, yet somehow returns for each new misadventure. Beckett sees paintings by Magritte: men in bowler hats standing on air; another with his face obscured by an apple. Beckett thinks: bowler hats against the void. The things we clutch onto. Of course. Someday he will use that.

He looks over at the dancer. Her eyebrows leap up like exclamation points when the Tramp is in danger, collapse again, to rest, when he is safe.

And the tenderness, too, in spite of it all.

Beckett is walking with the dancer through the park. There is snow on the ground and their coats are open, flapping. They are carrying warm cups of Styrofoam, looking for a bench.

The dancer hands him her cup and runs and skids on ice. *Wheeeee* she says, hair and scarf rising through the air. She motions for him.

Beckett stands on the path, clutching precious lattés. The day is wide and bright. Ice, black and treacherous, crackles up at him, reminds him his legs are not what they were. He thinks what he has always thought, turning back, refusing to go on. He helped Joyce's failing eyes in the fading Paris light, held off Nazis, has won the Nobel Prize. But nothing was ever hard as this. He wants to cross to where the dancer is, offer her the warmth in his hands. But there is a cold sheet of failure stretching off into the rest of his life. He is afraid to fall, to not stand on the cruel and rotting earth. He wants to not walk and never run and nothing move, the same not-want he's negatively yearned for his entire nothing life.

Beckett hears the trees whisper, once again, their old slanders, their ancient innuendoes: *No Beckett, you can't do it, the nothing's all you get.*

Beckett closes his eyes. He thinks of the dancer, calling. He listens, not moving, quiet. He hears the silence that always wants him, waiting, its call to surrender and slide in. But then, in the distance, something softly calling. Again, closer, echoing in his chest. Then stronger, louder, an explosion, an airplane roar inside of him, a deafening shouting *Yes.*

He steps forward, slowly, the other foot: Beckett is walking toward the dancer! Here comes Beckett, striding, moving, flailing, losing his balance— no, upright again, a few more strides, Oh Beckett, you hockey star, you can do it, your victory, your belonging in that *yes.* The dancer is waiting, cheering, here she is; Beckett, smiling, laughing, so close now, inevitable, he slides into her arms.

Ah Beckett, for so long, for so long you have waited. Rest now, gentle creature, rest now in this peace.

He brings his lips down to kiss her. It startles her, her hand on his chest, pushing back.

"Oh Beckett," she says. "I hope you didn't think... we're going to be like *that?*"

Beckett is at a Country & Western bar. Cigarette smoke clings to stained carpets and exposed wooden beams. Men with belt buckles and cowboy boots line dance with women in checkered skirts. Someone shouts "Yee-haw." Beckett is in the corner, jotting in his notebook and reading *The Anti-Christ, Theatre of Cruelty* and *Men Are from Mars, Women Are from Venus.*

After drinking seven beers, Beckett decides he will participate in karaoke. He approaches the Portuguese woman with the mustache and asks to see the songbook. His glasses slide down his face. He is outraged they do not have the fugue he is looking for. He asks for Wham! instead.

"Wake me up, before I go-go," he repeats many times, in German, before the uncomprehending room.

When they drag him off the stage, he is screaming about the void. They throw him into a garbage bin in the alley. Beckett sits there, blinking, looking out into the night, the lid resting on his head. A breeze carries the smell of wet coffee grounds, spoilt milk, kitchen oil.

Beckett thinks: A sour wind, a rough draft: language, transform this degradation. I think I'll call it *Endgame.*

Beckett is walking up the drive to his house. It is six in the morning; out all night again. He looks at the mailbox. Perhaps today, he thinks, a message will come. He opens the metal lid. Instead of letters, a family of tits is nesting. Bronze, mewling, hungry with life.

Beckett closes the lid and reaches for his notebook. Dear Postman: drop letters between doors. Birds not to be disturbed.

Beckett sits on the stoop, watching the rising sun. He lights a cigarette and pages through his jottings. He looks at his last entry:

Here I end this reel. Perhaps my best years are gone. When there was a chance of happiness. But I wouldn't want them back. Not with the fire in me now. No, I wouldn't want them back.

COLD FRANCE

AND OTHER PERMUTATIONS

by WYTHE MARSCHALL

EVERY FRANCE

THERE ARE MANY FRANCES. The France that you see on your map or happen to inhabit is a fine one, but it is just one of thousands, millions even. To understand them all, you must examine a wide cross-section. The following is a sampling of all existing Frances.

COLD FRANCE

France is cold. Even in the summer, even in Corsica and Perpignan, the wind blows only snow, and dogs will not venture far from the hearth. During the day, people from Germany and Spain visit and make polite conversation about the indoor gardens and taxes, but—as soon as the Night Bell strikes and the first rays of dark creep over the rooftops of Paris like burglars on the job—everyone who is not native-born slips back to a warmer spot and silently shakes his head as if to say, "I'm sorry, France, but you are too damn cold today." This rarely lets up. Even in the depths of a bombardment by cosmic rays, even given the microwave, Tae Bo, and space heaters, France on the whole is cold—inside, outside, under the blanket, and behind the ears. Only when a good thaw comes and the ice melts do you see people in the streets. Of course (and this is more than legend), most people outside France do not know it, but the street-people are only there to see the coming of the next ice.

SLOW FRANCE

France is very slow. The French move at a fifth the speed of Americans; a third the speed of Russians; the same speed as Romanian doctors. France is full of people who have stopped trying to move. Their sounds are less interesting than wind. They hoot halfheartedly and coo vaguely because they don't have the energy to wail properly. At least, thinks little Marie as she brushes her hair over the course of ten hours, our hair is better—and it is. Because each follicle has so long to think over each new molecule of French hair, each French strand is shinier, stronger, and more fit to entertain at parties than other, foreign hairs. So when you get it in the mail, please remember: Whatever you do, don't cut your French hair.

DOG FRANCE

Everyone in France is a dog. The French, collectively, lick themselves. They have too much hair. Their noses are black and, when healthy, moist, like the Seine. They do not eat croissants often because they cannot bake. They therefore have little commerce, except in dug-up bones and fleas. Flea-trafficking is a crime punishable by barking and humping. The French enjoy short walks, short naps, short fucks, long meals, and short lives. If they live too long, they grow confused and cantankerous and must retire to the underneaths of porches and verandas. They fear technology, except in the form of food. They will eat anything except each other. They should not eat chocolate.

WHALE FRANCE

France is a huge whale, with tiny castles built on its top and bottom sides and fins. Paris is inside the blowhole, protected from France's mighty gusts by storm windows and heavy shutters. Often, Jacques forgets to bring a bungee cord and carabiners when walking down the Rue Estienne and is blown straight to Belgium, which is a halibut of immense girth. One day, they say, France will overcome Belgium and finally make it to Sweden, which is also a whale, though of a more agreeable and daintier bent, and then the world will see the birth of a new country. Jacques does not know if it will be named Freeden, Swance, or some other hideous combination of the two, but he plans to be blown away by whatever choice the people of the new combi-nation make.

DARK FRANCE

France is dark. Even when he looks directly at the sun, Jean cannot see it through the haze of bats. Sometimes, millipedes and rodents infest lighting fixtures for no apparent reason. Because they have little food, they soon die out. In the meantime, nothing can be done. What is the meaning of dark-ness? thinks Jean. He wants to move to another country, but he cannot see what ticket to buy at the station. A badger walks into him in the woods when he is on vacation. They both are very surprised and apologize, although they do not understand each other. Perhaps the badger is German. Because Germany is not as dark, many people prefer it to France. Others, fearing capture by the authorities, or simply to get away from an often bru-tally lighted world, migrate to France and set up shops selling fake candles and used matches in bright, new matchboxes. No one knows why light is so scarce. Jean thinks it has to do with the water, but his wife says he is being paranoid. Because the water, too, is dark, no one can really say.

RED FRANCE

France is rosy, ruby, scarlet, carmine, sanguine, cerise, crimson, and pink. It is full of apples and galoshes and cold-bright noses and newborns. Things tend to be bloody. A man in the east walked to the store and returned with several deep wounds. Few people will tell the story similarly, but it appar-ently had something to do with the fish he bought (a red herring) and a sword (corundum-crusted hilt; rusted guard) he used as an impromptu knife when he (the bloody man) could not afford the entire fish (the red herring). Whether all of France is like this or not is hard to say; most people do not leave their houses for very long. The rain is mostly Skittles, but it is not fun like in the commercials and no one runs to basket hundreds of the candy particles at a time. Since you always know what you are getting, there is lit-tle entertainment value in a wet day.

SPONGE FRANCE

Everywhere you go in Montmartre you see people soaking sunlight into bricks, happiness into candy, and love into memories. Everything in France is porous, you see, and everyone spends every minute trying to save everything. If you stand too long in one place, you will slip inside France like a drop of water spilled in the desert. If you move too quickly, you won't absorb anything, unless you are from France, but—either way—France and its people will absorb you. If, however, you find a quiet spot in a café on a lazy Sunday afternoon and sit for a few minutes at a time, occasionally rising to buy another espresso or latté or to check the weather or to watch a football match, then you will bear a great gift when you leave France: The football players' jersey numbers will be tattooed onto your eyes; your feet will smell like daylight; your coffees will always taste like vacation; and you will marry someone who reminds you of that girl in the pink sundress by the soda fountain, the one who winked at you twice already and is playing footsie with you (her Mary Janes versus your sensible loafers) from across the café floor.

YOUNG FRANCE

Everyone in France is young. Little Adrien, nearing forty, is really only twenty-seven. Astrid looks like a white China doll, though she is well into her eighties. Matthieu still eats pears after skipping school on Wednesdays. He is a thousand. Colette died on Tuesday, but she looks great. She has no wrinkles. She loves pickles. She is young at heart, but you'd never have to guess it, as she is also young at body. At her funeral, Thierry and Margaux weep like babes, then kiss violently and run off. They say "nuh-uh!" when a friend tells them to stop being rude. Victor married Sabine because she is an excellent wrist at quarters and can drink more than most mountain rams. France is not known for mountains, except of the very young variety. Every mountain is a volcano and erupts daily. No one lives in mountainous regions except the very, very old, those who wish they were from Bulgaria or Modena or a fishing resort on a Micronesian island. Because France is so young, no one has heard of it, and commerce is difficult. Candy is the preferred currency. This sometimes makes Margaux weep, for she is allergic to sugar.

TENT FRANCE

France is a tent. If you live on the underside of the tent, you are an Underer. If you build a house on top, you are a Parisian. If you straddle the poles, by way of clever rigs of pulleys or simply strength (the kind bred into you by years of straddling and generations of rigging), you are a true Frenchperson. Your accent is deep, like the caverns below France that no one will traverse. Your demeanor is sharp and inspired, like that of a cave-troll or other denizen of the Below-France that even the bravest Frenchperson fears more than death. It is said that mushrooms shaped like spears grow under France. It is said that the trolls use these mushrooms to pick off low-hanging Underers at night. Parisians have nothing to fear. Their crops always grow straight and strong, and they enjoy as much sun or moon as they want, for they each carry on their backs smaller, man-portable tents used individually to block out one person's fill of star- or other celestial body-light. Paris is a utopia. Under-France is a ghost town. Only cowboys and American soap opera stars move there. Pole-France is the true France. Pole-France is the most likely to fall into Italy or spawn another Napoleon. Pole-France is really all there is of Tent-France. When Louis XVI neared his death, he moved to Pole-France and sat on a stool hung from a lion's back until a cave-troll took notice and fought the lion. When the lion won, France became a glorious place forever and ever. Sadly, Louis fell.

MERRY FRANCE

In France, even death is hilarious. When Carlo the Spic shot his bastard brother James in the face, everyone laughed. "Oh, that James!" or "Oh, that Carlo!" There was very little crying at first, then people doubled over and guffawed until the tears came. Carlo was pleased. He sold the movie rights and moved to the States. People in France like laughing. Everything that happens, from rain to oil spills, is great, grand news. "Did you hear? There are *people* in *Luxembourg!*" Everyone laughs. Intonation is not necessary. One man simply said "fox" until all of Limoges had died from heart seizures and wistfulness. A few people wish France wasn't so funny. They are labeled insane and carted off, to be examined and righted, and ultimately thrown out with the last night's discards.

RICH FRANCE

Bayonne is paved with virgins' blood imported at five thousand francs per goblet from Sweden. Nimes is solid gold, every last inch of every street and café in the city molded from one huge cauldron of liquid metal. Dijon is home to a mustard plant the size of Mars. It weighs the earth down in an odd way, and Russia often complains. The Rue de la Condamine, meanwhile, is crowded with renegade oil barons and dust-farmers who have scant millions to spend on their mansions in the country and their wives and their mistresses and their mistresses' mistresses, for everyone in France is rich enough to be a lesbian. Everyone in France is rich enough to be unhappy. People buy despondency from Jews in Serbia. People cultivate crops of self-righteousness and un-fame. People snort pure hatred. Rich France is full of professional assholes. One man sold his dairy farm for a huge spiked gauntlet. Another invented a robot to send cute rodents into space. Rich France is also lazy. People seldom shower, and their kisses taste like ash because they don't bother smoking. They just purchase large numbers of saffron-flavored Cubans and chew them, half-lighted, until their cheeks rot and the poor people in Andorra have to clean up the mess.

FAT FRANCE

Bordeaux is full of gelatinous people. The rivers of Europe are clogged with French spittle and fart. Few people wander out of doors, for fear of too-rapidly falling skydivers and would-be standers. Most French roll about on their backs and thighs, using crutches made of granite to prop themselves awake at Université lectures and symphony performances. Japanese cars have to be doubled in size for the French. Many Ukrainians make their livings selling eggs stuffed with butter to French dogs, who are in turn sold by the British to those French in need of cheap larder-stuffers. Even carrots here are rich in calories. The upside is that everything French tastes like fun. The air is salty. The sea is a piss-yellow limón-liquor substance that threatens to give the Spanish an ulcer. The Dutch buy French bark by the pound and shuck it for sport. Fat France is alive with its own fatness. Everyone loves it, because everyone is equally fat. Not one molecule is out of place, too big or too small. Fat France is equal France. *Vive la graisse.*

JUMPING FRANCE

Everyone in France is jumping. No one can stop moving. Even buildings shoot up and down, shaken by the jumpers within. American rappers have no effect at concerts. Trampolines are garbage here. Scientists in Roma study the Calais Bounce, the Lourdes Vault—even the Lyon Leap. In Kyoto, companies pay for research on the Marseille Hurdle, the Cannes Bound, and the Grasse Caper. The Polish, especially, feel a cultural draw towards the Arles Skip, the

Vézelay Hop, and the deadly Rouen Spring. No one refuses to jump. Members of professional jumping leagues regularly propel themselves and/or one another into orbit. Traversing the space above France is dangerous. Mountains fly like blowdarts; geodesic domes like pinball-halves. Everything moves. France is jumping, and the French wouldn't have it any other way.

BEAR FRANCE

Bourges was once home to a Great Bear. Onomatopoeically named for his mighty roar, Ahr-Uhr was the largest mammal ever born to the world of men. Far before the time of Jesus, prophets already spoke of his power and grace. Beggars sought his advice. His breath healed the sick. His knowledge of horticulture transformed France from a cesspit of Gothic barbarism to an enlightened center of silk trading and philosophizing. In Nancy, one man was born who hated Ahr-Uhr. He waited past Buddha, past the births and deaths of da Vinci (who left Firenze for the Great Bear's cave) and Shakespeare. Eventually, the man from Nancy decided to strike. He built a great slab of meat from sinew and dog-gut and thousands of cattle, slaughtered by the dozen and stacked end-to-end-to-end until a great trench of meat crisscrossed the nation. Ahr-Uhr could not resist. He ate and ate and ate until his intestines ruptured. His head is preserved at the Louvre. No one touches his huge eyes, fearing his last memories. The man from Nancy moved to Holland and is sometimes very lonely. No one thinks of France anymore, not even the people who dwell there. They just spin silk in silence and curse cows without speaking.

GAY FRANCE

The Rue de Rivoli is filled with couples necking. Cross-hatched, up and down, to and fro, dancing and singing and licking, people move, in heat. The summer sweat can't match the tears of joy. The airy music can't drown out the moans. People are meeting and rubbing, standing up, falling down, laughing. Some people hate each other but still fuck. This is not just Gay France; it is Sex France, Man France, Woman France, Man-Woman France, Woman-Woman-Dog France; it is Orgy France and Romantic Evening France. Does this mean that every type of coupling is equally real and unreal? That every lover is the same, regardless of gender or species or age or religion? Are these hippies? Are they in hell or heaven? Are they ghosts of nymphomaniacs? No one in France pauses to think about it. They are too busy with the matters of flesh. Carnality is the euro here, and every man and woman is a robber-baron.

MIND FRANCE

France is all in your head. Both Notre Dame cathedrals—imaginary. Cardinal Richelieu—never existed. Even French cats aren't entirely real. No one built a castle in France, though she might tell you she did, especially after a glass of pastis made thick with lamb gravy and fried potatoes. None of these foods are known in France, because France is a lie. Dostoevsky, Cervantes, and El Greco banded together and invented France to prevent a third World War. Bill Clinton allowed France to join NATO to stop the Russians from advancing into Poland again. The Pope christened France a nation out of brotherly love for all people, even those who do not, technically, exist. Many people concentrate on imagining France at any given time, so it is real. Discussion of France comprises the bulk of Internet traffic. Everyone has a .france site; everyone maintains at least one "French" personality online. Nearly all dating occurs via MindFrance.net. People pretend to be Alain-Alexandre and Aimée but are really Motomochi and Gzifa. This doesn't seem to matter, except to the deluded who actually believe in France. They hide in chat rooms and spew insults at those who will not pay homage to the glorious *fleurs-du-lis*.

DEAD FRANCE

This is not the France you go to when you die in a different France. This is not a France full of hippies following a legendary band from villa to villa, eating baguettes and chain-smoking unfiltered Kools. This is not a France of Hades, Pluto, Satan, God, Gimokodan, Hermodr, Emma-O, or any other deity. This is not a dark France, not a light France. This is hardly a France you'd want to inhabit, even if you were a true Frenchperson with a wine-fortified will and the balls of a cougar. This is not a France of laughter or tears. This is not a France below a sun, nor near a source of heat, nor cold at all. This is not what you think of when you don't think of France. This is not an anti- or un-France. This is a non-France. This is not a France at all.

AFTER THE DISASTER

A LOVE STORY

———

by BEN EHRENREICH

1

AFTER THE DISASTER no one went to the Natural History Museum anymore. Crowds still pushed their way into the Met and the Modern for the first few weeks till every last painting, sculpture, mobile, and video installation was stolen, slashed, smashed, or shat upon. Across the park, though, things were quiet. People had been there. They had left signs, traces, trash. Graffiti stretched improbably over the domed ceiling of the planetarium. The gift shop and cafeteria had been looted. Kaleidoscopes and maps of the solar system and plush stuffed hyenas lay strewn about the floor. Not a crumb of food remained. The big blue whale had been cut down and sprawled broken on the floor of the cafeteria. Squatters apparently had at some point taken up residence in its cavernous fiberglass belly, leaving behind beer cans, ashes, and a shit-stained bedroll. Like Jonah, though, they were nowhere to be found. Whoever had been there had not been particularly ambitious, or rapacious, or mad. For when Bruno returned one last time to wander the museum's marbled halls in search of Mildred and the giant squid, his heart aflutter with lust and longing, he found that the now-dusty glass-encased displays of silverbacks and okapis, bison and antelope, lions and emu, each arranged in perfect nuclear family units, were entirely undisturbed. Who had time for nature anymore?

He first encountered the squid by accident, weeks before the world as he had known it so effortlessly dissolved. He had no idea what he would find. He wandered into the museum to avoid a storm that, in the middle of a peaceful walk through the park, had broken without warning or apology. He stayed only because he knew that, despite the posted $9.50 "suggested contribution," the kind-eyed folks behind the admission desk would let you in for a quarter, a penny, or a dime. Bruno's pocket contained two nickels, a dime, three pennies, and two crumpled dollar bills. Not without some pride, he paid with a dime.

Still soaked, his hair sticking to his forehead and his shirt clinging to his sunken chest, Bruno dragged himself up a flight of wide marble stairs. He found himself in the Hall of Biodiversity, where he marveled at the many forms of life, large and small, furred and smooth, striped and spotted, every one of them irrevocably dead. A herd of stiffened pachyderms, feet raised, tusks lowered, tentlike ears eternally at attention, stood in the middle of the room, frozen in mid-stomp. Stuffed sharks swam suspended from the ceiling. Along the walls formaldehyde-bleached lobsters sulked in oversized Mason jars beside legions of fluorescent blue beetles, dried fungi, glass-eyed rodents, and lacquered frogs. "Cartilaginous fish," announced a placard.

At the end of the hall stood a single uniformed guard, his hands clasped loosely behind his back. A dim blue light shined sullenly forth from the corner behind him. Its source, Bruno saw, was a low tank, about twelve feet long and three high. Inside it was the giant squid. Four Korean children in bright rain slickers walked by, paused long enough to observe the squid and, screeching in exaggerated disgust, scurried off.

Around the tank on all sides were blocks of italicized text in white letters on a navy background. Before even glancing at the tank's contents, Bruno read, "The giant squid has never been seen alive in its natural habitat." The squid, he saw, lay in an ethanol-filled casket, its white, papery flesh peeling as if sunburnt, flecks of its skin littering the blue bottom of the tank. It was surely dead, and very far from home.

"The giant squid is the largest of the invertebrates," he read on. "Females can reach seventy feet in length." This squid, however, was male and only twenty-five feet in length, though it looked much smaller. In truth, only the two tentacles were that long, and they had been folded back to rest upon the squid's lifeless head. Its white and pulpy arms were tangled atop one another, an orgy of chalk-white eels. Each one was lined with round, once-lethal suckers, now arrayed haphazardly, comically even, a drunken chorus line of pupilless eyeballs. The creature's dead eye was enormous and terribly sad, a grey and faded lump of useless meat, loose in its tattered socket.

Bruno did not notice Mildred at first. But she lingered on beside him as others came, took a quick look, tittered for a moment, perhaps flashed a snapshot or two and moved on. Despite the closeness of the air in the museum, she wore a thick, black, woolen overcoat, which hung baggily over her wiry, almost brittle frame. After staring wordlessly at the squid for a spell, she turned to Bruno and spoke. "Amazing, isn't it?" she asked, letting a smile race across her lips and swiftly disappear, leaving her face awaiting Bruno's response with blank expectancy. A long white hand emerged from the wide sleeve of her coat and shook a strand of hair from her eyes.

Bruno was not accustomed to speaking with strangers, especially those of the female sort. Truth be told, he was not lately accustomed to speaking with anyone at all. Nonetheless, he grinned with as much warmth as he could muster and nodded his assent. Mildred's face relaxed. There was a softness to her eyes that spread into the harsh lines of her cheekbones and chin, almost blurring them when she smiled, which she did once more. Breaking her gaze, Bruno turned again to the squid's cadaver, its flesh heavy and wrinkled, bloodless and white.

"Did you know that they're bright red when they're alive?" Mildred asked. "A deep scarlet." Her green eyes widened as she said it.

"I had no idea."

Mildred pointed to the long tentacle that stretched limply to the end of the tank before doubling back again. "The males carry sperm in there," she said. "I read this. In a magazine. They shoot it through the tentacle—the penis is somewhere else, I don't know where—but they shoot it through the tentacle when they meet a female. And the females can hold it there, in their tentacle, until they're ready to fertilize themselves."

Bruno watched Mildred closely. Was this a come on? Her eyes gave nothing away, staring as they were at the squid and not at him. "How do they know when they're ready?" he asked.

Mildred considered this for a moment, then shrugged. "I suppose they just know. The article said they probably travel alone, giant squids. It can be so long that they won't see another squid that whenever they see one they mate, because it might be the only squid of the opposite sex they'll ever see. I guess you'd call it mating. They know this because they found a female once with sperm still in her tentacle. She never used it."

"I wonder if they enjoy it," Bruno said, and was embarrassed to find himself blushing.

Mildred at last looked up. "Squids?"

"Yeah."

She shook her head. "I don't know. I hope so."

The guard standing next to the tank shifted his weight from one foot to the other, brushed at his mustache, and glanced nervously from Mildred to Bruno.

Mildred wrapped her fingers lightly around Bruno's upper arm. He tensed it involuntarily. Her nails, he noticed, were painted blue. "What do you like about the giant squid?" she asked.

Bruno felt his cheeks redden once again. "I didn't know anything about them until today. I guess just that, that no one knows anything about them."

Mildred pursed her lips and nodded. "The mystery," she said. She let her hand fall from his arm. His bicep was warm where her fingers had been. "What about you?" he asked her. But Mildred's only answer was to flash a tight smile and ask him the time. He told her it was four fifteen and she said she had to run.

"Nice to meet you," Bruno said.

"Nice to meet you," said Mildred, and turned to go.

Bruno waited for the storm to clear before leaving the museum. It was dark when he at last shuffled down the steps and gazed up at Teddy Roosevelt in bronze, mounted high on his horse, one hand on his gun, flanked on both sides by loyal, naked, and manifestly noble savages, Indian to his left, African on his right, facing down an invisible enemy floating above the trees of the park. Inside, Bruno knew, was the squid, slowly disintegrating in its long, blue tank. And somewhere, perhaps not far, was Mildred.

He circled the block twice, peeking into each cafe and corner deli, then extended the radius of his search by one block and then by two blocks, until a cab sped through a puddle on the corner of 77th and Broadway, coating him with inky muck. He gave up and commenced the long trek home to save on subway fare. Bruno slogged through the park, which smelled of rain and rotting leaves. He walked all the way down and across town through streets that smelled of rain and garbage and of good hot food he couldn't afford, over the bridge which smelled of rust and urine and through one last piss- and trash-stinking mile to his home, cursing himself all the while for not at least asking her to join him for a cup of coffee in the cafeteria, right there under the ridged white belly of the big blue whale. How often do you meet someone, he asked himself, someone you can really talk to?

That night Bruno dreamed of the ocean. He dreamed of infinite blackness and cold. He breathed the frigid water as if it were air. With each breath the cold filled him to his very center, which was darker and colder than even the depths of the sea. There was no above and no below, no light anywhere. None of the fish had eyes. They were white and bloated and the shadows beneath their scales were blue. They didn't swim but drifted, directionless. His legs and arms were tangled in long belts of rubbery kelp. Ice-white shrimp nibbled at his fingertips, his nipples, his shrunken prick. And he heard a sweet sad song, the moaning of the waves, and the water turned scarlet, warm and thick. He saw Mildred swimming past him, her limbs, like his, trailing kelp. She smiled at him. Between the strands of seaweed he could make out her small and purple nipples, the sharp shadows of her ribs and her jutting hip bones, black tendrils of pubic hair floating across her thighs. As she kicked her legs he spied her labia, scarlet in the scarlet sea, the hollows of her knees, and the sole of one arched foot.

When Bruno awoke his face was wet with tears.

There was no hot water that morning. In the shower Bruno stood far from the stream, and as far as he could from the mildewed shower curtain. Shivering, he looked down at his pale body, at his knobby knees, his shriveled, bouncing cock, at the small black hairs on his wrists. He thought of the giant squid, of its tangled legs, dead in its casket, not red but white and trapped forever. He thought of the white flesh of Mildred's wrists peeking out from under her baggy coat, of her long white neck beneath her straight black hair. He rinsed the soap from his body and dried himself.

That afternoon Bruno returned to the museum. He paid his dime, walked upstairs to the Hall of Biodiversity, past the pack of pachyderms, the lacquered frogs and bottled lobsters. Mildred was not there, but the giant squid remained. It had not shifted so much as a tentacle.

Bruno lingered by the squid for an hour. He paced in front of its case. He looked for her in the cafeteria, by the great mammals of Africa and the mammals of the Americas, by the dinosaur skeletons and by the Indian canoe, but he did not find her. He left the museum. He bought a hot dog with everything and ate it on the damp marble steps, following Teddy

Roosevelt's cold imperial gaze above the treeline and across the park.

Five days went by before Bruno returned to the museum. It was again a Tuesday, as it had been when he had first seen the squid and first met Mildred. From the very end of the Hall of Biodiversity he saw her, still wearing her baggy coat despite the weather, her head slightly bowed, her face hidden beneath her hair. He quickened his pace, wanting to run, but not wanting to be out of breath when he arrived at her side. Soon the pachyderms, with all their ancient bulk, blocked his line of vision. He passed the father, his proud tusks raised in challenge, the mother just beside and a little behind him, and between the sturdy legs of their long-dead offspring he could see Mildred's feet—her pale ankles bare, sockless in red sneakers—as they swiveled round and she walked away. When Bruno emerged from behind the wrinkled posterior of the last juvenile pachyderm, she was gone. He hurried past the squid, which he almost expected to acknowledge him, to point with one of its eight legs or two tentacles and let him know which way she'd gone. But it did not, and he did not see her in the hallway behind its long case. He didn't see her on the stairs, or in the gift shop on the landing, or in the great muralled hall below. He loitered outside the ladies' room, left the museum and circled the block not once but three times, all to no avail.

So Bruno walked back up the stairs to await her return to the squid. Its white eye lolled in its socket like a rotting scallop, pupilless, unwinking and dead. Giant squids have larger eyes, Bruno read, than any other animals. The eye of the giant squid can grow to fifteen inches in diameter. There was an image of such an eye beside the text on the display case, perfectly round, the size of a dinner plate, its pupil still intact but without an iris, colorless. It looked nothing like the flaccid white eye of the squid preserved beside it, an eye which communicated nothing, not even death.

It would be wrong to say, in retrospect, that the disaster came without warning. There were rumblings and there were whispers. For those who look for such things, there were signs. The moon did not always complete its full circuit; more and more gunshots, screams, and screeching tires could be heard in the night; the sun rose an hour late one morning, then two hours early the next; everyone had the same mild flu; bond prices fluctuated wildly; pigeons and squirrels were more skittish than usual. But Bruno noticed none of this.

He sat in his kitchen on a bentwood chair he had found on the street and opened a can of squid. The chair's wicker seat had been torn out, so he sat as lightly as he could on its wooden frame. He dumped the can's contents—six squid, each about five inches in length, floating in brine dyed purple with ink—into a bowl. They smelled like a shallow tide pool on a hot and windless day. In death, their skin was scarlet once more, if only because their own ink had stained it so. They had been cooked prior to canning until their flesh was so brittle that they broke when he handled them. Their bodies tore into neat, papery rings, exposing a grey substance that the can's label described as "viscera." Inside the squid, surrounded by this viscera, was a transparent shard of cartilage, like an elongated arrowhead, called a quill. It was the closest thing to a skeleton the squid had. He brought the bowl of squid to the table and carefully sat down on the broken chair. The squids, he noticed, still had eyes, with tiny black pupils intact.

Bruno returned to the museum each of the two following Tuesdays and once on a Saturday, but he did not see Mildred again. He continued to dream of her, sometimes in the awful solitude of the deep, as on that first night. Sometimes she would take his arm in her hand on the street or in the halls of the museum and kiss him or whisper something incomprehensible in his ear, then run away. She was always barefoot in his dreams. In the mornings he remembered her feet, long and white. One night he dreamed she came to his apartment. They stood in his kitchen, by the sink. She was fully clothed, in her coat as always, but Bruno was naked. Her eyes were red and inflamed. She caressed his penis with her right hand, which was very cold, and scolded him for not having been gentler with the canned squids, for breaking them right there by the sink. The quill he had removed from one was still on the counter, pointing at him accusingly. As he felt himself approaching climax, he saw that the skin of his cock was beginning to peel in her grip, like the dead flesh of the giant squid.

The disaster fell that Monday, and Bruno stayed indoors for the next two weeks. At night the western sky was bright with distant fires. Tremors shook the windows in their panes. With each muffled boom Bruno's furniture leapt about the floor. The winds didn't let up till the weekend, and Bruno couldn't sleep for their howling through the streets. He lay on his lumpy mattress watching the sheetrock glow again red and yellow as another blast gripped the city. And as the cracks in the plaster once more cast their shadows stark above his head, he wondered about Mildred, if she was warm enough, if she was safe, if she'd gotten sick, if she had enough food to eat and clean water to drink, if she'd been hurt, if wherever she was she ever thought of him.

Bruno paced and counted the linoleum tiles on the kitchen floor. There were nineteen of them, and, he was fairly sure, 461 ceramic tiles in the bathroom. Bruno read old newspapers, even the ads. He did all the crosswords. He did push-ups and sit-ups and jumping jacks. He used an extension cord as a jump rope until the downstairs neighbors fired a shot through the floor. It left a small hole, which he patched with a rag. He wrote a letter to his father who died when he was four, then thought better of it and tore it to shreds. He sat on the edge of the bathtub and wept and slapped himself in the face. He counted the tiles again. There were 456. He filled the margins of the phone book with sketches of Mildred and of the giant squid and of Mildred and himself together wrapped in the squid's eight legs and two tentacles until all his pens ran out of ink. He took the back off a transistor radio and tried to figure out how it worked. He pulled the motor out of his deceased refrigerator and later reinstalled it, none the wiser for his efforts. He masturbated repeatedly into the same dirty sock, imagining Mildred's breath on his navel, her long hair in his eyes, her blue-painted nails pulling on his scrotum.

Bruno trapped cockroaches in empty tin cans, thinking he might need them one day. He soaked stale bread in water and ate it with salt. He opened his last can of corned beef on Thursday and ran out of sardines on Sunday morning. He ate a few spoonfuls of cold beans from the can with crackers twice a day after that and cut back on the push-ups and masturbation.

The morning after the night that Bruno took his final swallow of beans, shook the last cracker crumbs from the bottom of the bag and licked them from his palm, the water gave out. The faucets spun round and round, but not a trickle poured forth. It was time, Bruno knew, to venture out into the world.

2

HE LEFT HIS apartment without giving much thought to his destination. He would follow his stomach, he decided. But in the end it was something else that led Bruno on his wanderings and he found himself, to his surprise, once again on the wide marble steps of the museum. Teddy Roosevelt had been removed from his high post and lay on his side in the middle of the street, still mounted on his now horizontal horse, contemplating the well-clogged gutters. The stone base of the statue had been shattered and Teddy's once faithful savage companions had apparently abandoned him.

Bruno climbed the stairs and pushed through the great wooden doors. The lobby was empty. Its floor was strewn with brochures and crumpled floorplans, which leapt about like tumbleweeds in the breeze that blew through the deserted streets and in through the open door. Before he got to the top of the first flight of stairs, Bruno heard it, a series of dull thumps unconnected by any discernible rhythm. As he rushed past the landing and down the darkened Hall of Biodiversity, he mistook the banging for the unsteady murmurs of his own agitated heart. But he found its source at the very end of the hall. There was Mildred, hacking away at the squid's tank with a crowbar. She had made no mark at all in the thick glass. Bruno was nearly at her side before she noticed his presence. She stopped in midswing and let the crowbar fall to her side. Her black coat had been thrown on the floor behind her and her T-shirt was dark with sweat. Her bony shoulders shook with exhaustion. "Will you help me?" she asked.

Bruno took the crowbar from her, swung it back above his head and let it fall with all his weight on the glass. The shock of the blow rang through his joints and the bones of his fingers, wrists, and elbows. It was all he could do to keep the crowbar from flying from his grip, but he had dislodged only the tiniest chip of glass. Another swing bore the same result. Bruno motioned to Mildred to follow him to the other end of the hall. Once there, he lifted her up, then jumped himself, and they swung from the end of the great ivory tusk of the largest of the pachyderms. It broke free with a crack and a moan and clattered to the marble floor. Straw spilled from the cavity they'd opened in the dead elephant's face. Its glass eyes did not blink.

They charged the display case with the broad end of the tusk. On their eighth or ninth try, their battering ram crashed through the glass. A wave of rank ethanol burst through, soaking them, and the giant squid, stiff and white, rolled with a thud to the floor. Mildred dropped the tusk, leapt into Bruno's arms, and kissed him noisily on the lips. Before he could respond, she was on her knees, carefully picking shards of glass from the squid's tangled arms. She looked up at him and pushed a knot of wet hair from her eyes. Two of the squid's arms were cradled in her lap. "You'll help me, won't you?" she asked. "I can't carry him home alone."

Bruno nodded.

"I live nearby," she said. "It won't take long."

The squid was heavier than it looked. Soft and fleshy as it appeared, death had hardened its body and stiffened its legs. It stank of ammonia and brine. They heaved the mantle and head onto Bruno's back. Mildred did her best to carry the extended legs and tentacles, but one or another of them kept slipping from her grasp. Before they reached the stairs at the end of the hall, Bruno stumbled and fell. The squid pinned him to the floor. Mildred rolled it off of him and helped him up. She lifted his chin and inspected his face for bruises. "Are you all right?" she asked.

Bruno took her hand from his face and held it in his. "I've been looking for you," he said.

Mildred gave his hand a squeeze and turned away. Something in her face seemed to dim. "This isn't going to work," she said, and Bruno felt a sharp, tight pain encircling his ribs.

Mildred looked around the long, dim hall. "Maybe if we wrapped him in my coat," she said, "we could just pull him."

The pain dispersed and warmth returned to Bruno's limbs and he pulled Mildred to him and kissed her. She smiled tightly, pecked him on the lips, then turned and ran for her coat, which she had forgotten by the broken window. "We have to hurry," she yelled over her shoulder. "He won't last long unless he's in alcohol and we don't want to be out after dark."

They rolled the squid onto the jacket, its legs and tentacles trailing off behind it. They buttoned it in, then each took one woolen arm and pulled. The squid, like a monstrous scarecrow, slid along the smooth floors to the top of the staircase. Bruno supported its body from below. The alcohol had quickly soaked through the coat and he could feel the animal's cold and surprisingly brittle form inside it. He backed it slowly down the stairs while Mildred guided its arms and tentacles. With each step, the bundled squid gave out a soft and squishy thud. "Be careful," Mildred said.

They pulled the squid across the wide lobby and down the stairs to the street. The air had chilled. The old stone apartment buildings and the tall glass office towers across the park glowed pink in the light of the setting sun. Above them hung the moon, pink too and abnormally large, a shade less than full. The sidewalk was trickier. The cement was not as smooth as the marble floors of the museum and they were forced to stop every few yards to disengage a corner of Mildred's jacket, or the slender tip of one of the squid's eight legs, from a hidden crack in the pavement. Three loud pops rang through the air, gunshots a few blocks to the south. Bruno froze for a moment, his eyes wide with uncertainty, until Mildred motioned him on.

A young boy, barefoot in shorts and a T-shirt, sprinted out of the park and into the street a half block ahead of them. Three older boys ran after him. One caught him by his shirt, which tore loudly as he was thrown to the asphalt. The others raced in and commenced kicking him in the ribs and face. They dragged him screaming back into the park by his ankles. Bruno stopped again and dropped the squid. "There's nothing you can do," Mildred said, and kept pulling.

They had made it almost to 83rd Street when a man dressed in camouflage fatigues scurried into the middle of Central Park West behind them. He stopped, spun around, and emptied an automatic pistol at his pursuers, who were still invisible around the corner. As he turned to run again, Bruno and Mildred heard another shot. They pulled the squid into the shelter of a doorway and huddled together, crouching. The man's head was thrown forward and his body crumpled to the asphalt. Bruno could not see any blood. Three overweight men in tattered police uniforms approached the body with their guns drawn. They prodded it with their feet, then, satisfied that the man was dead, took his gun, boots, and jacket before returning in the direction from which they'd come.

Bruno and Mildred held each other tightly, each with one arm wrapped around the squid. She stood up first and tried to pull him up, but Bruno just looked at her. "Come on," she said. "Get up."

He tried to laugh, but what came out was more of a stifled retch. "It's not like this in Brooklyn," he managed. "I had no idea."

"Two more blocks and we're home."

At the corner of 85th Street, Mildred told Bruno it would be just two blocks more. The muscles in his back and thighs were cramping. His clothes reeked of ammonia and decay. They stayed close to the buildings and ran when they had to cross the street. As they crossed 89th, Bruno felt the squid suddenly grow heavier. He gave it a sharp tug and, just as Mildred screamed "Wait!", commenced pulling. His burden felt surprisingly lighter. Bruno kept moving until he heard her voice again. "Wait," she repeated, her voice firmer this time. He stopped and looked back. The squid's head, arms and tentacles had broken off from its body in a single clump and lay limply alone on the sidewalk. Only the mantle was still wrapped in Mildred's coat. A tentacle had gotten caught in a storm grate and wrapped itself around the steel grillwork. She pried it loose, then sat, crouching with the tentacle in her hand, shaking her head. "I'm sorry," Bruno said.

A burst of shots from an automatic weapon rang out nearby—Bruno couldn't tell from which direction. He pulled the squid's head under the overcoat, shoving it into the detached mantle as best as he could. Another shot echoed across the avenue and Mildred sprang up and began pulling. "We're almost there," she said.

On the next block Mildred stopped in front of a short, brass-railed staircase. They lugged the squid to the top of the stairs and through a varnished mahogany door. It was harder now that the squid was no longer in one piece. Mildred rushed them through an elegant, wood-paneled entryway and up three more flights of stairs. She had to stop every few feet to unravel the squid's tentacles from the carved wooden pillars supporting the banister and to reinsert its head into its body. "The door at the end of the hall," she said, and produced a ring of keys from the pocket of her jeans.

The apartment was dark, but Bruno could make out tall bookshelves along a distant wall as he and Mildred stumbled in. The carpet was soft beneath his feet. He let himself fall against the wall and slid into a slump on the floor. "Not yet," Mildred said. "Just help me get him into the bathroom. Then you can rest all you want. Please."

But Bruno did not stir. "What's going on out there?" he asked.

"I want to put him in the tub. It'll only take one more minute."

Bruno looked up at her. Her arms were wrapped around the squid's eight legs, which she supported from below with one raised knee. She was shaking with fatigue. The squid's arms shimmied soggily in hers. "Is it always like that?" Bruno asked.

Mildred at last let the squid drop to her knee and from there, carefully, to the ground in front of her. "Didn't you know?" she said, "Where have you been?"

Bruno shrugged helplessly. "It's quiet in Brooklyn at night."

Mildred unbuttoned the coat which the squid, in two pieces now, was just barely wearing. She stared at the half foot of empty space separating the squid's head from its body, then closed her eyes and leaned her head against the wall. "At night it's bad," she said, "like you saw. At first it was like that in the daytime too, only much worse."

"What were they going to do to that kid?"

Mildred abruptly stood and wiped her palms on her jeans. "I don't know," she said.

She took Bruno's hand and helped him up. The squid's flesh glowed blue in the dark. Its white eye rested limply on the carpet. The smell of ammonia had gotten stronger. They wrapped it again in the coat and each grabbed an end. Mildred led the way around the corner and the squid slid heavily between them.

The apartment was bigger than it had at first seemed. They passed through three large rooms before Mildred opened the door to the bathroom.

She produced a cigarette lighter from a shirt pocket and lit a wide red candle sitting on the sink. Mirrors on two walls reflected the flame about the room and Bruno could see all three of them, Mildred, himself, and their ghostly companion, all the same shade of pale orange. In one corner of the room was a low black porcelain tub, the fancy kind with jets set into its sides. They heaved the squid's tail in first, propping it up against the edge of the tub and letting it drop noisily over. The head, arms, and tentacles remained on the floor. Mildred shook her head. "I can't believe you fucking broke him."

Bruno lifted the giant squid's head into the tub and maneuvered it back inside the mantle as Mildred struggled with the arms and tentacles. Barely the first yard of them fit in the bathtub. The bulk of the stiff and tortured mass stuck straight out above the bathroom floor and rested on the lid of the toilet across the room.

From a cabinet beneath the sink, Mildred pulled a cardboard box filled with blue-labeled plastic bottles of rubbing alcohol. She handed a bottle to Bruno and opened one herself, pouring its contents into the tub. They emptied all twenty-four bottles, but the resulting puddle was barely an inch and a half deep. "Shit," Mildred said.

She sat on the edge of the tub, bit her lip, and absentmindedly caressed the squid's extended arms. "We'll have to use water," she announced.

"You still have water?" Bruno asked, but before the last word had escaped his lips, Mildred had twisted the taps and the tub had begun to fill.

"There's no hot water," she said, "but there's plenty of cold."

"Do you have any salt?"

"What for?"

"Add it to the water, like brine. Maybe it'll keep longer."

Mildred hustled off to the kitchen and came back with a can of Morton's salt and another candle. She emptied the can into the tub. "Help me stir it."

Bruno pushed the sleeve of his shirt up to his elbow. He got on his knees beside her and pushed the cold liquid around the tub. "Is it supposed to smell like that?" he asked.

"Like ammonia?"

Bruno nodded.

"To keep them buoyant, giant squids have these little pockets of ammonium chloride solution in their muscles, like balloons. It's lighter than water, so they float. They don't have air bladders like fish. Otherwise they would have to keep moving all the time to keep from sinking."

"Like sharks."

"I guess," Mildred shrugged. "I don't know about sharks. If you want to clean up, there are clean towels in the closet behind you. I'll give you some privacy."

Once she had closed the door behind her, Bruno stripped off his clothes and splashed his face with cold water. He rubbed soap onto a washcloth and scrubbed the dried sweat and the stink of ammonia and pickled rot from his body. He bent to wash his face again and, for an instant as he straightened, in the mirror behind him he saw the squid's arms and tentacles rise from the tub and toward him. When he turned, the squid had not moved. He laughed to himself and wagged a finger at it. "Stay," he said.

The door opened suddenly and Bruno scrambled to cover himself. He dangled the washcloth over his crotch. Mildred laughed and threw him a towel. "Sorry," she said. "I thought you were done. It's my turn."

She held the door open for him. As he bent to grab his wet clothes from the floor, she told him to leave them, that she had dry ones he could wear. She handed him a candle. "I'll be out in a minute."

In the first room he came to, Bruno almost tripped on a low, glass-topped coffee table. Beside it was a plush velvet couch. He put the candle on the table and sat to wait for Mildred, listening to the rush of water running behind the bathroom door. He let himself sink into the couch and imagined Mildred standing naked in front of the sink, the giant squid in the tub behind her. He imagined her bare neck and the harsh curve of her spine glowing orange in the candlelight. He imagined the broken squid beckoning to her from behind with a single raised tentacle.

When Bruno awoke the next morning, he found himself in an unfamiliar room. The walls and ceiling were paneled with a warm, dark wood and carved into intricate geometrical moldings. In one corner stood an antique wooden desk with dozens of very small drawers. There were two well-stuffed chairs upholstered in velvet, and a glass-topped coffee table on which sat a single unlit candle. He lay on a deep, soft couch made of the same fabric as the chairs. Under his head was a pillow and he was wrapped in a duvet, beneath which he wore only a damp towel.

On one of the chairs, Bruno found a neatly folded stack of clothes. There was a pair of men's worsted dress pants and a white cotton shirt, white boxer shorts, an undershirt, and a pair of black silk socks rolled tidily into a ball. The boxers were two or three inches too wide at the waist, as were the pants, which barely fell below his ankles. The shirt's sleeves didn't reach his wrists though the neck was a good inch wider than his. On each cuff were embroidered the initials *RG* in tight silken script.

Holding his pants and underwear up with one hand to keep them from slipping down his hips, Bruno inspected the rest of the apartment. The floors of each room were covered with Oriental carpets and the walls with ornately framed paintings and prints. Bruno recognized one of the paintings from books he'd had to study in school. The next room over was apparently a study. Its walls were lined with bookshelves filled with sturdy old leather-bound volumes. The room itself was dominated by a heavy oak desk, atop which sat an open laptop computer, its screen lifeless, its keys coated with dust. The study adjoined a dining room, furnished with a long, linen-covered table and twelve tall-backed chairs, which opened on one side to a kitchen and on the other to the living room, high-ceilinged and sparsely furnished, one wall giving way to a huge bay window with, largely hidden by heavy drapes, a view of the park. The moon, nearly full, still hung pale and low in the morning sky. Save the shimmering of the leaves in the wind, nothing moved, in the park or in the streets.

Bruno was standing by the window, the drapes pulled back, gazing out over the city, when he felt a hand on his shoulder. He spun around to find Mildred, her hair still tousled with the night's odd angles. Her eyes were ringed with dark circles, but she had pulled her face into a smile that was by all appearances genuine. "Good morning," she said.

"Good morning."

"Do you want some coffee?"

"You have coffee?"

"Only a couple pounds are left," Mildred said, "but this counts as a special occasion."

"How do you mean?" asked Bruno, who was not altogether certain that his feelings for Mildred were reciprocated. Was it the squid's presence she wanted to celebrate, or his own?

Mildred did not answer, but asked again if he wanted coffee. "Sure, of course," Bruno replied, "but how are you going to make it?"

He followed Mildred into the kitchen where she produced a small camping stove and gestured to a cabinet filled with propane canisters. "There's enough for at least a year if I'm careful," she said. "Plenty of food, too."

She opened a door beside the refrigerator that led into a long and spacious pantry, its shelves stocked with food. There were heavy bags of rice, dried beans of every size and color, boxes and boxes of pasta and crackers, shelf after shelf of canned goods—no Vienna sausages or sardines here, but pâté de foie gras and spring lamb stew, vichyssoise and Alaskan crabmeat. There were tins of truffles, jugs of deep green olive oil, boxes of chocolates, bags and bags of venison jerky, salted cod, mixed nuts and dried apricots and cherries. One corner was filled with five-gallon jugs of water stacked to the ceiling. Beside them were piled cases of wine, a few boxes of scotch and a few of cognac, even a case of champagne.

In his astonishment Bruno could form no words at all. Mildred smiled slyly, twisted the valve on the stove, lit a match, and then watched the burner leap into flame. "This apartment belonged to a man who was privy to information that almost no one else had access to. He was able to begin preparing long before anyone knew there was anything to prepare for."

"Where is he now?"

"The day after it happened I ran out to the museum but I couldn't get in. They were fighting in the street right out front. When I came back I saw them leading him away at gunpoint. There were six of them, in real uniforms, new ones. They'd pulled a pillowcase over his head, but I knew it was him from his walk, the shape of him. They put him in a jeep and drove off."

"Are these his clothes?"

"Yes," Mildred looked at him and raised one playful eyebrow. "I'll find you a belt." She stared at the blue flame of the camp stove and said, almost forgetfully, "I was his secretary."

"And he let you stay here?"

Mildred did not answer, but lifted the coffeepot from the burner and took two mugs from a cupboard above the sink. "There's no milk," she finally said. "Do you take sugar?"

"Yeah," said Bruno. "Two."

When he'd finished his coffee, Bruno felt a rumbling in his lower intestines and excused himself. There was no window in the bathroom, so he lit the candle on the sink with a book of matches Mildred had left there for that purpose. It was with a shock of remembrance that, as the light splashed about the mirrored room, Bruno saw once again the fractured squid lolling in the bottom of the bathtub, its arms shooting out over the end of the tub like the branches of a stunted and terrible tree. In his awe of the apartment's riches and his anxiety for Mildred's affection, he had forgotten the silent companion that had brought them together. But there it was. Its limbs swayed in the flickering candle light; its head and tail bobbed in the brine. The ammoniac stench had not faded. Bruno pushed the beast's stiffened legs from the toilet seat, dried it with crumpled toilet paper, let his pants fall to his knees without unbuttoning them, and sat. He had not eaten enough in recent days for his bowels to be very fruitful. He sat on the toilet and groaned, his thighs shuddering and in the process occasionally brushing a cold, slime-slicked tentacle. When he was finished, he washed his hands and dabbed with moistened toilet tissue at the spots where his legs had made contact with the creature's corpse.

Emerging from the bathroom, Bruno found Mildred sitting on the couch on which he had slept, her elbows on her knees and her head in her hands. The pillow and duvet were gone. Mildred looked up and, seeing him, brightened. "Try this belt on," she said. "We may have to poke an extra hole in it. Richard was a little thicker than you."

"No, this is okay. How do I look?"

She covered her mouth with her hand. Cinched tight at the waist, the slacks bulged out above the belt but barely reached his ankles. "You look good," she said. "A bit like Huck Finn, but good."

Bruno tried to laugh. He couldn't think of anything to say. He rolled up his sleeves and pushed a stray shirttail into his pants. He crossed his arms and combed at his hair with his fingers. He uncrossed his arms. "Are my clothes dry yet?" "I don't know. I haven't checked. You don't like these ones?" she laughed.

"No, it's not that. They're fine. It's only, I just thought that when the other ones dry I could go."

"Where will you go?"

"I don't know."

"Back to Brooklyn?"

"I guess."

"Do you have any water left there?"

"No."

"What about food?"

"No. Not anymore."

"So why go?"

"I just thought…"

"What did you think?"

"Well I didn't know if you…"

Something hard and bright shined in Mildred's eyes. Seeing it, Bruno found himself unable to finish his sentence.

"You know, after all this you still haven't told me your name," Mildred said.

"It's Bruno."

"Bruno," Mildred repeated. "My name is Mildred. Would you like to sit down?"

"Sure," said Bruno. He lowered himself into an armchair.

"Not there." She patted the couch beside her. "Here."

In the daytime they pulled open the heavy drapes and let the cloud-occluded sun fill the rooms with light as best it could. They walked through the apartment naked, or nearly so, lounging in unbuttoned shirts, french cuffs flapping at their wrists, with cashmere socks to warm their feet as they shuffled across cold parquet floors. They rarely spoke, but napped and read to themselves from the heavy, leather-bound books they found in the study and on oak shelves in the bedrooms.

And when Mildred would shake her hair from her eyes, put her book down on the carpet and gesture to Bruno with a crooked finger, he would cross the room and join her on the couch and their hands would find each other under their unbuttoned shirts. Their lovemaking was gentle and leisurely, filled with fluttering kisses and the lightest of caresses. At times they barely moved, but held each other, stroking one another with an eyelash, a lock of hair. Bruno learned to love every corner of Mildred's body, each hair under her arms or between her thighs, the scars on her elbows and knees from girlhood tumbles, the sad, lost look in her eyes when he put himself inside her. Even when he was not holding her, the glow of her touch remained on his limbs and on his face, a quiet, quivering joy.

The bliss of Bruno's days was interrupted only by trips to the bathroom, which he took as infrequently as possible. The twisted squid in the tub chilled him. The fascination he had felt for it, locked away, unchanging in a museum display case, had turned to revulsion under such close quarters. The cloying scent of its slow decay, which had begun to creep in beneath the ever-present stench of ammonia, sickened him. He felt its legs writhing and reaching for him every time he turned his back on it to pee. The odors of the giant squid lingered in his nostrils for an hour after he left the room, and for the length of that hour he could not help closing his heart to Mildred, regarding even her smiles with suspicion, finding in the traces of warmth her hands left on his body, no matter how tenderly, only disgust.

Bruno and Mildred did not share a bed. She assigned him a bedroom, its walls painted green, and took another for herself. They retired each night to their own rooms after watching the rays of the sun fade out the window, over the park, across the face of the motionless moon. Bruno never questioned the arrangement.

When she came to him at night, though, she came on like a fury. He would wake, startled, with her hands and mouth on him, her hair warm and wet and slick, her fingertips wrinkled, haunted by the smell of ammonia. She did not kiss his lips or his face, but pulled with her teeth at his nipples, at the flesh of his stomach and thighs, at his bony shoulders. The moonlight cast dense black shadows beneath each of her ribs and below her jutting hips. She seemed to move in fragments, like a filmstrip slowed. She took him into her mouth almost brutally, she shoved a brusque finger into his ass, she pulled him quickly into her. Their bodies slapped together, all bone and collision, and the sheets whispered in protest beneath them. But no sooner had Mildred's back arched and a long broken gasp escaped her, than she slid out of the room in silence, leaving Bruno, shaken and drained, to contemplate the slow movement of shadows on the ceiling as the damp sheets grew cold beneath him.

Bruno could never get back to sleep on the nights she came to him, and could barely drag himself through what little activity was required by the following day, speaking rarely to Mildred, longing for solitude and wide open spaces. But some nights he slept peacefully, uninterrupted by nocturnal visitors, and awoke with a smile on his lips that only grew wider when he rose and first cast eyes on Mildred. And there were the nights Bruno feared most of all, when he was visited only by dreams of drowning, of Mildred diving, pulling him into the depths of the sea. He would dream of walking the streets at night, stumbling in the dark and falling backwards into a puddle, long white tentacles holding him down, sputtering for air as the black water filled his lungs, and would wake, gasping, his hair wet and tangled, the sheets soaked and twisted. He would lean out the window to suck in the night air, but he could not escape the stench of ammonia and rot, which had sunk not only into his pores and nostrils, but deeper still.

On the fourteenth evening after their reunion, Bruno and Mildred opened a bottle of champagne to celebrate their first two weeks together. They ate a full tin of pâté de foie gras, spread on hard and salty crackers, and washed it down with Veuve Cliquot, warm and from the bottle. They lit far more candles than necessity required, piled cushions on an aging Oriental carpet and made love on the floor, as if in slow motion, swallowing each other's smallest movements like the last drops of sweet fresh water on earth.

Afterwards they lay sprawled on the floor, a tangle of limbs, and opened a bottle of brandy. They passed it back and forth, licking from each other's chest and chin whatever spilled from the bottle's neck. "How much," Bruno asked, "would this have cost us before?"

"You mean the cognac?"

"Yeah."

"I don't know. In a restaurant, maybe twenty dollars a glass, or a snifter, they call them—something like that."

"For one glass?" Bruno laughed. "I always thought it was a bum's drink. That's what they drank on the corner, by the liquor store where I lived. E&J from the bottle. No snifters."

Mildred kissed him and took the bottle from his hand. "This is not E&J."

"Did you ever," he asked her, tracing with one finger the line of her jaw, her neck, her bony shoulder, "order a twenty dollar glass of brandy?"

She shook her head. "No, but I served them."

Three muffled blasts sounded in the distance, and Bruno and Mildred were silent. They stood, naked, arm in arm, and looked out the window. Fires glowed on the horizon to the north. Smaller ones burned here and there in the park beneath them, the scattered camps of squatters or soldiers or bums. Two strange white stars arced soundlessly above the squatting moon and on across the sky, then a third. They hit the earth and the distant fires flared white, a premature and insufficient dawn. A few seconds later the sounds of the explosions followed, three faraway thuds, hollow and deep.

"They're mortars, I think," Mildred said. "Maybe something heavier. I don't really know. In the Bronx, it looks like." She turned to retrieve the bottle of cognac. Bruno took it from her hand and drank.

A tear fell from his eye. "Why?" he said, gesturing to the world outside. "Why all this? What happened?"

Mildred smiled weakly and wiped the tear from his cheek. "Politics, I guess." She pulled Bruno to her and hugged him. "It's late," she said. "Let's go to sleep."

"Wait," Bruno said. "First tell me, why the squid?"

She stiffened slightly in his arms and stepped away. "What do you mean?"

"Why is it here? Why did you take it?"

"We took it, remember. Because it wouldn't have lasted in the museum. It was only a matter of time before vandals got to it."

"But why did you want it?"

Mildred shrugged and smiled sadly. She turned her back on Bruno and pulled a shirt from under the cushions piled on the floor. She buttoned it slowly. "I'm too tired for this, Bruno, and a little too drunk. Tomorrow."

She kissed his brow and walked away.

Bruno did not sleep that night. He lay in bed and tried without success to impose some order on the thoughts chasing each other furiously about his mind. He got up and stumbled to the bathroom, intending just to pee, but the rising stench of the putrefying squid turned his booze-uneasy stomach and he found himself on his knees before the toilet, brandy and sharp undigested bits of cracker burning his throat. He rose too quickly, felt the cold touch of the squid's rot-slicked tentacles on his naked back and fell to his knees to vomit once more.

He did not go back to bed, but returned to the window. He stood for hours, shivering, warming himself only with brandy, watching bright shells scar the sky before bursting silently aflame in unseen streets. A skirmish broke out in the park. Screams and gunshots rose in the thin night air. The fighting spread into the street just a block away. Shadowy figures ran and dodged, taking cover behind cars long abandoned. The clatter of boots four stories below, muzzle flashes and groans. A bullet ricocheted off the bricks a few yards from the window. Bruno threw himself to the floor, hid his head under a pillow, and wept.

He didn't fall asleep until dawn and awoke shortly thereafter on the rug, still naked, his head throbbing. The apartment, save Bruno and the giant squid, was empty. Mildred's bed had been made. Bruno washed himself without lighting the candle above the sink to avoid seeing what he knew lurked behind him in the tub. He held his breath until he left the room. No sooner had he dressed than he lay down again, reclining on the living room couch. Picking up an open volume of Melville from the floor, he began reading where Mildred had left off: "...curling and twisting like a nest of anacondas, as if blindly to clutch at any hapless object within reach. No perceptible face or front did it have; no conceivable token of either sensation or instinct..."

The words fell through Bruno's eyes but stuck to nothing. He read them again and again found his mind drifting off between clauses. He put the book down and closed his eyes. Would Mildred return? Bruno paced from room to room, twisting the untucked tail of his shirt in his fist. The smell of the rotting squid, sharp and thick, had spread throughout the apartment. Bruno pulled the bathroom door shut and opened all the windows. The curtains billowed in the cross breeze. Cloudlets of dust and hair tumbled across the table tops and the parquet floors. Slipping a cashmere sweater over his shirt, and a tweed jacket over the sweater, Bruno leaned out the window.

The park was quiet, the streets abandoned. A greasy snake of smoke stretched above the trees on the other side of the reservoir. Bruno yelled Mildred's name into the empty city, but heard not even an echo in response, only the thin whimpering of the wind. He collapsed into the sofa, hugging himself and rocking slowly, certain she would not be back.

It was the jiggling of the lock that roused him. He scanned the room for a weapon and, finding none, scurried into the kitchen. He met Mildred in the hallway, a carving knife in one hand, a hefty tin of vichyssoise held high above his head in the other. Mildred, looking out from under the two cardboard boxes she had clutched to her chest, did not flinch. She smiled, amused, and said, "Put those down and help me."

Bruno happily complied, taking the boxes from her hands, putting them both on the floor and hugging her tightly as she tried to wriggle out of her coat.

"Where did you go?" he demanded, and before she could answer added, "I was so worried. I didn't think you were coming back."

"You thought I would leave you?"

"I didn't know."

"Where would I go?"

"Where did you go?"

"I had to get more..."

Bruno interrupted, "How could you go out alone like that? You know how it is out there."

Mildred waited. "Do you want to know where I went?"

Bruno nodded. "I'm sorry," he said. "I've just been worried."

She picked up one box and asked Bruno to get the other. He followed her to the bathroom, where she put the box on the toilet and lit the candle. "I can't believe how lucky I was," she said, her eyes glowing in the flickering crimson light. "It didn't take long at all." She opened the box and pulled from it a plastic bottle of rubbing alcohol.

"You got two cases?" Bruno asked.

"For a pound of coffee and a box of chocolates," Mildred gloated, smiling broadly. She emptied the bottle into the milky fluid, clotted and rank, that obscured the lower half of the giant squid, then opened another.

Bruno tried not to look at the broken corpse, which was now covered in a mucilaginous layer of rot. "Where?" he asked.

"In that little triangular park over at Broadway and 72nd. People meet every day to trade what they can. You just have to pray you don't get robbed coming or going, and that the militias or the cops don't show."

When they had shaken the last drop of ethanol from the last bottle, Mildred blew out the candle and, grinning mischievously, pushed Bruno into the hallway. She unbuttoned his shirt, let his trousers fall to the ground, and tugging gently at his penis, which was already hard in her hand, pulled him to the floor.

After fifteen minutes, the knots of Bruno's spine ached from grinding into the hard wood floor. Mildred rose and fell above him, her hands pushing against his chest, her body shiny with sweat, but Bruno lay still, no longer rising to meet her thrusts. "I'm getting sore," she said, slowing her pace.

He lifted her off of him. "I can't do this with that thing in there."

Mildred reached behind her and swung the bathroom door shut. "Do you want to go in the other room?"

Bruno sat up, leaning his back against the wall. "I want to know what it's doing here."

Mildred stood and pulled Bruno's shirt over her pale back, which was covered, like her neck and face, with red splotches from the pressure of Bruno's fingers. Shaking her head with irritation, she walked off down the hall, buttoning the shirt as she went. Bruno followed, and found her lying on the sofa, her legs crossed, angrily staring into the book open in her lap, tapping its cover with blue-painted nails. "Why did you bring it here?" he asked.

She closed the book. "You wanted it too. Don't pretend you didn't. You kept going back to the museum. What brought *you* back? And don't give me any shit about 'the unknown,'" she sneered.

"I wanted you. I was looking for you."

"Well, you found me." She picked up the book again, her jaw clenched, and began to read. They did not speak for the rest of the day.

Before the hollow evening light had fled the city entirely, Mildred retired to her bedroom and closed the door. Bruno, who had for hours been sitting on the bare floor in the corner of the living room, his head sagging between his knees, fetched the brandy from the kitchen pantry. The bottle was still half full despite the previous night's efforts. He sat on the velvet couch and drank, watching the shadows lengthen and mingle until they had invaded every last inch of the room. He watched the stars appear one by one, leisurely, like guests to an all-night party. He watched the moon brighten, its rays hardening and chasing the shadows from a slowly shifting trapezoidal patch of carpet, from a table top, from the sole of his bare foot.

All was still. No shells arced through the moonlit sky, no blasts shook Bruno's jaw. Not even a gunshot rang out above the park. Bruno tilted the brandy into his mouth. He could smell, from two rooms away, the heavy, acrid stench of the squid. It was time, he decided, to leave.

In his bedroom, Bruno removed the worsted trousers, tailored shirt, and V-neck sweater and donned again the threadbare corduroys, T-shirt, and windbreaker he had worn the day he left his home in Brooklyn. He kept only the cashmere socks, pulling his sneakers on over them, knotting one lace where it threatened to tear. He thought of leaving a note, but could think of nothing to write, and left, pulling the door closed quietly behind him.

It was colder in the street than Bruno had imagined. He had not been outside in weeks, and opening the windows occasionally had made him only vaguely aware of seasonal change. The wind rattled the few dry leaves still clinging to the trees in the park. Bruno buttoned his jacket, pulled up its collar, and headed downtown. Better to avoid the park, he decided.

It would rain, Bruno was sure of it. Every once in a while it would rain. He would go back to his old place and collect rainwater in pots and pans on the fire escape. He would trap pigeons and squirrels and catch fish in the river with a bent safety pin and a ball of twine. He would twist chain-link fences into crab traps. He had been fine before Mildred, and would be fine after her. He would bathe in the river. He would shit in a bag and save it for fertilizer for the garden he would grow, if only he could find the seeds.

Two men stepped from the park into the street a half block ahead of him. They were walking downtown. One wore a dented policeman's cap and what remained of a blue dress uniform. A pistol hung low on his hip. The other wore what appeared in the moonlight to be a pinstripe suit, topped with a motorcycle helmet. A shotgun, its stock and barrel sawn off, swung from his hand.

Bruno kept tight to the side of the building, taking shelter in its shadow, and slowed his pace, stepping as softly as he could. He would be fine in Brooklyn. He had never had much—what would really change? Winter was coming, but he could sew a coat from the hides of squirrels and rats, use their sinews and tendons as thread. He had grown flabby these last weeks, but he knew his body and mind would soon be leaner, stronger. He could defend himself if he had to, but who would bother him? What did he have that anyone would want to steal?

Three more men appeared a block or so ahead, heading uptown. Two of them wore dark blue shirts adorned with epaulettes and badges, tattered jodhpurs tucked into soiled boots. Bruno could not see the third for the shadows, only the silhouette of the rifle slung over his shoulder, an absurdly long ammunition clip protruding from its breach.

Bruno ducked into a shallow doorway, then peeked his head out. The two groups had stopped to confer. They turned to walk together uptown. In a few seconds, they would be at Bruno's doorway. He tried the door, but it was locked. He was ten yards from the corner of 92nd. If he ran away from them, he would have to run straight for nearly a full block before he could turn onto 93rd. He breathed in deeply, stepped out of the doorway and turned to his right, walking directly toward the five policeman, trying once again to stick to the shadows. Before he had walked two paces, one of the men put his arm in the air, and all five stopped. The first raised his rifle to his shoulder. Bruno crouched and sprinted for the corner. As he flung himself around the bend he heard a bullet shatter the bricks of the building beside him, then another.

Bruno ran, zig-zagging, avoiding the moonlight, his heart pounding faster than his feet. Another shot rang out and the air beside his ear was suddenly warm, then cold again. He dove behind a stoop. His pursuers stood in the middle of the intersection, guns drawn. Bruno edged himself out, keeping low, hoping the shadows would conceal him. He had only taken a half dozen steps when the bullets began to swim again through the air around him, crashing into the sidewalk, spraying his calves with pebbled cement. He dove behind the next stoop, heard three more shots, then a voice, "Save it."

Bruno crouched in the dark, shivering. His pants, he noticed, were wet in the crotch, and warm. They soon grew cold in the night air. The moment he was sure the men had gone and was certain his legs would hold him, Bruno stood, walked around the block, and headed back uptown.

Without looking first for Mildred, hoping instead that she was sleeping and would not notice he had been gone, Bruno went straight to the bathroom, stripped off his soiled cords and underpants, and threw them in a corner. He breathed through his mouth and kept his back to the tub. He lit the candle and found a washcloth hanging beside the sink. Soaping it, he felt something touch his thigh. A chill rose through his body as he imagined the squid rearing in the tub behind him, reborn. But he saw nothing in the mirror save his own reflection, the flickering candlelight reflected orange in his panicked eyes. And whatever it was that brushed again across his legs was firm, and, though cold and wet, not slicked with slime. Bruno turned.

Propped up in the tub, crowded by the squid, lay Mildred, one pale arm intertwined with the squid's twisted limbs, her flesh wrinkled from soaking and almost indistinguishable in the dim light from the creature's own, except for one dark nipple, floating above the foul alcoholic brine. Her other arm hung over the edge of the tub, grasping now at Bruno's knee. Her head lolled, hair woven into pillow of stiffened tentacles. Her eyes were half open, and less than half awake. "Bruno," she moaned. "I dreamed you left me."

Bruno knelt beside the tub and kissed Mildred's fluttering eyelids closed. He cradled her head in his arms, watched his tears splash in the hollows of her cheeks and, for a moment at least, did not even notice the cold and oozing corpse on which his forearms rested.

CHARITIES

by STEVEN STIEFEL

MY LANDLORD, the Egg Lady, decides I'm a pervert when she walks up to my stoop and sees my gay friend Paul giving me head in the living room.

A couple days later, she's out clipping her hedges. "I can explain what you saw the other day," I say to her while branches and leaves fly all over the place. Her hacking shears have two-foot blades, and I can tell that she hasn't been able to get out of her head the image of me with my pants down. She gives a stubborn branch a really good hack.

"Mr. Astinopolous, what you do on your own time in your own apartment is your own business." Her name is Mrs. Eggleston, but I think of her as the Egg Lady because she's kind of oval and mostly wears whites and ecrus, which help along the Egg theme. She talks in a gruff, kind of hard-boiled way that makes you think Humphrey Bogart has possessed Janet Reno's body.

"That won't happen again, because I'm not like my friend," I say.

"Mr. Astinopolous, you might consider drawing your blinds and shutting your doors."

She thinks my name is David Astinopolous, but it's not. The only ID I had when I moved out to LA was the fake one I used to use when I was in college, which I got from my oldest brother's friend. His name is really

David Astinopolous. Once you accidentally hand your landlord a fake ID, you can't really tell her it's not your real name; that's why David Astinopolous is the name on my lease.

After I had rented from her for a while, I asked her to call me Bret Cameron—only I told her this was my acting name, not my real name. She mostly bought that, but she keeps using the "Astinopolous" part because she thinks I need to stay in touch with my Greek roots.

"Anyhow," I say, picking a hacked up leaf off my tongue, "I just want you to know that the fridge seems to be acting up a little."

"If you'll check your lease, Mr. Astinopolous, you'll note that the apartment does not come furnished with a refrigerator."

"But it was there when I moved in."

"The refrigerator *happened* to be in the apartment. It's not included in the apartment, Mr. Astinopolous." I really wish she'd stop calling me Mr. Astinopolous. She says it in a condescending parent-voice, the same way the judge did when I got busted for being a prostitute. I don't dare explain to her my prostitution story and how David Astinopolous has a record in L.A. County. It certainly wouldn't help out my case about not being a pervert. I—Bret Cameron—am not a prostitute, either. One night, I was just dressed skimpily and waiting for a bus on Santa Monica Boulevard after my car broke down. But—I know—that sounds so stupid, I must be lying.

Of course I'm broke, so there's no way I can afford to buy a new refrigerator. My money from my breath freshener commercial ran out, except for enough for next month's rent. At this point, food's not really within my budget. It's about sixty degrees inside the refrigerator, so when I do buy something, I can only keep it for a day or two. I keep thinking I'm going to eat spoiled food and die, and then won't everyone be sorry?

I'd ask my parents for the money, but we're having a war of wills to see who can bear to see me starve to death. So far, they're winning.

When I get back inside, I break down and give Mom one more try. "I figure I won't be able to buy any more food after Thursday," I say to her on a reversed-charges call. This isn't the same as asking for money. It's just hinting.

"You should probably get a job before you're too weak to work," she says. Mom's more of a comedian than a Mother Teresa. I think a trip to Calcutta might help her cut loose the clamp on her Christian charity.

When my call-waiting beeps, I tell her I have to go. This used to piss her off, but lately she's just glad to end the call.

It's my gay friend Paul calling to say he left some crap when he was living with me. While he was down on his luck, I let him move in, even though he never paid any rent. Paul likes to act like we've had some big breakup, but all that ever happened was I let him give me pity head one time.

I ask Paul how he's doing, and he tells me he wants to come by some time when I'm not around to get his stuff. I tell him I won't be home tomorrow at noon, so we make a date.

Paul comes by an hour after we finish talking. "I thought you'd make a point of trying to be home tomorrow, so I came by now because I figured you'd be gone," he says.

"I'm here now, but I have a meeting with my agent, Eva, tomorrow."

"I know her fucking name!" Paul says, and his neck gets those bulgy little worms in it. Paul's a little bitter because he introduced me to Eva, a big commercial agent, and then my career took off with a breath freshener commercial, before it nose-dived. Paul's career has never taken off at all, and that culminated in him crawling between my legs. "Well, it looks like you've out-manipulated me once again," Paul says. He has a brand new, wash-that-man-right-out-of-your-hair hairdo that makes him look like an alert hatchling. "What do you want from me this time?"

I feel a little like I've been tricked into starting a knock-knock joke. "I thought you came by to get your stuff," I say.

"If you think you're getting a blow job out of this you're out of your tiny little mind." He collapses on the scene-of-the-crime futon like the very thought of it exhausts him.

"Why don't I go get your stuff for you?" I say, just to make sure I keep my pants on. I root around in the bedroom for any junk that looks like it might be his, and bring out a box of party hats and stage props.

"I know there was more," he says.

"Do you remember any of the things you're missing?"

"Don't put this off on me!" he almost screams. "I know you've got some of my clothes, but I am not going back into the bedroom with you!"

"Okay. If I find anything, I'll mail it to you."

"Don't think I'm giving you my address." Paul nudges the box with his shoe, then leans over and pulls an eye-patch out of it. "What have you been doing since I left?"

"Not much," I say.

"I got a haircut," he says, snapping the eye-patch into place.

"It makes you look younger," I say, but don't mention the baby bird part. "My refrigerator is busted and I have to get a job."

"APLA is hiring a driver."

"What's APLA?"

Paul roles his unpatched eye at me like I'm a twit. "It's an AIDS charity. Call them and tell them you're a friend of mine." After he says this, he clenches his fists a little bit. He stoops over and picks up the box. "There," he says. "I hope you're happy. Once again you've manipulated me into doing something for you that you couldn't do for yourself. Tell Sergio I miss him, and I'll talk to him soon." He huffs out the door, and the screen door bangs a couple times.

I sit down, dizzy from all my manipulating.

I go see Sergio on Monday. He's a cool enough guy with long teeth and manicured nails. "Who does your fingernails?" I ask him.

"You're going to fit in well around here," he says, examining his hands with newfound respect. He gives me a tour of the place, showing me the warehouse and all the offices. He keeps a hand on my back most of the time, leading me around like I'm blind and might hurt myself. "Rodney will be showing you the route." Sergio inhales and bites his lip, and I can tell something's up.

"Is there anything I should know?"

Sergio puts both his hands on my hips. "You're very perceptive, you know?"

"I've studied body language and cues."

"Are you a psychologist?" he asks, a little impressed.

"An actor."

This seems to impress him even more. "Oh, but they're really the same thing! You have to be so in tune to people."

"Yeah, except psychologists help people, and actors are mostly in it for themselves."

"But you give the gift of laughter and tears. That's a skill that will really be beneficial around here."

At this point, I think I could probably put "serial killer" on my resume, and Sergio would say, "You make people feel special by choosing them!"

"Anyhoo, Rodney doesn't know that we're going to fire him as soon as you learn the route, so keep that under your hat. He has AIDS and he's not very trustworthy. There are rumors flying that he's a drug addict."

"Won't he get suspicious when he sees me in the truck with him?"

"We've told him that we're getting him an assistant."

Some of these charities can be so devious, I think. "Maybe I should sort of boot him out the door when we're flying down the freeway?" I suggest.

"You're so funny!" Sergio guffaws, and sort of grapples with one of my butt cheeks. "We'll see you tomorrow!"

The next day, I show up early, but Rodney is nowhere to be seen. Finally, he strolls in about a half hour late. I'm sitting in the truck so he can't take off without me.

"What d'you want?" he says, like I've come to shake him down. He's about five foot one, and he looks like a stick-figure gangbanger—everything about him is small except his ears. He spends a lot of time trying to keep his pants up. Even in the truck, he yanks on them either out of habit or to keep them from sliding when he moves.

"I'm your new assistant," I say. This makes me feel a little crummy—stealing a job away from some guy with AIDS will do that to you.

"Cool," he says. "Some of the stuff we have to pick up is kinda heavy. I been tellin' them we need two guys."

We have the downtown route. In the mornings, we drive around and pick up all the donated stuff and take it back to the warehouse. In the afternoons, we go around and do all the deliveries to hospices. Sometimes we make home deliveries.

During the day, we ride around and chatter about the music we like, all the drugs you have to take when you've got AIDS and all the drugs that got you into this mess in the first place. "I can't afford to buy my meds retail," Rodney explains. "You know how it is. That's why this job is so cool. When we make the home deliveries, you get to know the caretakers, and if you kiss ass, you can usually get the dead guy's leftover AZT for cheap."

He tells me he'll cut me in for a third of the AIDS drugs. "I'm not HIV positive," I tell him.

He looks at me like I'm a leper. "Then what's your angle?" he demands.

"I needed a job."

"This is a shit job!" he almost explodes. His tiny body holds on to the steering wheel, and it about flips him out the window he's changing lanes so fast. "I don't even know anyone HIV negative," he says. " 'Cept my mother, that whore."

Most of the day, Rodney bosses me around like I can't figure out how to pick up boxes. "Put it right there," he says, pointing to the back of the truck, as if I'll screw it up on the thirtieth box. "Man, they should have teams doing this work all the time, it goes twice as fast."

When he's not bossing me around, Rodney tells me how he used to be a guitar player in a punk band that never got signed. "I wasn't much into the fame game, ya know. The record companies are all fucked. I was only in it for the music. And the chicks and drugs." He looks at me and smiles, and, right then, he doesn't look quite so sick. "Well, it was the dudes, too—a hole's a hole when you're fucked on heroin."

After work I'm exhausted, not from the work, but from trying to make Rodney think that I'm as cool and self-destructive as he is. We decide sometime we'll go listen to some garage bands and get some smack—the good shit. Then I tell him I'll see him tomorrow, and I go write a bad check at Mayfair for all sorts of food I haven't had for a couple weeks, like Cheetos and Pepsi. I decide this probably isn't a crime, since I might get paid before the check bounces.

That night, I eat all of an extra-large bag and drink three cans of Pepsi. I'm lying around in my living room, wondering if the combination is toxic and whether I should go to the emergency room to get my stomach pumped, when the phone rings.

It's Paul.

"Have you been calling me?" he demands.

"No," I say.

"I've been getting a lot of hang ups, and I figured it was you."

"I don't even have your new number," I remind him.

"It's 310-659-9080," he says, then pauses in a kind of icy way. "There. You've done it again. Now that you have my phone number, I'm sure you'll use it to encroach further on my life." He hangs up. I sit there holding the receiver for a minute, wondering why people always seem to get so nutty after they give you a blow job.

I go to the refrigerator to crack another Pepsi. It's like the refrigerator has been putting off its death till I get there. The motor in the back makes a metal clank that goes on for several seconds, then there's a little "poof" sound and a smell like appliances on fire. Then everything goes quiet.

I take all the stuff I just bought out of the refrigerator and lay it all out on the counter like a buffet. I decide I can't eat six packs of cold cuts, two dozen eggs, three semifrozen dinners, a gallon of milk, some apples for vitamins, and a half gallon of Häagen-Daaz.

I load all the cold groceries into a bag, and go back to the Egg Lady's place behind my building.

"Hi," I say when she answers the door in a big ivory-colored housedress. She doesn't say, "Hi," so I have to keep talking. "I just bought all these groceries and then my refrigerator died on me."

"We have already had this conversation, Mr. Astinopolous."

"I just mean that I wondered if I could maybe put some of this stuff in your refrigerator until I get one?"

"How long will that be?" she says like I'm some no-talent actor without a job.

"I won't buy any more food after this is gone," I promise. I guess I look so stupid and pathetic that it cracks her tough shell. "Very well," she says.

The next day on the truck, I'm telling Rodney about how nasty the Egg Lady can be.

"Man, you have a place to live?" he says, his big ears working overtime, and I can see the wheels starting to churn in the small space between them. Before he can complete his thought and get moved into my living room, I scream, "Watch out!" He swerves into the next lane, almost taking out a battered pickup loaded down with lawn-care equipment.

"Man, what are you screamin' about? There's nothin' there!"

"I thought I saw a cat," I say, sort of feeble-like.

He goes off on a tirade about all the drugs I must be on, and then how I'm not on enough drugs and I need some to chill me out, all of which is a much better thing to talk about than his not having a place to live and my having one.

"I'm taking you to see a friend," he says.

A few minutes later, we pull up beside MacArthur Park. "You wanna come with me?" Rodney asks.

"I think I better stay with the truck in case someone tries to break in."

"Good idea," he agrees. "Give me ten bucks and I'll be right back."

"I don't have that kind of cash." I open my wallet and show him all I have is two bucks for lunch out of a vending machine. He snatches that from my wallet. "You better hope Angelo's in the mood to have his dick sucked or you ain't gettin' high, pretty boy."

Rodney leaves me with the truck, feeling like I'm about two minutes away from a felony drug charge. I think about cruising off and leaving him, but that's probably bad karma. I look around for cops, and think about my night in jail on prostitution charges. I get the feeling that déjà vu's coming any second.

Several minutes later, Rodney comes ambling up to the truck, clutching his pants so they don't fall down. His eyes are bright and he holds up a bag with small white chunks in it. "Scored some crack, lover!" he says, all sing-song.

He smokes up while I drive the getaway vehicle.

Later, I'm talking to Mom on the phone. "What did you do today?" she says.

"Went down to MacArthur Park and bought some crack."

Mom plays it way cool. "And how did you pay for that on your budget?"

"Angelo—the dealer—takes oral sex instead of money." I don't say "blow job" because I always watch what I say around Mom.

"I'll tell your father; he'll be so proud."

"And my refrigerator busted," I say.

"Honestly, I don't believe a word that comes out of your mouth these days," she says. My phone calls home keep getting shorter and shorter.

Then there's a knock at the door. I half-expect it to be the cops tailing me back from MacArthur Park. Instead, it's the Egg Lady with a frozen dinner and pliers. "Mr. Astinopolous, I brought you this," she says, holding out one of my Budget Gourmets, all microwaved.

"Thanks," I say. "This rice one is my favorite."

"I felt I was a little brusque yesterday," she says. "So I wanted to do something to make up for that. Can I take a look at your refrigerator?"

I invite her in, then kind of glance around to make sure I didn't drag in some evidence of Rodney's crack purchase. I realize this is kind of stupid, but if you know the story about that Telltale Heart, then you understand why you keep thinking you're going to get arrested even though you're not a prostitute.

"Yes, this is shot," she says after she examines the back of the refrigerator.

"The light in it still works," I point out.

"So it does." She sets the pliers on the kitchen sink. "I've been thinking that maybe we could work out a compromise on the refrigerator."

"Sure," I say, spooning rice into my mouth.

"If you could procure a truck, we can exchange this refrigerator for a used one that works. I'll pay for it and you can reimburse me 50 percent, payable over the next few months."

"Great!" I say and give her a big surprise hug. Once I let her go, she shifts her housedress back into place and gives me an awkward pause. "I'll see if I can procure a truck for Saturday morning," I say.

I talk to Sergio, and he tells me it's okay to borrow the truck. I just have to sign it out and pay thirty cents a mile, which seems fair.

"How's it going with that lunatic Rodney?" Sergio asks.

"Pretty good. He doesn't suspect a thing," I say, so he'll keep thinking we're in cahoots.

"You let me know when you're comfortable with the route," Sergio says. "As soon as you take over, we raise your pay to ten bucks an hour." He cackles like a James Bond villain, which is pretty creepy when you have long teeth like his.

Rodney and I work out the rest of the week together, him pointing at boxes and me putting them on the truck or taking them off. On Thursday, he gets so tired from bossing me that I think he's going to pass out. I ask him if he wants to pull over and smoke up. That perks him up, and he pulls down an alley off La Brea. I roll down my window and sort of hang my head out so I won't get addicted.

He takes a couple long sucks on his pipe while I look around, checking the alley for déjà vu. After he finishes, he stretches out in the cab like a big-eared cat in the sun.

"You're a cool dude," he says. "You're not like the rest of those fags." He slips off his sandals and runs one of his dirty feet up my jeans. His toenails are orange and bumpy. "Maybe I'll let you screw me some time." His half-baked eyes watch my face as his cracked toenails work their way up my inner thigh.

I contemplate letting him give me a little pity head, but then I remember where that gets me. "That stuff always messes up relationships," I say and pat his foot.

"Yeah, man. We like each other too much to fuck it up." He gives my crotch a little foot squeeze. "C'mon, let's roll." He swings around, happier and more energetic than he's been all day. It makes me think doctors should start giving out crack to people with bad diseases.

On Friday, we go to the hospices in West Hollywood and drop off boxes of food and water, linens, and adult diapers. At one hospice, Gloria takes us into the supply closet. "Put the linens right there," she says and points to a corner. "Yeah," Rodney echoes. "Right over there, big guy."

Gloria wears glasses that make her eyes look like they've half exploded out of her head, and she talks in a very loud whisper, as if she's a librarian in charge of dying people.

"I'm gonna go say 'hi' to a couple friends," Rodney says and wanders back into the sick ward.

"I've personally seen a hundred and sixty-three people die here," Gloria whispers. "I've made a commitment to myself to stay here until I've helped five hundred."

"That's great," I say to her, even though this type of counting seems a little satanic. "I haven't seen anyone die, and I hope I never do."

"You can't ignore reality!" she whispers real loud. "It's attitudes like yours that got us into this health crisis in the first place!"

This makes me a little mad, but not quite mad enough to call her a bug-eyed corpse counter. Instead, I just go out to the truck to wait for Rodney. Pretty soon, he comes chugging out, holding up his pants. He stops to catch his breath so he can summon the effort to climb up into the cab. "Why don't you drive," he says. "I feel like crap."

"How was your friend?" I ask as we cruise down Fountain.

"I don't know none of those ghouls. I was after this." He digs into his pockets and pulls out little bottles of medicine. Some are pills, some are liquids. From his other pocket he pulls out some clean syringes and his crack.

"You stole medicine from dying people?"

"Don't give me that load of crap," he says. "These hospices get all the money they need. It's people like me got nowhere to go."

"It's wrong to take that stuff."

"I got it for both of us. Keep it up, and I ain't cuttin' you in for your third."

I shut up because I figure I can at least take my third back to the hospice.

Rodney counts out the vials and pills. He pops the glove compartment and sticks my share of the stuff in there. "You can sell yours or keep it for when you get AIDS. Doesn't matter to me."

He lays his head back against the headrest.

"Are you okay?" I ask him.

Before he can answer, he starts to spasm and jerk. The vials in his hands begin to rattle together, and then all his drugs explode all over the cab. His eyes roll back in his head, and I'm convinced an alien's going to pop out of his belly.

I think about trying to help him myself, but I don't know any kind of CPR, or even if that's what he needs. My mind goes blank on where all the hospitals are. Instead, I turn the truck around and head back to the hospice, holding onto Rodney, trying to keep his head from banging against the door.

I honk the horn like a maniac, and Gloria comes running out, her eyes bulging out even more. "What's the meaning of all this noise?" she demands, like it might have startled one of her patients away from dying.

"He just had a seizure," I scream. I look at him. Now he's just lying there, not twitching at all.

"Well, for God's sake, what's he doing riding around in a truck?" She reaches into the cab and scoops Rodney out and carries his limp body into the hospice like he's some little kid who fell asleep on a long drive.

Gloria puts him in a bed.

"Is he going to be all right?" I ask her.

The look she gives me over her glasses means I'm a total moron. Her normal eyes aren't bulgy at all, it's just the glasses. "He has AIDS," she says, whispering her loud whisper. "He's going to die."

"I can't just leave him here," I say, thinking she'll tattoo one of her numbers on his forehead the second I go. "I have to take him back to the office."

"If you take him, he'll die. You leave him over the weekend, and we'll see how he's doing. He's in need of constant medical supervision. There's nothing you can give him."

I start to tell her that he responds pretty well to crack, but I can see where that will lead me. Instead, I just sort of slink back out to the truck.

Back at the office, I tell Sergio that Gloria is helping Rodney. Sergio gets a bit disconcerted. "Well, the angel of death has added another soldier to her army," he says, sadder than I would expect.

I make *tsk*, *tsk* noises.

"Anyhoo, it looks like you'll be taking over the route on Monday," Sergio says brightly, finding a silver lining. "I'll let payroll know about your raise." He tells me I can take the truck home with me, so I don't have to come back over in the morning to get it.

At home, I'm so beat and depressed, I crawl into bed with some crackers. I don't even have enough energy to go over to the Egg Lady's to get a frozen dinner.

The phone rings and it's Paul calling to tell me that my reverse strategy of not calling him isn't working. "But that's not why I'm calling," he says. "I just wanted to let you know there are no hard feelings." To prove the point, he wants to fix me up with Trish. She's a hot bimbo who likes sex a lot. Normally, this type of thing is right up my alley, but I tell him I'm too tired to even talk about it.

"You are so clue-challenged," he says with so much force that the wind whistles through his teeth. "How dare you spit on my olive branch?"

I try to explain about Rodney starting to die, but he cuts me off.

"Does everything always have to be about you?" He slams down the receiver.

I wake up the next morning with something pounding inside my head. It takes me a little while to realize it's the Egg Lady at the front door.

"Mr. Astinopolous, I've been knocking for five minutes," she says. "I thought we had an appointment to go procure a refrigerator."

I pull up the truck and use the dolly to load the dead refrigerator into the back, while the Egg Lady climbs in the cab.

It's only when I open the door to the cab that I remember all the drugs that Rodney stole. I sit in the driver's seat, sort of sheepish, while the Egg

Lady shifts all the pills, vials, and needles. "I kind of work in the medical supplies delivery business," I explain.

"Is it common practice to leave the supplies lying willy-nilly in the cab?" she asks.

"No," I say. "That only happens when Rodney, the guy I work with, has a seizure." Just like when I tell Mom too much truth, the Egg Lady shuts right up.

We go up through the hills by Silverlake and Eagle Rock. The Egg Lady knows where there are charities that sell used refrigerators "for a song." The roads are tiny and steep, and it's hard to believe that we're still in Los Angeles. I keep expecting the truck to tip over and go cascading down the cliff, or I think we'll turn a corner and find some undiscovered native group, shut off by the hills from the rest of civilization.

Once we get over the hill, the Egg Lady steers me up to the loading dock of an orphan charity. She bosses me around and tells me how to unload the dead refrigerator just like Rodney would. "Is something the matter?" she asks me while I'm staring into space right at her.

"You just reminded me of a friend," I say, but don't mention the part where he's a big-eared crack addict in a coma.

Inside the charity, she finds an avocado-colored refrigerator that works except for the ice maker. She tells the orphan guy that he's taking advantage of people with his prices, and argues him down to the point where I think he's going to throw in a couple orphans just to get rid of her.

In the truck, she looks at me like she's just read my mind.

"I won't be gouged," she says as we pull out.

"I usually don't mind so much if it's for orphans."

We take off, driving back up the hills. The Egg Lady tells me to take it easy. She's afraid the new refrigerator is going to start banging around the back of the truck and take us "pell-mell" over the cliff.

The Egg Lady picks up one of Rodney's vials. She gets real quiet and examines it for quite a while. "Mr. Astinopolous, isn't Thorazine an AIDS medication?"

"Yeah," I say. "The place I work for helps out AIDS patients."

"That's very good," she says, her voice a little more quivery than it should be. "Would it be possible for me to make a donation?"

"Sure. We always need supplies."

The quiet in the truck gets real heavy. I can tell she has something on her mind, but she's sort of the type who keeps these things to herself.

Just when I think she's going to change the mood and boss me around about my driving, she says, "Mr. Astinopolous, what is it like for a man to love another man?"

If you look at my list, this is the bottom thing I would expect the Egg Lady to ask me. "You can call me Bret," I say, since this is a first-name-basis question.

I wait so long to answer that she has to ask again. "Bret, please. Tell me what it's like for you to love another man."

"Men are pretty much the same as other people," I say.

"Of course, I was married for years," she says. "So I know about the intimacies between a man and woman." Her hands have gotten all fidgety, and she's digging around between the cushions of the truck. "My husband died of a severe heart condition twelve years ago. But it's very important for me to know what it's like for a man to experience the love of another man."

Since the Egg Lady has been a witness to all my man-on-man love, I don't feel like I know anything she doesn't. I think about Paul and how he's always chased after me, pretending he hates me. "It's, um, like a compelling desire," I say. "It's something you can't get rid of no matter how hard you try. You know how it is when you haven't had something to eat for a long time, like Cheetos, and you wake up in the middle of the night and can't stop thinking about it even though you know they're not good for you, so you have to go out right then and get some?"

I look over at her to see what she thinks of this as an answer.

From between the cushions, she's pulled out a little white crystal clump, and she's staring at it through her moist eyes while she twirls it between her fingers. I almost turn the truck pell-mell over the cliff when I realize it's one of Rodney's crack rocks.

I slow way down and look at her face, watching her finger the crack rock. "Many years ago, I learned my eldest, Brian, had relations with men. I could never understand it."

While she talks, I can hear Rodney telling me that a hole is pretty much a hole. "The whole thing's pretty much the same no matter who you do it with," I say, talking so fast I can't get enough air. "I mean, most people are like other people, except some people are a little bit different."

She brings the crack rock right up close to her face, and I almost start to hyperventilate. I pull the truck over onto a gated driveway, so I can concentrate a little better. I'd like to be a little more help than I've been, but even more than that I want to get the crack out of her hand.

"Brian died three years ago," she says, so into her own thoughts that she doesn't notice me wheezing. She puts her fingers with the rock against her lips, and it looks like she could pop it right in her mouth like a Tic Tac. "I don't know for sure it was AIDS. He moved away many years ago, and all I was told was that he died of a respiratory ailment. His friends were very cold to me." She blinks her glistening eyes.

"That's too bad," I gasp, but I really mean it, thinking about poor Rodney, so sick he can't keep his pants up.

"I don't know if Brian had a companion or if he was alone. No one ever told me what happened when he died," she says. "So, can you see why I would ask you these questions? I really want to understand, and maybe you can help me." The tears begin to flood down her face, and she wipes her eyes with the back of her crack hand. "As I got to thinking about my horrible reaction to your lovemaking," she says between sobs. "I realized I was being given another chance. Do you understand what I'm saying, Mr. Astinopolous?"

I think about the real David Astinopolous, who lives in Lubbock with his plump wife and a passel of kids, and I decide that, since he's already been a prostitute in L.A. County, there's no reason a small part of him can't also be a gay guy who forgives an old woman. "I think maybe I do," I say for him, and my breathing steadies.

She lowers her hands into her lap and bows her head, sobbing quietly. I put one arm around her shoulder, and with the other hand, I reach out for her hand with the crack rock in it and try to pry it out of her grip. The touch of my hand reassures her, and she rests her forehead against our meshed hands. We stay that way for several minutes, her warm body heaving. She doesn't even notice when the crack bursts into a million pieces and the grains crumble down all over the cab.

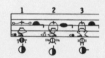

THE GENERAL

by JOHN HENRY FLEMING

FAMOUSLY, THEY FELL upon their swords when they could not defeat the invading army, leaving the occupying force unchallenged and the citizens to be brutalized, to be raped and tortured and maimed and drawn and quartered, or tarred and feathered, or whatever form of humiliating and excruciating torture was available and popular at that time.

All fell, that is, except the general, who did not need the ritual suicide to secure his place in history. The general only pretended, allowing the sword to slip between his arm and torso like an actor in a community theater who might be forgiven for not really wanting to kill himself for the sake of verisimilitude. *I am only a general*, he thought, as the sword sliced through the sleeve of his uniform, *which is to say that I am only generally engaged in things, only generally to blame for the deaths and the general defeat of the general forces of the alliance. It does not mean that I, for example, am specifically to blame for any of the individual deaths* (so many of which he had witnessed the horrific specifics—the last breaths gasped through red, red roses that bloomed on slit throats and gaping chests, the last words still hanging in the air and then falling suddenly under the unexpected weight of becoming Last Words but creating anyway just the kind of show-stopper performance that a general, for example, would have desired in victory but now must settle for in defeat, with the bloodied multitudes falling in military precision upon the swords they had carried halfway across a continent through trenches and razor wire as dead weight not useful in battle and not designed for anything but the falling on of which they were now specifically engaged in). *Nor*, he thought, *does it mean that I am to blame for the specific grieving of the individual families*, many of whose tears would anyway be washed away in blood, silenced by rape, evaporated by torture. *Nor am I responsible for my own specific act of cowardice*, the completion of which is fast approaching, *but damn that hole in the sleeve and the stained earth* (funny how he'd begun to think *soiled soil* and pulled up short, understanding with a general's skill of lightning-quick decisiveness that the thought might—he might later have thought—*soil* the solemnity of the act—and he owed them a solemn exit, he'd always said he did). *I am only ensuring a general conclusion*, he thought, *to a battle already lost in specifics not specifically of my own doing.*

And in such manner the general struck the soil, his head bouncing in the general fashion of his dramatically obedient and now suddenly discharged troops (though his bounce was a bit livelier perhaps, the grunt and the curse not cursed to be his Last Words thank God), whereafter he waited a few moments with his eyes closed until all the Last Words were exhaled and then fell in the dirt or were swept away by the wind, and a general and strangely affecting silence settled on the open plains.

Unnoticed, he dusted himself off and left the battlefield, conceding the shame it would be if there were no one left to write a general history of this war and place it squarely in the general scheme of things.

THE NUMBERS

by Andrea Dezső

HOME

On the other side of town, where we live, the apartment buildings swallow up the gardens whole, so we play around construction sites, in long ditches, among gray plastic pipes and half-finished staircases with one end anchored to the ground, the other soaring to yet-missing floors.

In the afternoons when the Factory blows the siren and the bent workers go home, fake leather bags trotting behind, blue, green, and brown, the site lies abandoned. We run, hidden by stacked-up walls of concrete, ready-made, waiting to be assembled into homes like ours, with two rooms, kitchen and bath, no hot water except on Sundays for two hours, with neighbors above and neighbors below, breathing, munching, snoring all around, with fathers who drink and argue and beat mothers who knit and cry.

We jump over lime lakes, climb on cranes, on still trucks, and when night comes patting black between pipes and ditches, houses and hills, we take flight from the fist of a sleeping bulldozer.

THE MODEL PIONEER

I like to close my eyes and pretend to see nothing, like the little blind lady who lives on the corner of Elbow Street. I stick out my arms in front of me, feeling my way around the house. Sometimes I crash into walls that weren't there with my eyes open. Last week when my mother took my sister Lili and me shopping for school uniforms I held on to her arm and kept my eyes closed, pretending she was a model pioneer who is helping me cross the street.

Teacher Oszer reminds us every day of the ten duties of a model pioneer, reading them out loud from a book:

1. A model pioneer loves his country and is ready to sacrifice his life for it.
2. He loves and obeys our fearless leader, the secretary-general of the party, president of this glorious land.
3. He studies, studies, and again studies to become a useful citizen.

Right after "4. The model pioneer celebrates holidays not with idle play but with patriotic voluntary work" is "5. He is compassionate. Helps his mother carry groceries home from the store, gives up his seat on the bus, helps blind citizens cross the street." There is a drawing next to the words in teacher Oszer's book that shows exactly how one is supposed to do this. The picture pioneer wears a tie trimmed with the red, yellow, and blue stripes of our flag, his uniform heavy with decorations. I don't have any decorations and Luminitza says I'm not very likely to get any since my parents are not even party members. I know she is wrong. This is not about my parents. I just haven't had the chance to do something truly heroic yet. She has six decorations already and wears them so close to one another they chime like bells whenever she moves.

Mamushka says blind people see with their fingertips and all it takes is practice. I like to teach my fingers the name my mother stitched in red script on my school uniform: "Eszter". My index finger likes to run the loops of the E, curl through the S, then buzz through the Z like a roller coaster.

There is a small space before the T where the letters don't connect, and when my finger falls in that narrow little hole I can hear again the doorbell my mother answered that afternoon, leaving the uniform with half my name done, needle sticking out of it, on a kitchen chair.

"Go and play by yourself or read something," she said before opening the door.

I lay down in the room with my eyes closed, teaching my fingers to read the woven roses of the rug. Mrs. Vago's voice came from the kitchen pale through the closed door:

"I cannot possibly have another one," and there were sobs hushed into cloth, and whispers, then she blew her nose.

"I have four at home already. All small. And my man is just like yours with the drinking and all... Where can I go? Someone told me to jump from a second floor window. My mother's aunt in the countryside knows of a plant… it's supposed to make you very sick but sometimes it works. They say…"

My mother's voice then, soft: "Hush. Hush now, Margit. A woman I work with at the Bread Factory knows of someone across the border who could do it. It's not illegal over there… You can get it for free in a hospital, clean, painless, the right way…"

"I can't apply for a passport for another year. I used up my travel option on that mandatory worker's exchange to Kiev last winter. And even if I could, they say it takes eight months and four bottles of vodka these days to get approved.

"They have new forms—Manci from the lab spent a whole week filling them out.

"First she went to the post office, called all their relatives long-distance for the models, ages, and plate numbers of their cars. Then she took the red eye to her husband's old folks down south to find out if they are still holding on to that rusty old typewriter from before the war. Had to give the serial number and a sample page of all the keys on white office paper. Suppose the old man gets the idea of typing something illegal then tries to get away with it.

"They want to know everything."

"They already know everything," my mother said, then they grew still.

My hand got numb trying to read the roses and in that silence there was a picture seeping up my finger of pioneers marching on the streets, singing:

"For centuries our ancestors but yearned
And for decades our heroes had to fight
For this glorious land to spread its wings at last
And ascend toward Communism eagle-like.
The Party, The Leader, Ro-ma-nii-ii-a,
The Party, The Leader, Ro-ma-nii-ii-a"

The boys and girls from teacher Oszer's model pioneer book were marching together with those from my school unit, decorations chiming with every step. I watched them clean up the trash from the park, quizzing one another on the birthdays of our heroes, then help every mother in town carry groceries home, red ties swelling in the breeze.

I must have fallen asleep because it was already dark when my mother came and put me to bed, the brand-new uniform laid on a chair next to me with my name stitched in red script on its breast.

LUMINITZA

Luminitza collects the green, star-shaped belly buttons of oranges. She keeps them in a shoebox, which she shakes every now and then to hear their belly button music. She says that her father works for the Securitate. They have special stores, people who work for the Securitate, in buildings unmarked from the outside where they enter using secret passes, where oranges, candy bars, and bananas are sold. We are afraid of Luminitza because if she doesn't like you her father can make a phone call, and he can get your parents to disappear one day on their way to work, never to come home again, so we swear to give her all the belly buttons we come by, even the ones we find on the street, but I haven't seen oranges for years and I never find anything valuable on the streets, yet in my dreams I sit under enormous, fragrant, blossoming orange trees in a faraway land, filling my pockets with green, star-shaped belly buttons for Luminitza.

TRUTHS

I wonder if God can see me when I hide in the closet under my mother's clothes, dark and scented, and murmuring tales from before I was. My mother says God can see you anywhere if he chooses to, you cannot hide from God, he sees through wood and wallpaper and sequined satin dress, through perfumed wrapping paper he sees, and through the skin, and through the bone-cage of ribs, and right into the heart.

I cannot talk about this in school because God doesn't exist there. My book says that astronauts rocketed up to the sky and didn't find anyone there. The children would laugh at me or get scared, for God is trouble for us pioneers, young and cheerful and committed to communist values.

And I cannot talk about God to teacher Oszer because I'd get her in trouble with my backwards superstitions and that's all right, since I know that we have different truths at home and in the classroom, truths that don't mix like the two sets of dishes at my aunt Eva's house, blue for dairy and red for meat, but we don't talk about that in school either.

SUNDAY AFTERNOON

A fly with a single wing is walking across the bedspread, humming a lop-sided buzz. It's nap time—a juicy slice of make-believe carved from the middle of the day; heavy, white sunshine slashed to thin strips of light shoots through the blinds, dust particles floating through like tiny galaxies.

The fly is moving fast, sticking its tongue out from time to time, tasting the fabric, disappearing on the black squares, reappearing on the red ones.

It's an easy one to catch with a cupped hand, and I hold it over the sheet to see better the small, hard body, thin black scratches for legs, and a veiny, transparent wing stirring the air with a half whirr. With a gentle pull I tear out the wing and hold it between two fingers to a ribbon of light, waiting for it to melt. When it doesn't, it occurs to me that I could press it between the pages of a book, the way I pressed flowers with Mamushka, so I tiptoe to the table, and carry a large, black volume to the bed. I find the wingless fly on the sheet, but it looks more like an ant now, and for a while I wonder if this is the way ants are made. It might walk better if it had four legs like dogs, or cats, or horses, so I turn the fly to its back, holding it down with a finger while ripping out its middle pair of legs. The legs are moving one last scribble on the sheet and I press them in the book carefully next to the wing. The fly doesn't seem bothered, although it is slowed down somewhat and there is a slight imbalance in its walk. It occurs to me: maybe it would walk easier on two legs, like people, or bears, or sparrows, although here an uneasy feeling starts to slowly squeeze my chest. Yet I yank the front legs out, and watch the fly topple forward, trying to drag itself away on its remaining pair of legs. There is a loud hammering behind my ribs as I set down the tiny limbs on the page. The last two legs come out with a delicate pop, or that might be my head growing noisy all of a sudden, the fly, a mere dark body with three clear divisions lying motionless on the sheet.

I don't notice when Mamushka comes in, only when she starts to wail, telling me that Jesus will punish me for tormenting his innocent creatures, and especially for pressing their body parts in his holy book, that now I finally proved to be an evil child who shouldn't be growing up in a decent family, but should be sent to an institution for the wicked, kept on stale bread and water, worked hard, and if I'm not asleep in an instant she will pack me up and send me to just such a place. She is wiggling her finger hard as she marches out of the room, leaving the door open to keep an eye on me from the kitchen, as I sink into a deep and tight and airless hole of fear.

I'm sure I will go to hell. Maybe it's true what they say, I was switched at birth while my mother was sleeping. If only I could pray to the baby Jesus, if only he would listen to me calling from the pit of sin, and I look up to the ceiling above my bed where I believe he would appear miraculously like in that holy picture in Mamushka's book, but there is nobody there except the three-armed chandelier, with the sticky, yellow strip of flypaper hanging from the middle, slowly swinging in the breeze, dusted with tiny bodies.

THE WISH

We all know it brings luck to spot a hearse or a chimney sweeper. But Luminitza claims your wish is guaranteed to come true if you see them both at the same time. All you have to do is twist one of your buttons around three times with your right hand while not letting either the hearse or the chimney sweeper out of your sight and wish away with all your might. You can't wish for more wishes and you can't wish for anyone to die. Those ones won't work.

That's how she got her bicycle, she brags, for Pioneer's Day, three days after she saw them, the hearse and the chimney sweeper, coming from opposite directions one Sunday afternoon on Elbow Street. "You need to have your wishes figured out," Luminitza says, "there's not much time to think when you see them, the hearse and the chimney sweeper," so she got her next few wishes sorted out and lined up, waiting.

Her first one will be for a real steel bell her father will mount on her bicycle, which she'll ring every time she rides and a child or a dog or a sparrow crosses her way. Her second will be for a pair of sport shoes, red leather with three white stripes on the side.

I peek both ways whenever I walk down Elbow Street nowadays, my wishes tucked away for when I'll see them at the same time, the hearse and the chimney sweeper.

Sometimes I wish I had a different face so when Mamushka's friends meet us they would not look at me with only their lips smiling and say "This one is the spitting image of her father," and she would not reply, "Unfortunately she seems to have his character too," and they would definitely not go on clicking their tongues, saying that my sister's face on the other hand is just like my mother's when she was a child, a real little angel.

Sometimes I wish for a girl I could walk with hand in hand after school down Liberty Street, take the corner at the Housewife Grocery, find the hidden entrance to the new construction site, and crawl in. We would run and jump, uniforms bubbling up around our waists, stroll among red pebble mountains and lakes of milky lime, and when we'd get tired we would rest in half-finished rooms braiding secrets into each other's hair. On rainy days I wish I'd find a small dog, teary-eyed and shivering and almost transparent, by the cemetery wall, one that would let me pet him and take him home inside my coat. Or a bird, smooth and green like a letter O, that would come to sing in my breast pocket every morning on my way to school.

But I can't explain these things to Luminitza, so when she asks me what I'd wish for if I see them one day, the hearse and the chimney sweeper, I say

I'd want a pair of original jeans, the foreign kind that says: *Made in China, Flying Eagle Brand.*

APARTMENT THIRTEEN

We live in apartment thirteen, and my mother says that's why we are so unlucky, my father is no good, she is stuck working at the Bread Factory, and there is no food to be found anywhere in town. She waits on lines that flow down the street and wind around the block, and when she gets inside the store, all they have left are hooks, empty shelves, and a whispered smell of meat. I told her that we should move but she said we can't with my father drinking his pay away. So I think we are stuck in apartment thirteen for now. Except we could pretend that it's a different number over our door. We could reverse the one and the three, or take them down. We could paint a lucky number in their place with shiny red paint, but my mother says that would be cheating, running away from our fate, and the way she looks at me I think she is afraid that bad luck would chase us down to take revenge.

THE NUMBERS

We got our numbers today. They are stamped with orange, three in a row on a square piece of dark blue fabric. Teacher Oszer handed me one and said: "This is you: 1735. Don't lose it and don't let your mother wash it in the machine—it might get erased."

I lay my number on my desk, 1735, as she explains that our mothers will have to fasten them to the arms of our sweaters, or coats, or whatever clothes we'll wear on the street. The numbers cannot be attached to rubber bands and switched between garments, nor glued to our coats. They need to be sewn all around the edges with small, careful stitches so they don't fray, and we are not to be caught on the streets without them at any time or we will be expelled.

The name of the school is stamped on top, it says No. 6 Elementary, in a half circle like a rainbow of letters, and underneath it's me, 1735. I wonder if I can keep my old name too or if I'll really be a number from now on, 1735.

Teacher Oszer says that from now on we'll wear our numbers to be recognized at all times. If we get into mischief on the streets, if we don't give up our seats to an old man or a pregnant woman, people can just look at us and write our numbers down, they can call the school No. 6 Elementary, and report that such and such did something or didn't do something, and that will mean trouble.

We are not in nursery school anymore, we'll be watched at every step, on every bus, and every street, in every park, so beware. And although not all of us are pioneers yet—that happens only to those who study hard and prove to be worthy—no one should think that school is all cheer and happiness, we'll have to work hard in class, do our homework, and not bring disgrace to the red tie.

I'd like to know if I'll be the same number next year or if I'll keep changing. 1735 is a grass-green number with long legs and a high-pitched smell of dandelion leaves, other numbers like 460 or 6844 are tree-bark brown, 1622 is peppered with gray like some moths, and there are a few plump, dark, velvety numbers, mysterious and full of the smell of roses like my mother's party dress: 9899, 968, 9669, but we weren't given any choices. I'd like to know if numbers start from 0 and who has to be that.

I hope my mother won't wash my coat without cutting the threads and carefully peeling it off the sleeve or I won't even be a number anymore. I should ask Teacher Oszer what happens then, what happens if a mother by mistake does wash her child's number to silence.

On my way home the old one-toothed gypsy woman who sells sunflower seeds by the school grabs my hand, the one holding my number, 1735.

"You got your number today" she whispers in my ear and laughs. My heart is going up and down, up and down and sideways as she rolls a tight cone out of a strip of newspaper and pours it full with seeds. "You don't have to pay," she says and her eyes are shiny with giggles. "It's a gift." And as she hands it to me I see a number much longer than mine written in blue on her inner arm, a number that disappears under the flowery sleeve once she lets go of the cone and pulls her hand back.

IN THE CLASSROOM

These are the correct ways of sitting in the classroom: hands laid flat on the desk, or clasped behind the back. Or one hand behind the back, the other raised in front, index finger crossing the lips right under the nose, like a bolt, like a lock, like a warning for silence. Legs parallel to each other or crossed under the knees. No swinging around is allowed. Postures erect, eyes up, shining with interest, or we will be tempted to talk, or doodle, or fall asleep during class. Then Teacher Oszer will take out her metal-trimmed wooden ruler and have us stand with outstretched arms, palms facing upward, fingers pressed together like small bouquets of candles sizzling and melting under the fire of her blows she calls "nailers."

Later—when she is in a good mood again as the entire class stands on one leg with both arms shot upward until the bell rings the end of the day—she walks up and down explaining she likes nailers because they hurt the most. I don't believe her for a moment because when she pulls my hair right by the ear it hurts just as much. And so does the crunching of my ears, soft and pink and pliable in her wrenching grip. And so do my tiniest, most hidden bones when she makes me kneel on kernels of dry corn in the classroom, facing the wall, but by then I feel a little dizzy and a little light, and like a soap bubble I slowly rise above the class, I'm Nadia Comaneci flying in a perfect arc over the cheering arms of the audience, I'm a bird.

I like to draw myself tying her to a splintery desk and pulling a brown paper bag over her head, filled with the plumpest and hairiest moths. I trace myself locking her up in a small place packed with thick darkness. I draw the outlines in black pencil, then color them, mindful to stay within the lines, a daily practice for a time when I'll be able to draw better, when I'll know how to paint lifelike people and rooms, skin and ropes, chairs and moths, when I'll make her look alive with fear, a puny shrunken person wiggling on a white sheet of paper.

LIBERATION DAY

Dana is marching in red, I am marching in yellow, and Zoe is marching in Blue, for those are the colors of our flag: red for the blood of our heroes, yellow for the crops, and blue for the mighty waters. Sitting on the pavement in a forest of flags and banners, three skinny drops in a river of tricolor trickling forward through the city towards the elevated tribune. There we'll deliver our much-rehearsed routine of delicate leaps and graceful bends, with fluttering kerchiefs that resemble blossoms from above. From up there we don't look like staggering kids ready to pass out from hunger, thirst, and sun; the shaded tribune with its many important eyes sees enthusiasm and might, group after group of eager pioneers ready to spill their blood should the cause ever call for it. We march across tar-covered streets softening to mush with the August heat pummeling down on them and scrawny little trees hung with fruits, apples, and pears, and plums in accordance with the secretary-general's newest decree. Our cities need useful fruit trees—he declared—instead of the outdated, bourgeois, ornamental ones. Before they cut down all the trees on the streets to replace them with twig-sized fruit-bearing ones, the city officials opted for the easy fix: decorate the existing trees with mixed fruits fastened to the branches with wire. Tired voices talk above our heads, then they don't, then they do again, about pigs raised at the villages of grandparents, children's grades, and outgrown school uniforms.

I have to pee so badly but there are no latrines anywhere in sight and the teacher in charge, an ample woman sweating profusely and fanning herself with a folded newspaper, snaps at me to hold it, we are almost there and then we can all go home. Dana says her tongue is a thirsty mushroom in a hot cave, Zoe says that her water is gone, she turns the bottle upside down to prove it, and that mushrooms don't grow in caves anyway, those are fungi and why don't we play twenty questions, make time pass faster, and I feel a sly headache sneaking up on me from behind, and close my eyes to watch colors bounce behind the lids, a built-in kaleidoscope. There is a pressure in my bladder as if there is no more empty space left in me, and I'm trying to imagine my mother in that river of faces, dressed in her Red Cross volunteer uniform waiting by her colleagues from the Bread Factory, smelling of home. I wonder if her turn has come yet to run and leap, rubber gas mask on, carrying someone on a stretcher, a pretend wounded in a pretend war we always rehearse for. My bladder is a balled-up hedgehog of pain, I'm nauseated, and bend my head to spill out the image of the cool-tiled bathroom of my home, fragrant with talcum powder and mint.

There is a resounding blast of cheering as we near the tribune; carefully chosen and strictly rehearsed words of ovation and warmest thanks bellowed to our party and its heroic leaders. There are two more groups in front of us, we are told, then there is one, then it's our turn, and we are suddenly in front of the tribune, Dana marching in red on my left, Zoe marching in blue on my right, we turn and bounce, petals opening and closing, kerchiefs swaying in the wind, red for the blood of our heroes, yellow for the crops, when my bladder's gate explodes and my waters break for I can't hold them any longer, thick, yellow rivulets rushing down my thighs, pulling a wide, dark trail on the pavement as I leap, as I sing, red for the blood of our heroes, yellow for the crops, and blue for the mighty waters.

VACATION

There are two kinds of vacationers at the beach: our kind and tourists. Our kind have official-looking work unit–approved tickets for everything we might ever need: travel, housing, even meals. When my mother finally brings the tickets home, Lili and I lay them out on the bed in rows. "These little red ones take us there, these yellow ones feed us, and these blue ones shelter us," Lili says.

Tourists are loud, blond, and foreign, with children wrapped in giggly colored clothes like expensive candy. They stay in the tall shell-shaped hotels by the beach and the ice cream vendor says that white silken sand is brought in at night by special trucks to be laid down wherever they walk. Tourists always hop on the beach shuttle instead of walking and leave the trash cans full of perfectly useable things: beautiful wrappers, slightly broken toys, glossy magazines full of glamorous pictures. Once I stood next to one of them on the bus and when she spoke each word came out of her mouth smelling of fresh strawberries. "It's the gum," Lili says, "they have a never-ending food called G-U-M, they can chew on the same piece forever if they want, and it always tastes like something delicious: mint, strawberry, bananas. Sometimes they blow their gum into balloons—once I saw a small child blow up an enormous gum balloon and get lifted slightly above the ground and get carried a short distance by it."

Lili and I like to play "Let's pretend we are tourists," lying on our side of the beach—the narrow one with small pebbles and almost no sand—with eyes closed, imagining blond curls flying around our faces and the frame of real sunglasses leaving enviable marks on our noses.

Tourists never look at us, but we always look at them, ready to observe and copy, as they sip frothy drinks out of shiny aluminum tubes, as they spread cream all over their bodies, as they talk in a sparkly language studded with Ss and Ts.

"Sutma katme tatamaxemaxamakme mek mek mek," my sister says.

"Satma katma," I respond.

"Sempa kom tatsamaxe pimp akam set tet metet," she insists.

"Sotka ma sutma kam pam tam," I give in with a sigh.

We keep pretending to be tourists when we go to our restaurant, the one that serves one kind of food only, as we eat the sticky, lardy casserole, as we fill our glasses with lukewarm tap water. We would like to pretend even longer but my mother snaps that she's had enough of our gibberish, she'll get a headache from us, it's her vacation too and she wants to enjoy it as much as possible. "So calm down both of you and let's just eat our meal in peace for a change," she says.

THE TRUE STORY OF THE BREAD FACTORY

When you walk across our flat little town, leave the Old Center with its plump, baroque townhouses and yawning parks behind. Cross the Old Bridge, pass the cemetery, and find our neighborhood of wobbly shacks and aging apartment buildings, abandoned gardens overgrown with raspberries, stray dogs, and banners with letters rusted to silence. You'll come across a crumbly fence that goes on forever, then turns to the left. Behind it hums a mint green cube, peeled to pink in places, with a flaking plate that says: "MUNICIPAL BREAD FACTORY—TOWARD COMMUNISM WE PROUDLY SOAR."

My mother works in that building. She wears the smell of bread in her clothes and tells us tales about the factory before we go to sleep.

Sometimes my mother cries because she is sick of her job, has been doing it since she was seventeen, since she replaced Mamushka at the shabby wooden desk.

She wants us to promise we'll never end up working at the Bread Factory, will never learn how to add up endless ribbons of numbers, nor memorize the ingredients of breads, cakes, and rolls, so that we won't have to sit in her seat padded with old rags against the wind that snakes in under the wire-glass windows.

Nor will we sit through endless meetings about how to increase productivity during the current five year plan, while the flour is slowly seeping away, in secret bags and bottomless pockets through favors and payoffs, and is replaced with stale feed grain in the bread. The sugar follows, then the eggs that make the buns smile, the oil and even the yeast, so the breads cannot puff up their cheeks anymore, but lay flat, sad, and gray like sour apologies.

Because of the "Most Committed Socialist Work Unit" contest, my mother has to work on Sundays, picking up broken bottles from the parks. And when autumn rains pull their sad curtains around our town, she rides on open trucks to help the peasants collect corn, beets, and potatoes.

She returns in the evenings with bleeding hands and field mice sleeping in her bag. She makes us promise that we'll do something better with our lives, although neither of us has any idea of what that might be like, since all the mothers we know are committed to one factory or another for life. But my mother says I'm good at drawing, and Lili is so pretty, she can even become an actress, we just have to be careful about where we put our talents like in that board game "The Thrifty Pioneer," where you have a single shot pretty early on, and can never go back if you missed.

Once my pioneer squad visits the Bread Factory, and we all get steaming, fresh breadsticks to chew on while my mother walks us through the stages of production, showing us all those magnificent machines, thrumming screechy songs while rolling, lifting, pummeling the dough, popping the breads onto the production lines, and the bakers glazed with sweat at the mouths of spark-spitting ovens leaning on long-stemmed paddles.

When Teacher Oszer gives us the assignment to write a true story titled "The Importance of the Bread Factory in My Young Life," everyone says they want to work at the factory among the heroes of the socialist cause. When I hear that I'm so proud of my mother, the hero. I imagine myself working at her side. I'd like to let my mind go out and find the words, red like flames, of awe. I'd like to write about how wonderful life will be working at the Bread Factory, but my mother made me promise so many times I never will that I don't know what to write so I skip the assignment altogether and get a gaping minus at writing with a warning for laziness. That's when I start to have nightmares. In them the Bread Factory is an enormous, deep, dark cradle where endless rows of pale, content mounds germinate on slow-moving production lines. I am a little lump of dough that is torn from a big, rotating, enameled dish by floury hands and placed on a line with thousands of others smiling in their sleep. I'm the only one awake and I want to find my way back to my dish through the one-way production line of the factory. The farther away I get the more desperately I try to get back, but I have no limbs and my body sticks to the line that brings me closer and closer to the ovens.

To chase the dream away I first try to ignore it, but it keeps sneaking back, so I crawl into my sister's bed after she falls asleep, and hold her, pretending she is a stuffed animal. I sing revolutionary songs, read cheerful pioneer stories that mention neither bread nor factories, yet when my mother turns the lights out in our room, I can't stop the sticky darkness from spreading over us, rows of loafs unable to raise, and over the click-clack of the gears that join and clasp under the production lines, dragging us in slow-motion towards those flame-hissing doors.

The dream keeps coming for days, then weeks, then a thought comes to my mind Monday morning on the way to school. I believe the Bread Factory wants me to tell the truth, pushing me and prodding me and not letting go until I do. Now I know how to get rid of the dreams. Tonight I will sit down at the kitchen table and write in bold script on top of an empty sheet: "The True Story of the Bread Factory." And the very first sentence will read: "Although I promised my mother many times to do something better with my life what I want more than anything is to work as a baker at the Municipal Bread Factory."

And when I'm finished writing I'll walk over to that crumbly fence that separates the factory grounds from my schoolyard. I'll wrap my story in a brown paper bag and bury it under a bush and when I'm done I'll toss dirt and old leaves on the ground above the spot so no one can ever find it.

CHECKLISTS

My mother checks the faucets, and the windows, and the gas stove, and the oven, and the TV, locks the door and checks that she locked it, then we can go. She returns from the staircase to check the door again, looks up from the street to see if she locked the windows, and asks Lili—once we are on the bus—if she shut the faucets in the kitchen. Maybe she forgot the plug in the sink and dripping water is collecting in it as we walk, as we take the bus— our minds carelessly set on pleasurable things—and will inundate the flat by the time we get back from our shopping. Maybe the Potis from upstairs will leave their faucet on and flood our rooms. She checks her handbag to make sure she has her wallet, and counts her money, and checks us to make sure that we are dressed properly, and nothing is hanging or disheveled, nothing is in a state of coming loose, that our faces are not smeared with food, our tongues are not sticking out, and our shoes are shiny. She asks me if I'm sure she turned off the gas, and especially the back burner where she made coffee, and she is really not sure at this point whether it got checked. We say yes, no, she sighs. She won't be comforted until we get home and she runs upstairs breathlessly and checks the faucet herself, the sink, the gas, the windows, the door.

And when we get home she starts worrying whether she left her wallet in the store, or any shopping bags on the bus floor, checking her money in her wallet, and we go back in our minds to the route we took, the streets we walked, the benches we sat on at the park, we check the contents of the bags, make inventory in abundant detail to determine that we have every-thing, and didn't forget anything, and we can move on, Lili and I to finish-ing our homework and my mother to her next chore.

THE GIFT

Judit's mother is a nurse and that's good because she can tell us to pretend that we need to pee real bad when our class gets shots at school with only one needle for all thirty kids. She teaches us to run away when the school nurse comes, to be afraid of jaundice and this new, secret, incurable disease that is not even supposed to be in our country, but those who have it still die tucked away in hidden hospital rooms, weak and big-eyed like newborn moths unable to fight even a cold. She boils her syringes and needles in a shiny, square box on the stovetop, and her needle squirts a tiny stream before she sticks. Judit's mother reminds Doctor Bota, the internist she works with, to change the patients' birthdates, since it's against the law for the pharmacies to give medicines to people older than sixty-five.

She gets gifts from her patients—yesterday a soap, a fluttery little scent like a small white flag sailing happily above. She lets us play with that soap gently, smelling it and pretending that we are ladies from those foreign movies taking long baths on carefree mornings in lion-footed bathtubs, using towels so big you have to be afraid of getting lost in them. We know to take good care of the wrapper, to touch it without crushing the folds, for tomorrow that soap will leave their house and go to Judit's language tutor as a gift, who will present it to the doctor who cured her kids of the flu by prescribing precious antibiotics, and that doctor will give it away to the sales clerk at the grocery store for extra meat or bread or oil, who will in turn give it to her neighbor as an appreciation for the somber black dress smuggled out of the clothing factory for the clerk's mother to be buried in. And by the end of all those travels the wrapper will lose its youthful gloss and look tired and aged and torn, and someone will wrap a clear piece of plastic around and tie it with a red ribbon, fashioned from a shopping bag, for a cheerful touch. But for now the wrapper is still newly hatched, crisp, cradled lovingly in our hands. We sip in all its details, the slippery, smooth surface decorated with elegant raised letters in gold, and the glamorous woman's face knocked flat unconscious from the pleasure of bathing with such a soap, but Judit is concerned that we might exhaust its perfume by smelling it too fiercely, so she gives it back to her mother, who carefully puts it away.

LILI

Lili is sitting and I am standing, and in-between there are grown-ups pressing us and each other to thin sheets. There is a smell of onions and of overheated bodies, a thin veil of domestic deodorant floating above the newvinyl odor of the bus seats. Clusters of people hang on all the doors that cannot close, and the bus, alarmingly tilted, ready to topple and crush us all, inches uphill with heavy sighs. There are conversations sprouting up and wilting fast in the heat about mock potato soup and the new breadrationing coupons. Someone says something critical about the transportation system but nobody comments since even we ten-year-olds know that it could be a staged attempt to provoke criticism of our party and government, only to have a reason to report the culprit as an untrustworthy, reactionary element, lukewarm in their beliefs and uncommitted to the red values. My body is embedded between a plump woman with short, permed hair and hot sticky breath full of neglected cavities, and a corpulent man with bulging, watery eyes, dirty nails, and sweat trickling down his temples. I can move my head and see the desolate concrete neighborhoods ribboning along the way, I can see Lili sitting by the window, staring ahead, separated from me by the heavyset man standing by her side, his eyes suddenly swimming upwards with delight, his hands moving to his crotch, pulling out something hugely swollen and dirty red, veins protruding between bulky fingers as he pulls back and forth, back and forth, back and forth on the shiny skin, inhaling, exhaling faster, faster, and there is a nauseating stench of spoiled corn grits when a sticky, gray river rushes out of him and onto Lili's chest.

My knees grow weak and there are words in my throat but all garbled up in balls making it hard to breathe, then it's our stop, we get off the bus, and stand in the empty station, Lili crying, sour-smelling vomit oozing down her uniform, she doesn't want to tell our mother she says, makes me swear on my pioneer honor I will never ever tell, even if I'll be mad at her one day, even when we're grownups, and later we lie together in our room, holding hands, and never talk about that day again.

NOVEMBER

I wake to screams of death again. You can't mistake those for anything else. When you hear them you know it's coming, you know it's the end, and that the one screaming knows it too. The sounds rush up and up, hit the low, gray ceiling of clouds, then tumble back down, resounding from a vast army of apartment buildings. First there is a continuous stream of bitter complaint, argumentative yet melodious, that escalates into a full-lunged screaming, shrieking, growling, and groaning. I know those screams, they are the ones that turn into knowing howls, scared, snarled. I can tell from how quickly the roar gets muffled into a wrinkled groan when the knife is finally used, and from the length of the struggled gargle that follows I know if it cut well. Sometimes the last sobs are short, quickly softening into a bloody murmur, but once in a while when the blade is dull or the killing arm hesitant they go on and on, those whispered wails, making smaller and smaller loops between snow and clouds, and I stuff fingers in my ears to keep out the picture of those sounds.

I don't look out the window to see the cloud-shaped patch of new blood on the snow. I see them every day on my way to school. Some are shaped like animals, some like castles, entire forests, or arguing peasants, and I often wonder if someone flying above our town would be puzzled at all by those marks at the bottoms of the concrete buildings, new shapes sprouting every day. Pig-killing season, November.

WE WALK

My mother says, "Your father is not coming back anymore," as we stroll down Victory Street one late afternoon. "Not coming back anymore" follows us as we walk hand in hand, my sister and I and my mother with my father's absence on her side.

He left a pool of broken glass on the rug when he fell head first into my mother's glass-front porcelain cabinet. My father often passes out in abandoned gardens by the edge of our neighborhood, and when he is found someone usually comes and knocks on our door. "Where this time?" my mother asks in her smallest voice while her eyebrows go up, up all the way, and the neighbor looks down and kicks the doorsill a little as he tells her, and my mother grabs her coat and goes to find him and bring him home from under the raspberry bushes, from next to the dead hedgehog, from underneath the snow. "Such a fine woman," people in our apartment block whisper behind her back, and "What a drunk, what a disgrace" behind his, and "How unfortunate, look at those two little girls, he should consider at least those," and they click their tongues.

"I told him, that's it, I've had it, he'll have to go live with his parents, no place for him in our house," my mother says as we turn on to Freedom Avenue, and we are almost at the place by the Old Bridge where my father passed out and we both fell off his bicycle after he had a couple of small red drinks at the Rapid Day Bar. My mother used to send me with him on errands and I had to keep track of where, how many, what color and size he had, so when we got home I could recite:

two tiny ones, transparent like water, at Bar Violet

a little bigger green one at Cosmos

three small red ones at the Rapid Day Bar

He talked a lot after those drinks and laughed too as he put me on the bar of his bicycle but his words ran into one another like giddy little rivers making up a language entirely new. Someone lifted me after the fall and someone took me home, and my mother screamed when she saw me without him, and I knew I should have not let him drink those red ones. I should have been a smart six-year-old and pretended to be sick or made up some reason to go home before he drank. I knew the way everything turned out with us muddy and bruised, the bicycle bent and useless was after all my fault.

My mother turns right on Independence Street, my sister and I follow, hand in hand and wordless. We pass the market and among heaps of greens I see the peasant woman my father got me to steal a potato from last year, one that looked like a sad face, and when I got caught he grabbed my arm and made me put it back and apologize to the woman, and later had me promise not to tell my mother.

There in the distance is the street corner where after a couple glasses he forgot me once when I was still little and didn't know how to go home on my own. And the fish seller is coming up after that, where we got a live carp once but decided to let it loose in the river. And beyond that is the newspaper stand where he got me a *Ray of Sun* children's magazine, and beyond that is the dam where he took us sledding on a Sunday two winters ago.

We walk. "He told me I should keep the TV for you children," my mother says and she suddenly picks up the pace, my sister's hand pressed hot in mine, and there are more streets and more stores that we pass, kerchiefed women selling flowers in front of the cemetery, a small dead bird by the curbside, and some stray dogs, but I keep my head high and stare at them without fear so they won't dare come any closer.

PELOMA

by CHAD SIMPSON

MY TWELVE-YEAR-OLD DAUGHTER Peloma kept trying to kill herself.

She tried three times, two years after my wife Marcella died in a car accident. The first two were kind of pathetic attempts, but still.

I blamed the counselors and myself. The counselors kept telling her that her mother was in a better place, that what was important was how Peloma lived her life, right now, and that she remembered her mother, and was happy; I went on and on about the afterlife. Peloma was smart, though. She knew better. But then she decided to hurry to that better place, where dead folks sing and walk on clouds and her mother wears large white wings and a halo as round and gold and perfect as the wedding band I still kept attached to my finger.

The first time she tried to kill herself, Peloma took seven aspirin and lay in a bathtub full of lukewarm water. She left a note on the seat of my recliner. I got home from Peterson Steel at five and found the note. It said: Dad, I took seven aspirin. Love, Pell.

As a part of my new position at Peterson Steel, I had to run two shot peen tumblers. I put small springs and Belleville washers into the tumblers where shot peen—tiny steel balls—pummeled the pieces until they were bright silver and hardened the way they were supposed to be. The machines did all of the work, which was nice, but I came home covered in shot peen pellets every day because when I opened the tumbler doors the tiny pieces of metal sprayed all over the place, like they were trying to make me as hard and shiny as the steel. Reading that note, I felt like I'd just spent fifteen minutes inside a tumbler and someone had jerked the door open and let me fall to the floor.

I rushed into the bathroom and found Pell sitting on the toilet with a towel wrapped around her shoulders, shivering. The tub was full of clear water. Shot peen fell from my work boots into the puddles on the linoleum. I grabbed a dry towel, wrapped it around Pell's shoulders, and held her so close to my chest my jacket left a quench oil stain on her forehead.

"It didn't work," she said. Then she stood up and dwarfed me.

At twelve, Pell was almost six feet tall and weighed close to two hundred pounds. That was the other thing I blamed for her suicide attempts: puberty. Puberty hit Pell early, just after she turned ten, just after her mother's car hit a pickup truck head-on at the top of a hill. I thought of what was going on inside Pell's body as a head-on collision between a sweet awkward child and buckets of hormones, which, like carbon monoxide, you cannot touch, taste, or smell. You could see the effects of the things on Pell's body, though. Before, she was big-boned and orange-haired, like Marcella. Then her breasts and her hips and her everything grew so that same orange hair was on top of a body that I'm sure the kids called fat, though I'd say was full-figured, like her mother's. By the time Pell and I stopped making monthly trips to the mall for larger bras and I'd already warned her ten to twelve times about the dangers of toxic shock syndrome (Pell insisted on tampons, said pads were for "girls," and I'd locked myself in the bathroom one night and studied the diagrams and the warnings that came packaged inside each little blue box), she was five inches or so taller than me and outweighed me by about seventy pounds. Less than a year after Marcella was gone, her physical double had appeared, though the new Marcella was clumsy, distrustful, and afraid of the new body she'd been given.

I had taught Pell about cup-sizes and how a tampon applicator works, but I still wasn't comfortable being a single parent, and I didn't know what to do about a suicide attempt. So that night I made chicken noodle soup and grilled cheese sandwiches. Pell ate a little and then said she was going to bed. I tucked her in and walked back out to my recliner. Pell's note was still on the seat.

I thought about calling Donna, the counselor Peloma saw the summer Marcella died, but I figured that would only make things worse. Pell hated

Donna. All Donna ever did during their sessions was ask Pell how she felt that day, on a scale from one to ten. Pell and I would joke about it on the way home. Early in the summer, Pell would say, "Five, five-and-a-half." As the summer went on, the number slowly rose, and her counselor decided we could discontinue the sessions. Like I said, she was a smart girl.

The next morning I made a big breakfast for Pell and left for work while she was still in the shower. I wrote a note to her and left it under her silverware, next to the plate of eggs and toast and sausages. It said: On a scale from one to ten, how are you feeling today? Love, Dad. I thought it might cheer her up.

I worried like hell about Pell, and I was having my own problems at work, too. I had worked in Plant Two at Peterson Steel, making hot-coiled springs, for fifteen years. But just before Marcella died I'd earned an A.S. at the junior college, thinking I'd maybe find somewhere to work where I didn't come home covered in oil and tiny steel balls. One of the stiff-collars got word I'd put two years of college under my belt and decided they could save some money by moving me into the quality-control position they'd just invented for Plant Two. Plant Two was four blocks from the other three plants that made up Peterson Steel, and the stiff-collars were tired of having to move the springs around to get them tested. They offered me a one-dollar-per-hour pay raise to take the position, which they'd thought they were going to have to pay some degree double my salary to do.

I balked a little, but the stiff-collars didn't give me much of a choice. They brought a bunch of equipment down to Plant Two from up the hill at Plant One and some twenty-four-year-old tie-wearing degree showed me how to use it. Before, we had gotten reports from and bitched about some nameless guy up the hill who decided our springs were shit. Now I had to do the tests and tell the guys I'd worked with for fifteen years that their Rockwell was off or their resistance was too tight, that they had to run another set of testers. Plus they told me I'd be in charge of the shot peen tumblers, which was a job usually reserved for someone on light-duty because of a back injury from dealing with the big jobs.

After Marcella died, the guys didn't know what to say to me. I'd never been one to say much on breaks, when we all sat around on empty upside-down paint buckets and stared out the open bay door at people going by on the street, living real lives. Once I became the asshole who told them they had to redo everything they'd already done, they started ignoring me completely. I was tired of being the asshole. I was tired of the silence that followed me around all day at work. The morning after Pell swallowed seven aspirin, I decided that I was going to lie and say that every spring I tested was perfect.

I collected sample springs all that day and returned them to the guys with the go-ahead on the run. Most of the guys didn't say much, but I could tell they were surprised. They raised eyebrows, looked at me sideways.

Toward the end of the day I collected two brake pad springs Jackson was working on for an important job. The stiff-collars were talking seven, eight million dollars if we got the contract. They were going to expand Plant Two and set up machines that ran only the brake pad springs.

When I'd finished the tests I carried them over to Jackson, who was tweaking the brake pad spring press with an Allen wrench. He saw me coming his way and looked like he didn't want to hear what I was going to tell him. In truth, the ends weren't square on the two I'd tested; they wobbled when I stood them on end—the press was bending the steel. And the machine said they were brittle, but I didn't care.

"They're right in the middle on everything," I said. "Hardness, length, everything. You're ready to roll."

"No shit," he said. He tossed the Allen wrench into a small pile of shot peen at the foot of the press.

"No shit," I said. And then: "Fucking run 'em."

Word spread about the run of good springs, and when we went to clock out at four-thirty, a few of the guys asked me how Peloma was doing. They'd seen her at company picnics and probably guessed she wasn't terribly athletic or popular at school, but they asked anyway.

"She just started taking piano lessons," I lied. "And I guess she's some kind of virtuoso. Her teacher says she's gifted."

"Well, fuck, Clem. You always said she was a smart one."

I walked out of Plant Two that day with a smile on my face, and when I got home, Pell had a meatloaf in the oven and the table set.

She wore a pink apron that was too small for her, the way it had been for Marcella. She stood at the oven door, and when she saw me, she said, "About a five, a five-and-a-half."

I shook pieces of metal off my clothes and showered. It felt good to hear the shot peen pellets fall from my ears and nose and butt crack and plink on the tub's porcelain. I used Pell's loofah to get at the quench oil lodged under my fingernails. I shaved and dressed in clean clothes and had dinner with my daughter, Peloma, who wore the too-small pink apron while we ate, and then asked me if I'd mind cleaning up because she had some homework to do, to which I replied, "No. No. I wouldn't mind cleaning up at all."

At home, all that week, I left notes asking, "On a scale from one to ten..." beside Pell's breakfast plate, and when I came home, she had dinner ready and had raised her self-ranking half a number.

At work, bars of steel were heated in two-thousand-degree fires and coiled by men or machines into springs. These springs were dipped in quench oil, hardened in long ovens, and sent through a shot peener, where tiny balls of steel scraped their edges clean. The springs were then pressed and picked up by me for testing. I gave the go-ahead on every set of testers I touched. Everyone was happy. When we punched out at the end of the day, I told the guys more stories about Peloma's piano abilities, how her teacher was thinking a concert was in order. And, sure, I'd invite every one of them if they felt up to it. We could all hear her play.

Then, seven days after her first suicide attempt, I came home from work and didn't smell anything cooking in the oven. There was another note on my recliner. It said: Dad, I'm off the scale. Love, Pell. I headed straight for the bathroom and found her there, on the floor. The water was running in the tub, but she hadn't used the plug, so the water just splashed into a small puddle and continued down the drain and into the pipes. Pell was sprawled across the bathroom floor, in her pink apron, with her arms stretched towards the toilet. She had nicked her wrist with the paring knife that lay near her hand; a half-dollar of blood pooled beside it.

I shook her awake, and she sat up. "I must have passed out," she said. Her orange hair was matted where it had been pressed against the linoleum.

I held her, pulling her face toward the same quench oil stain on my jacket that had marked her forehead a week ago. I knew I was going to have to call Donna. But first I found the bandages over the sink, next to the blue box of tampons, and dressed the small wound on Pell's wrist with antibiotic and tape and a square of gauze. Then I made tomato soup and grilled tuna salad sandwiches. We ate, and Pell went to bed early.

Once I could tell Pell was asleep I called Donna at her home number, which I got from an automated directory at the mental health center. I told her what had happened, and she insisted on coming over right then.

I showered quickly. The shot peen sounded like small bombs exploding when they left my body and landed in the tub. I left the quench oil under my nails.

I had never actually met Donna before. The people at the mental health center said they liked to work with children without interference from the parents. I didn't object at the time.

I dressed in pajama pants and a T-shirt and waited for Donna on the front porch. She was a short, stout woman with curly brown hair and large eyeglasses. She wore a dress and low pumps that made her calves look heavy. I met her halfway down the sidewalk, between the house and the street.

She whispered and cupped her hand at the side of her mouth, like she didn't want the neighbors to hear, when she asked, "Where is Peloma now?"

"She's inside the house." I whispered, too. I almost raised my hand to my mouth but caught myself.

"How is she doing?" Donna asked.

"She's sleeping. She ate some dinner, though." A light wind blew, and Donna shivered. Leaves fell from the trees.

"Good. Good," she said. She looked around at our neighbors' houses, keeping her hand near her mouth while she talked. She wanted details about Pell's suicide attempt that night.

I described the cut, how she was lying on the floor when I got there, the tub trying to fill with water. Then I brought up the seven aspirin and Donna's hand dropped; her voice grew loud.

"She tried this last week?" She raised her hand again as a shield and lowered her voice. "You definitely should have called me." Donna went on about how unusual this was for someone Pell's age. She reeled off some statistics and recommended we admit Pell to the treatment facility in Indianapolis, an hour south. I didn't like the idea. I didn't want to admit that Pell's problem was serious, that it was something I couldn't find a way of handling, even if it was. But she made me feel irresponsible for not calling the week before. She blamed my negligence for part of what was happening to Pell. I asked Donna to come by in the morning so we could discuss it with Pell face-to-face.

I didn't sleep that night. I sat in the dark and wished hard that Marcella were around. I wanted to ask Marcella how she dealt with puberty when she was Pell's age. I wanted to know how she'd acquired the confidence she had when I'd met her and how I could help give that same confidence to Peloma. I wanted to ask her what she knew about dealing with loss and grief.

I called in sick in the morning and made waffles and bacon for Pell's breakfast. Donna rang the doorbell while Pell was still in the shower.

Right away she started talking about a court order and late night phone calls, about how Pell was going with her to Indianapolis.

"It's seven-thirty in the morning," I said.

"Everything is already set. They just want to observe her at the facility for a week or so. It'll be fine."

Pell stopped in the hallway on her way to the kitchen when she saw

Donna. Donna walked towards her. "Good morning, sweetie," she said. It looked like the counselor was going to hug her.

"Dad," Pell said.

I told her it was all for the best, that Donna was going to help her, that she wouldn't have to stay long in Indianapolis.

Pell didn't cry or throw a fit the way you'd expect a twelve-year-old to. She just walked back to her room and packed a bag. While she was gone I asked Donna if I could come along for the ride, and she said I could but that once Pell was admitted at intake I wouldn't be able to see her until six o'clock that night.

I thought that if Peloma's problems were somehow caused by me, I should give her an hour alone with Donna in the car and some time at the facility without my interference, hoping that they could undo whatever damages I'd begun. I walked back to Pell's room and told her I would visit her that night in Indianapolis, that she should be good, and listen to what the counselors have to say, that I wanted her to get better. Pell packed her bag without looking at me.

Donna reached up and put her arm around Pell's shoulder when they walked down the sidewalk to Donna's car, and they were gone.

I called in sick to work every day, and every night I visited Pell in Indianapolis. Each time I went, a man dressed in khaki pants and a button-up shirt walked her to the visiting room, where we were left alone. I feigned seriousness each night, and said, "On a scale from one to ten, ten being the highest, the best..." Pell laughed, every time. The place was clean and Pell didn't complain about anything, except for wanting to come home. It was the same trick, she said, of making them believe she was feeling better. I wanted to know if she actually was feeling better, but I figured that if she wanted to come home, that maybe I was doing something right, that maybe I wasn't damaging her the way I thought I was. So I didn't tell her not to lie to the counselors, but I did tell her to listen to them, and that I hoped she really was feeling better.

On the sixth day Pell'd been gone, about an hour before I left to visit her, Donna called and said she was bringing my daughter home. I'd have her back in two hours.

I wanted to put Pell's room in order before she and Donna arrived. The room wasn't dirty, but I fluffed the pillows on her bed and hung clean clothes in her closet. I dusted her dresser and straightened the wooden jewelry box that had belonged to Marcella, and the tiny glass figures Pell kept on top of it.

I was putting away her clean bras and underwear when I found the opened envelope with the card inside. I didn't think I should open it, but I didn't know of anyone who would send Peloma a card. The outside of the card was navy blue and gold, covered with stars and half-moons. On the inside, the card read: Why are you still alive?

I thought hard about the card. I don't think the people who made it intended for the message to be mean. I think it was supposed to be life-affirming in some way. More like: There is a reason you are still alive. What is it? Now go out and do that. But it's not the kind of card you send an overweight, suicidal twelve-year-old. I went to slide the card back and found a whole stack of them behind a wall of crumpled underwear. Each envelope was addressed to Peloma and each contained the same exact card. Not one of the cards was signed and not one of the envelopes had a return address. I looked at each card and each identical message, trying to figure out who was sending them to my daughter and why they would do such a thing, until I heard a knock at the door. I re-stacked the cards, stuffed them into the drawer, and ran down the hallway to the living room.

Pell rolled her eyes in Donna's direction and carried her bag to her room. Donna was all smiles. She motioned for me to join her on the front porch.

"I think this has been the best thing for Peloma," she said. "She says she's feeling wonderful. That it was just a rough patch and now she's through it."

I spoke loudly, so maybe Pell would hear me and appreciate Donna and Donna's help the way I seemed to. "That's great. Really. You've been such a help." I put my hand on her back to get her going towards her car.

"Let me tell Peloma goodbye," she said.

"I'll be right here." I stayed outside. The trees were almost empty of leaves. The yard around me was full of them.

I thought that maybe I could ask Donna for some answers about Pell, some real answers, not just the same self-evaluation responses that Pell had been giving her. I thought maybe I should tell her about the cards Pell had been receiving, that she would want to discuss them with her. Then I figured that if Donna had the real answers I was looking for, she wouldn't be working as a counselor for the mental health center. She would be writing books and making television appearances. She wouldn't be Donna at all.

Donna came out of the house more chipper than ever. "The doll's asleep," she said. "Good night, Clem."

I waved her out of the neighborhood. Inside, I checked on Pell. She was asleep, still in her clothes, on top of the comforter. I told her good night from the hallway and closed her door.

The next morning I made everything—omelets and toast. I wrote the same note and placed it under her silverware. I waited for Pell to get out of the shower, told her to have a good day, and I left for work.

Jackson stopped me outside the door to Plant Two. I thought maybe he was going to ask about my illness, see if I was feeling okay. "What the fuck, Clem?" he said. "They sent back those brake springs every day last week. Snapped in half. Been at least twenty of 'em dropped off in your office."

"They were fine when I tested them," I said. "They passed specs."

"Well, we already got ours," he said. "They've been waiting to give you yours."

The stiff-collars came down from Plant One with the twenty-four-year-old after lunch. They checked the calibrations on my machines with some of the springs that hadn't snapped, the "good ones." The "good ones" hadn't broken but they were bent almost in half; they were shaped like question marks.

The twenty-four-year-old told me that the springs were a mess and asked what I'd been doing down here.

"What *have you* been doing down here?" the stiff-collar said.

"I've been out for the last week," I said.

They explained that the run they'd had painted and performance-tested were from a few weeks ago, when I was still working.

"Then I have no idea what's wrong with those springs," I said. "I haven't got a clue."

"Why don't you take the afternoon off," the stiff-collar said. "We'll look into this and get back to you in the morning."

At home, I found another envelope for Peloma in the mail. It was in the same handwriting as the others, without a return address. I threw it in the trash can and started an early dinner.

When Peloma got home she said, "A six, a six-and-a-half." We ate. She did the dishes.

The rest of the week went well. I left notes for Pell and her self-rating improved daily. She made dinner, and I washed the dishes while she did her homework. At work, they discovered the power had gone out one night a few weeks earlier during second shift. The stiff-collars had run some numbers and were guessing that the springs in the K-30 furnace, where they're heat-treated after the quench oil application, were baked brittle while the furnace cooled after the power went out. I was off the hook. But I was still lying about all the tests I was running on the new springs we were making.

The morning of the day Peloma attempted suicide for the third time, the stiff-collars came to see me again. They'd received another shipment of broken springs.

"I don't know what to tell you," I said.

"Think about your job here," the stiff-collar said. He went on about how they probably couldn't fire me, because of the union, but they could make my job a lot "less fun."

I whistled for the rest of the day. I even stopped at the press for a while and helped Jackson put some brake springs into boxes. I didn't test one of them.

While we were clocking out, the guys were appreciative of my lack of effort, even if they had gotten their butts chewed by the stiff-collars. They knew their jobs were safe. And the paperwork pride of that big contract was a luxury for the guys who didn't have to do the real work.

I told them that Pell and I were planning the concert, that we were having tickets made. They were going to have to pay to see my virtuoso play. Everyone laughed.

At home, I took my jacket off and shook the shot peen out of it on the front porch. Inside, there was no sign of Peloma. On my chair, another note read: Dad, I'm on the roof. Love, Pell.

Behind the house, the ladder was leaned up against the gutter. I climbed up and found Peloma standing beside the chimney, which was made of bricks almost the color of her hair.

We were one story, maybe twelve feet, off the ground.

I didn't know what to say to Pell, but I was glad I got to her before she twisted her ankle or sprained her knee. "Come on, Pell," I said. "Let's go inside."

"I'm going to jump, Dad," she said. "And you can't stop me." Gooseflesh covered her arms up to her elbows.

"You're right," I said. "I can't really stop you."

Pell walked gingerly down the slope of the roof toward the gutter. The gutters were filled with wet leaves. I squatted and began pulling handfuls out and throwing them onto the ground.

"You could help me out with this," I said. I kept throwing wet leaves onto the blanket of newly dead ones that surrounded the house. Pell did the same. She was careful not to lose her balance when she squatted at the edge of the roof, and she removed the leaves and tossed them confidently to the ground.

We worked our way around all four gutters, not saying anything to one another. When the gutters were clean, Pell seemed to remember her reason for being on the roof. She walked to the side we'd begun cleaning on, and stood with her toes hanging over the gutter.

"Nice trick, Dad," she said. She was a smart one. "But I'm still going to do it."

I looked around. I hadn't been on the roof of our house for a long time. We weren't high off the ground, but I could still see quite a distance. I saw Peloma's elementary school and her junior high and the high school she would go to in a few years. I saw the roofs of my neighbors' houses and the inner branches of trees, where birds had abandoned their nests.

"Let's take the ladder down," I said. "We'll probably fall off one of the rungs anyway."

When she didn't say anything, I walked over to her. She told me to stop or else.

I stood beside her. She shook from the knees up, told me not to come any closer. It was a short distance to the ground, really. I could see the veins in the dry red and orange leaves.

"I mean it," she said.

I took her hand. Her fingers trembled against mine, and my fingers trembled a little against hers, too. I squeezed her hand and let out a slow breath, like when I slide open one of the shot peen tumblers, just before I pull out the hard and shiny springs.

And together, we jumped.

Downtown Gagarin Town

Cosmonaut #1 was a dreamer. He had dreamed since boyhood of strapping on a pair of rocket-powered gossamer wings and flying toward the moon. But he was also a regular guy—albeit one with a monumental smile—who was born in 1934 in the backwoods of the Smolensk region near the town of Gzhatsk. While most Russian towns named after Soviet figureheads have long reverted to their pre-Revolution names, Gagarin Town will never become Gzhatsk again.

THE PEOPLE OF PAPER

by SALVADOR PLASCENCIA

SATURN

FEDERICO DE LA FE discovered a cure for remorse. A remorse that started in the river of Las Tortugas.

Every Tuesday Federico de la Fe and Merced carried their conjugal mattress past the citrus orchard and laid it down at the edge of the river. Federico de la Fe would take out his sickle and split open the mattress at the seams while Merced sucked on the limes she plucked from the orchard.

Merced sent Federico de la Fe across the river to cut fresh straw and mint leaves while Merced pulled straw, wet with urine, from the open mattress.

For the first five years of their marriage Merced felt no shame in having a husband who wet his bed. She got used to the smell of piss and mint in the morning. And she could not imagine making love without the fermenting stench of wet hay underneath her.

When Little Merced was born, Merced joked about Federico de la Fe giving up his cotton under-briefs in exchange for cloth diapers like the ones their daughter wore. But instead both child and husband slept in the nude, curled around Merced. The ratio of mint leaves to hay was increased, and although Merced feared chafing, she spread white sand on the bed to absorb the moisture.

But Merced grew impatient when Little Merced learned to use the chamber pot and Federico de la Fe's penis continued to drip on the sheets. "This is the last straw I'm putting into this mattress," she told Federico de la Fe at the river. "A wife can only take so many years of being pissed on!"

Federico de la Fe went to the botanica to find a remedy because he could not think of anything sadder than losing Merced. The curandero behind the counter gave him a green ointment to rub on his groin and two boiled turtle eggs to chew. A remedy designed to cure his enuresis.

As Federico de la Fe chewed on the shells and meat of the eggs and spread the salve, he felt the weight of an outside force looking down on him.

LITTLE MERCED

The medication failed. My mother got up from the bed and wiped the wet sand from her back. She left my father as he slept and I stared at her long and tangled hair.

When my father awoke and discovered that my mother was not in the house or in the river washing herself, his sadness began.

"Merced, it is just you and me," he said with a voice that was sore.

My mother was gone and my father chased goats and sheep to bring me milk. At night, instead of sleeping nestled between my mother's breasts, I slept next to my father and felt the wet warmth that had driven her away.

It was not until I turned eleven that my father discovered a cure for his decade of sadness, a cure that he never revealed to me. With his sadness the cure also took away his need for washed sheets and fresh straw and mint leaves.

"If only I had stopped when you were a little girl and your mother was still here," he said with a sense of nostalgia, but his sore voice had healed.

Two weeks after losing his sadness, my father told me to put my things in the pillowcases that my mother had stitched. He said that we were going to Los Angeles—where he could work in a dress factory and I could go to school and learn about a world that was built on cement and not mud.

SANTOS

Half an hour before the Guadalajara Tag Team Title Belt began I went into Satoru "Tiger Mask" Sayama's dressing room to review our strategy. His tiger mask hung on the side of the mirror while he sat on the couch shuffling his flash cards.

"Burro," he read from the front side of a flash card and then flipped the card to read the hiragana writing. Satoru Sayama had mastered the arts of Brazilian jiu-jitsu, aikido, and kendo and was now working on the ancient romantic art of Spanish.

I went over the setups for the flying cross chop and the diving plancha attack.

"Hai, hai," Satoru nodded and continued with his flash cards.

As I left Tiger Mask's dressing room I heard a voice coming from a crack in the brick hallway that had grown into a hole.

"Señor Santos?" I looked through the hole and saw a man and a young girl behind him holding two pillowcases.

"We are going to Los Angeles but before we go I want my daughter to see the last of the Mexican heroes." He lifted his daughter so I could see her and then put her down and walked away.

From the top rope, as Tiger Mask held down La Abeja Negra—so I could deliver my diving plancha—I saw the girl with the pillowcases and her father eating roasted peanuts. I delivered the plancha and then tagged Tiger Mask, making him the legal man in. I watched from behind the ropes. Tiger Mask executed his Japanese tirabusón submission hold and the peanut shells fell from the girl's lap onto the adobe floor where her pillowcases rested.

I thought that perhaps I could follow the girl after the match. But she had come too late in my life; I was an old man and she was just a young girl with flowered underwear. Instead, I tagged, so another narrator could follow her.

SATURN

When Merced left, Federico de la Fe fell into a depression that was cured ten years later by accidental circumstances. An itch had developed on the back of Federico de la Fe's hand and no amount of scratching could relieve it. He resorted to hand-feeding opossums and sticking his bare hand into beehives. The bites from the opossums and the stings from the honeybees temporarily relieved the severe itching. But it was not until Federico de la Fe resolved to stick his hand into the wood stove—where Merced used to cook tortillas and boil goats' milk—that the itch completely disappeared.

Federico de la Fe put his hand in the embers until it hurt so much that he could not feel his sadness and instead smelled only his singed flesh. After he wrapped his hand with an old scarf and rubbed on the green ointment that the curandero had given him, he wrote down all the things the fire had cured, prefacing them with Arabic numbers:

1. itch
2. bed wetting
3. sadness

Federico de la Fe's only regret was that he had not discovered fire ten years earlier. Every night, when the sun hid underneath the flat earth and Little Merced slept on the dry straw bed, Federico de la Fe went into the kitchen and lit the stove so his remorse would not return.

LITTLE MERCED

My father said that before we could go to Los Angeles we had to see the last of the Jaliscon wrestling heroes and partake in the long tradition of Lotería, a municipally approved form of gambling permitted in the form of long bingo cards with patriotic and religious icons instead of numbers.

I dragged the two pillowcases as I followed my father to Don Clemente's Arena. I walked through the hallways and blood from the morning's cockfights seeped into the cloth of the pillowcases.

I remember my father lifting me and making me look at a man who wore a silver-and-sequins mask. Through his eyeholes I could tell that he was a very handsome man, but a sad one with a lonely life.

In the arena we watched the match from the third row. My father bought me a bag of roasted peanuts and I asked for limes to squeeze into the bag.

"Your mother used to eat limes all the time," my father said, "they started rotting her teeth after a while." I promised not to eat too many limes. "Just this time," I said and he conceded two limes from his brown travel bag.

I ate the roasted peanuts soaked in lime juice and watched Santos tag Tiger Mask and step out of the ring. Perhaps it was my imagination—or the stench of the dead roosters underneath the seats—but I felt Santos', sad eyes staring at me.

After Santos and Tiger Mask defeated the Abejas Negras, we left the arena and followed a group of old ladies to the Lotería tables in the cobblestone park at the center of the city.

LOTERÍA CALLER

At the beginning of the night before the first game started I had to announce the rules and pretend I had a ridiculous name. I said:

"I am Don Senilla de la Silla. Your caller for tonight's Lotería.

"Sixteen beans per card. No more, no less. You buy two cards you get thirty-two beans, three cards forty-eight, four cards... you get the picture.

"I'll pull a card from this deck and then I'll announce the image. If the same image appears on your designated playing card, put a bean over that square. Once you fill the sixteen squares, call 'Lotería.' I will then go to your table to confirm your card and award you the cash prize of eight hundred pesos and a porcelain statue of our savior the Virgin of Guadalupe."

There was nothing spectacular about the night Santos and Tiger Mask defeated the Abejas Negras. The same people that were at the table every night were there holding beans in hand—the only exceptions were a couple of gringos and a man and his daughter whom I had never seen before. The young girl was pretty, but like her father, had terrible luck when it came to Lotería.

I started the game and the first card I drew was:

SATURN

Federico de la Fe did not win a single game of Lotería. He thought that perhaps an evil omen was at work because the only pictures he ever placed a bean over were that of the devil and the grim reaper which looked like this:

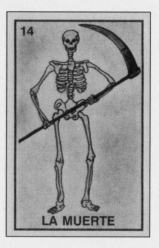

Little Merced did not win a game either, but none of her cards pointed to any signs of evil or premature death. Just benign images of watermelons and banjos.

Just before midnight they left the cobblestone bingo park and headed to the red-bricked bus depot that had slabs of tepetate rock as floors.

They boarded bus No. 8 on its north route to the border city of Tijuana. Federico de la Fe led Little Merced by the hand into the last two seats at the back of the bus—next to the toilet stall. Little Merced shoved her pillowcases beneath her seat and fell asleep across the burgundy cushions that smelled of sugar cane.

Ten minutes after the bus pulled out of the brick bus depot, four miles into the trip, Federico de la Fe looked out the window and then down at his daughter. He felt a slight inkling of the old sadness and feared that if he fell asleep he would soak his seat.

Out of this fear, Federico de la Fe went into the toilet stall and pulled out his sickle and heated it with a bit of phosphorus until it burned red. He lifted his wool Sunday shirt and pressed the glowing red sickle into his stomach until the sadness receded.

LITTLE MERCED

I bought three limes from an old salt Indian who sold fruits and blocks of sodium to people as they left the bingo park. I hid the limes in my pillowcases and pushed them underneath my bus seat.

I fell asleep and did not wake until four hours later as the bus meandered the curves around the Chapoltemec canyon. My father, who could sleep through almost anything, snored, but I could still hear a woman talking in a baby voice. I looked over the seat and saw a woman wearing a wool Indian poncho with bits of twigs tangled into the thread. She was talking to a slobbering baby who moved only his lower lip.

"He's meditating. He was born in a meditative state," the woman said. "At first I thought that he was brain dead; even the doctors said that he was as dumb as a turnip." She went on and explained that she had nearly poisoned him. But, as she was buying rat food for her baby turnip, the curanderos behind the counter looked into the baby's eyes. The curanderos told her that the baby was actually a very powerful soothsayer who was concentrating and meditating. "One day he will break his trance and add to the parchment texts of Nostradamus," they said.

"I know it seems like he is dead inside but just yesterday I looked in his eyes and I saw the history of the world on the inside of his retina. I saw us as jellyfish and apes, and then Columbus, and then a world where honeymooners sleep in glass cases.

"And it's not just this world. Sometimes I see Saturn and stars and planets that telescopes have never been pointed at. The universe whirls around in his head, and one day he will be able to tell us about it."

I wanted a glimpse of the future; I thought that in the contained vastness of the baby's head, maybe, I could spot my mother's black hair. I wiped the baby's slobber with my sleeve and stared into his eyes to discover a little about what the infant Nostradamus saw.

BABY NOSTRADAMUS

SATURN

Bus No. 8 arrived in Tijuana five days after it left the city of Guadalajara.

During their five-day journey, they ate a bit of salted pork, which Federico de la Fe had instructed Little Merced to put in her pillowcase, and a few corn cakes that Federico de la Fe carried in a nylon bag. Three days into the trip, Federico de la Fe discovered lime shells underneath his seat—but didn't think much of them. He figured that they had probably slid under his seat as the bus climbed the mountains of Culiacán.

During that journey, Federico de la Fe thought about dress factories and the technology of a world

that would learn to soak color into the gray celluloid world of Rita Hayworth.

"Baja California, Tijuana," the bus driver announced and spat out a wad of chewed sugar cane. Federico de la Fe patted Little Merced's head to wake her up.

"We're here," he said, and Little Merced reached underneath her seat and grabbed her two pillowcases.

As they walked down the aisle, Little Merced said goodbye to the Baby Nostradamus and his mother. At the front of the bus was a woman, made of paper, who insisted on giving Little Merced a hug and a kiss before she stepped out of the bus. Federico de la Fe at first resisted the woman's affections towards his daughter, but then saw Little Merced open her arms and embrace the woman.

LITTLE MERCED

After peering into the Baby Nostradamus's eyes, I moved toward the front of the bus and sat next to a woman who was made of paper. She said nothing was left of her people, except for her and her creator. And she had left him passed out in an old factory with thousands of paper cuts on his hands and arms.

She seemed sad. I looked at her newsprint arms and at the green construction paper wrapped around her ankles and asked if I could touch her. She nodded. I put my hand on her arm and gave it a slight squeeze, expecting it to crumple and collapse. It was warm and I could feel the blood climbing up the veins into her fingers and then racing back into her heart.

I wanted to know her name so I could preface whatever I said by addressing her properly and not as "the woman made of paper."

"In the rush and havoc of my creation I was never christened. I do not know what a proper name should be," she said, and asked me if I could name her.

I named her "Merced de Papel" after my own name, which was given to me by my mother. Merced de Papel asked me where my father and I were going. I told her that we were going to Los Angles so he could work in a dress factory and I could go to school and learn about a world built on cement. Merced de Papel was going to Los Angeles too, but for different reasons. She heard that Los Angeles was the last refuge for those who had lost their civilization and were afraid of the rain.

MERCED DE PAPEL

Once the rainstorm ended I walked around the puddles and remains of the paper people. I saw Antonio, our creator, passed out by the door of the old factory, his hands bloody.

I touched him and even splashed him with a bit of water but he did not wake.

In panic and loneliness, I set out for the nearest city and ended up in Guadalajara. I found a man who wore spurs on his boots and prodded steer through the middle of intersections and I told him my story. He bought me a bus ticket and told me that I should head to Los Angeles to avoid the thunderstorms and potholes.

On the bus, a young girl—who was made entirely of meat and wore flowered underwear—told me about the city I had just left and jokingly told me not to look back or I would turn into salt.

"You remind me of my mother though I haven't seen her in years," she said, and laughed. She went on to christen me "Merced de Papel." After feeling my arms, she said that I was warm and not a soggy roll of Sunday news as she expected.

She went back to her seat and fell asleep next to her father. When we arrived in Tijuana her father walked her down the bus aisle but before she stepped out she told me goodbye and hugged me.

"A baby Nostradamus is at the back of the bus," she whispered in my ear before she left with her father. I looked to the back and saw a proud mother holding a retarded baby with dangling arms and legs and a dripping mouth.

SATURN

In Tijuana, Federico de la Fe exited bus No. 8 and felt the hovering force pressing down on him. He felt that he was being constantly watched from above; at times he felt eyes from three different angles staring down at him.

Federico de la Fe—who once lived along the river of Las Tortugas—had heard that in the north, where water was scarce, they made mechanical tortoises and turtles that walked around, ate insects, and laid aluminum eggs. He felt fortunate because after feeling the strange eyes on his back he had immediately found an old repair shop where they worked on Japanese cars and mechanical turtles and knew that he could find shelter under the density of metal. And after a bit of pleading and explaining with one of the mechanics he opened the chain-link gate to the yard and crawled into an abandoned lead shell that not even the most powerful narrator in the universe could penetrate.

LITTLE MERCED

I bent down to look into the lead shell.

"Merced, I know that I'm wrong, but I feel as if you are one of the people that is constantly looking at me."

I told him that someone had to watch over him and that there was nothing wrong in that. But he refused to come out of the shell. He gave me some money and told me to leave the pillowcases with him. He handed me a shopping list to which I added in very faint writing, "limes."

I figured that the inside of the lead shell was very cold and that explained why my father wanted three quarts of petroleum and a box of phosphorus sticks.

I asked one of the mechanics, whose black and greasy hands made him look very much like an astrologer, if he could point me to the market.

He was reading an old cloth copy of *Centuries* and, though Mexico was a country of Francophobes, he read a bit of the rhyming quatrains to me in French and then drew me a map to the market.

I followed the map to a market that had given up on salted pork and beef and packed everything in ice, and distilled its petroleum into gasoline and naphtha and shined its limes with a layer of wax.

I bought a small box of salt, six pounds of frozen pork, bread, a box of matches, three quarts of gasoline, and a small bag of limes— small enough to hide in my blouse.

When I returned to the mechanic shop my father was still underneath the lead shell. Through the small opening, where the robot turtle used to poke its head, I gave my father the gasoline, matches, and a pork sandwich.

MECHANIC

I was calibrating the sprockets of an old tortoise when a man of southern features and complexion entered the shop asking to borrow one of the lead shells on the yard. Cereno, who refused to work on the turtles, was working on a Japanese engine block. He ignored the man and instead focused on the young daughter's knees.

I used to crawl underneath the lead shell to think about different mathematical configurations for making the turtles function more naturally. It was absurd, but I feared some hovering entity that seemed to know everything about me, even the ideas I had yet to patent. In the shelter of the shell I felt free to think, and free of any infringement on my theories.

Naturally, I felt some sympathy for the man and I agreed to let him use the shell. His daughter, who smelled of citrus, was kind enough to humor me as I read to her silly rhyming quatrains from the erred prophet Nostradamus.

"I've looked into Nostradamus's baby eyes," she said and cracked a small smile. I laughed and drew her a map that she could follow to the supermarket.

While the daughter was away I saw her father come out of the shell and look up at the sky. After praying briefly he crawled back inside.

SATURN

Federico de la Fe came out of the lead shell while Little Merced was at the supermarket buying groceries and the materials necessary for Federico de la Fe's remedy for sadness.

Federico de la Fe looked up at the sky. His black eyes moved a little to the left, toward the direction of Saturn. And as he looked at Saturn he said:

"I'm not coming out again until you go away. All these years I felt you watching me and mocking me as I peed in my bed and dreamed about dress factories and of my Merced. But no more. I won't be part of your stupid story anymore."

And after yelling at the sky, Federico de la Fe crawled back into the lead shell.

LITTLE MERCED

I laid out a salting bed, made out of the *News of the World* and a couple advertisements for transmission fluid and engine seals. I spread the salt on the newspapers and rolled the pork and then wrapped it in the newsprint and slid it into my father, who still remained in the metal shell.

I unbuttoned my blouse while hiding behind a rusting truck and took out the bag of limes. After eating one and throwing the peels into the cabin of a rusting truck, I noticed a tribe of Glue Sniffers walking toward the yard and I quickly put the limes away.

They were selling wallets and knapsacks made of string and glue that they wove through whatever chunks of leather they would find. My father had said that the Glue Sniffers were not like other Indian tribes. Some of them were not even Indians. It was a tribe made out of orphans and runaways. And when the world was poor and starving they became sad and would stop pounding and stitching leather and sniff glue instead.

When they approached me with their tan purses I told them to wait while I went and got my father.

I poked my head into the shell and felt the fumes of gasoline and the stench of burned phosphorus in my nostrils. I told my father about the Glue Sniffers and he said to let a couple of them in. A Glue Sniffer who had fair skin and wore duct tape around his waist went into the shell accompanied by a dark but tall Oaxacan Indian who had one eye lost in meditation like the Baby Nostradamus.

While they met with my father I looked through all the different bags the Glue Sniffers had made and occasionally turned to look at the lead tent, but all I could see was a red glow that pushed three shadows out of the shell.

GLUE SNIFFER

What was to be a gradual transition from rubber cement to fire began in the lead shell of a man who was planning a war against omniscient narration and had discovered a different cure for sadness. His name was Federico de la Fe.

I explained to Federico de la Fe that I had to wrap my stomach because I could no longer control it. Misueño, who used to be a Oaxacan Indian before he left and joined us, shaved the hair from my belly and wrapped my belly and lower back with gray tape.

Federico de la Fe nodded and told us that he used to be from a river called "Las Tortugas" where they had turtles made of meat and not of sprockets and coils; and that while he lived on that river he had once come across a Glue Sniffer who explained to him the purpose of liquid adhesives, which was to dull sadness.

He said that there was a better way. That his cure did not upset the stomach or cause nosebleeds; and that it did not tear away at the body where one could not see.

I pulled my pants down and Misueño took off his shirt. Federico de la Fe rubbed gasoline on my thigh, on Misueño's stomach, and then poured a puddle into the palm of his hand. He spread it on his chest and lit a phosphorus stick and the flames spread. After the flames faded and the black on my thighs began to turn pink, the sadness that I felt was replaced by blisters and pus.

After Misueño and I left the lead shell, I continued Federico de la Fe's treatment for a week and I regained control of my stomach. I wrapped my thighs with gauze and threw my jar of glue away.

SATURN

LITTLE MERCED

By the time my father left the lead shell, he smelled like the old Japanese combustion engines that the mechanics worked on. His face was fuzzy and he had developed an allergic reaction to the lead tent; his neck was blistered and his palms seemed to be peeling. He asked for a tin tub with hot water and soap; but before he stepped into the water he looked up at the sky and said that the air felt lighter. I agreed, but could not explain why.

"We are going to Los Angeles," he said when he was shaven and clean and no longer smelled like a machine. We said goodbye to the mechanics and one of them quoted Nostradamus. After we went to the market we sat in the middle of a roundabout watching all the cars and salting pork.

We packed the pillowcases with meat and guava juice and walked toward the border. We passed a honey garden and factories where Chinese men shoved meat into aluminum cans. There were a couple of teenage Glue Sniffers who tried to sell us tasseled purses and leather knife cases. I said, "No, thank you," and continued walking until there was only loose dirt and chaparral.

When we came across a white chalk line that ran from the Pacific shore to the Rio Grande, my father looked around to see if anybody was following us or watching us through telescopes. When he felt that we were alone we stepped over the chalk line and walked toward a world built on cement.

PREGNANT GIRL SMOKING

by JAMES BOICE

WALKING MY DOG one day through a strip mall after the rain, pregnant girl walks out of the baby clothes store, lights a cigarette. Girl, obviously pregnant, pretty far along, looks to be anywhere from seventeen to twenty-two, steps out of the baby clothes store, puts a cigarette in her mouth, asks me walking by for a light. Pregnant girl with some traces of acne stands in front of a baby clothes store with unlit cigarette in mouth, says to a guy walking by with his little black dog, Excuse me, do you have a light? The rain stops, the world is wet, she pops out of the store with a baby in her belly and a cigarette in her mouth, hair just there, unkempt, hanging in her face, she kind of brushes it aside as she asks a stranger for a light. Girl lays on her back on a basement floor with a big eager kid on top of her, grunting into her shoulder, a couple zits on his back, a promo for a new Fox show that she probably won't watch on the TV, six months later she's looking for a light for her cigarette in front of the maternity store. Bong hits with a guy she went to or goes to high school with, in the basement of his parents' house, gets pregnant during *The Simpsons*, stops eating, starts smoking, gets up to a pack a day, and, never owning a lighter, asks strangers to light her cigarettes, in public. What you do is you take it out of your mouth as a guy walks by, say to him, Excuse me, do you have a light? kind of waving it as if to clarify the question. I halt because I don't want to be disliked and it is enormous-looking, fills up my entire vision, like a size 100 or 120 or something, but it's not, and I reach into my pocket and then am holding my green lighter in front of your face and you lean your face in and get it lit and lean back and say with smoke, Thanks. He puts the lighter back, this time in the pocket of his jacket, and his dog is trying to jump up on her, and says, Yep, and yanks his dog's leash and kind of laughs apologetically and says to it, Kemmon, bud. Girl starts going in the other direction, guy looks back when he gets to the corner, seeing her waddling away in her ugly oversized T-shirt, kind of does a laugh that says, It takes all kinds. Shakes his head, wraps his dog's leash around his hand a couple times to shorten it, waits for the light to change.

Slightly overweight girl hides her low self-esteem by talking loudly and intimidating the pretty girls, gets out of high school, wastes around her parents' little house and her hometown, the broken spirit of strip malls and the radiation from cell phones breeding tumors in your brain, the bland cynicism of chain restaurants, the neon God of their signs miles high above the heads of the people standing around in herds outside, staring at nothing, exhausted by it all and just wanting a table at Chili's, the cold monster void of Wal-Mart with its constant anesthetic blip-blip-blip of buying, but it doesn't numb everything, not the MTV in her friends' parents' basements, which they watch when no one's playing X-Box or whatever, not the sting that comes from wishing you were on the other side of the screen, part of that cool pretty world but looking around (Oh my God, is this my LIFE?) and knowing you never will be. Doesn't numb the telemarketing job, the getting knocked up by some guy she knows and hangs out with sometimes, the running over somebody, the getting strangers to light her cigarettes, a way of sort of dragging the world into helping her destroy this thing, making the world her hired gun, taking some of the blame off her own shoulders because you can't smoke if it's not lit, doesn't eat mostly because not eating is easier than eating. Not doing something is easy. Eventually has the thing, a limp skeleton of a boy that they snatch away from her ASAP and put on a breathing machine, she asks how it is but doesn't really get a straight answer. He lives, grows into a pale sick toddler with spots who for awhile needs braces and crutches to walk, which one kid kicks out from him on the second day of third grade, becomes a pissed-off, undersized, late-blooming teenager with spots, crutch-free now but with a loud mouth and an intimate knowledge of the layout of the juvenile court building and an ever-present inhaler, does the dishes for his mother after dinner every night, yells at her almost every night, remains a virgin (involuntarily) until age twenty-three when he finally gets in the pants of this girl at work, sells weed to high school kids. Pregnant girl smoking in strip mall. Pregnant girl steps out of the baby clothes store with a cigarette. Pregnant girl gets guy walking by to give her a light, has the baby, it does her dishes, she grows old without a pension, dies at age sixty-six because she can't afford the cost of the prescription drugs she needs. Has sex on a basement floor on a Wednesday afternoon, gets pregnant, tries to make the world destroy the baby it gave her, it doesn't work. His name is Darrell and he went to the other high school and wears this stupid shirt that looks like tin foil and as the commercials come on he leans forward on the couch on which they sit side by side (elbows sort of touching) and puts the bong on the coffee table and fiddles around with the bag of weed, looking up at the screen every now and then as he packs the bowl, laughing sometimes at commercials that aren't very funny. The screen is tiny and far away, a little TV/VCR combo, on the other side of the basement, one square room that isn't finished, concrete and two-by-fours and exposed wiring and an old couch and a coffee table and a thin red rug on the ground, and that's it, that's all this basement is. She laughs a little at the same commercials too, even though she doesn't really think they're funny, weak little stoned giggles, and she doesn't want another bong hit but whatever, she's too high to really want to say anything and she doesn't want to disappoint him and it doesn't seem like he wants to talk either and she doesn't want to make him talk if he doesn't want to, so she just watches the back of his head and his shoulders, breathing, and he's breathing too, through his mouth, she can hear it, and for a second they are both breathing, in unison. He's big, everything about him is oversized, like his shoulders and his back and his facial features and his voice, which, when he isn't too stoned to speak, carries over everyone else's, and he makes her feel small, which is good, that is what she likes most about him, that she's small around him, and when *The Simpsons* comes on he laughs and so does she, but she is only laughing inside she thinks, isn't laughing audibly, out loud, she thinks, or is she? Want this? Ummm, taking the bong. His dad is upstairs, she can hear the floor creaking. She chokes on it and Darrell laughs and she smiles as she exhales the rest and says, Shut up. But he doesn't hear her and she realizes it is because he was laughing at the show, not at her choking. What's going on tonight? she says. …Anything? Um… I don't know. Fuck during the next commercial break, he breathes into her neck and her ear, which is loud, ends before she expects it to, he jogs into the bathroom with no clothes on, closes the door, she's late for work. Months later she's pregnant and starving herself and smoking, sticking her middle finger out the window and screaming whenever she drives by Darrell's house, goes to a baby clothes store for the first time for some reason one day, just looking, it doesn't mean anything, just for the hell of it. Has the baby, it's a boy, there it is, small, lives, does the dishes after dinner. It rains all of a sudden while she's in there, makes the parking lot and highway outside green and gray and glassy, this cold autumn rain that makes her feel like she should be late for math or something, and this thick warmth floods behind her nose and eyes, and nothing is anything, and if there is a God which there is b/c He is good and beautiful, help her now b/c she doesn't know which hand is which, and when is what, and who is why, she doesn't know where she is anymore. And she closes her eyes and tries hard to fight off the horror swarming through her, the lady behind the counter starting to take notice, and she starts thinking about the time she was at a red light and a crazy lady with crooked glasses and gross teeth appeared outside the car and opened her passenger door and climbed in and she spoke in gibberish and called her Stephanie even though that's not her name and said something about needing a ride. A ride? No, get the hell out of my car. What are you doing? Stephanie, akchgb chbdh ghfy. Just give me a ride, dear, right up the street there. Gbfhfnfj, Stephanie. Hgbdfhdh. The light's green, come on, get out of my car. You don't just. Bfgdbchxj! Take me to the Food Lion up the road there, Stephanie. Hfbdsjdmcn... They're honking at me. Hear their honking? Hear them? They're honking at me. Get out. They want me to go. AAAACK! ACK! Christ, okay. *Okay.* You fucking *bitch.* Close the door then. *God.* But the lady, possessed by demons and with no chance in hell, was already climbing back out of the car and running around to the front, enormous glasses dangling from an ear, and they didn't have any lenses in them she'd noticed, and the lady was laying down in front of her car, apparently not intending to move, the cars behind them were still honking and a few were starting to go around, the drivers uglifying their faces in her direction and grumbling to themselves. BAHFBFJC AAAACK! FOOD LION!! STEPHANIE!! AAAAACK!!! She could still hear the lady down there under her bumper somewhere, and could smell her still also, she smelled like shit, like unwashed body, a person stripped to the most elemental human status of pissing and shitting and stinking and needing rides, and was this what *happens*? Was this what we were born for? Was this what becomes of us, our lives? And where she was on her way back from, she was on her way back from the doctor's where she'd just found out that she was going to be having a baby. And hearing that a life is forming slowly inside of you. And the concept of breeding, of birthing a new human being. So, even though she could have easily gone around too, her foot began easing the gas pedal down and the car began moving forward, rolling just a bit, and the whole time she could still hear this meth-addicted creature screaming gibberish down under her bumper, and then under her tires, something about Stephanie, which might or might not have been her daughter, now that she thinks about it. And as she pressed harder and harder on the gas, running over the lady, she decided at the same time to stop for a pack of cigarettes, to start smoking today, had never been a smoker before, had looked down on smoking as weak and disgusting and detrimental to good health. The idea of someone growing inside of you. Someone depending on you for health and nourishment. Blind faith in you. Absolute trust. Two people falling with one parachute, you have to pull the cord. Drove over the lady, heard nothing, no cracking of bones or lensless glasses breaking, no tortured shrieking, her car didn't sort of rise and fall like going over a speed bump which is what you'd expect running over someone, nothing, no confirmation of death, no sensations to come back in future nightmares. Looked back in her rearview expecting blood and a broken body and horror, but there was nothing but road, the crazy lady wasn't there, the crazy lady was nowhere to be seen, the crazy lady had left, the crazy lady was *gone*. Stopped a little ways down the road at a 7-Eleven and got a pack of cigarettes, Camel Lights, because it was easier to pronounce than Marlboro and she didn't want to mispronounce the name and expose herself as a novice, smoked one on the way home, lit by a sad-looking Mexican guy with white paint all over him, held it awkwardly between her fingers, careful not to drop, didn't eat until two days later, almost fainted twice in that time, nothing in the paper about any dead homeless ladies found, cleaned her upholstery, bought an air freshener for her car that looked like a little pine tree that dangles from the rearview, bought the new Jay-Z but only like three of the songs on it were good, went to the baby clothes store where she is now, staring and touching the clothes for hours, rain assaulting the windows and everything outside. She walks out of the store with a cigarette in her fingers, asks a guy walking by for a light, gets one. Girl, pregnant, stands smoking in front of a baby clothes store, back arched with the cigaretteless hand over one kidney, belly protruding, stumpy legs doughy, a puddle between her feet with a plastic fork in it, dirty oversized T-shirt making it look like she has no pants on, in a strip mall right off the highway, and her name is Angela, is twenty years old, drives her mom's ten-year-old white Taurus, which is parked in the lot somewhere.

You are born limp and gray, get off life support, drop out of high school, lie to the kids you sell weed to about getting laid a lot, get your GED at age nineteen, finally have sex for real at age twenty-three when you're now a tele-marketer, play Playstation 9 and smoke weed instead of sell it and post tough-sounding expletive-laden posts on Internet video game message boards and almost get fired every couple months because you just sit there, screwing around thus until your late twenties when for some reason you sign up for junior college and find in your studies a refuge, a place to hide from your self-loathing and hideousness and for the first time ever you are actually comfortable and stop just sitting there, your blood replaced with diesel fuel or something, always front row, hand always up for questions, notebooks filled, assignments turned in days early; use your good grades at junior col-lege to transfer up, eventually graduate near the top of your class from the respectable state university that you pay for with student loans, cut off con-tact with your fat mother who has married and divorced a guy with a mus-tache who works at the Pizza Hut, decide you want to save underweight babies, apply to a decent medical school, three tries later you even get accept-ed, meet a girl there, you both become doctors and get married, get placed, pay off your student loans over the years, get your own practice, save lives.

You have a baby, he has a couple kids of his own, doesn't talk to you, doesn't let your grandkids talk to you, saves lives. Sends you money one Christmas, w/ a note that just says MEDICINE, to help pay for your prescrip-tion drugs because you can't pay for them because you have no insurance, money which you instead send to a tanned man on TV who speaks to Jesus personally, doesn't come to see you on your deathbed which is just your nor-mal bed, is too busy saving babies born premature or born addicted to heroin, babies born to mothers who smoked, is too busy saving lives, your last couple weeks your nurse pretending not to hear you talking out loud to him, as if he were standing right there, holding your clammy hand and say-ing, Mom I love you.

Angela dies, son becomes a philanthropist, donates some of his fortunes to the arts which he doesn't know much about really but it seems like the thing to do lately among his peers and they congratulate him on his gen-erosity, is one of the plaintiffs who sue R.J. Reynolds for something like $7 billion and win, uses some of the enormous amount of money he gets to set up trust funds for each of his three grandchildren (all healthy, athletic) and for the Cambodian girl he and his wife adopt and bring to America, away from land mines. Dies a happy old man playing golf, able to say that he never paid for sex and never strayed from his marriage once, his obituary in *Time* because he was so well respected. Dies a cheerful, sane, able old man still on speaking terms with his children and his wife of fifty-two years. The funeral is more of a tribute than a mourning, with a former Supreme Court Justice showing up, and when one of his great-grandchildren asks one of his children on the way home from the funeral why Pappy was so popular, the answer is, He saved lives. Angela looks at herself in the rearview mirror in the parking lot before going in, straightens herself up a little so she doesn't look too much like she just let had sex, feels good, feels wanted, is warmed by thoughts of Darrell and of seeing him later, will call his cell phone after work tonight, will talk to him on her way across the parking lot to her car, will make plans to maybe stop by and see him, hang out, just see where it goes, no pressure. Hello? Hi, it's me. Who's this? It's me. Angela. Oh. Hey. What's up. Nothing. Just getting off work. Oh really? What are you up to? Uh, nothing much. Cool. Might be having some people over later. Oh really? Yeah. Hey can I call you back later? I'm pretty busy right now. Yeah, sure. Do you have my number? Uh, I'm sure I do. I'm sort of waiting for a call right now, though. So. Oh, cool, okay. I'm going out tonight too. So. Uh, just call my cell. Okay. I'll call you later. Okay. I just have some parties to go to tonight. So. I'll have my phone on me. So. Alright. Yeah, I'll hit you up later. Cool. Bye, Darrell. Peace. That was fine, that conversation was good, it went fine. She goes to the parties, but they're not parties, just some kids sitting around in their parents' basements, keeps her phone in her hand so she doesn't miss it if it rings, but it doesn't. Does he have my number? He must not have it. He thought he had it but he doesn't. He's trying to call but doesn't have my number. I'll call him, he must have lost it or never had it. No, don't call him. Not tonight at least. Asks one of Darrell's friends who is there, very casually, Dude, do you know if Darrell has my number? By the way. What? No. I don't know. Because he was going to call me but. I don't know, dude. I don't know. Leaves, stares at herself in the bathroom mirror for one hour and thirteen minutes, goes to bed, Darrell never calls the next day or the next and doesn't answer his phone, she finally talks to him the next week. One month later, while doing something like folding laundry the way she learned to fold when she worked at Belk for two weeks, or changing her mom's like fifty-two-year-old cat's litter, something ordinary, because that's when these things occur to you, Angela knows she is pregnant. Something womanly inside tells her. Schedules a doctor's appointment for the next day to confirm it, calls Darrell on the way, nervous because of the way the last conversation with him went (a week after they did it), gets his voice mail which is a clip of some rap song, leaves a message for him but forgets what she's said as soon as she's said it. The nurse is cold and almost mean to her, the doctor has big brown eyes that never look away from hers, and he's balding and she is pregnant, checks her phone for messages as she comes out of the doctor's, there are none, she thinks about driving through Burger King but doesn't have any cash on her. Crazy lady at a red light, runs her over, disappears, buys cigarettes, smokes the whole pack, throws up from it before falling asleep, and it feels great for some reason. Darrell never calls back, she never tells him she's pregnant, but he finds out from other people, convinces himself it isn't his, there are rumors, gossip, everyone knows everything about everyone, Angela doesn't bother him about helping out or doing a paternity test or anything. He eventually moves out of town with some buddies, gets married, has kids, is a good father to them, can't help but wonder every time there is a knock at the door if it will be some strange kid calling him Daddy. Dies of prostate cancer in his late forties, his kids have kids have kids have kids, etc.

And then finally talking to big stoned Darrell one week exactly to the day (and within thirty-seven minutes, she notes, of the exact time, too) after they had sex on his parents' basement floor during *The Simpsons*, the one where Bart turns himself into a fly using this machine thing, the episode always bringing back all sorts of mixed contradictory emotions years and years later whenever she sees the episode again. Hello? Hey it's me. It's Angela, I mean. ... Hello? Stop calling me, yo. Giggling in the background, is it girls' giggling? Not girls' I don't think, it sounds like guys' giggling, his friends, he's trying to impress them, they've been making fun of him because of me and now he's trying to save face. Fuck you, Darrell. You're like *obsessed* with me. You're like *stalking* me, yo. What are you? Psycho? (More giggling in background, the bubbling of the bong, Ned Flanders' voice, someone saying something to Darrell, to which he responds, Seriously.) Seriously, Darrell. Seriously... fuck you. Whatever, yo. Stop calling me. Take a hint. ... Seriously. Quit stalking me. For real. Stalking you. I've called you like twice in. I... don't want... you in... my life. And before he hangs up on her she hears someone in the background go, Slut! and someone else go, You fucked *Angela! Ha ha ha!* Angela goes to work that night, is pregnant the next month, tries to destroy the thing growing inside of her like an alien by smoking like it'll make her money and starving herself, it doesn't work, she becomes The Pregnant Girl, evokes whispers wherever she goes like some sort of wind trailing behind her carrying things people can't believe: I can't believe she smokes. I can't believe she doesn't eat. I can't believe it was four guys at once and she doesn't know which one is the father. I can't believe she poked holes in Darrell's condoms. Etc. Gets pregnant, starving doesn't work, the baby is born anyway, survives, Darrell flees, baby rises from the ashes of juvenile delinquency to medical doctor who saves the lives of countless babies, rich, with a soft-smiling, watercolor-painting woman for a wife who watches TV with her head cocked, kids who love him, grandkids who think of him as a god, dies old and ripe on the putting green with an obituary in *Time* magazine that mentions his philanthropy work. You fucked Angela. I can't believe she smokes. Saves the lives of countless babies.

That's how you do it. Smoke a cigarette. Walk out of the baby clothes store, ask me for a light, walking my dog. Twenty years old and pregnant, don't carry a lighter, make strangers like me do it. Do your best to make yourself as repulsive as possible and you still end up pregnant somehow at age twenty, ask a guy walking by with his dog, me, for a light, and I give one to you, the whole way home I wonder why I did it and who you are, and this is what I come up with, here you are:

At Home with Mother, Gagarin Town

Gagarin Town is a Graceland for all the Russian cosmonauts who followed Yuri. They came to pay respects to Yuri's mother, herself an icon of Soviet Motherhood, until her death in 1984. They still come to drink the cold fresh water—said to ensure one's safe return from the cosmos— from the Gagarin family well beside the recreated log cabin in the nearby village, Klushino, where Yuri was born. Neil Armstrong, the first man on the Moon, once placed a gold coin in the foundation of a local Yuri museum and declared: "Gagarin called us all to the cosmos."

THE LAST WORDS
ON AN AEROGRAM

by SARAH RAYMONT

THE HORSES ARE GONE:
THE PLEDGE TO MY DAUGHTER

MY BREASTS ARE OLD SOLDIERS

1. YOUR BODY, THE BUDDY BUSH

2. YOUTH, WHAT I HAVE LEFT OF IT,
   WAITS INSIDE MY ORGANS FOR THE FINAL VOID

3. WHEN YOU KISS, YOU ARE SHINGLING HIS HOUSE

4. YOUR DEFENSES ARE DOWN IN THE SHOWER

5. CHEWING AND SWALLOWING

SPEED IS TECHNOLOGY

1. GET ON TOP OF THE WORLD

2. YOU WANTED TO FLY

3. RAIN IS SOUND THAT'S ROMANCE,
   THE SNOW A BREATH ON YOUR SHOULDER

4. YOUR PERSONAL ANTHEM

5. CAULKING THE BATHTUB

THIS TOMB IS MINE
1. TAKING CARE OF YOUR SKIN
2. HOW TO ENJOY A FRESH APPLE
3. FORTUNE-TELLING CHILDREN

DEATH IS A STRONG POSSIBILITY
1. HOW THE MOON CAUSES PEOPLE TO DISTANCE
   THEMSELVES FROM THEIR OWN ACTIONS
2. SPRINKLE PRIVATE TIME ONTO YOUR HEART
   AND ZIP IT IN

THE HORSES ARE BACK:
THE FINAL ADDRESS

THE HORSES ARE GONE:
THE PLEDGE TO MY DAUGHTER

Dear Daughter,

These men are merry. They are glue-eyed behind beards. They cannot wait to mount their horses. The nighttime crickets are silenced as the hooves beat down the path, like the sound of applause before the audience dies down, and the moon sits in the sky, easy to peel, if only I could see it. And the whole night belongs to me.

By now, you and anyone else who once knew me have long forgotten what I look or sound like. I cannot help but laugh when I hear the sound of my own voice. I know very little about my captors, or the reason they have got me in here, but I am growing more and more convinced as the days wear on that my end is near. Death is a strong possibility. I would do anything for you, you see, and I would keep doing it until I was the best, until there was nothing standing but us. We would have the whole cleaned-out world set on a table before us, and it would be an exquisite meal.

Do you know what I wake up to every morning? My tomb. They let me pick this one out, choose between this and a room the size of a football field. It was so big I could not see to the end. There was a pool and a sunken kitchen with ancient wooden spoons of all different sizes. There was a bathroom and the windows were lined with smashed pots where herbs once grew; I could smell the dying rosemary. I could tell by their pride that it was once the room of the last great woman. When you grew up as I did, part of you wants to keep that comfort. But your father saw to it that my childhood was the punch line of some cruel joke. So when I told these men which room I picked for my keeping I could read off their faces: I won. When they escorted me to my tomb, I said, "You are not in my world." I said, "I will finally be dead," and they drove a bar on the other side of the door and set me in.

I know now that we are all just humans, scared ones, but people are different here. The men are convinced they have to fight, and they cannot wait to be killed for having fought. I get the sense that, in their minds, death is the next best thing, better than living, as if they are all very old, having led proud and amazing lives. Except these men are fierce. They ride open-mouthed. They yell all the time, and sometimes they laugh. I have started to believe the two are the same.

My head is a spinning top that is condemned to streams of a language that I will never understand. I rouse each morning to the sound of the men returning from their night's activities. They are costumed as if they have just fought a war, though it is very possible that they go out and combat one another. I am certain they are training me for my last night. Just after sunrise, I am helped into a beribboned dress, not unlike the dresses your grandmother fancied, with a matching ribbon for my hair. You should see these shoes—they tie around my feet like ballet slippers. I can feel my childhood self, open mouthed with envy. It feels great to make myself jealous—you should try it sometime. It is a healthier pastime than being jealous of others, that much I can tell you.

I stopped asking questions long ago. The Ritual For My Conclusion makes sense to me, every part of it. Even the long thumbnails, their offbeat costumes and pointed spears. And when the tomb door is unbolted in the morning, when we all have a laugh, I realize that I am still alive, that they have not killed me just yet. It is an odd little victory. Mine is a simple tomb, but roomy. I have a pen with me and this aerogram that I keep pressed against my stomach. I made myself get used to writing in the dark and I am hoping that this will be posted after they are through with me.

I feel safe telling you what I really think. I feel like I am moving very far away. This makes me sad. I miss your body, your voice, but the truth is, everyone loves the bad years: because we can talk about how your father died and left us, so that we were nothing but four trembling eyeballs on a rock. Because we miss those times, do we not? I hope that my words will make you understand certain things about the world later on in your life.

Now I know I am finally part of something important, that I am ready for the sacrifice. That is what makes these times so dear to me, as a mother.

For I realize this is the only chance I will ever have to say anything worth-while to you, with my head as clear as it is. You are probably wishing for a report that describes my captors' peculiar astronomy tools and impressive genitalia, but you were always more academic than I am, and anyway, this is between a girl and the mother who stuck around her for most of her life. The mother who eased the girl into waking while the sleep demons were trying to steal her back. I am sure that your life is the best thing I have done yet, and I know you are wondering why I am no longer in it. It was not a choice to start with. I have made some bad decisions. It was not supposed to be this way. Usually when you make a bad decision things only get worse. Your memories start feeling embarrassed for you.

I became your mother so you would not grow up looking at your face in the morning with too many questions. The truth is, I would do anything for you, child, and if it is okay by you I am going to keep calling you that. You did not take to me in the beginning, so your father daubed his cologne behind my ears. We knew you were smart, even then. You would point to get the facts out of your system, saying, "That monkey is my mommy," or, "The moon is in my hand." Your father and I would just stare at each other, amazed, because you could not read so well, so we had no idea where you were getting your information. But you loved your books, and any fancy-booked professor could recognize your taste—you would eat the books spine first and finish off with the index. Pretty soon we were paying late fines to the library because it took you too long to pass them. But then we joined a book club and you got your fill. And the doctor said your colon was as clean as the Black Forest in the dead of German winter.

I know you might get a little lonely in this world, but remember that you have just as much of a place in it as any of us. I know you were born dif-ferent and that it is not even my own fault. But when you scratched "Mommy" on to the hood of a car with a rock, you named me for life, for everyone to see. And that wasn't even my car. That is why you should take my advice as a gift, like the best and last Christmas you will ever get from me. And I believe you can push past this business of having to perform all the time, acting as if things are so terrible, as if you are defective, which you are not. You are the proudest thing I have ever seen a lot of.

Perhaps you are wishing that your birth was a hoax. At one point I know I did. But it was not: You are here, and some people know about you. I feel a little guilty for never giving up anything of my own for you. I did not risk a thing, until now, and I am about to pony up the only thing I have really got a hold on in this world, me.

I want you to firm up, stake your place, and grow into a huge bush that can withstand a cicada storm. The stronger you are, the more resilient your leaves shall be. Think that everything you fertilize yourself with is going to make up your parts. So be wise about what you throw to your insides, and you will be better for keeping out the invaders. Enemies cannot push past a woman in complete conversation with her body; they do not know where to interrupt.

Mine is a life doomed to the sound effects of men. I have been in here for quite some time. And judging by their enthusiasm, I doubt very much that tonight is a rehearsal. So tonight I pledge to tell you everything. It is because I do not want minutes to turn themselves into secrets, and no one has the ears that you do. I know that yours are large and beautiful. They are made out of stars. In being my daughter, you have promised to hear me out, whether it is my day, my dreams, my breakfast, or my mother. You have promised that no word I say will ever go ignored.

This world gets hard and people in it are mean. It might look different to the rest, but we two are the same. It is just that you were given the boat with the holes in it. You are always going to be scooping the water out. Your life is about saving yourself the whole way, or you will die much sooner than you have to. Death does not have to be around the corner, waiting to topple your plans and devastate the space where you used to be.

There is no sleeping for women like us.

Good luck,
Mother

MY BREASTS ARE OLD SOLDIERS

1. YOUR BODY, THE BUDDY BUSH

A man is a sugarhouse, small enough to crush with your palm. And he will spread the leaves and see your branches. Right now I am imagining that you still have not done this sort of thing before. Promise me that you will behave in such a way that you won't pack the experience, once it is over, in the bottom of some trunk you will push under the bed in shame. One night, when you are feeling cruddy about yourself, perhaps you will be tempted to slide this trunk out and go through each of the regrets just to wallow in your inability to make good memories and your propensity to be boring. So avoid this altogether by imagining yourself telling me all about it, without having to lie.

Your body will be handled, groped really. In turn, he will take his clothes off and let you touch his body. Control your shaky face because that will most likely be the first thing to scare him away. Take off your glasses so he can look into your eyes. But not too deep, as a man is liable to steal something that you might not know you had. Then it will be too late, he will be out the door, your face goopy from what is now irretrievably lost. Watch his hooks. Any word you say, any gesture you shoot off with your body is a missile. I learned that from your father.

I know you might not want to hear this, but because he is gone, and because I have not much time to go, I think it is important you know what your father was built like. God yanked hard and long on those testicles of his, they quit just before the floor. And that playdough cock with its dumb face; imagine having to lead your life with that thing inside you. It was a life without dignity, a life on my stomach two pages into a book, or enough time to soap up my hair and wash it twice. What I recall of my marriage is misery under the covers, and your father's ass up like a porpoise, farting a two-gun salute in my honor. Do not get upset in hearing these things: a girl should know these things about her father; it eases her past wanting to fuck him.

2. YOUTH, WHAT I HAVE LEFT OF IT, WAITS INSIDE MY ORGANS FOR THE FINAL VOID

When I was still a child, running flat-chested laps around the swimming pool, I enjoyed giving my friend—whose home I owned with my bare feet and soggy swimsuit, whose cabinet I raided of its snack food artifacts—great big titty twists with my fists. Sweet girl with her brown hair and unafraid smile. Sweet embarrassment for having so much. I did not yet have anything that would indicate to me how sensitive the skin would be, that she was not lying when she said that it killed, and that her grimace was real. I would swear up and down with the kind of bravado that made me into the victim, ending on a tearful "never again" until she relaxed her arms out of the shield that crossed her chest. The minute she let them down, I would grab and turn her as if she were a doorknob filled with cream cheese and hope. As if our differences could be smoothed over with a simple hand transfer. I rarely refer to my breasts anymore. My breasts are old soldiers, and they sit cross-legged on my chest.

3. WHEN YOU KISS, YOU ARE SHINGLING HIS HOUSE

This is not beauty of art, this is your war, and this is the time when animals are being born howling into the world by the minute. When the boy you are kissing is startled, you should take your hands and move them to the back of his neck. Lick his lips.

Time your hand movements with the speed and pressure of your tongue, which by now has made its into his mouth. Let your fingertips target pressure points on his back that make him feel alive and unrecognizable. It is important he disregard his old self. Feel as he arches and livens. You may pause for a moment and show him your nice eyes, but do not hover.

When you kiss a boy, show him there is a lot on the way, that your breath is a mere abbreviation of long, complex songs that will tell the history of every promise ever made.

4. YOUR DEFENSES ARE DOWN IN THE SHOWER

Do not be aggressive toward your body. I encourage you to take off your clothes, draw a curtain, and get wet. It is permissible to take more than one shower a day. Many activities presuppose getting clean. Engaging with leaky children, roughhousing with animals, and nature's rough elements are just a few possibilities that beg a shower to realign your nerves.

Many people sing or whistle while showering in an attempt to reconcile their helplessness and fallen senses, as if theirs is the only sound there is. But the sound of water is so loud that anything can be happening around you, but in the shower, all you are is nude and wet. The shower that is beating your back has access to the stress that impedes your movement and ultimately inspires you to think less of yourself. Your muscles are right beneath the skin, and they tend to tighten and knot. Skin is your entire surface and nobody really cares about your pain.

5. CHEWING AND SWALLOWING

Since they only feed me once a day I try to make my food last. I chew very slowly, getting a feel for the hazard I am about to introduce to my body. Then I bring it back up. I do this a few times so the end result is a smooth paste on my tongue that can last one hour.

I pray in bed after a whole day has happened. First the necklace around my neck goes into my fist like a penny or a spongy penis. The same necklace that used to help me win at bingo. And though the necklace is not as strong in the magic and luck arena as it was when I used to win, when it's in my hand it wipes the smile right off my face and enables me to ask for those whom I love so fiercely to be protected, always.

SPEED IS TECHNOLOGY

1. GET ON TOP OF THE WORLD

I know this might go against whatever notions you might have of sharing and taking, but recently I have recognized the quality everything good shares. It is called speed. And it does not care about fairness or making sure the low-luck families are squared away with their share. Speed is going to make sure I die soon. Speed is about hustle, and everything that is slick and fast is on its way to something important, even if it has to kill a few sea lions or childhood dreams in the process.

Forget pity, it is technology you should join up with. Call it an instinct, but you are going to get left behind if you do not learn to move. You are going to miss everything if you stay slumped, and your mother is not around anymore to rub out your bruises or push you into one of her big hugs. Now your noise is for no one, so get your legs into shape and use them more. You should get sore; hear what your muscles are saying. That pain is prayer.

What I mean by all this is that you should go out there and figure out what the hell is going on. Get on top of the world. Get me a computer and put it on my grave if you have to, because even I want to catch up. You know, part of me regrets not being more up-to-date; I am not a fashionable mother just yet. Your father played such a minor role in the outside world, so small that everything he picked for your shaping was pretty much at random. And sometimes he ended up lucky: he found a prestigious beer to call his own, and I had a friend or two from my childhood who hung onto me like a monkey swinging from the scars on a tree.

2. YOU WANTED TO FLY

We used to set you up in front of cereal boxes and you would have your information for the whole month—your color TV. Your father aimed for the most educational cereals possible. He did not want you reading all the crap they put out there that turns kids of the nation into zombies, all lined up as if they knew what war is, eyes yellow and fire coming from their brains.

You set up the boxes around your head as if they were dominoes. You peered over the tops to say good morning. The high-fiber boxes were best. With the Audubon information on their backs, they introduced you to a new bird every month. At the start of each month, you had a new favorite bird that you named and loved. You wanted to ride them, and then you decided you could fly.

3. RAIN IS SOUND THAT'S ROMANCE, THE SNOW A BREATH ON YOUR SHOULDER

I would rather be in bed all the time, my eyes shut tight and the room filled with the sunshine of a brand-new day, if that is what the weather is cooking up for breakfast. As long as there is a window to remind you what is inside and what is out, all weather is tolerable.

Five a.m. is a glowing wonder. Surrender your head to the pillow and watch the seasons of the sky duel for you. Sometimes that feeling of being the loneliest person in the world is second only to the beauty of space.

4. YOUR PERSONAL ANTHEM

When I was young, I loved The Song. When my friends and I sang together, I would complain at first, or feel like hitting the person who suggested it for activity. But only because inside I was delighted. Once we got started and our voices hit the ground I embraced the song as if it were my own mother trying to live. The songs were about animals, or the hard luck of a guy who goes swimming only to find that later, his clothes are all gone... the goof-ups of man, really.

Often the songs were just melody wrapped around silly words. The question was, who could get it all out the fastest without letting parts of the word crumble? I always won. But I faked that winning at song-singing was second to my real interest in scarves or men or the night. If I had a book of every song I used to sing, with the lyrics on each page, it would be a soft book. Each page would be oily from the amount of time I spent thumbing each song and not washing my hands first. The book would have the dirt from my whole life on it.

5. CAULKING THE BATHTUB

Caulking the bathtub should be done whenever you feel that your bathtub is unsanitary, which should be often. Since bathtubs are smooth and are constantly hit by steady streams of water, they give off the impression of being clean, of being self-cleaning. They are not. You will feel this when the shower curtain tries to pull you into its skirts, when it whispers its humid promises right into your body. You respond right back with the best of you, with the bleach, the sponge, and the caulking gun. Get down on your knees and be sure the caulking gun is unclogged. If it gets jammed, try running a Q-tip with a little turpentine over it.

THIS TOMB IS MINE

1. TAKING CARE OF YOUR SKIN

Old things are outdated. They belong to kings and queens. They live alone. New things jump for joy, for they have just been born. They say to themselves, I am born now, so let me live. They are clean and their holes are not yet filled. They have not started taking any pills. Between you and me, they are the lonely ones. The new things are wise, they are wiser than Moses and all the Jews. If they could, they would rant. They would tell us about the future because they have just happened. They would say, "No, go back," or simply just shriek. When you are down below the ocean or locked in a tomb you feel like this. You feel fear and all the weight of the world on your face.

I am irritable, older. My hands are dry all the time from the lack of fresh air. The sky hates me. I am sure that the sky-lovers would hate me even more. I am the wrong kind of queen. Take me to the moisture and soak me in it. Make me a milk bath and brush my hair. Let me rub my back against a tree for some time; it is getting to be winter and I am itching all over. Put special leaves into a tub for me, the kind that color the water. They will help my muscles and soften my parts.

2. HOW TO ENJOY A FRESH APPLE

If it is autumn, apples are dropping from their trees. Look down—there on the ground lies an apple you should have taken advantage of. Only now it is pushing up between your toes, rotten.

I have learned that apples taste best when eaten outside. Leaning out an open window will work if you are too high up to get out. Just be sure the white of the apple hits the outdoor air before it goes into your mouth.

There is an apple for you. There are so many different kinds, but do not feel overwhelmed. Sample as many as you can and soon you will be picking out your favorites. You will know when you make the right decision: a right decision can rain coins on your head.

3. FORTUNE-TELLING CHILDREN

Do not fear the effect you will have on children. In fact, you will have little to no effect on their daily lives. Your prophesizing burrows into their sub-conscious and is the stuff of their dreams or play talk, not their day. Your whisperings will give them the knowledge that they are set apart. Listening to you will make them understand certain things about the world later on in their life. But do not feel any responsibility for this. They will think they are chosen by forces higher than you, better than their own families or the city they come from.

If you are bogged down by your day, or if your head aches from going unheard for too long, locate a special child, the kind you would fear, who stares at you from all the way across a room, over its parent's shoulder. By the way the child reaches for you, you might guess that this child likes you more than it likes its own mother.

One time, I held such a child captivated for a full hour beneath the din-ing room table. She brought me to an empty room, because her legs did not work, and there she was able to lie comfortably on her stomach. She was out of earshot and could not be seen by her mother. Her mother so wanted her to make every attempt to stand on her feet, in the hopes that her legs would strengthen and then she would be able to walk like the rest of the girls in her school. The little girl told me she was tired, that she did not mind her wheelchair, and she loved all the secrets she could see from the floor.

As we cast spells on the world, the girl's tiny hands fished objects from my pockets. She found a picture of you in my purse, balled it up, and moved it to the chest pocket of my jacket. She told me to touch it when things got bad. She stared in my eyes, fearless, assuring me of her undying protection. Her sorcery was uncanny. Those eyes had all the strength her legs failed to give her, and she gave it to me, free of charge. She waved goodbye through the mail slot as her mother accompanied me down the walkway.

Her mother was delighted that I spent so much time with her imperfect daughter. Her mother acted as if there was New Hope For Her Legs. But I walked away knowing it was I who received the blessing. Every now and then, I still touch the place where she put you in my pocket and I know that I have enough spells in me to keep me special until I die.

DEATH IS A STRONG POSSIBILITY

1. HOW THE MOON CAUSES PEOPLE TO DISTANCE THEMSELVES FROM THEIR OWN ACTIONS

The moon is perfect, despite the fact that people blame all the plane crashes and wrongful humpings on its shape. When the moon is full, you are free to kill.

2. SPRINKLE PRIVATE TIME ONTO YOUR HEART AND ZIP IT IN

I have always followed my gut with people. You cannot ever predict the hassle someone can become. By the time you see that they are a threat, summer is over and it is cold and sad; you feel weak.

For some reason there are no set times of the day, like meals, that would curtail the urges a person feels to share themselves with others. I embrace honesty, I do, but I rarely receive it. Someone finds me and then I have to watch him or her as they try to open themselves up. However, I end up on their nerves, like a rash all over my body.

If people were funnier, I would not have to be so critical all the time. I would not have to be constantly using myself as an example. I am getting tired. I've forgotten how to laugh. I was so ready to hear about blunders, the time when a fall onto the street brought the crossing guard to her knees and set a whole slew of schoolchildren snickering on the curb. I was always waiting to hear. Somehow, I missed all the little things a person's pride keeps far away.

THE HORSES ARE BACK: THE FINAL ADDRESS

Dear Daughter,
The sun peeks through my tomb like marmalade.

Do you ever think that the reason there is so much blood crushed into every surface is because there are not enough signs in the world that there is magic afoot?

I bless these words into my space, these shrines, and I will them to work their way into your life. I know that you need me like a hole in the head. It is tricky: Without you I'd fall apart, a plank going backwards onto the cement. I am so scared of falling. I am so scared of flying off and there not being a tree for me to grab hold of.

There is no reason to shout. And you understand me perfectly well, do you not, and you need my council. But I have asked you to listen for so long

I wouldn't be surprised if the sound of my voice has made you rough. I am tired of turning my head and staying awake as all the voices tumble out of me. I am tired of having to tell everyone everything I hear. I want to smell like roses. I want to save the winged creatures and show them the patch of sky they should exit through. I wish at least one of my index fingers had an eye on its tip. I have tried, violently some times, to grab at myself through the cloth I wear, but it does not bring me any closer to you.

I wish I could make wind, make sense. I wish I could make a house for us to live in. I wish I could take things back and find what is lost. I wish that there was a place to go where these lost things fell into place, where I knew what a woman was, where I would not erupt, where someone would take my shoulders and laugh along with me.

It is quite possible that you are the devil who stands over me with a pillow. Was I ever a prophet? Was there a quickness about me that would suggest that I never cared in the first place? And all of a sudden it hits me strong—I do not know you. It occurs to me that you should not be in my life, that perhaps you are harmful. Without my secrets I feel like part of me has already dropped off and is flying close to heaven.

I could stick around and continue to hump the world along with everyone else, or I could ease myself into the crater and go with dignity. I have lived what is far and impossible. And I am a person whose throat is now eroding into her lungs.

Sing, early sun, with your wet kisses and mourning skirt. For I am the maker of color, I created sound and you are the child who is my daughter.

And when you look at a church in the dark while it is misty, you'll see me having tea with the plain folk.

The ocean is an earth-hot boiling spring with an old worn-out bridge between us, but bear down and have faith—when luck swings your way all the lost items of your life will line the road like jewels.

Goodbye,
Mother

Let's Go!

On the 12th of April 1961, a gleeful Yuri shouted "Let's Go!" (Poyekhali!) as he was launched from the dusty steppes of Kazakhstan's Baikonur Cosmodrome to become the first human to see with his own eyes that the Earth was indeed round. While careening around the planet at a speed of 28,000 km/h, he reported back: "I am Eagle!" and "I can see the clouds! I can see everything! It's beautiful!" and "I am feeling great! Very great! Very great! Very great!" Meanwhile, Radio Moscow interrupted normal broadcasting to play the song "How Spacious is My Country."

THE DEPORTEES

by RODDY DOYLE

CHAPTER ONE
THE REAL SLIM SHADY

JIMMY RABBITTE KNEW his music. He knew his stuff alright. Jimmy was slagging Moby before most people had started liking him. He once heard two kids on the DART talking about Leftfield, and he was able to lean over and tell them they were talking through their holes and know that he was absolutely right. Jimmy knew that Radiohead's last album was so bad that it was cool to defend it—but he didn't. Not Jimmy. It was too important for fashion. Hip-hop, jungle-country, big beat, swing—Jimmy loved and hated it all. But he was thirty-six, with three young kids and a wife who was six months pregnant and tone-deaf.

He stood at the bathroom door and listened to her in the shower.

—FORGIVEN, NOT FORGOTTEN. FORGIVEN, NOT FORGOTTEN. FORGIVEN, NOT—

Jimmy spoke.

—Are you singin' that because it came into your head or because you like it?

—Shut the door after you, Slim, said Aoife. —FORGIVEN, NOT

FORGOTTEN. FORGIVEN—

There were seven hundred and thirty albums in the house, and Jimmy knew where to find every one of them. He'd bought most of them himself. Twelve had been presents, and one of them had been in the house when they'd moved in. *Brothers in Arms* by Dire Straits, on the floor when they walked in, and Jimmy would have fuckin' left it there. But Aoife had picked it up.

—Oh, I like this one.

And they still had it. He knew where, kind of hidden between the blues and acid jazz. He'd been tempted to smuggle it out and lose it, but he loved her and he'd never caught her looking for it. They were married nine years and in that time she'd brought exactly six albums into the house, and that didn't include Nick Cave's *Murder Ballads*, which he'd given her for their anniversary.

But it did include the *Titanic* soundtrack.

Jimmy had refused to file it in the Soundtrack section.

—Why not?

—I'm giving it a section of its own, he'd said. —Utter shite.

She'd laughed.

—You're such an eejit.

And they'd made love on the kitchen table, while Celine Dion rode the vast Atlantic.

Now, Jimmy shut the bathroom door—

—NOT FORGOH—TEN—

and he went downstairs to the sitting room. He stood in front of the telly.

—Do any of youse like the Corrs?

—Yeah!

—No way.

—Cwap.

He went into the kitchen and turned on the radio. Lite FM.

—For fuck sake.

He attacked the dial, until he found "Pet Sounds." That was better. Lambchop. Up With People. Great music no one had heard of. Jimmy shut the kitchen door and turned up the volume. St. Germain followed Lambchop—I WANT YOU TO GET TOGETHER. And Jimmy lay back on the kitchen table.

It was months since he'd been to a gig. Months. He used to go to gigs all the time. He used to *make* gigs. He'd managed bands, some great ones. There was The Commitments. ('The best Irish band never recorded'—*d'side*.

'Shite'—*Northside News*.) There was The Brassers. ('Sex and guitars'—*In Dublin*. 'Shite'—*Northside News*.) Great days, when twenty-four hours weren't enough, when sleeping was a waste of time.

Now, he had the kids and sleeping was an impossibility. He never woke up in the same bed; he'd even spent a night in the cot, because Mahalia, the youngest, had refused to stay in it.

—*Not* my comfy bed. *That* my comfy bed, she'd yelled, pointing at *his* comfy fuckin' bed.

It was past midnight now. He'd been listening to *The Marshall Mathers LP*. That was another problem. A lot of the stuff he liked had the Parental Advisory sticker on the cover, so he had to wait till the kids were asleep.

He crept into the bedroom.

—FORGIVEN, NOT FORGOH——TEN—

She'd been waiting for him. Married nine years, and they still slagged each other. He got into the bed and slid up to her back, and wondered which she'd noticed first, the gut or the erection. He'd been putting on the pounds; he didn't know how. He never ate and it was ages since he'd had a pint, weeks, months—fuck.

—How's the real Slim Shady? said Aoife.

—Not too bad, bitch, said Jimmy. —Grand.

—Why the sigh? she said. —Are you okay?

—I'm grand. It's just—

—Oh wow, she said. —There's a kick.

She took Jimmy's hand and put it on her stomach. He waited for the baby's next kick. He was suddenly exhausted. The kids would be coming in soon, climbing in on top of them. He tried to stay awake. Kick, for fuck sake, kick. He was gone, and awake again. Did it kick? Did it? Stay awake, stay awake.

—I'm thinking of forming a group, said Jimmy.

—Oh Jesus, said Aoife.

CHAPTER TWO

NORTHSIDE DELUXE

WHAT SORT OF a group, but? That was the question.

But, actually, it wasn't.

—You're not serious, said Aoife, after Jimmy made the announcement in bed that night.

There was silence, long enough for the baby to kick Jimmy's hand twice and for Jimmy to regret having opened his stupid big mouth.

—Are you? said Aoife.

And *that* was the question.

—There's a kick now, said Jimmy. —That's some left foot he has on him, wha'.

—*Are* you? said Aoife.

—Well, said Jimmy. —Yeah. I am.

—Why?

—Well, said Jimmy.

Another kick.

—You know. Me and the music. You know yourself.

—Why now? said Aoife.

—It just came up, said Jimmy.

—Stop being thick, Jimmy. Why *now*?

—With you pregnant and that?

Another kick, this time from the baby's mother. It didn't hurt but Jimmy didn't tell her that.

—Stevie Wonder's wife was up the stick when he recorded *Innervisions*, he told her instead.

She said nothing. She didn't move.

She loved that album. Or, so she'd said, anyway. Mind you, no one loved music the way Jimmy loved it. He'd met Simon Le Bon once—at least, he'd said he was Simon Le Bon—in Café en Seine, in town, years ago, and he couldn't believe it when Le Bon couldn't remember the name of his own first album. It was just as well, because Jimmy had been going to tell him it was shite.

Still nothing from Aoife.

Jimmy kissed her shoulder, and sang.

—FORGIVEN, NOT FORGOTTEN. FORGIVEN—

—Jimmy, said Aoife.

—Yes, bitch?

—Get out of the bed.

He climbed into the top bunk in the boys' room. Marvin, the eldest, had got in beside his brother, Jimmy Two, in the bottom bunk, and soon both of them would go into Jimmy and Aoife's bed. It was the same every night. So, this wasn't unusual; he was just a bit early. But it was different tonight, and he knew it.

It was the first time she'd ever told him to get out.

He listened. He thought he heard her crying. But he couldn't be sure.

He couldn't hear anything. He'd tell her in the morning. He'd bring her a cup of tea and tell her he hadn't been serious. Which was true enough. He really didn't want to go through it all again.

It was the only time he'd ever been really depressed, in the weeks after The Commitments broke up. It was years ago now, before he'd met Aoife, but he could still feel it. There'd he'd been, sorting out their first record deal, with Eejit Records, and the next thing they'd exploded, just like that, blood and egos all over the shop, no more band, no more record deal. He hadn't gone out for weeks after it, hadn't spoken to anyone or listened to anything, especially not soul. The Brassers' breakup hadn't been as painful. The vocalist, Mickah Wallace, went to Mountjoy for eighteen months, for robbing his uncle's Ford Capri.

—Me ma bate the head off him for reportin' it, said Mickah. —But it wasn't his fault. He didn't know it was me that robbed it.

—Why did you do it?

—I didn't know it was his, said Mickah. —How was I supposed to know he'd bought a fuckin' car? Sorry about the band but.

—We'll wait for you, said Jimmy.

—Yeh'd fuckin' better, said Mickah.

But by the time Mickah got out—he did the full eighteen months, the first man in the history of the state to serve his full sentence—Jimmy was three weeks away from getting married and The Brassers weren't even a memory.

Then there was Northside Deluxe, Jimmy's boy band. Years before your man, Louis Walsh, invented Boyzone, Jimmy came up with the idea of getting five good-looking lads together and grooming them for stardom. He held auditions in their new house, with Aoife there to point out the contenders. But, by the end of the fifth night, after a hundred and seventy-three young men had walked in and walked out of their fridgeless, cookerless kitchen, Jimmy had to conclude that there wasn't one decent-looking young fella on the northside of Dublin, let alone five.

—God love them, he'd said.

Aoife had been taking notes.

—Ninety-two of them sang "I'm Too Sexy," she told him.

So, he really didn't fancy going through it again, the nonstarters and bloody endings. He really didn't want it. He didn't have the time. He didn't have the energy. He was happy enough as he was.

When Aoife got up the next morning, she found Jimmy and the kids on the kitchen floor, surrounded by hundreds of CDs.

Jimmy smiled up at her and put his arms around the boys.

—Dad's forming a group, said Marvin.

—Oh Jesus, said Aoife.

CHAPTER THREE

WIGS IN THE WINDOW

IT HAD BEEN a tricky few days.

Jimmy didn't want to go back into band management, he really didn't. He didn't want the grief and, as well as that, he couldn't come up with the music—there was nothing out there that he could really get worked up about. With The Commitments, it had been soul—James Brown for breakfast, Otis Redding for dinner. Jimmy was the first man he knew to own a Walkman and he'd deliberately missed buses so he could hear all of "Prisoner of Love" or "Down in the Valley" without having to turn the volume down while he paid his fare.

He liked a lot of what he heard these days but nothing that he really wanted to wade into and drown in. But, still and all, there was something that kept pushing at the back of his head—do it, do it, go on.

And Aoife felt mean for coming between Jimmy and his schemes. And that made her angry because he shouldn't have been having them at this particular time. She was six months pregnant, for God's sake, and retaining water like a camel. There were days when she could hardly move, when the sweat ran off her like rain. But Jimmy's schemes and plans, the way he could build dreams with that mouth of his—these were what she'd always loved about him. The man had literally talked his way into her knickers an hour after they'd met.

She wanted to kill him.

They avoided each other.

He washed the dishes, even some that hadn't been used. He bathed the kids until they were wrinkly and faint. He told them bedtime stories that went on forever. He saw Aoife looking in as they all lay on the big bed, cuddled up, listening to Jimmy.

—Once upon a time, he said, —there was a pixie called P.J. who wanted a career in band management.

She didn't laugh. She didn't smile.

She was gone.

She sat in the kitchen and tried to think of nothing.

He came in and went behind her without touching her chair. She heard him fill the kettle at the sink.

—Tea?

—Yeah. Thanks.

He sat at the other side of the table.

—So, he said. —How was your day?

She smiled. She couldn't help it. She looked, and he was smiling at her. And she cried. The boiling kettle sounded exactly how she suddenly felt. A flood of wet happiness and relief poured up out of her. She held her hand out, across the table, and he took it. And she got ready to tell him, Go ahead. Form your band. It's why I love you.

She wiped her eyes with her free hand and looked at him again. And she caught him looking at the CD rack in the corner, between the fridge and the wall.

—Jimmy!

—Yes, bitch, sorry— Yeah?

—Can you not even look at me for a few seconds!? Do I look that bad!?

—No, said Jimmy. —You look gorgeous.

She screamed, and stood up.

—Listen, you, she said. —You think you know everything but you don't. For your information, Stevie Wonder's wife was not up the *stick* when he recorded *Innervisions*. It was *Songs in the Key of Life*, and you can stuff your fucking tea.

Aoife never said Fuck or Fucking.

She left him alone in the kitchen. They hugged twenty minutes later, and had another row. And they rolled that way all week. It was desperate.

Jimmy was on his way home on the Friday. He was walking down Parnell Street, on his way across to Tara Street Station. The car was being serviced. Marvin and Jimmy Two had filled the petrol tank with muck from the front garden.

—It was an experiment, said Marvin. —Petrol comes from the ground.

—Not Irish ground, Marv, said Jimmy as he pushed his hands deep into his pockets so he wouldn't strangle him.

Anyway, he was on Parnell Street, walking past one of the African shops, when something in the window grabbed his attention. Wigs or something, a string of them hanging there. He walked across for a closer look—he'd get one for Aoife, the pink one there, for a laugh—and someone walked straight into him, sent him flying.

—E'cuse me!

A Romanian, a young fella, Jimmy could see, as his head hit the edge of the path and an Italian bike courier rode over his hand—an Italian who'd been in Dublin for a while.

—You theeek fockeeng eeee-jit, he roared as he dashed across to Marlborough Street.

Jimmy's head was hopping as he stood up, helped by the Romanian kid and a big African woman. His hand was in a bad way too, fuckin' killing him. But he was grinning.

Jimmy had his group.

CHAPTER FOUR
THE HARDEST WORKING BAND

HE TYPED, ONE-HANDED, onto his laptop. "Brothers and Sisters, Welcome to Ireland. Do you want the Celtic Tiger to dance to your music? If yes, The World's Hardest Working Band is looking for you. Contact J. Rabbitte at 087-22524242 or rabbittej@banjo.ie. White Irish need not apply."

Could he write that? He didn't see why not. It was his fuckin' band. But he deleted the last sentence. A couple of old-fashioned Irish rockers would look good onstage with the rest, especially when they were touring abroad. Touring abroad—Jesus. Jimmy could hardly stay sitting at the kitchen table. He read over the ad again. It was going into the *Hot Press* classifieds, where The Commitments ad had gone.

He'd explained it all when he'd got home that night—about the wigs and the Romanian kid and the Italian prick on the bike.

—How did you know he was Romanian? said Aoife.

—His jumper, said Jimmy.

The kids admired the tyre-tracks running across the back of his left hand.

—It must have been a good bike, said Marvin.

—Only the best, said Jimmy.

He got Marvin and Jimmy Two to design a flyer and an A4 poster for him. And, while the lads got dug into the artwork and Mahalia annoyed them while they did it, Jimmy stuck on Rubén González and he danced with Aoife in the space between the table and the door, and between them, seven months of unborn Rabbitte, give or take a week.

—What's the weather like over there? said Jimmy.

—Lovely, said Aoife. —Grand. But I'll have to sit down in a minute.

—D'yis like the music, kids? said Jimmy as they swung by the laptop.

—Cwap, said Jimmy Two.

—Poo, said Mahalia.

And Marvin didn't disagree.

But Marvin had a great head on him, a genuine chip off his da's block.

—How will we get people to stop and read it? Jimmy asked him as he looked over his shoulder at the poster.

—Put a picture of a nudie woman on it, said Marvin.

—You will not, said Aoife.

—Nudie man then.

—No, said Aoife.

She was having a breather; the trot around the kitchen had flaked her. And she'd stood in the cat's litter tray. The cat, Babyface, had died a month ago—lung cancer, God love him—but the kids wouldn't let Aoife get rid of the tray.

—Nudie nothing, said Aoife.

But, even as she lay down the law, Marvin was putting the word *nudie*, repeated, red blue, red blue, in a glowing rectangle around the ad copy. Jimmy took up the laptop and showed it to Aoife.

—Does that pass?

—Okay.

She laughed, and hugged Marvin and Jimmy Two and Mahalia's imaginary friend, Darndale.

It was three more weeks before the *Hot Press* ad would become public. But he spent the next Saturday with Marvin and Jimmy Two, with Mahalia in her buggy, sticking the A4 nudie ads on poles in Temple Bar, in the African shops on Parnell Street, in any pubs they passed, on DART station doors, anywhere they were likely to be seen and gawked at. They were still sticking up posters, on Molly Malone's bronze arse at the bottom of Grafton Street, when Jimmy got his first call.

—Mine!

Mahalia wouldn't give him the mobile. Jimmy gave her his keys and guaranteed her two Loop-the-Loops, one each for herself and Darndale. She let go of the phone.

—Hello, said Jimmy.

—Nudie? said a male voice. On the DART, Jimmy guessed.

—Rabbitte Talent Management. How can I help you?

—Interested in the band, said the voice.

An Irish voice, vaguely Dublin, vaguely MTV.

—What instrument d'yeh play? said Jimmy.

—Guitar, vocals. Drums, a bit.

—D'yeh like The Corrs?

—Yeah, sure; cool.

—Fuck off, so, said Jimmy, and he handed the phone back to Mahalia.

A disappointing start maybe, but Jimmy was on his way. He needed coffee.

—D'yis want a cake, kids?

—Yeah!

—Cool!

—Big cake, this big.

—Okay, he said. —Let's go to Bewley's and terrify the tourists.

He'd just pointed the buggy at the caffeine when he got the second call. Mahalia threw the mobile at him.

—Thanks, love. Hello?

—Yes, said the voice.

Jimmy waited, but there was no more.

—Are yeh ringin' about the band? said Jimmy.

—Exactly, said the voice.

It was an African voice, kind of southside African.

—Are yeh interested? said Jimmy.

—Yes.

—D'yeh like The Corrs?

—We are not acquainted.

Jimmy's phone hand was shaking.

—What instrument do yeh play?

—To whom do I speak?

—Eh. Jimmy Rabbitte.

—Mister Rabbitte, said the voice. —I am my own instrument.

Jimmy punched the air.

—We'd better meet, said Jimmy.

—Exactly, said the voice.

CHAPTER FIVE

THE KING

THE FORUM WAS a surprise. Jimmy had walked and driven past it but he'd never seen it. It didn't look like a pub; it was more like a café, and as far as Jimmy was concerned, there were enough of those things in Dublin already.

But, once he was inside, it was a real pub, and a good one.

Portuguese-looking barman, Spanish-looking lounge-girl, Chinese-looking girl on the stool beside him, good-looking pint settling in front of him, R.E.M.'s new album on the sound system—sounded good, although maybe a bit *too* like an R.E.M. album—African locals chatting and laughing, Irish locals chatting and laughing. Jimmy tasted his pint. Grand—and just as well, because it wasn't fuckin' cheap.

—Mister Rabbitte, said the voice.

Jimmy turned on his stool. He was looking up at a tall black man.

—You are Mister Rabbitte, the man told Jimmy.

—Yeah, said Jimmy. —That's me. Jimmy.

They shook hands. It was hard to put an age on him. Late twenties, Jimmy reckoned, but he could have been older or younger. Serious looking. The man didn't smile.

—You know my name, said Jimmy. —But I don't know yours yet.

—Robert.

He stared at Jimmy.

—King Robert.

Jimmy did well; he didn't laugh or even smile.

—Will you have a pint, Your Majesty?

No smile from your man.

—Yes.

—Guinness?

—Exactly.

Jimmy ordered the pint from the Latvian-looking barman who'd joined the Portuguese-looking one. The place was getting busy, beginning to nicely hop. Jimmy turned back to King Robert.

—Your English is very good, by the way.

—As is yours, Mister Rabbitte. You speak it like a native.

And now Jimmy stared at *him*.

—I will now sing, said King Robert.

And it happened. After the births of his kids and maybe, just maybe, the third time he'd ever had sex, this was the best, the most fantastic fuckin' moment in Jimmy's life. A black man standing six inches from him opened his mouth and sang "Many Rivers to Cross." Jimmy died and went straight up to heaven.

And when he came down back to Dublin three days later he had the rough makings of a band. He had King Robert on vocals. The man was probably mad, but he'd bought his round and he'd sung "Many Rivers to

Cross" so well and convincingly that, for three great minutes, Jimmy had forgotten that the nearest river to them was actually the Liffey.

He had a drummer from Moscow; Jimmy had his name written down somewhere—a student in Trinity. He'd played for Jimmy over the phone. An hour later, he had a girl from New York who'd said she could play the bass, preferred guitar, sounded gorgeous over the phone, and promised him that she wasn't white.

—D'yeh like The Corrs? he asked her.

—No, I do not.

—You're in, said Jimmy.

—That it?

—Yeah, said Jimmy. —As long as you're on the level about not being white.

—I have got to say, she said. —This is not a conversation I have had before.

—Welcome to Ireland, love, said Jimmy.

So, three down, eleven or twelve to go. Jimmy was beginning to see and hear the band. And the phone kept hopping.

—Droms.

—Sorry, pal, you're too late. We already have a Russian drummer.

By the end of the fourth day, post-King Robert, he'd added a djembe drummer from Nigeria, and another singer, a young one from Spain.

—What was her voice like? said Aoife.

—Don't know, bitch. But her name is Rosalita.

—So what?

—Springsteen wrote a song about her.

—Did she tell you that?

—No, said Jimmy. —I told her.

Aoife's laugh had little sharp corners on it.

—I'm only messing, said Jimmy. —Her name's Agnes.

And Aoife went to sleep.

The latest addition, half an hour ago, while lying here on the bed, was a guitarist from Roscommon.

—D'yeh like The Corrs?

—Fuckin' hate them, boy.

—D'you like black music?

—Fuckin' love it, boy. Not the rappin' though; fuck that.

Jimmy lay beside Aoife. He was buzzing, way too excited. He wouldn't sleep.

But he was well gone, fast asleep, when the phone rang, the mobile on his chest, where he'd parked it after he'd recruited your man from Roscommon.

Aoife was digging him with her elbow.

—Jimmy!

—Wha'?

The phone, he heard it.

—Jesus; sorry.

It must have been two or three in the morning.

—Hello? said Jimmy.

Nothing.

—Hello?

—Nigger lover.

—Who is it? said Aoife.

Nothing else. No more words. Just the horrible space at the other end of the line, and someone waiting there.

Jimmy turned it off.

—Who was it?

—Just a playback message; sorry.

—For God sake.

—Sorry.

Aoife was asleep again.

But Jimmy wasn't.

CHAPTER SIX

FINGER FOOD

JIMMY DID NOTHING about the phone call. Yeah, he was furious and a bit scared, but he didn't know what to do about it and he didn't want it interfering with him. He hoped, half-decided that it wouldn't happen again. It was just some creep out there, killing the night. But he made sure that the kids never had the phone, to be on the safe side.

—*My* phone! said Mahalia.

—Mine, love, said Jimmy. —Daddy needs it for his work.

—Want it!

The doorbell went, thank Christ, and he escaped.

The phone was still hopping, three weeks after he'd put up the posters. And the *Hot Press* ad was out there catching fish as well. And the local word was out: Jimmy Rabbitte was forming a group. They were coming to the door.

This time it was kid, a young fella of about fifteen.

—Yeah? said Jimmy.

—Can I be in your band?

—What's your name?

—Pedro.

—No, it isn't, said Jimmy. —It's Wayne. I went to school with your da.

—Can I be in it, anyway?

—Sorry, said Jimmy. —Tell your da I was askin' for him.

He shut the door.

The bell again.

Pedro again.

—D'yeh want to buy a wheelie-bin?

—No, thanks, Wayne.

A nice kid.

—D'yeh want to help with the equipment? said Jimmy.

—Serious? said Wayne.

—Yeah.

—Ah, thanks, m'n.

—No problem, said Jimmy.

He liked to see enterprise in the young; it was a great little country. And he was having a ball.

There'd been no more midnight phone calls.

He was driving Marvin to a match in Malahide when he saw the Romanian. More importantly, he saw the accordion on the Romanian's back. A guy about his own age, selling the *Big Issues* at the traffic lights in Coolock, strolling down the line of cars when the lights were red. Jimmy rolled down the window.

—Want to join a band? he said.

—Want to buy a magazine? said the man.

—If I buy one, will you join the band?

—For sure. My son, too.

He pointed at a kid walking another line of traffic.

—Plays trumpet. Very good.

—Fair enough, said Jimmy. —Hang on till I park the car.

—What about the match? said Marvin.

He was changing into his gear in the back of the car.

—We've loads of time, said Jimmy.

And he was right. He signed up the two Dans, father and son, and Marvin won two-nil; he didn't score but he passed the ball to the fella who passed it to the fella who scored the second one.

It was weird, thought Jimmy that night. He was lying in bed; the phone was off. If it had been an Irishman with an accordion, he'd have run him over. Up to the moment he saw it on Dan's back, he'd hated accordions, everyone and everything to do with accordions. But Dan had played his, a Romanian jig or something, on the side of the road, just down from the Tayto factory, and Jimmy had loved it. He'd left the Dans with his number, their number in his pocket, and the promise that he'd contact them in the next couple of days.

—I'm thinking of getting all the band together, said Jimmy, now.

—Fine, said Aoife; she was drifting off to sleep.

—Here, said Jimmy.

—Fine.

—I thought, maybe, we'd have some finger food, said Jimmy.

—Fine.

—So, said Jimmy. —Will you handle that department, or—

She screamed.

—Or I can go to Marks & Spencer's, said Jimmy. —No bother.

—Jimmy!

—Yes, bitch?

—The baby!

—What baby?

—The bay-beee!

—Oh Jesus! The baby. Is it comin', is it?

—Yes!

—It's a bit early.

—Jimmy!!

—Right, love; I'm in control.

And he was. Head clear of the band, accordions, tours of the world and the midlands. He phoned his parents, checked on Aoife. She was staying in the bed, less jumpy now that they were getting ready to go to the hospital. He put on the kettle, packed her bag, flew around the bedroom and bathroom as she told him what she did and didn't need. What did she want with a hair-dryer, for fuck sake? But he packed it, said nothing.

His parents arrived.

—Did you get your remote control fixed? said his Da.

—Shut up, you, said his Ma.

They watched at the door as Jimmy helped Aoife into the car.

—Don't worry about anything here, said his Ma.

Aoife smiled out at them, and they were on the road to the Rotunda.

—How're yeh doin'? said Jimmy.

—Okay, said Aoife.

—It's alright, said Jimmy. —I can cancel the band meeting.

He was grinning when she looked at him.

—Aretha if it's a girl, he said.

—No way, said Aoife. —Andrea. FORGIVEN, NOT—Oh, Christ; Jimmy! Stop the car!

Here?

Fairview.

—Stop!

—It's only up the road!

—Stop!!

CHAPTER SEVEN

THE TRACKS OF MY TEARS

SMOKEY WAS BORN right under the pedestrian bridge in Fairview. And thank Christ for mobile phones. The head was well on its way—TAKE A GOOD LOOK AT MY FACE—when Jimmy heard the ambulance and, suddenly, he felt confident enough to deliver the baby himself. The shakes were gone; he was in control, all set to catch the head.

—Jimmy!

—Right here, love.

—Jimmy!

—Looks like a boy from here, love.

But the lads in the ambulance hopped out and took over and, with her arse hanging over the bus lane, Aoife gave the one last shove and Jimmy was spot on; it was a boy. A beautiful, red, cranky boy, already giving out shite about the state of the public health service. There wasn't room for Jimmy to get in at Aoife, to hug and adore her, but he laughed and whooped and hopped over the park railings. He waved at the kids up on the pedestrian bridge.

—What is it? yelled one of them.

—Boy!

—Ah, nice one. Well done, mister.

—No problem, said Jimmy.

And he meant it. He was a da again, a father, and it was just fuckin' wonderful, what he'd always wanted, what he was on earth for. Marvin, Jimmy Two, Mahalia, and now this one, delivered by Jimmy himself, more or less, another boy, another star—Smokey.

—Brian.

—Wha'? said Jimmy.

—Brian, said Aoife.

They were in the back of the ambulance, on their way to the Rotunda.

Fair enough, Brian was her father's name, and he was sound. But, Brian? As the ambulance took a sharpish right onto the North Circular and sent Jimmy flying and the baby squalling, he ran through his Stax, Chess, Hi and Atlantic albums, mentally flicking through all of them, but, for the life of him, he couldn't find a Brian, not a drummer or a sound engineer, not even a fuckin' sleeve designer.

But he said nothing.

They made it to the Rotunda. Smokey was checked and weighed. Seven pounds, no ounces.

—A fine boy, said the Filipina midwife.

—Can you sing? said Jimmy.

—Jimmy, said Aoife.

But she was smiling at him as she fell asleep.

It was four in the morning. AND ONCE MORE THE DAWNING JUST WOKE UP THE WANTIN' IN ME-EE, Jimmy sang it to himself as he walked out onto Parnell Square. A great song that. The first country song he'd ever liked. By Faron Young. Faron Young. Not *Brian* Young.

But it was all great. The seagulls were up, and no one else. He had the world to himself. He'd left the car in Fairview; he'd walk.

His phone rang in his pocket. That would be his da. He flipped it open.

—A boy, he said.

He recognised the absence of voice, remembered it too late.

—Nigger lover.

And Jimmy dropped, he actually fell to the path, and cried. He couldn't stop. He was exhausted, angry, hopeless. He cried. He couldn't explain it, not really. Just some sick bollix, getting his life from his late night calls, a sad bastard with nothing and no one else, but Jimmy couldn't help it, he couldn't stop. That evil out there, on a night like this. He looked at the windows across the street. He searched.

The phone rang again. It was his own number this time.

—Well?

His da.

—Boy, seven pounds, said Jimmy.

—Grand, said his da.

—I'm on my way home, said Jimmy.

—No hurry, said his da.

Jimmy felt better. He walked to O'Connell Street.

The phone again. His da again. Jimmy knew the routine.

—What I really meant to ask was, will you get us a bottle of milk on your way back?

—No problem, said Jimmy. —Seeyeh.

It used to irritate him, the absolute certainty that his father would come back with the last say, sometimes funny, often not, but always certain. It used to really get on Jimmy's wick but he'd copped on a few years back, when his own kids started arriving: it was love.

He was grand again. He wasn't tired anymore either. He was wired, raring to go. When the kids woke up he told them the news.

—So?

—Cool.

—*I'm* the new baby!

He brought them to the zoo.

—Look at the baby monkey, Mahalia.

—No!

And, while they wandered the zoo till it was time to bring them to meet their new brother and Mahalia refused to look at anything under the age of twenty-seven, Jimmy made some calls.

—So, tomorrow night; okay.

—Yes, said King Robert.

—D'you think you'll be able to find it?

—For sure, said Dan.

He was bringing them all together.

—Got a name for this band? said the young one from New York who wasn't white.

—Yeah, Jimmy lied.

He had the rest of the day to think of one.

CHAPTER EIGHT

VIGILANTE MAN

THEY WERE ALL there in the kitchen, their first time together.

Jimmy Rabbitte: manager.

Kenny Reynolds: guitar.

Gilbert Boro: djembe drum and scream.

Agnes Bunuel: vocals.

Kerri Sheppard: vocals and guitars.

—Am I black enough for you, Mister Rabbitte? she asked when Jimmy climbed over the kids and opened the door for her.

—You're grand, said Jimmy. —Come on in.

In actual fact, she was hardly black at all, but she did have dreadlocks. And she was gorgeous.

Dan Stefanescu: accordion.

Young Dan Stefanescu: trumpet.

Leo Ivanov: drums.

Last to arrive was King Robert. Marvin had opened the door and the three kids were staring up at him.

—Hey, Mister, said Marvin.

Don't mention his colour, Marv, said Jimmy to himself; please.

—Who do you follow? said Marvin.

—Follow? said King Robert.

—Support, said Marvin.

—I follow Bray Wanderers, said King Robert.

And the kids fell around laughing.

—Don't mind them, said Jimmy. —Come on in. No problem getting here, no?

—Your directions were adequate, Mister Rabbitte.

It was quiet in the kitchen, just Dan and Young Dan chatting together and Kenny trying to chat to Agnes. And it got even quieter when King Robert walked in after Jimmy. He stared at them all, gave them a long, hard second each. Even Jimmy was sweating. He filled the kettle and introduced everybody. They smiled, and nodded, or didn't smile, and didn't nod. He filled cups and mugs, handed around the coffee and tea. Then he tried an old trick, an icebreaker he'd used when The Commitments first met. He got out the Jaffa Cakes.

—Soul food, he said.

It didn't really work with this gang, though. The dynamic was different; they were older, foreign, the country was too prosperous, they weren't hungry—something. Kenny from Roscommon was the only one to dive at the plate.

This was no party. Jimmy was all alone there in the kitchen. There was no spark here, no energy at all. They were stiff, nervous, ready to leave. King Robert stood against the wall, well away from all of them. Gilbert was looking at the back door. It wasn't going to happen; Jimmy could feel it. But he pressed on.

—So, he said. —The music.

They looked at him.

—Woody Guthrie, he said.

—Pardon me?

—Listen to this, said Jimmy.

There were eight in the kitchen, not counting himself, but it wasn't the full band. He needed bass, more vocals; he needed age and protection. And belief.

He was working on it.

He played "Vigilante Man" for them. A Guthrie song, but Woody wasn't singing this one. That was for later. Jimmy played them The Hindu Love Gods—three-quarters of R.E.M. backing Warren Zevon. Released in 1990, it was the fifth CD Jimmy had ever bought. "Vigilante Man" was the last track.

—HAVE YOU SEEN THAT VIGILANTE MAN?

They listened. And Jimmy watched them loosen and fall in love. It was music they wanted to play; he could tell already. It rolled and growled; it was angry and confident, knocking shite out of the enemy. Agnes was tapping her foot. Young Dan was tapping the dishwasher. Kenny was tapping his belt buckle.

—WHY WOULD A VIGILANTE MAN—

King Robert's ear was aimed at the nearest speaker, already taking the words.

—CARRY A SAWED-OFF SHOTGUN IN HIS HAND—

It was over.

—HAVE YOU HEARD HIS NAME ALL OVER THIS LAND.

And Jimmy was pleased with himself. He'd done it again. He had his band. He had the music and the name. He looked at his watch: half-seven. His mother would be coming in ten minutes. She was looking after the kids so he could dash in to see Aoife and Smokey. They were coming home from the hospital tomorrow, so he had to go on to his brother Darren's house in

Lucan, to get the crib and a few bags of baby-grows and other stuff. And there was nothing left in the fridge for the kids' lunches for school tomorrow, so he'd have to stop at the 24-hour shop on the Malahide Road on the way back. And his da had said something about them going for a pint. And, before all that, he had to help Jimmy Two with his Irish homework and Marvin with his sums.

But Jimmy was a satisfied man. This time the silence was comfortable.

—That's the kind of thing yis'll be playin', said Jimmy. —Alright?

—I fuckin' like the bit about the shotgun, said Kenny.

Kerri the Yank got ready to object but, before she got to words, King Robert started singing.

—OHHH—

HAVE YOU—SEE-EE-EEN THAT VIGIL-ANTEE—

MA-AN.

And that was it. The nine people in Jimmy's kitchen were all together.

—So, said Kerri. —Who are we?

—The Deportees, said Jimmy.

—Fuckin' ace, boy, said Kenny.

CHAPTER NINE

DUST BOWL REFUGEES

IT WAS COLD and damp. And it was cheap.

—I'll take it, said Jimmy.

In fact, it was free. An old hairdresser's, Collette's Unisex, it had been stripped of everything except the sink brackets, a lot of sockets, a couple of posters, and the mould behind them.

It was perfect.

His sister, Linda, had found it for him. She worked in an estate agent's. Craig, her boss and boyfriend, had said that Jimmy could use it until some daw took it off his hands.

—He must be a good lad, this Craig fella, said Jimmy.

—He's a prick, said Linda.

—Why are you with him then?

—Ah, he's nice.

So, just like that, they had their rehearsal space and, just like that, they were rehearsing. They were stampeding along behind King Robert— WE-ELL, THEY CALL ME A DUST BOWL REFUGEE-EE-EE—while the rain hammered the roof. It was different this time, not like The Commitments.

—Why are you doing it? Aoife asked him.

It was three in the morning. Aoife was feeding Smokey and she'd nudged Jimmy awake, for a chat. It was three weeks after she'd come home from the Rotunda.

—I'm not sure, to be honest with yeh, said Jimmy.

He sat up in the bed.

—But, I'll tell yeh. It's different this time. I've a feeling about this one.

—Good, said Aoife.

—WEH-ELL, I AM GOING WHERE THE WATER TASTES LIKE WINE.

These people were musicians already. They were grown-up; even Young Dan had years of living and music behind him. They knew how to listen. They could climb aboard a tune. AND I AIN'T GOING TO BE TREATED THIS WAY. Yeah, sure, there were egos in the room. Kerri had arrived with seven guitars—LORD LORD—and King Robert wasn't happy with Woody Guthrie's diction.

—He is uneducated.

—Fair enough, Your Majesty. But just sing AIN'T, will yeh. AM NOT doesn't sound right.

Gilbert had already missed one rehearsal. Leo was the gentlest, nicest drummer Jimmy had ever met, so he'd probably explode soon. And Kenny was a danger to himself and the community; he was running a snooker cue up and down the neck of his guitar while he kneeled in front of his amp. But it was fine. He knew why he was doing it and they respected that. And Jimmy liked it. There was a tamed wildness in the room that was producing good noise.

He hadn't worried about playing Woody Guthrie in his raw state to them. He put on "Blowing Down That Dusty Old Road," a version of an old blues song that Guthrie recorded in 1944, and he knew they'd get it; they'd hop on the possibilities and make the song theirs. WE-ELL, YOUR TWO-EURO SHOES HURT MY FEET. A folk song could be huge. Jimmy told them that and they knew what he was talking about. AND I *AIN'T* GOING TO BE TREATED THIS WAY.

The *Hot Press* ad delivered his bass player. Another woman, a Dubliner.

—Northside or southside? said Jimmy.

—Ah, grow up, would yeh.

Her name was Mary.

—I used to be called Vera Vagina, she said. —I was in The Screaming Liverflukes. We played the Dandelion Market. U2 supported us. Remember?

—Yeah, Jimmy lied. —And look at the fuckers now, wha'.

She shrugged.

—Yeah, well.

An old punk, with two kids and a husband in the bank, her hair was still purple and standing up.

—Just when the rest of me is beginning to sit down.

She was great and here she was, walking the strings, loving the sound, loving the company. It was already a full sound, just their third time together. No shoving for the front, no real showing off. Agnes sang into every second line—YE-ES, I'M LOOKING FOR A JOB WITH HHH-HONEST PAY. Young Dan's horn went YES YES, NO at the end of each vocal line; his da's accordion was a swooping, laughing whinge. AND I *AIN'T* GOING TO BE TREATED THIS WAY.

After he'd locked up the Unisex and said the goodbyes, Jimmy went to his da's local.

Paddy Ward was his da's idea. He was a traveller who'd married into a settled family.

—But he forgets now and again, said Jimmy's da. —He wanders a bit. But he's sound.

They watched now as Paddy Ward walked in, solid and slow, a big, impressive man with hair that took managing and a jacket that hadn't been cheap.

Jimmy's da spoke first.

—How's it goin', Paddy?

—Not so bad, Jim.

—This is my young fella.

—Don't I know him.

—I hear you can sing, said Jimmy.

The man said nothing.

—D'you want to be in a group?

And the man spoke.

—I was sixty my last birthday, sonny. You took your fuckin' time.

And he sang.

—IT'S BEEN—SEVEN HOURS AND FIFTEEN—DAYS—

And Jimmy died again.

CHAPTER TEN
SMELLS LIKE TEEN SPIRIT

—HAVE YOU ANYTHING against blacks? said Jimmy.

—What about Hello first, Jimmy?

—Hello, Mickah. Do you have anything against blacks?

—No, said Mickah Wallace.

—Grand, said Jimmy. —D'yeh want a job?

Mickah Wallace was a family man these days. He had three kids he adored, and he was also very fond of the two women who'd had them for him. They lived near each other.

—Saves on the petrol, said Mickah when he met up with Jimmy, for the first time in years. He was on the Ballygowan. He didn't drink or smoke these days.

—I don't even say Fuck anymore, said Mickah.

—So, said Jimmy. —D'yeh want the job?

—I have a job, said Mickah. —I've two fuckin' jobs.

—D'you want another one?

There'd been no more phone calls since the night Smokey was born but the first gig was coming up and Jimmy didn't want to leave anything to chance or Nazis. He wanted Mickah on his side.

—What kind o' job? said Mickah.

—Well, said Jimmy. —The usual.

—Ah Jaysis, Jimmy; I don't know. Those days are kind of over, yeh know.

Mickah worked on one of the new green wheelie-bin trucks.

—Yeh should see the stuff they put in them, he told Jimmy. —How d'yeh recycle a dead dog, for Jaysis sake?

And he delivered for Celtic Tandoori, the local takeaway. Fat Gandhi, the owner—real name, Eric Murphy—gave Mickah three nights a week.

—We go to the same church, said Mickah. —He's sound.

Mickah was a born-again Christian.

—It's been the makin' of me, m'n. I owe it all to the Lord.

Jimmy told him about The Deportees, and about the late-night/early-morning phone caller.

—What would the Lord do about it, Mickah? said Jimmy.

—Hammer the shite out of him, said Mickah.

—So, you'll take the job?

—Okay.

—THE NEW SHER-IFF WROTE ME A LET-TER. They were really hopping now, playing the walls off the Unisex. COME UP AND SEE ME— DEAD OR ALIVE. They were ready.

That was Paddy Ward singing. King Robert had been very reluctant to hand over the space behind the mike, but he was listening now, and watching Paddy's mouth—I DON'T LIKE YOU-*RRRR* HARD ROCK HO-TEL. Paddy put his hand on King Robert's shoulder, the King stepped in and they brought the song home together—DEAD OR ALIVE—IT'S A HARD RO-OO-OAD.

Kenny had objected to Paddy when he'd turned up a few nights before.

—Is he what I think he is? said Kenny.

Jimmy was ready.

—He's a traveller, yeah. Have you a problem, Ken?

—Eh—

—Cos we'll be sorry to lose you.

—No, no, fuck no. It's just, it's unusual though. A, a traveller, like. In a band.

—Look around you, Kenny, said Jimmy. —It's an unusual band. That's the whole fuckin' idea. Are you with us?

—God, yeah. Yeah. Thanks.

Jimmy watched Kenny now. He was lashing away there, in some kind of heaven. Kerri played rhythm; Kenny was free to roam. And he did—he went further on that guitar than any traveller ever did in a Hiace.

They had eight Guthrie songs now, and some more to make up the gigful. "Get Up, Stand Up"—Gilbert's choice; "Life During Wartime"—Kerri's choice; "Inner City Blues"—King Robert's. It was beautiful, pared down to djembe and voice. —MAKE ME *WANT TO* HOLL-ERRR.

—Want to, King Robert explained, —not Wanna. Mister Marvin Gaye was a genius but his diction, I am sorry to say, was very bad.

"Hotel California" was Dan's; "La Vida Loca," Young Dan's, and a good one from Agnes.

—I'M—SEEENG-ING IN THE RAIN—I'M SEEENG-ING IN THE RAI-NNN—IT'S A WON-DERFUL FEEE-LEENG—I'M HAHHH—

—Fuckin' nice one, said Kenny.

He was a bit in love with Agnes. His own choice was "Smells Like Teen Spirit."

—You're jestin', said Jimmy.

—Why not? said Kenny.

Jimmy looked around the room.

—Who'll sing it?

Before they had time to mutter, Paddy Ward stepped forward.

—I'm the man for that job.

And, sixty last birthday, Paddy grabbed the mike.

—LOAD UP ON GUNS AND—*BRING* YOUR FRIENDS. Mary's bass went with him, and Leo caught up and kept them company. IT'S FUN TO LOSE AND—TO-OO PRETEND. Kenny hit the two famous notes— DEH-DUHHH—and disappeared behind his hair so he could cry in peace. HERE WE ARE—NOW-WW-WWW—ENTER-TAY-NNNNISS. Inside an hour, they had it broken. A MUL-ATTOHHH—AN AL-BEEEN-OHH. It was all theirs, a brand new thing. A MOS-QUEE-TOHH—MY LIB-EEDOHH. The walls were sweating—YEAHH—Paddy was gasping on the floor, and Jimmy made the announcement.

—You're playing on Wednesday.

—Will that be football or tunes? said Paddy.

They all laughed, but they were leaning out for more.

—Tunes, said Jimmy.

—Please, where?

—It's an unusual one, said Jimmy. —But it'll be great for exposure.

—Where?

—Well, said Jimmy. —You know the Liffey?

CHAPTER ELEVEN
CIVIL WAR

IT WAS A FUCKIN' disaster.

They played on a raft below the new pedestrian bridge, the warm-up act for a sponsored swim that didn't happen. The thing was cancelled because of reports of rats pissing in the water at Lucan.

—Wiel's Disease, the organiser, the husband of one of Jimmy's cousins, told Jimmy on the mobile. —It's transmitted by rats' urine. Anemia, sore eyes, nosebleeds, jaundice. And that's just for starters.

Jimmy was standing on the bridge, trying to hold onto a rope. There was an inflatable bottle of Heineken on the other end of the rope, a giant green yoke, that kept bashing into the raft. Leo's high-hat had already gone into the water. And the wind was making waves that Jimmy had never seen on the river before.

—Rats' piss? he said. —Jesus, man, if you took the piss out of the Liffey there'd be nothin' left.

—I know where you're comin' from, said the cousin's husband. —But we can't take the risk.

—So you're at home and we're fuckin' here.

—I'm at work.

—Whatever.

—Sorry, Jim, but the medical advice is to stay out of the water.

—Ah, go drink a glass of it, yeh fuckin' bollix.

Jimmy pocketed the mobile and concentrated on the rope. The Heineken bottle was charging at the raft again. Mickah was at the south side of the bridge, guarding the gear; they'd caught a couple of young fellas trying to toss Kerri's spare guitars into the river. Jimmy looked at the raft. It was up against the quay wall, in under the boardwalk, being lifted and dropped by those waves. Paddy was on his knees, searching for grip. Leo was lying across his drums; he'd given up playing. Agnes was trying to grab the boardwalk rail and climb. The gig was well and truly over, although King Robert wouldn't admit it yet—WE-ELL, THEY CALL ME A DUST BOWL REFUGEE-EE—and Jimmy was in trouble.

He helped them all and their instruments over the quay wall, back onto solid land.

—Well done. Yis were great.

But he got nothing back for his efforts, just wet-eyed glares and angry words diluted by seasickness.

—I do not like these kind of concerts, said Dan the elder as he wiped his eyes.

—Sorry, Dan, said Jimmy.

—Yes, said Dan. —Me too.

The two Dans held each other up as they walked away. King Robert was gone before Jimmy had a chance to say anything to him. Paddy was falling into the back of a taxi. And Kerri slapped Jimmy.

—With her guitar strap, Jimmy told Aoife later, in the bed. —Across the back of me legs.

—Show, said Aoife.

—There's nothing to see, really, said Jimmy.

—Show me anyway, said Aoife. —Ouch.

Smokey had just bitten her nipple.

—Brian, Brian, Brian, said Aoife.

—Just like his da, said Jimmy.

—Jesus, I knew you'd say that, said Aoife. —So, what'll you do?

—Don't know, bitch, said Jimmy. —What d'you think?

—Phone them all, apologise, and ask for another chance.

—No way, said Jimmy.

But he did. He stayed at home from work the next day, sick, and tried to contact all of them. It was easier said than done. Some had no phones, and Leo and Gilbert weren't living where they should have been. And, seeing as he was at home, Aoife went into town—her first adventure since Smokey'd been born—and she left Jimmy to look after the kids.

—That'll teach you to mitch, she said, the wagon, as she took the car keys from his pocket.

—Spuddies! said Mahalia. —Now!

They listened, all of them—Mary, Kerri, Paddy, the Dans, Agnes. They were all ready to give it another go.

—Under a fuckin' roof, though, boy, said Kenny.

And Jimmy was getting excited again. Later on, after dark, he went out and tracked down Gilbert. The African guy who answered the door to his old flat stared at Jimmy for a long time, then sent him on to another flat, in a house of flats off the North Circular.

—When will be the next concert? asked Gilbert.

—Don't know yet? said Jimmy.

—Before Friday? said Gilbert.

—Wouldn't think so, said Jimmy. —Why?

—I am being deported, said Gilbert.

—No, said Aoife when Jimmy asked her if Gilbert could stay with them for a while.

—He's nice, said Jimmy.

—No.

—You'll like him.

—No.

—His family was wiped out in the civil war, said Jimmy.

—There's no civil war in Nigeria. You should be ashamed of yourself, Jimmy Rabbitte.

—Okay, okay, said Jimmy. —I'll tell him.

He got out of the bed.

—Jesus, Jimmy. Can it not wait till the morning?

—Not really, said Jimmy. —He's up in the attic.

CHAPTER TWELVE

FAT GANDHI'S BACK GARDEN

JIMMY WAS RIGHT. Aoife did like Gilbert. She made him a rasher sandwich, and one for herself, and nothing for Jimmy—

—Only two left; sorry—

when Jimmy got him down from the attic.

—Was it cold up there? she asked him.

—No, said Gilbert. —It was quite comfortable.

—See? said Jimmy. —I told you.

—Shut up, you, said Aoife. —He didn't charge you, did he? she asked Gilbert.

—No, said Gilbert.

—I wouldn't put it past him, said Aoife.

—That's a fuckin' outrageous thing to say, said Jimmy. —Are you eating the rest of that rasher?

It was Mickah who got them the next gig. His born-again pal, Fat Gandhi, owner of Celtic Tandoori, was organising a party for his daughter's twenty-first, and he'd given up looking for a local band that would promise to play only songs of a suitable nature.

—They're not coming into my house so they can sing about the devil and blow jobs, he told Mickah as he double-checked the order. —Ah, look it, I'm after putting in too many samosas. So, anyway, I'll have to fork out five hundred for a disc jockey.

—I have a band for yeh, brother, said Mickah. —Kind of a gospel group.

—How much? said Gandhi.

—Four hundred and ninety-nine, said Mickah.

So, they were The Deportees again, and on the road, all three miles north, to Sutton and Fat Gandhi's back garden. In the meantime, Gilbert stayed at Jimmy's. He slept on the couch, and was up before the kids every morning. He made their school lunches, sneaked in stuff that Aoife would never have given them.

—What's in yours?

—Two cans of Coke and a Lanky Larry.

The kids loved him.

—Again! said Mahalia.

Gilbert whacked his head with the spatula.

—Again!

They explained the situation to Marvin and Jimmy Two.

—And sometimes, if the bell rings, he might go up to the attic.

—Rapid, said Marvin. —Like Anne Frank.

—A bit, said Jimmy. —Happier ending, but.

—And don't tell anyone, said Aoife.

—No way.

—Good lads, said Jimmy. —I'm proud of yis. Here.

He put his hand in his pocket.

—It's alright, Dad, said Jimmy Two. —This one's on us.

Gandhi's back garden ran the length of a good-sized supermarket, right down to the sea.

—Big, said Dan the elder.

—Slightly smaller than Nigeria, said Gilbert.

Gilbert was wearing shades and a silver wig that Aoife had bought for her sister's hen party.

—Hey, Rabbitte, said Eddie. —You said there'd be no more outside gigs.

—There won't be, said Jimmy. —Look.

Then they saw it, the circus tent; they'd missed it.

They lugged the gear the long way, around the house, escorted and growled at by Fat Gandhi's dog, a mutt called John the Baptist. They were set up, in front of the dance floor, plywood sheets that didn't quite meet, when the guests started poking their heads into the tent.

—There's all sorts in there, they heard a voice from beyond the flap.

Gandhi himself stuck the head in.

—Are yis alright for samosas?

—Grand, thanks.

Gandhi looked at Mickah.

—Why are they dressed like that, Michael?

They wore dungarees, all of them, and felt fedoras, unlaced runners or docs.

—It's just, their look, said Mickah.

—Ah, said Gandhi.

Jimmy had bought some old cardboard suitcases and covered them with stickers—Lagos, Dublin, Minsk, California, Budapest, and Trim. The cases were piled in front of the mike stands. Mickah finished hanging the banner, BOUND FOR GLORY, painted by Marvin and Jimmy Two.

The tent began to fill. The relations were first, the aunties and uncles, a granny, wheeled in by Gandhi's wife.

—They'll hate yis, said Mickah.

Then the birthday girl, a surly looking young one, and her pals; they began to outnumber the aunties and uncles.

—They'll hate yis as well, said Mickah.

—Shut up, Mickah.

They stood and stared at The Deportees. Not a smile among them. It was suddenly very hot in the tent.

—Better get it over with, said Jimmy.

He nodded to King Robert, but before the King could grab the mike, Fat Gandhi had it.

—Lord, said Fat Gandhi. —We thank you for this day. We thank you for the gift of Orla and the joy that she has given us every day of these twenty-one wonderful years.

Gandhi smiled at the birthday girl but she was staring at the plywood.

—And we thank you for Orla's sisters, Sinéad, Ruth, Miriam, and Mary.

More eyes hit the plywood.

—We thank you for the food and refreshments. And, last but not least, Lord, we thank you for the talented people behind me here who have come from, well, all over the place, to entertain and inspire us. And I'm sure they'll do their level best. Amen.

He handed the mike to King Robert.

—It's all yours.

—Exactly, said King Robert.

CHAPTER THIRTEEN

DRUGS AND CHRISTIANITY

KING ROBERT TOOK the mike from Fat Gandhi.

They were ready and nervous, dying to take on the silence that was sucking the air from the tent. King Robert lifted his arm, and dropped it. Leo smacked the drums, and the world ended; the dead arose and Satan stepped into the tent. So Gandhi thought, until he saw John the Baptist falling out of the bass drum.

While Gandhi brought the Baptist up to the house, to see if he could sedate him with a mix of Pal and paracetamol, King Robert tried again. He lifted his arm, and dropped it.

And they were The Deportees.

—HAVE YOU SEEN THAT VIGILANTE MAN?

They roared into the song. Paddy joined King Robert at the mike.

—HAVE YOU SEE-EEN—

THAT VIG-IL—

AH-HANTI MAN?

Jimmy watched the walls of the tent pushed back by the power of the sound. One of the aunties dropped her glass. Jimmy watched it hit the plywood, but he didn't hear it smash. He watched faces, and feet.

They were winning.

—HAVE YOU SEE-EE-EN THAT VIG-IL-AH-ANTI

MA-AN—

There were feet tapping, no one charging to the exit. They were curious, and some were already impressed. Agnes was singing now too.

—CAN YOU HEAR HIS NAME ALL OV-ER THIS LAND—

God, they were good, the real thing. They looked, sounded, *were* it— Jimmy Rabbitte's band. Kerri was sex on a stick up there, and so, mind you, was Mary, in an early-middle-aged very nice kind of way. The dungarees suited her, and so did the anger.

—WHY WOULD A VIGILANTE MAN—

But why was she angry?

—WHY WOULD A—

VIG-IL-AH-HANTI MAN—

Then Jimmy saw the answer right beside her, the ghost of Kurt Cobain. Kenny was whirling and dangerous; he was losing it. Jimmy looked at Kenny's eyes; they weren't there at all. He'd taken something.

—CARRY A SAWED-OFF SHOTGUN IN HIS HAND—

He was tearing around, not a drop of sweat on him. He knocked into both Dans, and sent the trumpet flying. Ah Jesus, thought Jimmy; before they'd even started.

—HAVE YOU HEARD HIS NAME ALL OVER THIS LAND.

They were falling apart already.

He found Mickah.

—Give us a hand with Kenny.

The two of them grabbed Kenny. He didn't resist, the stage was tiny— they had him out of the tent in a few big strides.

Jimmy held Kenny's face.

—Kenny! Kenny! What did yeh take?

—Wha'?

—What did yeh take? Come on.

Jimmy pushed the back of Kenny's head, so he had to bend over.

—We'll have to make him puke.

It was Kenny who answered, not Mickah.

—Why?

—To get the fuckin' drugs out of you.

—What drugs?

Jimmy let go of Kenny.

—Did yeh not take anythin'?

—No.

—Well, why were yeh goin' mad in there?

—I was enjoyin' myself, said Kenny. —Sorry, like.

—That's okay, said Jimmy. —Just, eh, take it easy, will yeh. You're not the only one up there.

—Yeah; thanks, said Kenny, and he ran back into the tent. Jimmy and Mickah followed him, in time to see the band launch into the next tune. Some of the aunts and uncles were leaving, but that was grand. The younger gang had room now. The bottles came out, the funny tobacco; hands grabbed hands, faces met faces and mashed. The birthday girl took off her jumper and threw it at the roof. Christianity had left the tent.

—SOO-LONG—

IT'S BEEN GOOD TO KNOW YEH—

This was dance music.

—THIS DUSTY OLD DUSTY IS HITTING MY HOME—

He'd hadn't known it when he'd thought of Woody Guthrie, ten minutes before that first band meeting, two days after Smokey was born. But that was what it was.

—AND I'VE GOT TO BE DRIFTING AH-LONG—

Dance music. Anything played by this band was dance music. They were that good. Jimmy looked at them. They were happy, sexy; they were cooking and Irish.

Paddy roared.

—I JUMPED THE GULLY—

Agnes and King Robert joined him.

—WE-EE SHA-LL BE FREE-EE—

—I JUMPED THE ROSEBUSH—

—WE-EE SHA-LL BE FREE-EE—

Jimmy whooped; it just came out.

—ACROSS THE PLOUGHED GROUND—

—WE-EE SHA-LL BE FREE-EE—

And they all sang now.

—WHE-EH-EN THE GOOD LORD SETS YOU—

FREE-EE-EE—

The birthday girl was bringing her arse for a walk in a clapping circle made by her friends and cousins when Fat Gandhi stooped, and stepped into the tent. His jaw fell.

And Agnes stepped up to the mike.

—THERE'S—

The clapping stopped.

—A PLACE FOR - US—

The birthday girl stopped.

—SOME-WHERE—

A PLACE-FOR US—

Gandhi stared at the stage. His jaw stayed where he'd dropped it. He'd just fallen in love.

CHAPTER FOURTEEN

SPIRIT OF THE NATION

AGNES HELD THE MIKE; her hands were shaking, her eyes were closed.

—THERE'S—

A TIME—

FOR US—

What she was doing was beautiful, but Fat Gandhi wasn't looking at her, or listening. His jaw still hung dead.

—SOME DAY—

A TIME FOR US—

Agnes's voice and song had brought the aunties back into the tent. But Gandhi didn't notice or care. He was in love. With Gilbert.

Gandhi knew the line: homosexuality was an abomination. He'd known it since he'd seen the light ten years ago, and quickly realised that his loud embrace of Christianity was very good for business. It bored most people, and frightened quite a few, but, even so, Gandhi's weird faith had made him suddenly respectable. Here was a man who could be trusted, a man who took the world seriously. So, he took it for what it was: golf without the exercise.

—SOME-DAY—

SOME-WHERE—

And he hadn't really looked at a man since.

—WE'LL FIND A NEW WAY—

OF—

LIV-ING—

But here he was, in love again. It had happened once before, when he was seventeen. The love of his life, he'd thought ever since, a student from Lyons, a tall lad who'd played table tennis like a gorgeous maniac and never leaked sweat that didn't suit him.

—WE'LL FIND A WAY—

OF FOR—

GIVING—

And here, out of nowhere, it was back.

—HOLD MY HAND AND I'LL—

The feeling, the longing.

—TAKE YOU THERE—

The happiness and misery, all thumping at Gandhi.

—SOME-HOW—

Propping him up and knocking him over.

—SOME-DAY—

Gilbert was drawing whispers from the drum. They surrounded Agnes as she stood there and, finally, opened her eyes.

—SOME—

WHERRRRE.

There was silence then. Gilbert straightened the silver wig. Gandhi was the first to clap; he had to do something—he brought his hands together with slaps that made his teeth, and everyone else's, rattle. The tent was full of whoops and applause. Gilbert and Leo thumped their drums, forced a rhythm on the crowd. And Paddy stepped up to the mike.

—LOTS OF FOLKS BACK EAST THEY SAY—

Gandhi knew: a Christian couldn't just walk away from his family.

—IS LEAVIN' HOME EVERY DAY—

And take off with a man, any man, let alone that particular man there in the silver wig.

—BEATIN' THE HARD AND DUSTY WAY—

He was stuck.

—TO THE 'PUBLIC OF IRELAND LIY-INE—

But not for long.

Gandhi was the big embodiment of the spirit of the new Ireland. Easy come, easy go. That was then and this is fuckin' now.

Right then and there, Fat Gandhi abandoned his religion.

But he didn't tell anyone.

Which was probably just as well because the birthday girl, his daughter, had decided that Gilbert was the second-best looking man in the tent.

King Robert took it from Paddy.

—ACROSS THE DES-ERT SANDS THEY ROLL—

Big Dan gave them a quick blast of *Lawrence of Arabia*, on the accordion.

—GET-TING OUT OF THAT OLD-DD DUST BOWL—

Gilbert let go of a scream.

—THEY THINK THEY ARE GO-ING-GG

TO THE SUG-AR BOWL—

Fat Gandhi and the birthday girl screamed back.

—BUT HERE IS WHAT THEY FIND—

Paddy took the floor behind the mike again. Kenny came out of his hair and saw the birthday girl's little sister staring at him.

—NOW THE GARDA AT THE POINT OF EN-TRY SAY-YYY—

YOU'RE NUMBER FOUR-TEEN THOUS-AND FOR THE—

DAY-YY-YY—

Jimmy watched eyes meeting other eyes, but he couldn't keep up. Paddy, Agnes, and King Robert sang huge.

—OHHH—

IF YOU AIN'T GOT THE DOH - RAY - MEEE—FOLKS—

IF YOU AIN'T GOT THE DOH - RAY—

MEEEEE—

And Kenny roared over Agnes's shoulder.

—That's fuckin' euros, boy!

The little sister blinked for Kenny; she'd never been called *boy* before.

—WHY—YOU'D BETTER GO BACK TO BEAUTIFUL GHAN-A—

OKLAHOMA, POLAND, GEORGIA, AFRIC-EEEE—

Jimmy was sent flying; a dancing auntie followed, and landed on his chest.

—BALLYFERMOT'S A GARDEN OF EEEE-DEN—

And she wouldn't get off him.

—A PARA-DISE TO LIVE IN OR—

SEE-EEEEEE—

Gilbert screamed again.

—BUT - BELIEVE IT OR - NOT—

The birthday girl was wearing Gilbert's wig. Jimmy rescued his phone; it was buzzing and biting his arse.

—YOU WON'T FIND IT SO - HOT—

He got the phone to his ear, just before the auntie's tongue got there.

—Jesus! Hello!

—Nigger lover.

Jimmy laughed, and held the phone in the air.

—IF YOU AIN'T GOT THE DOH - RAY—

MEEE-EEEE -

He was still laughing as he stood and dried his ear. And he watched as Kerri the Yank took the microphone from Paddy.

CHAPTER FIFTEEN

I'M CHECKIN' OUT, GO'OM BYE

—HELLO-O? KERRI SAID to the mike.

—Hello, said every man in the tent, except Jimmy and maybe ten others.

Young Dan led off this time—DOO DEH DEH—and they all went after him.

—Hello-o, said Kerri. —Is this Harlem seven seven seven eleven?

—Yeah!

—John? said Kerri. —Is this you-ou-ou?

Young Dan took off his fedora and put it over the bell of his horn.

—WA-UH-WAH-AAAH—

And Kerri started to sing.

—I THOUGHT I'D PHONE YOU—

I HOPE YOU AIN'T SICK—

—DOO DEH DEH

—COS I'M CHECKIN' OUT—

GO'OM BYE—

It was great, brilliant, better than Jimmy could ever have expected.

—NICE TO HAVE KNOWN YOU-OU

YOU WERE—

MY BIG KICK—

—DOO DEH DEH—

He'd been getting a bit bored with Woody Guthrie. All that dust, it got on your wick after a while.

—BUT I'M CHECKIN' OUT—

GO'OM BYE.

That was the thing about this gang. They'd play anything and make it theirs. A nursery rhyme, a rebel song, a good song, or any old syrup served up by Westlife or Mariah Carey, they'd give it the slaps and turn it into three or four good minutes of jumping, swaying, hard-rocking loveliness.

—YOU TRIED AN OLD TRICK—

—DOOH - DEH—

They'd slow it right down, or laugh it into life.

—YOU FOUND A NEW CHICK—

—DOOH - DEH—

Here now, they'd hopped from Woody Guthrie to Duke Ellington, and no one had noticed.

—BUT I WAS TOO SLICK—

—DOOH - DEH—

They were happy up there. And Jimmy knew: they were staying.

—I'M- IN- THE-KNOW—

YOU'VE - GOT - TO - GO—

THE - CAKE - IS - ALL - GOIN'—

Jimmy's right.

—TOO BAD OUR BLISS—

The Deportees will stay together.

—HAS TO MISS OUT LIKE THIS—

For years and albums.

—I'M CHECKIN' OUT—

GO'OM BYE.

They'll get better and quite well known. They'll tour Wales and Nigeria.

Some of them will leave, the band or the country; others will join, and some will come back. Leo will leave, home to Moscow. Kerri will be the second to go. She'll have a baby, and another, both girls, and she'll write regular articles for the *Irish Times* on the joys and demands of stay-at-home motherhood. Kenny will leave, and come back.

—I only went to the fuckin' chipper, boy.

Gilbert won't be deported. He'll out-sprint the Guards on Grand Canal Street, outside the Registry Office. It'll be a close thing. The Guards will have the tail of Gilbert's jacket in their fingers when they'll be stopped; the flying weight of his future daddy-in-law will deck the pair of them. And Gilbert will marry the birthday girl. Jimmy will be the best man, and Fat Gandhi, out on his own bail, will be their chauffeur for the duration of the honeymoon, a month-long tour of our great little country.

—Did you have mountains like them in Nigeria, Gilbert?

—No.

—They're something else, aren't they?

—Yes.

—YOU TRIED AN OLD TRICK—

There'll be no more little Rabbitte's. Jimmy will have a vasectomy.

—YOU FOUND A NEW CHICK—

A birthday present from Aoife. And it will hurt. Especially when Mahalia drops the *Pet Sounds* box set into his lap, half an hour after he gets home.

—S'oop John B!

But he'll recover. He'll be upright in time to lead his band into the studio for their first recording session, a surprise novelty World Cup hit, called "You Might Well Beat the Irish But We Won't Give a Shite." Jimmy's share of the royalties will buy half a wide-screen telly, and a box of Maltesers for Aoife.

—I love you, Jimmy.

—I love you too, bitch.

—How's the war wound?

—Not too bad.

—BUT I WAS TOO SLICK—

Their first album will be big in Chad and banned in parts of Texas.

—I'M - IN - THE - KNOW—

YOU'VE - GOT - TO - GO—

THE-CAKE-IS -ALL- GOIN'—

Mary's son, a scrawny kid called Zeus, will replace Kerri. Agnes will go home to Seville for Christmas, and come back with a drummer from Cabra. King Robert will join Fianna Fáil—the Republican Party. He'll be the city's first black alderman, and the first mayor to sing "Let's Stay Together" on Bloomsday.

—TOO BAD OUR BLISS—

The second album, *Dark Side of the Coombe*, will be the classic. Tom Waits will fly in, to sing with Paddy.

—HAD TO END UP LIKE THIS—

Talvin Singh will guest on three tracks, Aimee Mann will sing on two. The two Dans will play with the Wu-Tang Clan, and Lauryn Hill will drop by. Bono will bring a pizza, and Eminem will bring his ma. Yo-Yo Ma will make the tea, and Jimmy will make his own day when he opens the studio door, finds Ronan Keating, and tells him to fuck—right—off.

—I'M CHECKIN' OUT—

GO'OM BYE-EEE.

108 MINUTES LATER

Yuri landed a short distance from where he first learned to fly in Saratov. It was said he was in the capsule when it landed, but in fact he had bailed by parachute. It was said he landed in a freshly ploughed field, but in fact he had landed too close to a secret missile division so the capsule was moved to a suitably ploughed field. It was said an old woman, a little girl, and a cow were the first to greet him, but in fact he had to convince pitchfork-armed farmers that he was not a spy. Nevertheless, it remains an unparalleled moment in human history.

TWENTY-MINUTE STORIES

The idea started with an exchange I had with Dave Daley, then the books editor at the *Hartford Courant* and now at the *Journal News* in Westchester. Daley, an extremely agreeable man whom everyone loves and whose enthusiasm for books is pure and boundless, was in the process of commissioning a number of original stories from many authors. He asked me to write something for the *Courant*, and I agreed, then dawdled and did nothing until the fake deadline was past and then the real deadline was approaching. I told him, desperate and pleading, that I couldn't write or finish an actual story in the time left—maybe half a day—but I could, if he were amenable to such a bold experiment, write a bunch of stories, each in twenty minutes, thus illuminating the creative process, the working mind, the limits of space and time. This load of bullshit he swallowed. So I wrote five stories in a few hours, and sent them to him. They weren't uniformly terrible, and the exercise went a long way to convincing me that sometimes speed is helpful, given that with such rigid time constraints, a writer is forced to just tell a story, without dawdling or overthinking or muddling it to the point where it no longer makes sense. So we began talking about asking other writers to do the same thing, write stories in twenty minutes, and given that, after all, we were only asking them for twenty damned minutes of their time, many many writers sent them along, largely because—again—everyone loves Dave Daley.

This whole experiment was completed over a year ago. Maybe longer than that. It's likely that few if any of the writers included herein even remember their stories, especially Mr. Wareham, who we understand is in the music business and probably remembers little in general. The results represented are all over the map, and include many stories that we're not printing here, sometimes at the author's request. And what did we learn overall? We learned that there is a reason why some great art is made under certain constraints, and even within such constraints, a writer can go a thousand different directions. Have we invented a new form? A kind of snappier Snap Fiction? Quicksnap Fiction? Is it the prose equivalent of haiku? These and other questions go unanswered. Thank you.

D.E.

J. ROBERT LENNON

HE NOTICED. He stared. She noticed. She smiled. He approached. She rebuffed. He offered. She accepted. He said, she said, he said, she said. They drank. They said. They drank. He touched. She laughed. They danced. He pressed. She kissed. They left. They did. He left. She slept.

He called. He called. He called. He begged. She refused. He called. He wrote. He visited. He called, called, called, called. She reported. He arrived, shouted, vowed, departed. He plotted. He waited. He visited. She gasped. He demanded. She refused. He grabbed. She screamed. He slapped. She ran, locked, called, waited. He panicked. He fled, hid, failed.

She accused. He denied. She described. He denied. She won, he lost. They aged. She wed, reproduced, parented, saddened, divorced. He bided, waited, hardened. Fought. Smoked. Plotted, planned. Escaped. Vanished.

They lived. She thrived, he faded. He wandered; she traveled. They encountered.

He sat, she sat, they ignored. He noticed. She noticed. He gaped. She jumped. She warned, he assured. She reminded, he admitted. She threatened, he promised. She considered. She sat. She asked. He told. He asked. She told. He smoked. She smoked. He apologized. She cried. He explained. He begged. He pleaded. She considered, resolved, refused. He stood. He clenched. He perspired. He spat. She flinched, paled.

He stopped. He slumped. He collapsed. She stood. She pitied. She left. They lived. They forgot. They died.

—March 28, 2002, 9:05–9:25 a.m., Ithaca, NY

DAVID EBERSHOFF
THE HAY FARMER AT DUSK

THE NAME'S DAVE BROWN, I'll be forty-five years old next week, I've been over on Darwin Road most of my life, and I'm not the hollering type so you wouldn't believe what I'm about to tell you if it wasn't true: I'm lying in a field with a three-ton International Tractor on top of my leg. You might be wondering if I'm in pain and I am and you might be wondering what I'm doing with a tractor pinning me down and it's simple, stories always are. I was out haying that farm on Fly Summit Road, the one the fellow from

New York bought last year. He's got some real steep fields and the tractor somehow slipped out of gear and started rolling back and I tried to jump but it was too late. I've been out here for most of the day, and I'm waiting for someone to come along but the trouble is I'm not sure who that's going to be. This fellow from New York, this here hay farm is just a country spot for him and his boyfriends. He comes up once or twice a month and they swim nude in the pond behind the barn and he's nice enough and he fixed up the place nice enough, put in flowers where there weren't flowers, and painted the shutters and all that, that's the sort of thing they do, and other folks got trouble with him but I don't. Let things lay, is what I say about most of life and most of men. But it's a Monday and he never comes up on Monday and I have no idea how I'm going to get out of here.

If I had a wife she'd be calling around about now but the wife left two years ago last Sunday and she took the daughter too, and the two of them send postcards every now and then from Phoenix. My dog Sophie's probably scratching at the door for dinner but she's a smart fat dog and knows to go down to the sty and eat old Penelope's turnips. Poor Penelope is a lame old pig and can only make it to the food pile once a day and has to suffer while watching Sophie eat her slop.

The field is a pretty field in a little valley and far off you can see the Green Mountains and if you're wondering why I'm not calling for help, well I told you that's not my style and besides I already tried and no one came. This was only my second week out haying, it's been real wet up here, but today was our first heat wave and my arms are red and my neck is burned and I can feel the skin on my face as if it'd been set to fire. Other than that, all of me is fine except my leg, the tractor is just leaning on it and it reminds me of the time I found old Penelope collapsed on poor Sophie. Had to take the poor dog to the vet and have her leg wrapped for a month. Penelope may be old but she's still nearly half a ton and now that I think of it I laughed at Sophie over that one and that wasn't too nice of me because I wouldn't want you to laugh when you find me here.

I always keep a little notepad in my pocket and a pen and on it I record the amount of hay and the field conditions and other things too and sometimes a nice thought comes to mind and I write it down, something about the wife or the daughter or something about how the place on Darwin Road no longer feels like the place I want to spend the rest of my life. Now I'm writing this here down for him who finds me because the leg is worse than I first wanted to admit, it's shattered to just about nothing beneath the tractor I can tell, and after another day of heat the puddle of blood will be dry and no one will think it's blood, they'll just think it's cracked mud. I don't have any water and the night sky is now a soft deep blue and the bugs are coming out, the fireflies are beginning to burn. The nights here are short in the summer and the fireflies twinkle until dawn and if you wake up in the middle of the night and look out the window without your glasses on it'll look like the whole blurry black world is exploding. This morning on the radio they said tomorrow's going to be even hotter, maybe up to ninety-eight, and I wonder how my old leg will do through that. I remember reading somewhere the story about the dog who chews his leg off to get free from a trap, but Sophie sure didn't do that when Penelope pinned her down. The notion's crossed my mind, in case you were wondering what was crossing my mind at the end, but I don't have anything to saw my leg off with. And in any case, it's something that's more an idea than something you'll actually ever do. The fellow who owns this place might be coming up for July 4th but I don't know and that's not for another few days and who knows what will happen between now and then and all I know is I'm a mile from anyone and the dark has come now and even though I hate to be the noisy type I yell out—Help me! Please! Someone! Anyone!—and it bounces back as fast as it left my lungs, and the echo is all I have, the echo and the night, and when you find this, when you find me, do me a couple of favors. Go over and feed Sophie and don't forget about Penelope, she'll need watering in this heat. And then if you would, call up the wife and the daughter, the number's taped to the phone in the kitchen, and tell them it's at least their duty to come home and put me in the ground.

—July 4, 2002, 9:36–9:57 a.m., Cambridge, NY

JONATHAN LETHEM

ZEPPELIN PARABLE

Everybody knows "The Caravan Barks and the Dogs Move On." Fewer know "The Zeppelin Sails and the Dogs Sniff the Gas Nozzles." This is how it goes:

THE POTENTIAL ZEPPELIN is in the field, lying sagged and helpless along the grass, a membrane painted with gay colors, struggling to assert itself, expecting to fly, unable yet.

The dogs are kept at bay in the parking lot in anticipation of the great moment. They pick boogers, call their spouses on cell phones, solve cross-word puzzles, crack puns, speculate, lap from water bowls, etcetera. In this they resemble the irascible poker-playing reporters killing time as they wait for the execution of the convicted murderer in *His Girl Friday*.

The gas flows from the pipes, which are laid in long sections of hose and fitted with nozzles. The nozzles connect to the inflow nodules of the vast baggy zeppelin. The gas comes from underground, from purportedly "great deep secret sources." The gas would certainly stay underground unless it had a zeppelin to fill, because the gas is by nature bashful, deferential, conflict-ed. Slowly the zeppelin inflates, taking succor and inspiration from the munificence of the gas.

Lift Is Achieved.

Ropes Are Loosened.

Hoses Disconnected From Valves.

Many Shouts.

Hurry, it's in the air!

No one can pinpoint the moment the bag becomes truly a zeppelin, thanks to the gas, but after so long a wait, a water-boiling interlude, this phase transition in fact seems to elude even the closest watcher: suddenly. Now there is much to do. We all adore the zeppelin when it sails, do we not? We are all ready to have our hearts broken. The dogs are loosed and rush baying into the field. The zeppelin is unbound from earth now, unfixed, a thing of the sky and beyond. It wants to go to outer space—not as a rocket would, but by drifting, by departing this world with our amazed and yearn-ing eyeballs in gentle tow.

There could never be enough of this.

If only X were here to see it!

The dogs have joined us now where we stand under the zeppelin's fuzzy shadow, the zeppelin soaring so gradually, yet now already beginning to depart the field, to incline for the mountains, there to be lost in the higher air—

Look! Great god, look! It's the mothership! Look! But the dogs have their noses to the ground. They're chasing traces, sniffing hoses, rooting for nozzles.

No, dogs, that's beside the point! The gas was only to fill the zeppelin—please, look, before it is too late.

One dog whines, finding a nozzle, and rolls over it in his excitement. Others come growling and grumbling, wanting a piece of the action. He's got a good one! This dog can really detect a strong whiff of gas, a tendril left behind in the quick disconnection of nozzle from socket.

Yummy, the dogs all say. Nasty, yummy gas. Gotta gotta get me some of that.

No, look in the air! we shout.

It's so beautiful!

Too late, gone. They missed it.

The Zeppelin Sails, and the Dogs Sniff the Gas Nozzles.

Twas ever thus.

Hey, man, these dogs don't even LIKE zeppelins! They like gas.

Cut 'em some slack.

Yeah, what were we thinking?

—June 15, 2002, 3:56–4:16 p.m., Saratoga Springs, NY

JENNIFER EGAN

To Do

1. Mow lawn
2. Get rid of that fucking hose
3. Wash windows
4. Spay cat
5. Dye hair
6. Do tarot cards
7. Pick up kids
8. Drop off kids at Mom's
9. Buy wig
10. See if small removable portion of fence can be cut QUIETLY
    a. Kinds of clippers
    b. Metal solvents
    c. Electrical devices
        1. How noisy?
        2. Flying metal chips?
        3. Danger of electrocution?
            a. Rubber gloves/goggles?
            b. Lethal?
                1. Sign will
            c. Does it make the body look really shitty at death?

          1. Get tooth capped

11. Send warning letter
    a. Newspaper cutouts?
    b. Get kids to write it?
    c. Write with left hand?
    d. Be vague. "Certain unpleasant things"

12. Mail letter
    a. Or drop it off while wearing wig

13. Renew meds

14. Investigate poisons
    a. Flammable
    b. Powders
    c. Gasses
    d. Pills
    e. Herbal
    f. Chemical
    g. Musical
        1. Ask kids
        2. Hamlet—ear
    h. Ingestible
        1. Cookies?
    i. Must look INNOCENT

15. Research cameras
    a. Affixed to fence
    b. Propped in hole cut in fence
    c. Small, undetectable
    d. Implanted in flowers
    e. How to use?
    f. Must be REASONABLY priced
    g. Take no shit from photo man
        1. Remind him of ruined prints

16. Pick up kids

17. Make dinner

18. Get ready for party
    a. Polka dots
    b. Black gloves
    c. Hair ribbon
    d.Veil
    e. Bring seltzer

f. Remind Lou of party

g. Plan two funny stories

h. Breathing exercises to prepare for seeing THEM

1. Kiss Kiss

    2. Hug Hug

    3. Remember: NO ONE CAN SEE YOUR THOUGHTS

—July 1, 2002, 12:35–1:00 p.m., in Central Park, NY

KATIE ROIPHE

ONE STEAMY DAY in July a friend and I walked into Dolce & Gabbana on Madison Avenue so that she could try on a dress for her wedding, which was two months away. She didn't want anything pouffy or lacy or beaded or floor-length. She didn't want to be a bride in any obvious or clichéd way. She wanted to be herself, only more glamorous and photogenic.

The salesgirls in black glided through the store. The floor shone. The sweaters were stacked so neatly it looked like you could build a new kind of sleek, shiny pyramid with them. On the rack, in between a pair of red leather pants and a shirt with turquoise feathers sticking out of it, hung the dress. It was a skintight backless white stretchy satin dress in exactly her size, a dress that could have been worn by a '40s movie star with a long pearl-encrusted cigarette holder.

My friend went without speaking into the softly lit dressing room to try it on. She floated out into the middle of the store. She put on her veil. She looked at herself in the mirror, and everyone in the store felt it. She was suddenly a bride. The salesgirls in black forgot to sulk. The price tag— $2,500—fluttered under her arm. You could feel it in the room, the rising female fantasy. Excitement. Bliss. We were all trembling with it. And then it happened. Blood started pouring out of my friend's nose. This had never happened to her before. It hadn't happened to me before that I had been around someone with a bloody nose. At least not since Sandy Vanderzee manipulating the school nurse in fourth grade. She could give herself bloody noses at will, but I think that is unusual.

My friend stooped over and cupped her hands under her nose. The salesgirls began to peel the dress off her, but it fit like the skin of an onion. There were men milling around the store, idly flicking at pricetags. But we had no choice but to peel.

Finally, my friend stood naked in the middle of the store, which glistened like a jewel. The men pretended not to notice. One of the salesgirls brought her tissues. Another took off her veil. There was general rejoicing that not one drop of blood had touched the dress: the white satin remained unbloodied and virginal. My friend, still naked, walked over to her handbag and reached in for her credit card. The salesgirls folded the dress reverently and put it in a garment bag.

Seven weeks later, my friend called off her wedding.

—February 8, 2002, 2:02–2:26 a.m., Brooklyn, NY

EMMA FORREST
GENTLE BEN

"WELL, I FIND him charming. If that makes me a gay man then I'm a gay man."

Dad, who had not unbuttoned his pinstripe blazer since he got back from work, leaned back in his chair, making its front legs leave the ground. His white satin yarmulke sat at a jaunty angle, like a cocktail hat Adrian might have designed for Rosalind Russell. My mother, ignoring his statement, said, "Stop tipping, Adam. Adam, stop tipping!"

He had tipped his chair on their fourth date and cut the back of his head open. Since he could not see the stitches, nor the scar they left, he had continued to tip. That it never happened to him again was, he felt, a vindication. "The only difference between a psychotic and a neurotic," sighed my mother, "is that a neurotic learns from their mistakes." Dad tipped back a little further.

"Adam, stop it!" she shrieked, throwing her napkin in alarm. When I was little and being too noisy, mum would put a napkin on my head and say it was the Quiet Hat and I would believe her and grow absolutely silent until she took it off. I looked at the napkin and decided to back my father.

"I think Ben Affleck is great."

"Yeah," snarled my sister, "except for when he's acting."

Sophie had been born the angriest child alive. I remember Dad driving us to piano lessons and Sophie, not yet five, belted into the back seat, asking, "Daddy, what street are we driving on?"

Dad, who was used to her abstract questions like "What's your favorite kind of glass?" looked up at the street sign and answered, "Ponsonby Place."

Sophie pondered this a moment and then, in her soft, sweet voice, said, "I hate Ponsonby Place."

"I loathe Ben Affleck," shuddered Sophie, as she helped herself to more potato. "He has a face I could never tire of kicking." Sophie, though nineteen, had yet to grow past five foot.

"Is Ben Affleck Jewish?" asked Dad, turning to me. "Because, you know, I think he probably could be."

Mum pushed back from the table. "Just shut up about Ben Affleck being Jewish. Shut up. It's never going to happen with you and Ben Affleck, okay?" Her voice was so shrill that Dad physically curled away from her.

"I didn't say I wanted anything to happen."

"Right," she said, trying to catch her breath, "then what's your point?"

"My point is that he's charming, and charm is hard to come by in this world. It's different from allure or charisma. It's not the same as bonhomie or simple joviality, which, of course, George Clooney has in spades."

Mother retrieved her tossed napkin, sat back down and, back rigid against the seat back, took a sip of diet cola.

"I'm not going to spend this whole dinner talking about Ben Affleck."

"Okay," said Dad, raising his eyebrows and returning his chair to the upright position, "Fine."

And so we were silent.

—July 12, 2002, 6:30–7:00 a.m., Los Angeles, CA
in my cousin Bobbi's kitchen

RICK MOODY

PHYSICALLY ADAPTIVE END USER INTERFACES
WITH HYDRO-INDUSTRIAL INDOOR APPLIANCE*

THIRSTY PHYSICALLY ADAPTIVE end user (A) flings Acme brand clay pigeon into the uninterrupted blue of sky. Childhood friend of physically adaptive end user (B) fires Remington 12-gauge in same direction, having loaded firearm with fancy peeled carrots. Carrots bounce harmlessly from clay

---

*After Rube Goldberg.

pigeon. However, jackrabbit (C) sees carrots, leaps from bushy undergrowth at carrots falling from sky. Local timber wolf (D), attached by rubber cord to red aluminum wagon, sees flying rabbit, catches rabbit in mouth, dragging red aluminum wagon (E) onto railroad tracks, where freight train carrying load of liquid nitrogen (F) and other inflammable products bears down on wagon. Train derails (G), rolls down mountainside, spilling liquid nitrogen and other inflammable products into valley where troop of Cub Scouts (H) are camped around fire, singing drinking songs. Inflammable cargo trickles to base of campfire, causing valley to burst into flames. Hot air balloon (I), moored harmlessly nearby, spontaneously lifts off in eddies of hot air, carrying away house cat, several Cub Scouts, seven volumes of diary of missing balloonist. Cat leaps out of balloon (J), in pursuit of passing flock of starlings, Cub Scouts leap after cat (K), causing balloon to rise further, over Continental Divide, until, in or around Los Angeles metropolitan area, balloon begins to lose pressure, landing in yard (L) of disgruntled independent film producer. Film producer, seeing deflated balloon in driveway, panics, drinks on top of antidepressants. Producer takes volumes of diary from basket (M) at base of deflated balloon, immediately recognizes, in hallucinatory state, that diary is *major motion picture.* Calls studio head (N). Studio head, engaged in attempt to eliminate starlings from attic of guest house by catapulting poisonous frogs (O) through louvered window, cannot hear film pitch by reason of bad cellular telephone contact, believes film producer is balloon store owner bringing over mylar balloon products for Sweet Sixteen of cocaine-addicted daughter (P), accidentally gives tentative green light to three-hundred-million-dollar project (Q) about the life of balloonist. Disgruntled independent film producer, doing dance of joy, falls from second-story terrace, hits head, dies. Pool belonging to independent producer dries up (R) for nonpayment of utilities, causing water vapors (S) to form clouds over body of deceased independent film producer (T), such that fast-moving tropical depression (U) gains strength and crosses Rocky Mountain region (V), showering several inches of rain on parched latitudes. Local aquifer fills (W), so that well in house of thirsty physically adaptive end user produces water (X), as shown in hydro-industrial appliance in garage (Y) where no water has lately been produced. He drinks.

—*January 15, 2002, 6:00–6:20 p.m., Saratoga Springs, NY*

ALEKSANDAR HEMON

DAYS

ON MAY 24, 1968, I was brought back to consciousness by cold water my Uncle Bogdan poured on my face. I had fallen into a ditch full of cow shit, mud, and yucky sludge. The cup was beaten tin, and I drank from it later.

On September 1, 1971, my father brought me a blazing-white sweater from his trip to Monaco. On the chest, there was a resplendent emblem for the Casino Royale.

September 7, 1971: my mother made me wear it to school. I was embarrassed because I stuck out, and some kids though that my family was rich. So after school, I rolled in the dirt behind the school. I told my mother I had been tripped by a bully named Ziojutro.

January 15, 1974: I had a dream in which hordes of armored knights were sledding. There were three knights per sled, and I could hear the din of clattering visors and squealing knights and swords and armors clashing when the sleds turned over. I couldn't see the knights' faces. Another part of the same dream—though what the relation was I could not tell—was the feeling that my big toes were enlarged to the size of a horsehead.

April 19, 1974: I wrote a poem entitled "Is This Death or Rebirth?" It was based on an untested assumption of mine that when you die, you go to a place thickly populated with dinosaurs and other gigantic reptiles.

May 9, 1974: I gave that poem to a girl I was in love with so much that I couldn't imagine her not being in love with me, and she wasn't. She thought "Is This Death or Rebirth?" to be weird, and it was.

July 29, 1982: I scored a goal with a bicycle kick. It was a school soccer tournament, played on a concrete surface. I dislocated my shoulder, and we lost.

October 3, 1984: I slept under my bed in the platoon dorm, successfully hidden from the platoon commander, who stupidly expected me to dwell over the freedom of our people and be on guard against the enemy, inner and outer. Neither the inner nor the outer enemy ever slept, but I did, every day, under the bed.

February 11, 1987: I got drunk on a bitter herbal digestive, normally consumed by the worst of drunks, who liked to believe that being wasted on a digestive was good for their ulcers. I wore a navy blue trench coat and my father's pseudo-Irish hat, which was thereafter marked by a barely visible vomit stain on its rim.

August 25, 1990 (a Tuesday): my girlfriend came to our date with a postcoital glaze over her eyes. There were so many fornication candidates (including numerous women) that I couldn't be jealous. I was just sad, because when I embraced her, it was like embracing an empty coat.

November 11, 1991: I saw my dog—a beautiful, flaming-red Irish Setter—running uphill (the same hill, come to think of it, down which the knights were sledding in my dream) with a unit of military police shooting with blanks, getting ready for the use of live ammo. I had let my dog out of the mountain cabin I was spending my time and wasting my mind in, because he started licking my face at 6 a.m. So at 10 a.m. my dog was running alongside military policemen with gas masks on. I couldn't see their faces, but I could hear their panting and the clatter of their helmets, as I stood outside in my pajamas and whistled, calling my dog. My dog ignored me, thinking it was all a game, the military police charging at the imaginary enemy. I whistled.

March 30, 1993: I told the story of my life to a restaurant manager in Chicago. I was trying to get a busboy job. He had a sword tattooed on his arm.

December 10, 1998: In a graduate Shakespeare class I pronounced the word *akin* as "achin'."

January 2, 2000: I washed my face with cold water and noticed that the toothpaste sprinkles on the mirror formed a pattern.

On October 23, 2002, in Chicago, I wrote this down—it took me some thirty minutes. After I finished, I felt quick emptiness looking out the window at the garage roofs and fences and back alleys, where kids in helmets rode their skateboards. The only thing moving in my room was a pot with a plant that calls itself snowstorm, swinging like a pendulum.

—October 23, 2002, 10:30–11:02 a.m., Chicago, IL

RHETT MILLER

I'LL SMASH HIS fucking head in with a rolling pin. The thought first occurred to me in the late '60s. Not long after we'd married. Just words. They had weight, though, heft. I wasn't even quite sure what a rolling pin was at the time. The phrase stuck. I'd hear myself say it in my head. Not in anger. Just driving alone. Or watching soaps. I'll smash his fucking head in with a rolling pin.

I took up baking. I guess it was a private joke. Very inside. I'd roll out crusts. Flour on the rolling pin. Wooden. Old School is what Jeremy would call it. OG. Legit. Our son the seventeen-year-old gangster. Only he's a puddle of a man. A sourceless stream trickling downhill.

Cakes are my favorite. No crust to roll, but the rising is a thing to see. Up and up. Not too long or it'll explode. I wish I had been a slut. I could have been. I declared other girls at my women's university sluts. I could have been had six ways to Sunday by any one of the guys who took me out in their cars to dinner and what have you. Only no what have you.

Till he came along. I'll smash his head in. The thought occurred to me years before I found out he deserved it. I guess I knew even before I picked up the phone in 1974 to call Time and Temperature and heard him whispering. To that slut. Cupcakes are good too. You pour them one-by-one into the paper cups.

I never let on that I knew, but I got good at listening. Hold the receiver upside-down so the mouthpiece is up over your head, lock the door so Jeremy doesn't walk in. In the '80s I stopped making pies altogether. No crusts, no rolling. I couldn't touch it. The words have weight though, right? They're heavy.

—June 7, 2002, 11:06–11:27 p.m., Los Angeles, CA

MYLA GOLDBERG

WE THOUGHT IT might be better to swim. Crumb tested the water with his foot while I sat on the raft, which was flimsier than either of us wished to admit. It's cold, he said, and I nodded. We already knew it was cold. The clouds were so thick it was impossible to tell day from night and I thought of Sweden, where I had heard the opposite happens, where the sun shines twenty-four hours a day, and I said, We're in the anti-Sweden, but Crumb only looked at me the way he always looks at me when I say something, which is to say he looked at me like I was some kind of talking insect and so I reminded myself it was really better not to speak at all.

The water had thick qualities, like Jello when it's only been in the fridge for half an hour and hasn't firmed up yet but is beginning to gelatinize. I thought about what it might be like to be surrounded by such water, how it would seem not like water but like something else, and this was not a pleasant thought and so I thought maybe it would be better to stay on the raft after all. I don't know what Crumb was thinking. After my anti-Sweden comment and having tested the water with his foot, he had been keeping his mouth shut and looking off toward the far bank as if he were alone on the raft or as if we were strangers in an elevator.

The goal, of course, was to get to the far bank, but we didn't have sticks or any other sort of paddle device and the current was straight and sure, like an arrow, so the raft wasn't going to take us there on our own, which is why the swimming idea, but then gelatin. I'm sure Crumb was thinking he would rather have been on the raft with anyone but me. It is difficult in times of stress to control the expression of the face and I think my facial expressions were beginning to bother Crumb but I could not help it. It is amazing how private a thing the face is and I began wishing I had a hood or something so that I could keep my expressions to myself. My face is my own, like my heart is my own. No one would ever think it right to see the heart, beating, which is not so different really from the expressions of the face. The inner being should not have to be revealed like that, in the twitches and stretches and curves of the face.

Suddenly Crumb said, I'm going, and slid into the water. I watched his weighty doggy paddle as he made for the far bank, the current carrying him so that his body described an oblique angle and not at all a straight line and I tried to project in my mind where that angle would intersect the far bank and whether his water-logged doggy paddling would hold out that long and I was not certain it would. I was not certain it would.

—May 24, 2002, 11:00–11:20 a.m., Brooklyn, NY

MARC NESBITT

THEY CAME CLOSE in the library, paused in an aisle, looking for the name Nunez, they just about kissed, and it was almost exactly nearly like something he'd seen in a movie once, which made it all the more important to him, and he imagined himself walking out and renting that movie that very night, as she walked away from him and turned at the end of the aisle.

Her breath had smelled of ice cream and onions and "Combined with the fumes from her face paint, it was quite overwhelming, I assure you," he said to Bonnard in the locker room. "Nobody talks like that," Bonnard said, and continued to hassan chop the man's shoulder blades. The man with the shoulders was the heavyweight wrestling champion of the contiguous forty-eight, known to the world as The Least Excited One. His signature move was The Shrug. *USA Today* described his style as the tai chi of grappling. He never attacked. People ran at him, threw him off the ropes, tried leg locks and clotheslines. He was a human noodle. Most offensive he ever got was to lean the shoulder a little. Kept beating people without really trying. I'm just not into it, he'd say, when people asked, which they didn't. He had a mask that stopped at the nose. Not a Zorro job across the eyes, but a skull-cap with eyeholes, and he always wore an 8:30 shadow. And the unitard. A light blue some people said was a denim, but it wasn't. He just wore it a lot.

Bonnard hands him one peanut butter cracker at a time as they walk down the gangway toward the ring. No music. The crowd nearest the locker room starts screaming and it swings around the arena. Before you know it the whole place is on its feet and beating their hands bloody.

"Ice cream and onions," he says.

"What?" Bonnard screams.

They're at the ring now, and Bonnard holds the ropes open.

In the opposite corner stands Hand Face, wearing an all-white bodysuit and a white mask with flesh-colored hands on it. The rest of his enemy's clan—known only as the Locusts—stand outside the ring, sucking on the edge of the canvas.

—May 31, 2002, 1:45–2:07 a.m., Jersey City, NJ

STEVE ALMOND
The Chicken Killer's Remorse

TWO MEN IN an office, a decent crappy little office in one of those new buildings off the highway. The man behind the desk, Wilkie, is wearing a white button-down with the company logo over the pen pocket, and pleated trousers. The man across from him, Huggins, is wearing faded overalls and boots caked with red mud. Wilkie has a square face and a neatly trimmed beard, a bit severe, like a Revolutionary soldier, though he is, in fact, an exceptionally friendly fellow. He smiles and says to Huggins: "Tell me about yourself."

Huggins says: "I kills the chickens."

"I'm sorry," Wilkie says.

"I kills the chickens. You asked what I did. I kills the chickens."

Wilkie seems briefly confused. He shuffles some papers on his desk. He smiles nervously. "Well, yes, the situation, Mr. Huggins, you see, the position we are hiring for does not involve chickens. It involves computers. Are you, if I may ask, familiar with the Linux operating system?"

"I already tole you, I kills the chickens."

"Yes, so I am given to understand. But familiarity with that operating system, and at least with the rudiments of HTML and Javascript, are minimal in a candidate for senior programmer."

Huggins squints and pulls a toothpick from his pocket. "Boss says I ain't good enough at killing chickens."

"Your previous employer?"

"Said I liked the work too much."

Wilkie gazes at his blotter. Though he is, by nature, a chipper fellow, it has been a long day of interviewing. "I think perhaps there's been a crossed wire here, some kind of mix-up."

"That's what he says," Huggins said. "Says, 'Boy'—he called me Boy—says 'Boy, I can't have you singing while you work. That will not cut mustard.'"

"If I may ask, Mr. Huggins: Do you know anything about the high-tech sector?"

"What he don't understand is I was singing hymns for them chickens. That's what it was. We'd run 'em through them machines and it was terrible what they did to 'em, just tore them little birds apart, ass first and on up the gut. And I mean that, sir. So's what I did, I'd sing to 'em, real soft, just these hymns we used to sing down there at the church. May the Lord lay you down gentle in the nest of paradise. Like that."

Wilkie glances at Huggins, whose eyes are shining. "Can you tell me whom you spoke to in HR?" he says.

"Says to me, 'Boy, can't have you serenading them chickens, now. Ain't good for morale.' Then tells me to collect my stuff. I said, 'What am I s'pose to do, boss?' He says: 'With a mind like yours, boy, I'd go high-tech.' I said, 'I gotta kill any chickens in that line of work?' He gives me a gentle little pat on the back and says, 'No sir.' So here I am."

"Yes," Wilkie says. "The thing…" Oh, he doesn't like this, not at all. "What it is…"

He takes a peek at Huggins, those shining eyes and the red mud on his boots. "We usually like a candidate who has a bit more experience, just in terms of the operating systems."

"You ain't even gonna check my references. I got references."

Wilkie hears himself saying: "If it were up to me," which is a curious thing to say, as it is, actually, technically, quite pointedly, up to him. But it is one of the things that one says—civility, manners, all the rest of that—and he flashes his lower management no-hard-feelings sort of grin, the one he rehearses sometimes at home, while his warm little wife waits for him in bed. And there's poor Huggins, digging a slip of paper out of the comb pocket of his overalls, a wrinkled slip of paper. Wilkie imagines this must be his list of references, which his applicant now casts onto the desk.

But it is not until much later, after Huggins has risen from his seat and walked slowly out of the office, after he has paused in the doorway and turned to tell Wilkie, with a mournful smile: "Well, I'll tell you this. No one likes to be let down, sir," after he has tracked bits of red mud onto the white carpet of the reception area, indeed, it is not until Wilkie himself has been "let go" seven months later, and has to clean out his desk, that he sees that the slip of paper is something altogether different.

It is a hand-written note, in blocky lettering, which says: "God asks only that you love all the creatures of His earth, from the serpents in the grass to the beasts of the fields to the birds of the air whose wings are blessed. Amen. Amen. Amen."

—February 13, 2002, 4:32–4:51 p.m., Boston, MA

JESSICA FRANCIS KANE

WHAT HE COULD say is that he doesn't have a glove. That he was the only guy cut from his high school baseball team. That he throws, in fact, like a girl. But he knows what they will say. Smiling and shaking their heads, It is not important. He'll look down, searching for another excuse. Please take him, they'll say again. Please take the boy to the park.

His huge purple laundry bag will be sitting between them on the counter. He started with just a few impersonal things, just shirts and pants he could have washed and dried but didn't have time to iron. It was a slippery slope. Now he brings everything: underwear, socks, sheets, towels—his slow corruption giving them their current power.

But how could they know this? They're about his age, he thinks, two Korean women who run the dry-cleaning shop around the corner from his apartment. He's not sure which one is the boy's mother; they both seem very solicitous about him. The shop is open six days a week from seven to seven and they are always there, always washing, drying, folding. The boy, he's probably nine or ten, helps a lot. He stands in the back sorting whites and colors, folding. He's a good folder. When he does a stack of T-shirts, he smoothes them with his palms so that the shirts are neat and stiff.

A few weeks ago, he saw the boy playing in the back with a baseball. To fill the silence at the register—the two women were having trouble finding his laundry—he made a casual remark. He said the boy had a good arm. The women smiled and nodded repeatedly, and he felt something changing, almost growing between them. A huge misunderstanding in the making. The following week they asked if he would take the boy to the park for a game of catch. It was raining, his automatic foolproof excuse. But he felt so guilty—these women washed and folded his underwear!—that he said he would take him this week. He may have promised. He would like to be the kind of person who could keep that promise, but he fears he is not.

—May 8, 2002, 2:36–3:00 p.m., Charlottesville, VA

GLEN DAVID GOLD*
COOP

IN 1943, GROUCHO MARX lived alone in Maine on a chicken farm he'd purchased with the proceeds from what the brothers swore was their last film, *The Big Store*. It had been a terrible film that no one had wanted to make, something rewritten from a Ritz Brothers program. Humiliated, Groucho had left California on a train, and since he was just another fifty-three-year-old man with thick glasses, he was ignored from station to station. He read books. He looked out the window. He called in for messages, and when there were none, he seethed. The worst place for anger is, of course, when it is worn on the surface of the skin. Groucho imagined it made out of that powder found on the wings of moths; touch it and the animal can no longer fly. But it had served him well, it was the fountain of his fame, and because he was Groucho, no one could touch it. It rendered him completely opaque.

When he arrived at his chicken farm, he found a caretaker's cabin at the edge of a nest of olive trees. It was deserted, and he collapsed onto a single

---

*This story contains a single sentence—a disputed sentence—found both in a Stephen Ambrose book (*Wild Blue*) and in his source material (*George McGovern Grassroots: The Autobiography of George McGovern*).

cot in the center of the room, and closed his eyes and listened for the sounds of chickens. It was the heat of the day, they slept, so he listened for sleeping chickens. A middle-aged Jew who had received no phone calls asking where he'd gone to, and he was on a cot listening for sleeping chickens.

He loved this. He hated this. He was asleep until he heard, definitively, the flapping of wings, which satisfied him for just a moment. Then he explored the cabin. There was a standing wardrobe, half-splintered at the joints, filled with uniforms—nurses' uniforms, valets' uniforms, perhaps something worn by the local fire department. And next to it was a stove. And along two pieces of plywood propped up by cinderblocks, armed forces editions of novels: *Forever Amber*, Faith Baldwin trash, movie star magazines (none with him featured), photographs of a man in uniform.

There was no telephone, no refrigerator, no shower, no plumbing. Groucho was for the first time in his life actually alone rather than just feeling that way. His plan was to stay for months, or until someone missed him enough to come looking, but he, it turned out, was hardly that patient. To wish to be a lonely farmer is much different than actually to be one, and three days into his exile, when he walked to town and at the soda fountain made his daily call and heard from his manager only that Chico needed money again, and had started looking for him, he snapped.

When he returned, he entered the cabin, and for a few moments there was no sound, except for the clucking of the chickens. Then the stove, uniforms on hangers, shelves of books, magazines, and photographs, all flew into the olive grove.

—June 1, 2002, 11:54 p.m.–12:15 a.m., Los Angeles, CA

ALICIA ERIAN

MARGARITAVILLE

IT WAS THEIR second marriage-counseling session, and Mary and Lawrence were late. "It's your fault," Mary said in the car on the way there, and Lawrence said, "No, it's yours," and they gave up almost immediately, knowing that neither of them would ever win.

At the session, their therapist, Nan Overton, suggested they discuss Lawrence's mom, who all three of them agreed was a terrible woman. "She talks constantly," Mary complained, and Nan said, "Let's let Lawrence begin."

Mary hated being shamed by Nan. It was always so obvious, what Mary should and shouldn't do in the sessions, but she couldn't seem to control herself. She was so excited to be there, to see Lawrence get in trouble for all the bad things he was always doing. Like defending himself when he was wrong, or not ever bothering to notice that Mary was hot.

So now he started talking about his mother, using too many words and telling all the least important details, as usual. Mary watched their money ticking away on the clock and wondered what the point was. Maybe all Lawrence needed was a punching bag and a speech coach. Maybe Nan had no idea what she was talking about.

"Mary?" Nan said. "What are you thinking?"

"Nothing," Mary said.

"You looked a little thoughtful there for a second."

Mary sighed. "Well, I guess I was just thinking that Lawrence could stand to economize verbally."

"Oh, fuck you," Lawrence said, which gave Mary an unexpected charge.

"Fuck you," Nan repeated, "is this the kind of language you guys use with each other?"

Mary and Lawrence nodded.

"It doesn't really bother me," Mary said.

"Me either," Lawrence admitted.

Nan nodded. All of a sudden her fax machine started going off and she jumped up to try to fix it. Mostly the problem was the noise. Mary looked at the clock and attempted to time the whole incident, wondering if she'd then have the nerve to demand additional seconds when their fifty minutes was up.

After Nan sat back down, she said, "Where were we?"

"Lawrence was having verbal diarrhea," Mary said. She'd meant it as a joke, but no one except her was laughing. Soon she stopped, embarrassed.

"What does it feel like when Mary makes jokes at your expense, Lawrence?" Nan asked him.

He shrugged. "I mean, I guess she's pretty funny."

After the session ended, Mary and Lawrence went across the street for Mexican food. Lawrence ordered a margarita, and when it came, Mary asked if she could have a sip. "You see?" Lawrence said, passing it across the table in an unfriendly fashion. "You always do that. You always want half my stuff."

"Fine," Mary said, huffing it up after her sip. "Don't share. See if I care."

A waitress came and took their order. Soon another couple arrived, and

Mary and Lawrence began listening to their conversation instead of making their own. The couple seemed to be on a first date, and the man was bragging about the success of his law practice. The woman seemed to be listening to him, because she kept saying, "Uh-huh, uh-uh." When the waitress came for their order, they used bad pronunciation to say taco. They said "tacko." This made Lawrence laugh a little. "What?" Mary said.

"Tacko," he repeated. "That's funny."

The man from the next table looked over at Lawrence then, and Lawrence looked away.

"You see?" Mary said. "That's what you do. You embarrass us constantly. In public places."

Lawrence sighed. The food arrived, and when he cut into his chile relleno, he saw that it was filled with shrimp instead of the beef he'd ordered. When the waitress came, he asked if she could take it back and get him the beef. She nodded politely and scurried away. Mary had ordered chicken enchiladas, and now Lawrence stared at them jealously.

"You want a bite?" she asked him.

"Okay," he said.

She cut off a bunch of different sections and pushed the plate so it was more at the center of the table, easily reached by both parties. "Thanks," Lawrence said. In the end, he ate most of Mary's dinner, along with his margarita.

On the way home, they listened to Mary's favorite hard rock station. In bed, they provided orgasms for one another, then turned away, their backs pressed together in a competitive style of sleep.

—February 27, 2002, 2:30–2:55 p.m., Brooklyn, NY

RYAN BOUDINOT

VACUUM CLEANER

WHEN I FINISHED vacuuming the house I went out to sweep the front walkway. The poured concrete bore the almost corduroylike ridges of the worker's brush. A child's name, *Hiro*, was fingered into the path's margin by the rosebush, the name of a child who must have belonged to a previous occupant of the house. After six years of living here I was still finding traces of their presence. Ripping up the carpet in the study that morning, I found a reddish stain on the hardwood beneath, the result of a painting accident or indeterminate chemical spill. Their books still sat on a couple bookshelves. In the basement I still found traces of the craft projects the woman did, a doily hidden under the hot water heater, a pipe cleaner, the odd googly-eye that never got adhered to a sock puppet.

Sweeping the front walkway, I became frustrated at the resistance of the dirt in those little ridges. Bits of beauty bark and curls of animal hair either got tangled in the broom bristles and refused to leave, or would simply get redistributed to other parts of the walk. Realizing my efforts were pointless, I retrieved a crusty yellow extension cord from the garage and plugged it into the foyer outlet, then attached the female end of it to the male plug of the vacuum cleaner cord. This gave me at least fifty feet to work with. I set the vacuum setting on "bare floor" and began vacuuming the concrete. One of the neighbor kids stopped on his bike, watched me vacuuming for a moment, then asked, "Are you vacuuming the walk?" I replied, "No," and that seemed to momentarily shut him up.

The walk looked great when I was done with it, and the vacuum bag was full. I removed it and tossed it in the trash, then replaced it with another. The extension cord gave me some more room, so I continued vacuuming the driveway. Little bits of gravel, a penny, got sucked all rattly-like into the machine. I vaguely wondered if this was detrimental to the vacuum, but if it could not handle this task then it had no business being a vacuum of mine. I could easily buy a new one. I ran it over a stubborn piece of beauty bark, and after the fourth or fifth pass when it still wouldn't pick it up, I bent down and broke the beauty bark into smaller pieces. That did the trick.

There were still some grass clippings that hadn't gotten sucked into the bag when the kid who mows the lawn last mowed the lawn. The grass was as short as the living room carpet, so I figured there was nothing wrong with running the vacuum across the yard as well. It picked up a piece of ice-cream wrapper trash that had blown in from the street. The vacuum formatted the grass into pleasing-to-the-eye rows. I fetched another extension cord from the garage and attached it to the first extension cord, male to female, female to male. This provided me enough room to reach nearly every corner of the yard. The kid was back, with two friends, and they stood straddling their bikes, quietly watching. After filling another bag, I turned the vacuum off and said, "Don't you kids have anything better to do than watch a woman cleaning her yard?"

"But this is the Nakayamas' yard," one of the kids said. It was nightfall and I was removing my sixth bag of dirt when the RV pulled into the pristine driveway, a family staring at me idiotically from inside.

—October 7, 2002, 9:41–10:00 a.m., Bellevue, WA

DOUGLAS COUPLAND
THE VANISHEES

ONE MORNING IN the not-too-distant future, 1 percent of the all the people in the world—60 million moms, dads, brothers, sisters, dog-owners, and friends—vanished. The vanishing crossed all national borders, beliefs and religions.

Nobody understood how or why the vanishing happened. All they knew was that the ones who vanished were either extraordinarily beautiful and/or extraordinarily intelligent—movie stars, Nobel Prize winners, fashion models, and astronauts.

As can be imagined, the chaos and fear created by the event was extraordinary, yet after some months, daily life on Earth managed to continue in its way. Crops were grown. Factories kept working. Newspapers were made. New kinds of microwaveable snacks were advertised on TV. Babies were born.

A year later, another 1 percent of people vanished, except this time there was no common thread. The vanishees might just as well have been selected by having their names pulled out of a hat, and it was after this second vanishing that human beings realized that further vanishings might be on the way, and that checks had to be put in place so that if somebody, say, at the control panel of a nuclear plant went missing, the transuranium core wouldn't go critical. Cars and planes developed systems to cushion the effect of a missing pilot or driver. Factories learned to shut themselves off. Canal systems and missiles were made as fail-safe as possible.

Sure enough, a year later another 1 percent of humanity vanished, and by this point, humankind was one seriously spooked species. It became hard for people to concentrate on anything long-term, be it a painting, the Olympics, or a presidential election. Beyond basic survival, life as we knew it began to grind to a halt.

Then the vanishings came more quickly, until at the end of five years, only 5 percent of the people on Earth remained. Curiously, much of this remaining 5 percent was composed of engineers and construction workers.

When the flying saucers appeared and the aliens landed, everybody was actually pretty happy, because now some sort of sense could be made of the vanishings, except that the aliens did no such explaining. Instead they used highly tweaked pharmaceutical molecules as a form of mind control to turn young and old into a single-minded cult—the remediators. Their goal was to remove every single trace that humanity had ever left on the planet's face.

Much of the great remediation was cosmetic, such as the systematic molecule-by-molecule deconstruction of cities and roads. But it wasn't enough that buildings and roads be removed—they had to be removed in such a way that no ecological trace of them was left: wood was mulched and stones and rock and concrete were turned to dust. Drywall was crumbled and used to deacidify lakes. Boxes of insecticides and pesticides from garages had to be burned in a way that left behind no toxins. The gravel and stone beneath railways and freeways was sifted and sorted and moved elsewhere in the continent where they made natural sense in the landscape. Graveyards and their coffins were erased, as were ski resort gondolas and Monet's garden at Giverny.

Of course the areas of larger cleanup were human traces such as garbage dumps, dams, and industrial and nuclear facilities. Dozens of generations of humans were born and raised with just enough knowledge, and just enough will, that they could spend their lives sifting backwards through time through layers of household trash, construction debris, and sludge. Clans of remediators were formed around the sorts of cleanup skills they were assigned at birth. The Aquamagnetics scoured the bottoms of oceans and lakes for metallic human evidence: bottle caps, car parts, and submarines. The Olivo-desalinizers specialized in removing salt crusts from deep within the soils surrounding olive processing factories, often in digs that went down thousands of meters. But to these human beings, linear time and pyramid-sized projects generated no awe. All that mattered was the ultimate repair of the earth. To eat only algae, rice, and beans and fix the planet was the best possible gift a human being could imagine.

Many thousands of years passed, and one could look down at the planet from the height of a 747 and see nothing but pristine continents, and at that point, every pop can and every cigarette butt and every piece of lead gunshot on the Earth's surface had been located and removed and dealt with. The vast underground coal and asbestos mines in the northern hemispheres had been scraped clean and then been collapsed into themselves. The Florida Everglades showed no trace of freeways. Chinese hydroelectric dams might just as well have never existed. New York City was a forest.

Every once in a while, a report would come in of a wedding ring located in the ocean off the coast of Greenland, or a nail hammered into the trunk of a thousand-year-old tree in Argentina; an emergency team would be dispatched, but the heavy lifting had all been done.

Nuclear waste proved to be the largest problem. The aliens refused to put it inside their spacecrafts, and they left the care of it to the engineers they'd kept behind, and to the subsequent generations of engineering overlords. Some of the waste was fired into the sun. Some was treated using deradiation techniques pioneered in the centuries after the vanishings. Even then, a further hundred generations of humans were required to dig and scrape into the planet's skin and remove and remediate all possible radioactive molecules, and the zeal with which they attacked this final chore would rival anything from any of history's purges or fatwas. And once humans were finished this detoxifying effort, their job was done. As foretold in a piece of fake prophetic claptrap written millennia before, the last remediators dressed in cornstarch jumpsuits, then they scattered themselves out equally into the landscape where they swallowed an organic poison and melted into the ecosystem.

History was now over. Human beings were over, until...

...early one evening, around dinnertime, when the original 1 per cent of humanity—the movie stars, Nobel Prize winners, fashion models, and astronauts—was returned to where it had been plucked from the planet's surface. They were left standing with their purses, briefcases, and whatever they were wearing at the time of the vanishing. They were given no rules or laws or guidance. Earth, to them, was like a brand new 2003 VW Jetta but without an owner's manual. What would they make of it? Would they trash it? Would they keep it clean and give it routine checkups?

And meanwhile, the aliens, bored of babysitting human beings and playing computer solitaire for 10,000 years, returned to their own home.

—June 2, 2002, 5:20–5:40 p.m., West Vancouver, BC

GABE HUDSON

TOOLS EVALUATION OF DRAMS BATTLE DRESS UTILITY

ELLEN MACKERAY
SPECIALIST IN NATIONAL DEFENSE
INTERNAL RESEARCH SUBCOMMITTEE

DATA:
Research Theme: Land Management—General
ID #: JL-92
Environment: Joint C37
Platforms: 00B, B-IMP, K7 M/I/W, UL-42
Variant: OWR
Security Classification: 12

FRAMEWORK ISSUES:
Featuring an interferomic, transference-to-readiness capability, the antimicrobial DRAMS-7421, equipped with a triangular tail adaptable to parachute option, represents a new generation of inflatable battle dress garments designed to ballet the soldier through sand-oriented environments. One objective of the DOD's Progressive Battle Dress Division, headed by Dr. Trinton, was to macreciate next-generation shock batons for the purpose of shuttling soldiers from their abbreviated bodies into Go-Dura-Life-Structures. A phenomena referred to by Dr. Trinton as "full personnel transplants." A shoulder-fired NetRifle was later added to the DRAMS-7421 ballistic repertoire. Regarding the deployed soldiers' evacuated bodies, these tissue receipts were closeted in a storage facility in Ft. Leonard Wood, where they are routinely injected with stealth particle light, rendering the intact skeletal and organ matter invisible to the naked, room-temperature, controlled eye.

PERFORMANCE ANALYSIS:
Municipal Guardian Assessment cited the 7421's War Performance as excellent, despite the fact that a team of reconnaissance Marines reported slow leaking out their DRAMS during exfiltration from the DMZ along Al Jouf. Following tabulation, with an overwhelming vote of 5-1, the leaked personnel portions elected to pursue their fleeing Go-Dura-Life-Structures, and lunge back on board before the Blackhawk lifted up. When later presented with a Democratic Multiple Choice Serviceman's Poll (DMCSP) regarding real-time effects of leakage during a compromised mission, three of the

Marines checked answer (B): *All of the above*, and one Green Beret checked answer (D): *A medal would not help.*

—*March 5, 2002, 5:58–6:18 a.m.., Washington, DC*

JUDY BUDNITZ

WE WENT TO the meeting for parents of gifted children. I went; Brad's late. Comes in, saying excuse me, excuse me, everyone staring at his pants. We're all sitting on two-foot-high kids chairs, knees up to our chins. Meeting is led by the gifted-child teacher. Doesn't call herself a teacher, calls herself what? An instructor? An enabler? A facilitator? A lubricator? A fluffer? (Instant forgetfulness, caused, my dentist says, by the mercury in my fillings, I should have them all replaced with a new amalgam that looks just like real tooth enamel, he can do it all right there in the office, the cost is minimal.) Says to call her Monique. Has a close-fitting cap of gray hair, glasses on a chain around her neck, a wide flat bottom. Brad sits down next to me, no more orange plastic chairs left, sits on the sour disinfectant-smelling floor. I can smell Brad, dry-cleaning, mouthwash, yeast. Can anyone else? Don't kiss me, please. Pretend you don't know me.

Flakes of dry scalp in his hair. Monique passes out photocopied lyric sheets and leads us all in song:

Oh, what is to be done with the gifted child?
Sing!
He is not like other boys
She is not like other girls
He scores in the 98th percentile
Standardized tests are his forte
He takes chemistry class with his elders
And speaks Latin like a native
He is prone to nearsightedness and the violin
He is given algebra two years
Before his peers
And calculus, O calculus
But sex education comes two years late
So as not to offend
The delicate

Constitution of the gifted child

In the morning I'm watching our gifted child, Alan. He'll be starting the gifted program now; the special classes meet in a trailer parked behind the school. He says the other kids call you trailer trash if you have to go there. I don't know where he came from, Alan. Where is the grubby tousle-headed boy with the snails, puppy dog tails, and Erector sets? With Alan, the seats of his pants wear out before the knees. Where did he pop up from? My definition of gifted child: one that doesn't come from you, out of you; it comes to you out of nowhere. Like a gift, see, or curse. From God, storks, aliens, or something. This morning I laid a T-shirt out on his bed, the one with robots on it. He's wearing it now with a white button-down shirt underneath, all the buttons buttoned. He's eating the Oat Blasters. Brad is trying to interest him in photographs in the newspaper, soldiers in fatigues.

The Oat Blasters are supposed to make a sound like machine guns when the milk touches them, but they don't. Alan is horribly disappointed by this. He made me buy them. Now we're making him finish the box. After they leave I go outside and pretend to pull weeds out of the lawn. I'm watching for our neighbor; she's always outside in her headscarf and muumuu, enormous gloves on her hands. She has no eyebrows, no eyelashes and moves slow as dirt. I think she is slowly dying. I would like to tell her what I've discovered—the power of the mind to control the body. I don't want to produce another gifted child. Brad wants me to. So I follow the rules, eat my green vegetables, my vitamins. Eat eggs, people tell me, eggs call to eggs. You'd think this was an old wives' tale, but I hear it most from the sports-bra ladies working the machines at the Y, them so full of conviction and Slimfast. I do all these things I'm supposed to, but I will it not to happen. I will it not to take root. I picture sperm like deflating balloons, their strings limp. And it seems to be working. I want to tell my neighbor this but I do not.

Alan comes home. He's still alive. I expect him to die at any moment. I don't know why. Soon they'll ship him away, stick his head in a vise to give it some corners, he'll work for the government in a top-secret capacity, they need man-boys like him. How was school, my gifted child? I hate it, he says. She made us write haikus. Can I hear one, I say. She gave us the first line, Alan says, and we had to fill in the rest, follow the pattern.

Five beats, seven beats, five, I say. I know the drill.

Summer thunderstorm, he says and stops. That's hers.

Go on.

Summer thunderstorm

Electrocuted horses
In an empty field.
Well, you got the beats right, I say. That's something.

—*April 8, 2002, 5:17–5:37 p.m., New York, NY*

JILL BIALOSKY
THE OLD LONGINGS

I WOKE UP and thought about the time
decades ago when I sat in a boy's bedroom in Santa Monica
and stared at his tropical fish in his aquarium all day waiting
for him to return. I sat on the bed and wondered if the myth was true,
if mother guppies ate their children.
I went into his roommate's room. I had heard him leave earlier that morning,
and went through his drawers, tried on his pants and T-shirts (he was my size)
and stood on his bed so I could see myself in the mirror above his bureau
and contemplated pilfering a pair of faded jeans (those were the days
where I had no money) but didn't.
I took a walk in the neighborhood, marveled that the sky could be so blue,
    so perfect,
and so unrelated to the gray mood I was in and made myself a peanut butter
    and jelly
sandwich and went back in his bedroom and watched the fish circle the tank
wondering what they did with their boredom, trapped
in a ten-by-ten tank filled with the same colored pebbles and algae, the
    same fish,
the same plastic mermaid, and cried because the boy had disappeared.
When he returned later that night, elusive, saying he had gone to an
    Al-Anon meeting
(he really said that), we messed around for a while, I read him a poem
I was working on, and we fell asleep. In the morning
I told him to take me to the bus station. What was the use? I was in love
with someone who would leave me alone in his apartment all day and most
    of the night,
a girl who had traveled all the way from Iowa City to Santa Monica to
    see him.

That's how it was then. I was always in love
with a boy who wouldn't have me and the ones that liked me got on
    my nerves.
If that boy walked in the door I'd still want him
to tell me about the tropical fish,
to tell me the name of each one, to explain how they do their harm.

        —September 3, 2002, 4:25–5:00 p.m., at home in New York, NY,
        watching my son's lone fish in its bowl

AIMEE BENDER

THE WOMAN WAS born with snakes for hair. But unlike Medusa, or any of her predecessors, these snakes were harmless. If you looked directly at them, you did not turn into stone, or butter, or salt. And these snakes were not evil raiders, or slithering boa constrictors, but instead simple garter snakes, evenly dirt colored, and often quiet. If you happened upon her when they were all sleeping, it just seemed like she had shiny and very thick locks, and only when they awoke, each raising a snake head and flicking out a tiny yellow tongue, did anything seem out of the ordinary.

As an old woman, the snakes changed too. They shed their brown skins for gray skins, so that she would fit in with the other old women, though three of the snakes had died by then, unable to keep up with the stubbornness of the rest of her body, and they hung down, dead weight. Soon, they would snap off and there would be a hole in her scalp line, something for her hairdresser, whom she paid very well, to contend with.

The snakes themselves were not a problem. The problem was the people. Lovers, waking up, suddenly acutely aware of what was on her head, found themselves amazed at their ability to move. But I should be stone! they all cried. No, she said, my snakes have no such powers. But the sight of those little reptilian heads raising up from her ears caused blood to freeze in some kind of fear, regardless. Only one man went the other direction and tried to employ the snakes in their sex life as a way to kink it all up but she refused that, too. They're separate from me, she said. It just wouldn't be right.

It's all power of suggestion. And she was a flexible sort. So when a Greek ambassador asked that she take a flight over, wearing a hat, and show up in front of their enemies in exchange for a cottage on an island, she agreed. She was middle-aged by then, and had seen her fair share of ups and downs. The hat she got had air-holes in it and was dramatically large so everyone on flight assumed she was crazy, or else into rock music. She flew first class and let the snakes out in the bathroom, where they gulped the air and scraggled their bodies as much as they could, weaving around each other, forming quick braids, then unraveling. They could curl up tight in ringlets or hang stick-straight. They were much more obedient than any gel or mousse. She could hear their hissing protests when she put the hat back on.

In Greece, she was escorted from the plane and taken to a large building, and from a huge picture window, the ambassador pointed at the approaching armies. We want you to do a standoff, he said. We will protect you. He dressed her in bulletproof clothing, and then over that placed the garb of old gods and warriors, so that she looked of an ancient time. She had to remove her watch, and Band-Aid, as they undermined the total appearance, but she left her hat on.

They're under there? he asked.

Yes, she said. They're ready to roll.

Fine, fine, he said. Now go climb up the hill. And wait there. And when you see the first soldier, remove your hat.

Where's my cottage again? she asked.

On the island over there, said the ambassador, pointing. You'll be able to walk to the beach and you'll be right next to an olive grove.

She shrugged her shoulders. This was worth the risk, considering her last lover had said the snakes were watching him as he made love to her and the pressure was killing him and she refused to wear a blanket or towel on her head during sex. Her parents had died. Her one sibling had always felt jealous and lived across the country and was a hairdresser for normal hair. She had an open field of time ahead of her, and facing off some warriors did not seem like such a terrible way to begin the next phase.

And are they bad people? she said.

No, the ambassador said. Not so bad. But we do not wish to fight them in this manner.

She climbed the hill and the Greek sun was warm and the water blue and the buildings white and the flowers yellow. The snakes were ready to jump right out of that hat. And so she stood on the hillside and when she saw the glinting foot of the first soldier, she removed her hat, and the snakes, delighted, relieved to be free, stretched their bodies out as far as they could, and recoiled back, and curled and straightened so that her entire head was a moving ball of lines and curves. Of springs and muscles. It was quite a sight to see. From his picture window, far away, even the ambassador felt his skin shiver up.

The armies believed in everything, and so they froze. They saw Medusa high on the hill and felt their skin harden into stone. They heard their hearts thudding deeply, and stopped cold in their tracks. The ambassador rode up on a mule and waved to them. I will free you! he yelled. If you promise to go home and stop this invasion! I will free you from the grasp of the return of Medusa!

With that the snakes stretched out again, towards his voice, so that her whole head had the look of an electrocution.

Someone dropped his gun, and the rest of them turned to look, and in that, they all realized they were not stone at all, not a bit, and they charged up again, toward the ambassador who dashed away on his mule. The woman with snakes for hair ran toward the nearest vineyard, and spent the night in between rows of grapes, listening to her snake hair quietly eating the spoiled ones, nearly raisins, baked from the sun.

The armies took over the ambassador's house and looked out from the picture windows. The woman wandered off to the ocean's edge and gave her hands and feet a good washing. People left her alone. The snakes did not like salt water, so she had to stay out of going too deep or they would gently bite her ear in protest. She had received an offer once, from an animal trainer. He had believed that with very careful cutting, he could remove the snakes from her head and they would mostly live. It seems that only their tails are wedged into your skull, he said, examining her closely with firm fingers on her scalp while the snakes hissed around his wrist. I could keep the snakes here, at the zoo, he said. You could visit whenever you wanted, I'll leave you a key.

The snakes untied his watch band. She thought about it all up until the point when he returned with a small scalpel and some local anaesthetic. No, she said. I can't even imagine it. No way. No. He looked vastly disappointed, as he had really been interested in getting that careful angle right, and was already writing the placard in his mind. Can I do one? he asked. No, she said. It's time for me to be going.

On her drive home, the snakes organized themselves into an elegant top-knot. She dressed in an evening gown while she made herself a small, modest dinner. They tumbled down on their own in curls and wisps while she got ready for bed, where she fell asleep to the gentle ssshing of their many voices.

—January 29, 2002, 9:11–9:31 a.m., Los Angeles, CA

DEAN WAREHAM

WHEN I WAS sixteen I took a trip to Europe with my friend Greg. He asked if we should take some acid with us, but I didn't want to be caught smuggling LSD into England. We had a budget of $800 each for five weeks, and were staying at youth hostels. Greg insisted that we should restrict ourselves to two meals a day to save money. We went to the London zoo, and by midday we were getting a little hungry, so we went to the cafeteria and waited till we spied a family leaving their table. They had left a plate full of french fries. Greg went over to the table and took them, but unfortunately the daddy of the family saw him take their scraps, and came rushing back over to the table. "I paid for those chips!" he said indignantly, snatching the plate from Greg and dumping them in the trash. His wife yelled at him to leave us alone.

We spent a week in Paris at the end of the trip, and were put up by the family of a friend of my sister's, named Nathalie. She was a year older than us and had short hair and she was very cute. They had a nice place near the Notre Dame cathedral. Nathalie came with us to the museums. Her older brother took us on a nighttime tour of the tunnels that run underneath the city of Paris. We saw the Louvre and the Pompidou, and Greg and I got into an argument as to whether or not Joseph Cornell could be considered a surrealist. "No way is he a surrealist," said Greg. "Yes, he is too," I said. "It says so on the pamphlet." Many years ago I read a book about Joseph Cornell. He lived with his mother his whole life, on Utopia Parkway in Queens, NY. And in one of his boxes there's a photo of André Breton. So that's pretty compelling evidence if you ask me. But Greg knew more about art history than I did.

Toward the end of our stay Greg confessed that he had brought the acid with him, a piece of blotter stashed behind the luggage tag on his bag, and he had been tripping every third day. Which explains why he wasn't so hungry, and why I got bored at the museums before he did.

On our final night in Paris, Nathalie came into my room and got into my bed. She had a scar on her hand, about half an inch long, but on both sides of her hand, where she had stuck a knife all the way through it one time. I think today I would recognize that as the sign of a disturbed young woman. We made out for a long time, and then we went to her room and took off our clothes, and then I got on top of her and we made love for about twenty seconds, and then I came on her tummy.

—July 15, 2002, 1:10–1:30 p.m., New York, NY

ASHLEY WARLICK

ANNE, 1985

THEY SAY GOODBYE in the parking lot of the Pocono Motel. He says he'll call her later that night, but she doesn't think he will because she's made him mad by leaving early, earlier than expected. He keeps looking over his shoulder at the hygienist he's brought with him from the office, a woman so neurotic she cannot leave a morsel of food on the table, and so she has spent the weekend cleaning up after his unfinished bacon and toast, the half of his pasta he couldn't eat. He and Anne laughed about it in bed, the thin, nubbled sheet pulled up, but now he's looking at the hygienist because he thinks Anne will try to kiss him goodbye. That would prove awkward, although how she's not sure. The hygienist is the one everybody thinks he's sleeping with anyway.

The hygienist knocked on his door at the motel this morning and he groaned, called out how he was not yet up, all the while pulling on his clothes from the night before, discarded on the floor. Anne just laughed, turned on the shower. He never gets in the shower with her and she wonders about that too, if it's just not something he thinks to do, or if there is a reason. She likes to shower with her lovers. There is a laziness to it she can find nowhere else in her life. And anyway, the hygienist would have seen her suitcase, the single bed slept in, the sheets pulling free at the corners.

In the shower, she found a tick on her finger. It looked like lint at first, without her glasses, and she brushed it off, but there was something sticky about it and she looked closer and could see it was alive. She wiped it on the shower wall and watched it for a while, coming back to life, finding itself where it was, and wet. Outside the bathroom, she could hear him and the hygienist talking; they had conference sessions today and she knew she should be going home. Her son had strep throat; her husband was convinced she didn't like him very much, or at the least found him unattractive, unfun, unfriendly, which was in some part all true. But this man she was with now, if you tied her down, she could not say much different for him.

So she would leave him, horribly, in the parking lot after breakfast, and the first hours of her day without him would be okay, even fine. She would get home, she would kiss her son, thank her husband. She would sit down at her desk and pay some bills. And then the house would get quiet, and she would play over the weekend in her head and sooner or later she would be desperate to get him on the phone. She would find a calendar and try and figure out when she could see him again, and by the time she did talk to him, she would tell him she loved him if he asked.

She gets out of the shower, and he asks what her plans are for the day.

She takes the towel from her hair, sits on the edge of the bed, the rumpled sheets, the night before, and then again, coming from sleep, he hovered over her, and she just wanted to do it all again, even before it was over, just again.

She says she is trying to figure out if she should leave now or after breakfast, and he turns to look at her, naked, wet, waiting on the edge of the bed while he packs.

"After breakfast," he says. "Please."

—May 12, 2002, 11:05–11:25 p.m., Greenville, SC

ANN CUMMINS
MUD

I WAS OUT the door and down the street before I remembered I'd forgotten to pay for my haircut, so I went back and was greeted by the refugee. They'd hired a refugee to do massage.

"Be good to yourself," she says to me. "Give yourself a treat."

She was a small, square woman, flat as a board in front and back, but wide. She took my two hands and led me as if I were blind past Bette, my hairdresser, who has always scared me a little and thrills me in her Cajun ways. "What?" Bette says. "Defecting?" She arches her red eyebrows.

"No, no," I say, and laugh a little.

We go through the door at the end of the hall, and right away I hear water running. It's dark, not pitch—dark, like twilight, the blue light of twilight—and I'm walking on cool stone slabs toward a pool, a pond, really, with a waterfall, and I'm thinking, How am I going to pay for this? But the refugee is laughing, her eyes little winks in her head, and before I know it she's got me in the mud there at the edge of the pond.

The mud is orange with little nodules in it, shiny, like drops of orange coral. The woman is packing herself in, and she takes a little nodule between her thumb and finger, squeezes it, and the nodule bursts—a whiff of tangerine. She holds her fingers to her nose, closes her eyes and inhales. "Try it," she tells me. "This is to forget," she says, "but there is one thing I can never forget. When they raided my village, they took a woman, strapped her four little babies to her four limbs and threw her in the river.

There, now I have told you, and you will never forget it either because there are some things scratched in the head, and that's one, but don't worry. Sonny. Your hair is so short. Do they call you Sonny? Don't worry about it a minute. It has already happened and it will happen again," and she leans back into the mud, and the mud oozes over her, pillows up around her neck and ears, dribbles onto her chest, and my neck, the aching in my neck and shoulders thatI didn't know I had, begins to ease. I do think about it as I settle into the mud—it's more a chocolatey orange sludge than mud, sort of a river of sludge we're in, it laps against my neck and cheeks—but I do think about it, about that poor woman and her fear and her great sorrow for her babies, and I think about my own little troubles, the job I'm about to lose, the bills I cannot pay—how much is this costing me, I wonder—it all seems to swirl around me, to pack me in, and little panics I didn't know I had swell then burst, and there is a pleasant tingling in my toes and fingers.

After a while we crawl like turtles through the mud river to a spot where we have a sideline view of the hairdressers, and it's funny because all the times I was sitting in Bette's chair, I never saw the mud. We lie on our backs, our arms stretched out, fluttering our fingers through the satin sludge, and my companion says, "Isn't this nice?" then, "I don't know how she does it."

"Who, Bette?"

"She gets more people in and out of that chair in a day than I see in a month."

"She's competent," I say.

"She's fast," the woman says.

"She's really very good," I say. "She's a golfer, you know."

"Is she? Does she have a golf beanie?"

"A beanie?"

"Does she have little socks for her clubs?"

I laugh.

"Does her license plate say 'Live to Golf'?"

I laugh again, though I feel bad about it. This woman is making fun of Bette, who has never given me a bad haircut, nor subjected me to dumb chitchat, an artist, Bette, who can wear red pants and look good, tall bony Bette, with her thick lips and her freckles, her wild copper hair—says, "Wha'd you do to your hair, girl?" every time she sees me, says, "This'll be trouble," then goes to work without a plan. A woman with talented hands and money in the bank. Has golfed every course worth golfing in America and Canada, too, to hear her tell it. "I'm pretty good," she'll say. An afford-able sport on a hairdresser's pay, which is fifty bucks a cut, ninety-five for a cut and color, a 10 percent tip's an embarrassment, go 20 if you want her to meet your eye, a half hour a cut, do the math, pretty good pocket money, you have to schedule in advance to catch her off the green, so every time I come in three weeks overdue, it's "What did you do to your hair, girl?"

"Yeah, she's fast," I say to my companion, and I'm thinking how she never cuts much, just enough to make sure I'll come back, and a little rage bubbles in me. "She's slick," I say.

But the refugee has forgotten all about it. "Who?" she says. She dredges her long hair back and forth in the mud. "Silt of the seven seas," she whis-pers. "I am bejeweled in tangerine teardrops, and do you know what, Sonny? My heart can't break. I've seen too much." She fists some mud, opens her mouth, packs her cheeks—"Good for the stomach," she says and grins, her teeth brown stumps, her eyes moon white, and my heart gives a little for what she's seen and what she knows.

Bette is singing along with the radio like she does. Now I'm inclined to harmonize. It's the mud, I guess. These little fevers come and go. I run my fingers through my hair, which worms mud-tucked around my face. I decide I will never worry again, which is a worry itself, the decision, so I kick up my heels, a stuck-in-the-mud can-can, and I waddle my hips: "Why these haircuts?" I shout, and it feels good. "Why these bills? I'm going to write my stuff in blood," I tell the refugee, who looks confused.

She is watching Bette, whose fingers sashay in and out of a small girl's hair, the child, a brown-haired, full-cheeked beauty making faces in the mir-ror. "Now you just relax, honey," I hear Bette say. "We're going to make you so pretty," and the child, all taffy, giving to the touch, lets Bette take her head—closes her eyes and lets the artist take her, and I think suddenly, I know those hands, remember them as if they are on my own head, finding the shape by touch. In spite of myself, I admire her.

"She could cut hair with her eyes closed," I whisper.

"A golfer you say," the woman says, and snickers, but her pettiness annoys me.

Bette is singing and toeing around the chair. I am ready to go. I wonder where my checkbook is. My hair is plastered to my head. It needs a little attention. She can work me in, I think. Bette's always very accommodating to regulars. I'll ask her to work me in, I'm thinking, then I notice the child is gone. Bette is sitting in the chair, her head lolling. She's twirling, and she's singing, "Too late. Too late. Too late." Tucks her chin into her shoulder, lifts her hair from off her face, and looks my way. Gives me one of those catty, Cajun grins. "I'm gone."

And she is. And now my fun's gone bad.

—*September 19, 2002, 2:13–2:36 p.m., Northern Arizona University, Flagstaff, AZ*

PETER ORNER

Miss Greenburger

JENNY HAFNER'S FATHER showed up at school in his pajamas drunk and roaring. The pajamas looked comfortable and lived-in, softened, the way pajamas should look. He wasn't wearing any socks or even slippers and even more amazing than his sputtering rumpus were his awful feet, not so much big as grotesque. His toes were black, as if for years he'd been stubbing them on the sidewalk. Nobody had ever seen Mr. Hafner's feet before, much less him in his pajamas, although of course it wasn't a secret that he was a raving public drunk (he was on the school board) so his sudden appearance in our classroom didn't come as much of a shock to anybody, except the new teacher, Miss Greenburger. Imagining her now, she was so young, so greenly bendable.

It was her first year teaching. It was fourth grade. She tried to love us all equally. She was like a new mother with twins, kissing one and then the other to not play favorites. She was almost pretty even though her nose didn't point directly at you. I loved her more for this. We all did. She taught us cursive though she said in most schools you had to wait another two years. She didn't waste a hell of a lot of time on math. Her breasts were like anthills that my hand craved smoothing. Her hair was short but still somehow got in her eyes. We all hated her name and once passed around a scrawled petition begging her to change it to something more appropriate to her delicacy and petite wrists. We refused to leave for recess without her. She was pigeon-toed. She wore swishy skirts that sometimes brushed our knees. Once she put two pencils behind her ears by accident. She said she hated chalk. We never saw her eat anything, so we left half-eaten Baby Ruths on her desk when her back was turned while she was feeding the turtles. She didn't grow her fingernails longer than ours. Sometimes she stopped in midsentence to look out the window. Some days her breasts were more like small balloons than anthills. We would have died for her, all of us, which is why I remain ashamed.

It wasn't his feet that got her. When Mr. Hafner ranted into Room A-14 that morning in late October, barefoot and foozled in his comfortable pajamas, his open fly allowing Miss Greenburger to see more of Mr. Hafner than she ever needed to see—she cried. She hunched over her desk and wept. She shrank more than we ever imagined she could. And we did zero. Maybe for a fleeting moment we were more interested in him than her. Prevaricators! You're not children, you're evil midgets! Or maybe in those two perfect months our love had waned inexcusably. I wish I could say. To our credit, we never talked about it after. We focused solely on our dereliction of duty. Yet that didn't absolve us then and never has. What would it have taken for one of us to stand up from his or her desk and go to her and block her view? After Mr. Hafner staggered away, Miss Greenburger thrust her head back and sneezed, viciously, her face awash in tears and snot. Marlin Lavanhar shouted Gesundheit! from the back of the room, but nothing, not even being polite in German could have brought her back to us then. She'd aged. We all had.

—April 7, 2002, 1:15–1:45 a.m., San Francisco, CA

DARIN STRAUSS

A True Story

MY GRANDMOTHER'S FATHER played first base for the Brooklyn Kings before they came to be known as the Dodgers. In 1907, '08, and '09, Manny Joseph was the only Jewish King, and he got razzed a lot during away games. Catchers would mutter "sheeny" and worse when he stood to bat; the fans yelled all the old insults.

Another Jew, Sandy Koufax—arguably the best lefty ever to pitch (or, *in*arguably if you're a Jew of a certain age)—won with the Dodgers half a century later. Koufax, a dutiful man, skipped a momentous World Series game to worship on a High Holiday. My great-grandfather held different priorities. On Yom Kippur in 1909, the Brooklyn Kings' Jewish first baseman sneaked from temple to sit for the team photo, of which I cherish a copy. Dapper in his straw hat and intricate necktie, he's the only player not wearing baseball clothes. And if he's seated there not exactly *handsome*, he does show off one of those rakish half-smiles so beneficial to the faces of good boys when they're acting naughty, or think they are.

The next season, on a Sabbath night, Manny Joseph played his best game. He went five-for-five and squibbed out the game winner, a dying quail of a pop-up that barely dodged the shortstop's glove.

"Thank God he didn't catch it," my great-grandfather said, for years afterward.

—June 26, 2002, 8:14–8:37 a.m., Marriott Room 1807, Minneapolis, MN

LAIRD HUNT

The Operatives Ball

IT WAS PART of their Organization's policy that operatives must fill out an application before seeing each other in anything more than the most leisurely and amicable way. They duly traipsed down to the local applications office and asked for the appropriate form. The individual behind the counter coughed. We're all out, he said. And why aren't you wearing your sunglasses?

We didn't think, said the man.

It was necessary to do so, said the woman.

In our free time, said the man.

You're on Organization property, aren't you? You're taking up Organization time, aren't you? said the individual.

How very true, said the woman.

But never mind that, said the man, when will you have the form?

They were told to try again the next day. That night the man assisted at a kidnapping and the woman led a small group into a trap. Neither engagement went off particularly smoothly. When they were finished, they happily honored the terms of a rendezvous at the bar they were in the habit of frequenting.

I'm tired, said the man.

Exhausted, said the woman.

Feeling sexy, though, said the man.

Entendu, said the woman.

They drank. Pretty soon they were drunk. Pretty soon they were in bed together. The next day they went back to the applications office and asked for a form.

No form, said the individual behind the counter.

But we have to have a form, said the man.

No, apparently you think you don't, said the individual.

That night the man was conked on the head and shipped off to another duty station, and the woman was tossed into a box. They both recovered. Ten years went by. They both did well, very respectably. By chance, they met up again. At an operatives ball.

You've grown so lovely and fat, she said, swooshing up to him.

As have you, he said.

They smiled and tittered as they looked at each other through their sunglasses.

I was actually under the impression that you were dead, said the woman.

I was told that you definitely were.

Well I'm not, said the woman.

Nor am I, said the man.

They giggled, moved towards each other, tangled shoulder holsters, danced a couple numbers, then left. They had only been in the dark for a few delicious all but undressed moments when they heard a cough and the lights came on.

—April 7, 2002, 6:43–7:03 p.m., New York, NY

STACEY RICHTER

My Funky One

I AM MAKING an effort to get Billy to call me "My funky one." I say: "Call me 'My funky one.'"

He says, "Okay, Funky One."

"No! *My* funky one. *My funky one!*"

Billy looks at me with no expression and says, "My funky one."

Billy has just returned from an airplane trip and is infatuated with the phrase: "All remaining cups and glasses." We are staying at my parents' for a few days while they are out of town. He emerges from the bathroom where he does his most ambitious reading and begins to talk to me about "prophets." He says: "This textbook says that many people question the legitimacy of prophets. They don't understand how prophets function in society; prophets take advantage of people."

He says this and I look at him. Billy has a friend with a very long beard. This friend likes to handle this beard—stroke it like a little cat—while he's eating or talking. It is disgusting. Then I realize Billy is holding my sister's economics textbook and understand that it's possible I've never understood anything anyone is saying. All remaining cups and glasses.

In the middle of the night we awaken to the sound of scurrying in my mother's office, just off the bedroom. An awful, trapped sound, and loud. Billy triangulates the noise to the garbage can under mom's desk and we cover it with a piece of cardboard and banish it to the hall. We think it could be a roach. Or it could be a mouse. But way down deep in my soul I know that it's a baby bunny, little, little, only the size of a quarter. Why? The yard is overflowing with bunnies; there is a bunny problem, and on two consecutive days a week before, when I was talking to first my mother, then my father, each interrupted our conversation with the same exclamation: "Oh my God! That's the smallest rabbit I've ever seen!" There may be bunnies in this house the size of crickets. There may be bunnies we could crush with our toes.

We get into a fight about the fate of the thing in the garbage can. Billy says let's just leave whatever it is in there, imprisoned. I want to free the bastard. *I never seen you looking so bad my funky one You tell me that your superfine mind has come undone Any major dude with half a heart surely will tell you my friend Any minor world that breaks apart falls together again...*

I go into my sister's room and discover a gold mine of seventies paraphernalia—her old high school bulletin board, where she stored precious shreds of her identity, now encased in lucite. Inexplicably, there are several references to adult movies, specifically John Holmes. Also, a stack of concert tickets. The Doobie Brothers, Kenny Loggins, Dan Fogelberg, Kenny Loggins again. But no Steely Dan. Where the fuck is the Steely Dan?

—August 17, 2002, 1:04–1:24 p.m., Phoenix, AZ

JULIE ORRINGER
THERE WERE THREE OF THEM

THIS IS A STORY about the youngest one. When I was nine, she fell down the stairs. This was at a vacation cottage at Lake Michigan. We were moving in. My sister had just learned to walk. In the one small room upstairs, my mother was unpacking while my sister explored. I stood at the bottom of the stairs. I think I held a small green suitcase, the kind kids get to pack and unpack by themselves. I was the oldest one. I stood at the bottom of the stairs and watched my sister walk in her duck-footed way, in the white baby shoes that were her first pair ever. She was looking down, smiling, saying a word to me I couldn't understand, one of a thousand secret words of her own devising.

She reached the lip of the stairs and she kept walking. Our mother saw too late. The floor fell away beneath my sister. Below her the stairs descended, but she did not observe their order. She fell forward onto her hand, her chest, her head, tumbling like a wooden doll, her hard white shoes making their dull sound against the stairs. I held my green suitcase, watching. I knew what happened when people fell down stairs. I'd seen it happen in movies. When people fell downstairs, they died. This was the moment I'd remember all my life: my little sister falling, her neck breaking, her body in its yellow dress coming to rest at my feet. This moment would define me. I would become tragic. Back at school, I'd be the girl whose sister died. I dropped the green suitcase, opened my mouth, screamed like nightmare-screaming.

At the bottom of the stairs, my sister raised herself and stood. The blue hall rug had printed its crosshatch upon her forehead. She looked up the stairs at my ashen mother, then at me. Wide-eyed. Unhurt. My mother flew down the stairs and picked her up, then threw a stinging slap across my face.

"Idiot!" she said. "Useless!"

And I was. I had just stood there. I might as well have killed my sister. I was ashamed of everything, my rock-stillness, my screaming, my own life. Next time I'd save her. I would never scream like that again. I would rise up and protect her.

When our mother died we knelt shoulder-to-shoulder at the burial, touching the casket as it hung over the black hole of her grave. My sister: twelve years old, pale, her fine blond hair caught in a clumsy braid. The men began to lower our mother's casket. They lowered it on chains that made a sound like the ghosts welcoming her down, like a jail claiming her forever, like a pain machine, like the morgue, like the worst horror of the longest night. My sister fell forward toward the casket and I caught her. I held her, trying to be eight years older. Still the casket went down. Nothing could stop us from falling. We went down. We lay on the grass. We crushed our faces into the wet dirt. This time, both of us were screaming.

—*May 16, 2002, 10:48–11:08 p.m., San Francisco, CA*

27 March 1968, 10:41 a.m.

During a jet training flight, Yuri crashed in a quiet forest known only to bears and mushroom hunters, near Novoselovo, 100 km from Moscow. The cause was ruled accidental, but soon other schools of speculation arose: that Yuri was abducted by aliens, that he was killed by a jealous Brezhnev, or that he had finally gone mad from something he had seen in outer space. The most ridiculous scenario had a drunken Yuri flying low and trying to shoot a moose with a rifle.

CONTRIBUTORS

JAMES BOICE is twenty-one years old and delivers pizza in Harrisonburg, Virginia. He has work forthcoming in *Fiction*.

ANDREA DESZŐ is an artist, designer, and illustrator in New York City. She teaches at Parsons School of Design. This is her first published fiction.

RODDY DOYLE lives and works in Dublin. His novels include *The Commitments*, *Paddy Clarke Ha Ha Ha*, and *The Woman Who Walked into Doors*. His latest book, *Rory and Ita*, is an oral memoir of his parents.

BEN EHRENREICH has worked as a journalist for several years, but has only recently begun publishing fiction. He is currently finishing a novel.

JOHN HENRY FLEMING is the author of a novel, *The Legend of the Barefoot Mailman*. He teaches creative writing at the University of South Florida.

ANDY LAMEY, a columnist for the *National Post*, lives in Ottawa, Ontario. This is his first published fiction.

WYTHE MARSCHALL, a Southern Motion Event, lives in Atlanta and attends college in Vermont. He is nineteen years old.

Photographer RENE NUIJENS (www. renenuijens.com) and writer STEVE KORVER (korver@cistron.nl) are both based in Amsterdam. They thank Troy Selvaratnam for being the rocket and Lava Design for making them look pretty. The photographs presented here are selections from an upcoming book.

SALVADOR PLASCENCIA was born in Guadalajara, Mexico, and now lives in Los Angeles. "The People of Paper" is from his just-completed first novel, about first love and paper cuts. This is his first published fiction.

SHANN RAY teaches in the Leadership Studies program at Gonzaga University and is a research psychologist for the Center for Disease Control. His wife wears the garment of praise; his two daughters shine like the sun. A version of "The Great Divide" appeared online in *Carve Magazine*.

SARAH RAYMONT recently completed the graduate writing program at the University of East Anglia in England. "The Last Words on an Aerogram" is an excerpt from a novel-in-progress. It is her first published fiction.

RACHEL SHERMAN works at the Print Research Foundation, researching WPA prints. She lives in Fort Greene, Brooklyn.

CHAD SIMPSON lives in Murphysboro, Illinois. He teaches composition at Southern Illinois University Carbondale, where he is in the MFA program. This is his first published fiction.

STEVE STIEFEL is a staff writer for *FLEX* magazine and a contributing editor at *Men's Fitness*. He is currently finishing his first novel.

TWENTY-MINUTE STORIES CONTRIBUTORS

STEVE ALMOND, who teaches fiction at Boston University, is the author of a collection of short stories titled *My Life in Heavy Metal*.

AIMEE BENDER is the author of *The Girl in the Flammable Skirt* and *An Invisible Sign of My Own*.

JILL BIALOSKY is the author of two collections of poetry as well as a novel, *House Under Snow*.

JUDY BUDNITZ is the author of *If I Told You Once* and *Flying Leap*, a *New York Times* Notable Book of the Year.

RYAN BOUDINOT's story "The Littlest Hitler" was published in *Best American Nonrequired Reading 2003*. He has written a collection of stories and a novel.

DOUGLAS COUPLAND is the author of several novels, including *Generation X* and, most recently, *Hey, Nostradamus!*

ANN CUMMINS teaches at Northern Arizona University. Her short stories have been published in the *New Yorker* and *Best American Short Stories 2002*.

DAVID EBERSHOFF is the author of *The Danish Girl* and *Pasadena*.

JENNIFER EGAN is the author of several novels, including *Look at Me*.

ALICIA ERIAN is the author of *The Brutal Language of Love*, a collection of short stories.

EMMA FORREST is a writer and journalist. Her debut novel is titled *Namedropper*.

GLEN DAVID GOLD is the author of several novels, including *Carter Beats the Devil*.

MYLA GOLDBERG is the author of *Bee Season* and *La Estación De Las Letras*.

ALEKSANDAR HEMON is a writer and journalist from Sarajevo. His books include *The Question of Bruno* and *Nowhere Man*.

GABE HUDSON is the author of *Dear Mr. President*, winner of the Sue Kaufman Prize for First Fiction from the American Academy of Arts and Letters.

LAIRD HUNT is the author of *The Impossibly*.

JESSICA FRANCIS KANE is the author of the short story collection *Bending Heaven*.

J. ROBERT LENNON is the author of several novels. His most recent is *Mailman: A Novel*.

JONATHAN LETHEM's most recent book is *The Fortress of Solitude*.

KELLY LINK is the author of *Stranger Things Happen*, a collection of short stories. She runs Small Beer Press with her husband, Gavin J. Grant.

RHETT MILLER, a founding member of the Old 97's, has released two solo albums, *Mythologies* and *The Instigator*.

RICK MOODY is the author of several novels, including *The Ice Storm* and *Garden State*, winner of the Pushcart Press Editors' Book Award.

MARC NESBITT is the author of *Gigantic*, a collection of short stories.

PETER ORNER is the author of *Esther Stories*.

JULIE ORRINGER, a Truman Capote Fellow in the Stegner Program at Stanford University, recently published a short story collection titled *How to Breath Underwater*.

STACEY RICHTER, author of the short story collection *My Date with Satan*, is a two-time winner of the Pushcart Prize.

KATIE ROIPHE is the author of several works of fiction and nonfiction, including *She Still Haunts Me* and *The Morning After: Sex, Fear, and Feminism*.

DARIN STRAUSS is the author of the novels *Chang and Eng* and *The Real McCoy*. He teaches at New York University.

DEAN WAREHAM is a member of Luna. Their most recent album is *Close Cover Before Striking*.

ASHLEY WARLICK is the author of *The Distance from the Heart of Things* and *The Summer after June*.

McSweeney's Books is proud to introduce a new series—
one part excitement and two parts education...

GENE JEANYUZ, TEEN SCIENTIST

*Gene has aced every test in school—but he's also had
a few adventures outside the lab! Read them!*

QUESTIONS FOR GENE?

NAME: _____

ADDRESS: _____

CITY, STATE, ZIP: _____

YOUR SCIENTIFIC DILEMMA: _____

Send queries, gifts,
and orders to:

Gene Jeanyuz
2217-A Roosevelt Ave.
Berkeley, CA 94703